FIRE
AND
ICE

Christopher Jones

To Don & Joan,
For giving the world
a beautiful daughter.
Enjoy the ride!

Chris

Published by Lulu Press, Inc.

For more information on the novel or author contact:

neoFutures
P.O. Box 3092
Grand Junction CO 81502-3092 USA

Or email: info@neofutures.com

First edition December 2006
ISBN: 978-1-84728-103-6

To Owl, *Astarte,* and spring butterflies

Agency Glossary

DARPA – Defense Advanced Research Projects Agency (DoD)
DIA – Defense Intelligence Agency
DoD – Department of Defense
JPL – Jet Propulsion Laboratory (NASA)
NASA – National Aeronautics and Space Administration
NCAR – National Center for Atmospheric Research
NCIS – Navy Criminal Investigation Service
NEST – Nuclear Emergency Strike Team
NFS – National Science Foundation
NOAA – National Oceanic and Atmospheric Administration
NSA – National Security Agency
USGS – United States Geological Survey
WPTC – Western Pacific Tsunami Center (Australia)

January 12, 2012
Thursday

0900 EST

The familiar chime sounded and the "fasten seatbelt" sign illuminated in the first class cabin. Most of the passengers were finishing breakfast or coffee except for the woman in seat 1A who only now pulled off her eyeshades and wiped sleep from her eyes. She rubbed her temples, moved her tongue in her dry mouth, and strained to hear the captain's voice, "…landing in ten minutes, the temperature at Reagan National Airport is 40 degrees. Thank you for choosing..." The woman straightened her business suit, opened the window shade, and observed the gray overcast Northern Virginia landscape creep closer.

She folded her blanket, repositioned her pumps awkwardly on her feet; she quickly brushed and pulled her blonde hair into a ponytail. She looked wistfully at the disappearing coffee service and hot towels. Then the tall black man in 1B offered her a stick of gum. She accepted the gift, smiled in slow motion, and examined the wrapper as she stuck the gum in her mouth. It was a blast of hot cinnamon and her eyes opened wide and watered. The wrapper read *"Esprit Ogun"* and she shook her head as though stuck in molasses. She sucked in cooler air. Flames flickered through the cabin window from outside and the plane began to shake. The woman turned to look at the face of her seat mate, whose mouth broke wide open into an ugly display of missing and rotten teeth. An overpowering fetid smell came from his breath. The woman's mouth formed a scream, but no sound emerged.

The flight attendant shook her gently on the shoulder, smiled, and said, "Agent St. Cloud, please put your seat upright, we are getting ready to land." She shook herself awake from the nightmare, pulled off her eyeshades and wiped sleep from her eyes. She rubbed her temples, moved her tongue in her dry mouth, and strained to hear the captain's voice, "…landing in ten minutes, the temperature at Reagan National Airport is 40 degrees. Thank you for choosing..." The woman opened the window shade and observed the gray overcast Northern Virginia landscape creep closer.

She folded her blanket, repositioned her pumps awkwardly on her feet; she quickly brushed and pulled her blonde hair into a ponytail. She looked wistfully at the disappearing coffee service and hot towels. Then her eyes opened wide in recognition and her head turned slowly to her right. The seat next to her was empty. She hesitated for a second, then reached into her coat pocket and pulled out a piece of spearmint gum. Her mouth broke out into a wry smile as the plane touched down.

As she waited for the jet way to connect and the doors to open, FBI field agent St. Cloud mentally reviewed progress on this latest case. Until a few days before, Karen had been on assignment in Hungary working with the federal police in Budapest. Her year had been fairly evenly split between Budapest and Washington, D.C. and she had been working with Hungarian and other Central European police agencies developing training programs. The latter had meant working with INTERPOL and other national civilian and intelligence agency recruits. The work was rewarding and she'd met a lot of interesting people. She'd even spent some time working with the Hungarians, undercover, on a couple of smuggling cases involving the Roma—gypsies—trafficking guns and drugs. It was cutting-edge work in a dangerous part of the world and she'd learned a lot. She'd even managed to get into a spot of trouble, but it had worked out.

Two days earlier, though it felt like a week, she'd been called home to D.C. The reason wasn't immediately clear, nor was Karen any closer to understanding why, precisely, she had become a central figure in the hunt for missing nuclear warheads. To be sure, she was past due for rotation and she was wryly suspicious that her military experience had a bearing on her reassignment. She was determined to get to the bottom of that question before the day was over. "May you live in interesting times," she growled as she launched herself ahead of the crowd leaving the plane and chuckled quietly.

She took a cab home from Reagan National and arrived home to a nearly empty, dusty condominium. The entry way was almost covered in shoes in loose little piles. The living room featured a single small end table she'd picked up in Vermont and piles of women's magazines, news magazines, and small islands of empty beer bottles. She smiled at the juxtaposition of glamour recycling materials. No evidence of Steven, she thought to herself, except by omission. Scattered dead houseplants were mute testimony to the end of her troubled five-year marriage to Steven, the year before, shortly after her posting to Hungary.

Karen found some beer in the refrigerator; nodded at the kitchen clock that showed 10 A.M., hauled her luggage into her bedroom, and turned on CNN. She grimaced, noticing it was domestic, not Hungarian beer. The news retreated into wallpaper as she unpacked, poked through piles on her bedroom floor for a clean set of clothes, opened cabinets in the kitchen looking for lunch (or was it breakfast?), and then found her car keys where she left them in the refrigerator. She was almost in the shower when a special bulletin came over the news.

"CNN presents this Breaking News development. CNN has learned that the toxic chemical spill outside of Baton Rouge has resulted in a continuation and expansion of the evacuation order for parts of three parishes in central Louisiana. Over 5,000 people have been affected by this evacuation, which began 4 hours ago due to a chemical spill at the Pharmex Chemical plant 20 miles outside of Baton Rouge. The Louisiana National Guard has been coordinating the evacuation.

"New Orleans' television station KUTB traffic helicopter arrived on the scene to get aerial footage of the disaster, but was chased away from the scene by National Guard chase planes. Our coverage from the ground will continue at the top of the hour. Stay tuned for an update of this unfolding story."

Looking a bit jet lagged and grungy, Karen shrugged her shoulders, got into the shower where she lingered after washing her hair, and then put on a touch of makeup. She wondered if coffee would have been a better idea than beer, but the shower was great therapy and cleared her head. The beer settled her stomach and nerves. All was well. Then a look of recognition came over face and she said aloud, "Missing weapons... Duh."

She fixed lunch based on a can of tuna, put on clean clothes, threw all her dirty laundry onto a large pile in the corner of her bedroom, and surveyed the house before heading out the door. She stared at herself in the entryway mirror.

"Girlfriend, you'd better hire someone to come in and clean the place up."

She shook her head and wondered to herself what the point would be without furniture. It wasn't as if she was about to start entertaining. Her thoughts drifted to the prospects of dating again and then she mentally kicked herself and shook her head even harder. She picked up the remains of what had once been potted ivy and smiled wickedly at her reflection.

In a mock Bronx accent she said, "Girlfriend, how can you be thinking about finding Mr. Right when youse can't keep a freakin' plant alive?"

Of course her car's battery was now dead, so on the cab ride into the District to FBI Headquarters, Karen stared down at a copy of the encrypted email message from headquarters 48 hours before that ordered her to pack her bags and get on a plane to Houston. She deciphered some of her small notes around the margins.

She looked up with a frown and thought to herself that this case was a different kind of trouble, and she could smell it, now recalling events of the last two days. The issue was not being sent home unexpectedly nor being sent immediately to Houston without a stop in D.C., it was both the clear urgency and obscure facts of the matter that gave her a sense of shadows moving behind the scene— and a sense of foreboding.

Almost 48 hours before, she made a quick job of packing up her small collection of personal effects in Budapest and caught the first available flight to the US. She flew directly to Houston via Amsterdam. Outside of customs at Bush Intercontinental Airport, two gray suits made a beeline to her, and asked her to follow, and escorted her to the door of an awaiting limousine, not the sort of government sedan she would have expected.

One of the suits held the rear door open for her and took her bags. Inside was someone she wasn't expecting either, an old acquaintance now also an Assistant Attorney General in the Justice Department.

"Hello Karen, have a seat." He smiled professionally.

Karen looked over her old college boyfriend. A few more gray hairs, but still a dashing figure, Alexander Hamilton was dressed in an expensive three-piece suit. They'd been friends and then lovers at Yale. Alex was a political science student, Karen a history major. Karen's father had been a Foreign Service officer and a Yale graduate himself, but Alex's family was old money and it was obvious even back then that Alex was on a fast track to a Senate seat or an upper echelon government position. He'd risen even faster than Karen expected, but they only exchanged Christmas cards. It might have something to do with the fact that Alex had dumped her for her best friend when she was a senior.

A warm smile crossed Karen's face. "Alex, look at you! You look great. How are Sandy and the kids?"

"Terrific. Sandy didn't know I was coming to see you, but if she had, I'm sure she'd ask me to say hi. Greta's in first grade; Allen's in third. Trying out for Little League already if you can imagine that?" His demeanor changed to business and he wasted no time.

"Look, we only have a few minutes." He handed Karen a manila folder stamped Top Secret. "We're putting you on a government plane to Lackland in a few minutes.

"Director Beal himself selected you for this assignment; it had nothing to do with me..." He actually looked a bit unhappy. "It was just a coincidence that I was sent down to brief you." He seemed to consider saying more on that point but shifted gears.

"We have a major crisis on our hands and for a number of reasons, some of which they wouldn't even tell me, you got the nod. Your military background and work with the NCIS and DIA are what they are looking for in an... evolving 'situation.'" He put quotes around "situation" with his fingers. She smiled crookedly at the mannerism.

Alex hesitated, "The point is that this is a NCIS and Air Force intelligence matter," he pointed to the folder that Karen now had open and was skimming, "and Justice needs someone inside to keep us informed. So, keep your nose clean and eyes open."

Karen ignored his inside joke. She was riveted upon what she was reading and shook her head back and forth.

Alex, her well-connected Brahmin bureaucrat rising star, was quiet for a while and let her read through the folder.

Karen finally looked up and asked incredulously, "Twelve nuclear Air Force warheads are missing?"

Alex definitely looked unhappy now. "So it appears."

"As soon as you find out what you can, find a secure line and call me here at the field office in Houston. You have 12 hours to report back. NCIS is already on their way to Lackland, but you won't be far behind. They have been told to liaise with you. Good luck, kiddo."

They pulled up in front of a small, unmarked Lear jet.

Karen smiled wanly, "Don't sleep too soundly," she said getting out of the car.

An Air Force official met her at Lackland AFB as she stepped off the steps of the small plane then made her wait in a small conference room not a hundred feet from the plane itself. The Agent in Charge, a large red-head dressed in civilian clothes simply identified himself as O'Brien, politely asked if Karen would review the documents assembled and if she needed coffee.

"Black, a little sugar... thanks." Her smile thawed the jet lag settling across her face.

The official Bill of Lading identified twelve tactical nuclear warheads SF-80/2000s, each weighing 280 pounds, minus launchers, loaded early in the morning the day before—en route to Kerr-McGee, the manufacturer, outside of Montgomery, Alabama. Additional Department of Defense paperwork indicated that the warheads were due for cleaning and recalibration. That seemed a bit strange to Karen—but what did she know about the care and feeding of fission weapons? She scribbled a note on her PDA to find out. The records indicated that each warhead was loaded at Lackland, onto a large AF cargo plane in an insulated, lead-lined steel crate about the size of a burial casket.

As the hours dragged on into the late evening, the paperwork spread out. Karen began to pace and to her knead her butt with her fists. She paced back and forth between a window open to the airfield and the table. Her face looked like it would break out in laughter, and then a frown, and then her head shook back and forth languidly.

On her PDA she scribbled: a) armory personnel and procedures, nominal, b) loading personnel and procedures, nominal, and, c) an AWOL Airman 1st class, discrepancy. She tapped the stylus on the edge of the PDA.

"Something anomalous, girlfriend."

Normally, Karen would be a good sailor and wait patiently until someone would extend the courtesy of telling her what the hell was REALLY going on. But her jet lag and time displacement were making her resentful and her normal bemusement with the absurdity of the universe evaporated. Her stomach growled audibly and she stood up abruptly and clicked the stylus into its place on the PDA.

She poked her head out of the room and looked at the startled airman outside the conference room and in her Second Lieutenant

12

voice ordered him to get O'Brien. Ten minutes or so later, when O'Brien returned, another familiar face trailed him, Bernard Snow, a tight-lipped Navy Commander, another blast from Karen's past—a co-worker from her early days right out of college during a stint in the Navy at DARPA. Although they hadn't purposely stayed in touch, they did seem to bump into each other frequently, once in Berlin and numerous times in D.C. The last time Karen saw him, Bernie was with NCIS.

"Hiya, Karen," he said amiably as he dropped down into one of the conference room seats. He didn't offer his hand and Karen continued standing.

"Bernie… staying out of trouble?" she cocked her head at him.

"It's not like I go looking for it. But the world is a dangerous place, so what can you do?"

Then he asked, "Have they fed you?" O'Brien, standing behind the Navy Commander, started to look uncomfortable.

"Except for caffeine, no—I have been kept hungry and in the dark."

"Okay, we'll fix that." He turned back and gave O'Brien some kind of look that Karen couldn't quite see.

"Just your luck, we are headed to the commissary. Harvey Ash will brief us. You know Harvey, don't you?"

O'Brien had left the room and the commander stood up and they both made their way outside where it was now growing dark. The young serviceman who had been outside the door was now sitting behind the wheel of a jeep waiting for them. The two swapped stories as they drove across the base.

Smoking a cigarette outside the nondescript low-slung building was Ash, another NCIS field agent that Karen knew during her Navy years. She remembered that he was a real prick—too many of them in the service. Thinking back, Karen wasn't exactly sure why she'd signed up for Officer Candidate School right out of college, except that she felt like her history degree hadn't given her what she wanted. And it was a rebuke to her father who wanted her to get a job in the Foreign Service or State Department where he had more connections than just about anyone—as a former ambassador. Karen ended up in Monterey, California for language school, then back to the East Coast to work at DARPA with the computer geeks.

For better or worse, she'd made a lot of friends, a few enemies, rattled a few chauvinists like Ash, and met lots of people in the intelligence community. It was after six years of naval service when she was being groomed for intelligence analysis work that she decided to leave the regimentation of the military for civilian life. Or maybe it was Steven's hounding. Not that he was any happier once she joined the Bureau… She laughed out loud as the sequence unfolded in her mind. The two NCIS agents looked at her funny.

"What's so fucking funny, sailor?" Ash snarled.

"Oh, it's not you asshole," she shot back and winked at Bernie. "It's the housekeeping. You can't get good help these days." What an incorrigible jerk she thought to herself.

Ash looked somewhat taken aback as though he had fallen through a crack in time, realizing the woman in front of him was now an FBI agent.

"Sorry," he said actually looking chagrinned. "We do need help. The evidence at this point is not very helpful. Except for a few obvious irregularities."

"'Bout the size of it," rejoined Ash. "But the lack of information at this point is an interesting fact in its own right. All we have are the lists: the inventory numbers and descriptions of the munitions; the manifest from the flight; the armory personnel and crew rosters. And that's it."

"So what's next?" asked Karen.

"Shakedown the armory people and the loading crew and look for anything suspicious," answered Snow, as though he already knew the drill.

"First we eat," said Ash as he flipped his cigarette into an ash can by the door. "The Air Force still knows how to feed its boys and girls well."

They walked into a large, well-lit mess hall, with rock music playing in the background. Karen didn't have a military ID card, but her FBI ID seemed to do the trick. The airman checking ID at the door didn't bat an eye. But they got a few dirty looks from the enlisted people cleaning up the buffet area. Even close to closing, the salad cart looked surprisingly fresh and since it was hours past Karen's normal dinnertime, she settled for a hot roll and salad smothered in blue cheese dressing. Even the roll tasted like it had just come out of the oven. Maybe it had. They ate quickly and in silence. If there hadn't been enlisted ears so close it might have been otherwise.

Karen faced the door and noticed that a baby-faced MP was talking eagerly to the airman at the door who nodded in their direction. The policeman approached, saluted, and asked, "Captain Ash?"

"Thanks," said Ash and simply held out his hand and the kid filled it with a brown file folder.

"Master Sergeant Waverly," began agent Ash, "thank you for mustering your crew this late in the day." It was nearly midnight. Not all the crew had actually been on base to muster, but the interrogations were going forward. Waverly looked calm and composed—despite smelling like a brewery—but some of the other enlisted folks waiting in the hallway appeared uneasy.

Waverly was dressed in a starched, neatly pressed Air Force uniform. He was a slightly graying, slim white man in his mid-forties. They occupied the CO's office in a rambling outbuilding on the edge of the air base and were interviewing airmen one at a time at a small conference table on the side of the office.

The non-com pulled a cigarette out of his pocket without asking and flicked open a Zippo and lit up. He exhaled and cocked his head.

"Yessir?"

"The C-5 your crew loaded yesterday arrived in Alabama missing the tactical nukes which you allegedly put on board," said Ash managing to make it sound like a challenge. The Master Sergeant's composure changed immediately.

"Christ Almighty," he said looking back and forth between the three agents, "I supervised the entire job myself. Everything went smoothly—well almost—and there wasn't anything out of the ordinary going on..." He reacted like he really had not had an inkling of why they'd mustered his crew and was starting to sweat.

"What did not go smoothly?" asked Snow.

"Well, Jonesie, er...Airman First Class Jones, sir, didn't show up which caused a little delay." This was in their background report. Normally a missing member of the flight crew wouldn't have mattered seriously, but there's always extra concern with nuclear payloads. "So the pilot made us wait around until they got someone to fill in for him. Kinda pissed us off, sir."

"Why's that?" asked Ash.

"Some of the crew had beers with him the night before last at the NCO club. Barnes said he'd joked about getting packed and to bed early. Jones had leave coming and was supposed to drive home to Houston to see his wife. The guys were riding him about going home to some free pussy."

Karen didn't blink, and the NCO didn't seem to care there was a woman in the room. But she smiled inwardly at rank and file insensitivities. Snow frowned, "His wife?"

"Yeah, the guy's a carouser and a real ladies' man. Well anyway, we were all a bit surprised to hear that he'd left the base last night, AWOL. The guys were ticked that he was out partying while we were waiting on the cold fucking runway." There were actually flurries as they spoke, a bit cold for San Antonio.

"Anything else you can think of that was not routine about this loading job?" added Ash.

"Come to think about it, there is. We usually load the heaviest gear towards the front and middle of a C-5. You know, trucks, tanks and heavy artillery, and other heavy equipment usually go in first. Balancing those monsters is a bitch. Today's load was made up of lots of crates and assorted ordinance on pallets. We take our time with that kind of stuff, but balancing the load is still a big deal. Usually, tactical pallets ride further in, but the loading schedule had the tactical pallets going in last—they're extra heavy." When he saw the blank faces of the agents, he added, "You know, because of the lead shielding?"

"Anyway, there is no rule against it, but now that I think about it, it did seem out of the ordinary. We were all getting annoyed with Jonesie by about that time, so I didn't give it much thought then."

Ash asked, "Whose responsibility is it to balance the plane?"

"The 'deck master' for that flight was supposed to be Airman Jones."

The interrogation of the rest of the crew followed the same pattern. One after another, each of the crew were ushered in, asked questions, and then led out a side door. The armory crew was also interrogated. Ash and Snow did all of the talking. Karen concentrated on taking notes and reviewing personnel files. She gave her PDA a workout and transposed all the names and numbers to run through the FBI databases. By the end of the evening her low battery indicator was blinking. The agents finished with the last interviews at 4 A.M.— all except for the missing Airman 1st class Jones. No particularly compelling evidence had turned up. A couple of the airmen, including Airman Second Class Barnes, had been rather short on answers. Maybe his lack of answers was due to being questioned at two in the morning, but only time would tell.

The agents collected their coats and Harvey Ash made a quick call on his cell phone.

"Okay, St. Cloud, we got orders to stick around San Antonio. They're getting a plane ready for you. Your ride will be here any sec."

As soon as Karen was on the plane, she had the pilot give her a secure circuit and she called the number Alex had given her earlier. She didn't want to talk to the guy, she felt so tired she was nauseated, but to her surprise, Alex answered.

"You're up early."

"No. We have been here all night working hard like you. What can you tell me?"

"Not much, I'm afraid. There is a missing airman, but nothing obvious came out of the interviews. What can you tell me?"

"All I can say at the moment is that there is unusually high signal intelligence chatter that the NSA has picked up. I'm sure they'll brief you at back at headquarters. That's where you are needed. We're flying you back to Houston to catch a commercial flight in about an hour.

"I see."

"The Assistant Director wants you in his office ASAP, okay?"

"Okay."

"Did Baton Rouge come up in any connection to anyone in the interviews?"

"Baton Rouge, Louisiana? No, not at all."

"That may be where the warheads dropped out of the C-5."

She let out a low long whistle.

"I really can't say much more at this time, as it is mostly under wraps… Uh, just keep your eyes and ears open for Baton Rouge."

"Aye aye, captain." She fell back on a slight jab at him from their sailing days on the Long Island Sound back in college.

"Have a smooth sail back to Washington."

"You, too," Karen said and switched off the phone. Moments later the plane was airborne.

In Houston a TSA employee met her at the base of the Learjet stairs, took her bag and escorted her to an electric golf cart. In minutes she was being led up a staircase at the end of the jet way and was quickly inside an empty 747.

"Agent St. Cloud?" asked the flight attendant who smiled at her. "You lucked out with a first class upgrade in the first row. Can I get you anything to drink?" She pointed at the empty seat. "It will be a few minutes before the gate opens for regular passengers."

Karen settled herself in and pulled her 9 mm Glock from the holster behind her back, dropped it into her saddlebag purse, stuck the purse under the seat, and was asleep in minutes. She never even heard the other passengers come on board.

Boulder, Colorado (0700 MST)

Leah Wilson banged away determinedly on the computer keyboard, as though emphasis would ensure that her colleagues would pay attention. The title said it all, "Confronting the Antarctic hydro-morphology regime: a climate change paradigm shift." She cut and pasted the completed abstract in front of the body of the paper and admired the look of it on the monitor. She made a small contented sigh and tapped the save button again for good measure.

Her gaze shifted to the desk and bookshelf behind it, the books obscured by their recent wedding pictures from up on Pikes Peak. There were pictures of her also recent doctoral commencement, with her mentor and now husband next to her in his own academic regalia. She noticed that she was in his shadow in the picture, as well as in her present academic life. She turned back to the paper as though focusing on it would elevate her status in the profession.

She had to remind herself that Jake Meadows was, after all, one of the fathers of the field of global climate circulation modeling. His influence was written all over her paper, she saw as she paged through it. Between the lines, it reflected what she had learned from him, and what he had brought out in her: a passion for research and love for theoretical and physical climatology. But she was beginning to come to grips with the circumstances of their relationship and the pall it cast across her own professional career. She wanted to be recognized for her own worth, her own contributions to her discipline. Her research and this paper would make it hard for the geophysicists and global climatologists to ignore her. She only hoped that Jake didn't take it too hard.

She opened up her e-mail to send him a quick message. Her mailbox was mostly full of National Center for Atmospheric Research

(NCAR) announcements and project reports from others in her post-doctoral research group. There was a backlog of messages from the Arctic team that she corresponded with, but no sign of messages from Jake. She looked up at a picture of the two of them in front of their San Francisco apartment. Her sigh this time was not so happy.

To Jake she typed: "I'm working my fingers to the bone on the sea level rise paper this morning. Remember to feed the cat. See you Saturday. Love you. Ciao."

She absently picked up a file containing materials for the annual meeting of the International Geophysical Society, six months away, and crossed her fingers that her previous paper would be peer-reviewed and published by the time of the meeting. She thumbed through the draft schedule to review the arrangement of paper sessions and panels that she'd flagged. She dog-eared the page listing the session she shared with four others on the topic "Sea Level Glacial Grounding." She smiled in anticipation of the stir that she thought she'd make. It was a good thing, she thought, first that the chair of her session was her friend Max of NCAR, and two, that the meeting was going to be in San Francisco this year. She absolutely hated airports and long plane trips. On the other hand, she loved her old but well-maintained '92 Corvette and burning gas with utter abandon along the Interstate at 90 miles an hour. The glove box was full of a small number of speeding tickets and dozens of warnings from motorcycle cops smitten by her long brunette hair and piercing blue eyes that sparkled when her dark glasses came down.

She double clicked again on her mouse and was instantly banging again on her keyboard. After twenty minutes of intense work she stopped to consider which charts and maps to include in the sea level rise paper. She looked up at the photo-mosaic map of Antarctica, which covered one wall. For a few minutes she lost herself staring at the enormity of the Ross Ice Shelf. Leah shivered—not about the cold, although cold it certainly was, but about the implications of her research. If she was right—and she was sure of that—there was evidence that the feeder glaciers, the larger ones a half-mile thick, were accelerating in speed. While that was not in and of itself a serious problem, other mitigating factors suggested a potential crisis of global proportions.

Beyond the computer desk, books, and pictures, the walls were all covered with maps, satellite images, and Post-its, and notes and newspaper clippings and other evidence of the evolution of her work and thinking. She inspected: her research ideas on Antarctic glacier disintegration as a result of global warming and highlights of her doctoral research at San Francisco State on the feedback processes between sea level rise and local climate variations (or microclimate modeling as she liked to describe it). A photocopy of her National Science Foundation grant award in Antarctic studies was on the middle of the right-hand wall. A news clipping from her hometown describes Leah's NSF graduate research project designed to explore the relationship between glacial calving—the process which creates icebergs—sea level rise in the South Pacific and southern ocean microclimates. There were scattered pictures from the season she spent at McMurdo Base in the Antarctic and on icebergs in the Ross Sea. Also on the wall was the picture of Jake that she took with her on that trip—before they were an item. There was a red lipstick kiss covering his head, now.

One of her latest charts based on satellite data showed alarming rates of accelerated calving, double and triple the rate of a few years earlier. But what dominated the left wall was image after image of sonar scans of the morphology of the Ross Ice Sheet basin. There were maps of the basin with the Ross Ice Shelf, without the shelf, with the approximate look of the shelf during the height of the last interglacial. The most dramatic of the lot had red magic marker X marks indicating active undersea volcanoes.

One side-view cutaway showed how the Ross Ice Shelf was actually a sort of super iceberg that sat partly over the Ross Bay and was partly grounded on bedrock that would normally be below sea level were it not covered with ice. It showed the seamounts and volcanoes that lie across the middle of the bay keeping the ice sheet from slipping into the sea.

An outline of the current paper was taped to the wall on her right: her plan to demonstrate that the accelerated glacial activity was not only speeding up the production of ice berg calving but was also effecting the volcanic ridges: first by depressing the surrounding terrain forcing more magma to the surface, and second by scraping the "surface" fissures and crust. She had firm evidence from satellite telemetry that these "hot spots" in the Ross Bay were heating up, but she was neither a geologist nor a volcanologist, so her speculations about the geomorphology might be suspect. She looked at the outline and visibly cringed at the thought that her volcanologist friends, especially her McMurdo pals, would see her as a carpetbagger.

Moreover, her conclusion that the whole ice shelf might soon be loosened enough to slide into the Southern Ocean was definitely going out on a limb. She smiled and thought to herself how proud Jake would be of her if she got *Science* to accept her article.

At roughly the same time in San Francisco, Jake Meadows looked over at a picture of Leah, and thought of her in a biblical fashion. He threw off the covers and stretched. Even at the crack of dawn he looked bored. His course preparation materials for his Climate Modeling class were still spread out all over the bed and floor. His laptop computer was perched precariously on the edge of the bed and still open to his multimedia presentation. He grabbed the laptop and pulled up NOAA-GOES satellite cloud imagery and then downloaded it to the university server. He grimaced waiting for the large data files to find their way through the clogged university ultra-broadband system, drummed fingernails on the titanium case, and then sighed with relief when the gray bar disappeared.

Jake slowly eased himself out from under the covers and reached down to slide on his slippers. He winced and glanced at the frost on the thin windowpane, with fog filling in the background. Sitting on the edge of the bed, he leaned over to touch a kiss to a picture of Leah on the nightstand.

"I miss you sweetie," he said and pushed himself the rest of the way up and stumbled a bit on the way to the kitchen in the direction of the brewed coffee aroma. He glanced at the alcove where Leah was usually already hard at work in the mornings when he got up, but she was, of course, in Boulder where she would be for most of the next three years of her post-doc position. He wondered to himself why waking up with her in the flat seemed to make the mornings go so much faster.

Jake lingered over his coffee, switched on the Weather Channel, and puttered around the apartment, picked up stray articles of clothing—mainly socks—and glanced at Leah's corner and let out wistful small sighs. He wondered if his classes were suffering; his teaching this semester was automatic, not as enthusiastic as it was normally. He had a smart bunch of students this term who seemed more excited by climate modeling than he was.

He wondered to himself how Leah's work was coming—she'd been awfully secretive about her research lately. In his mind's eye, he saw her long slender fingers pounding away at her keyboard. If there was one thing that annoyed Jake about her it was the way she attacked her keyboard when she was working intensively. He followed his way up her arms in his mind and wished he had her in his arms.

A garbage truck rumbled by in the street out in front of the building and Jake's eyes came back into focus. He took a few sips of coffee, plucked the last pair of dirty socks from the sofa, started to soak a pile of dirty dishes, and toasted a bagel. Studying the calendar, he crossed off the last few days and circled Saturday when Leah would be back for the weekend. He grabbed kitchen hand towels and threw them into the hallway on top of a pile of dirty clothes.

The Weather Channel bleeped a weather warning on the bottom scroll: heavy fog warning. As he finished washing dishes, Jake watched the swirling fog outside the small kitchen window. The crystals of frost in the corners were almost all melted and he seemed entranced for a few seconds.

For no obvious reason, he looked at his reflection in the window. "Antarctica," he said, as if it were the answer to a question.

Buenos Aires, Argentina (1120 AST)

Late morning shoppers and office workers out early for lunch crowded both the street and sidewalk of Avenida Florida, the famous pedestrian-only street in the heart of the city. Signs of the vibrant economic situation were everywhere, with new trendy boutiques showing off the latest fashions from Paris, New York, and Shanghai. The plainclothes detective pulled her shopping bag prop closer and jostled a few other women shoppers as she skirted outdoor restaurants and sidewalk cafes.

Sandi Gusman was dressed like any of the downtown secretaries from accounting or law firms, in pumps and a longish gray skirt. It was summer and the warm weather made her bulky cotton jacket seem a bit out of place, but it hid her arsenal and radio well. She tugged at her earphone, determined to work its way out of her ear canal and dismissed the strange looks she got as other window shoppers caught her talking to herself in a boutique window.

Normally she loved "la Florida," but not today.

"Suspect entering a shoe store between Corrientes and Sarmiento," she reported. She eased her way across the narrow street so she could watch the entrance in the reflection of a shop window.

Her earphone responded, "Raul is covering the alley."

"Copy that," she said and nodded.

22

She moved to the next shop, a tiny stamp and coin store. An angled display-case window afforded her an even better, less conspicuous view of the shoe store. Within another minute her man stepped out of the door and walked directly towards her. She avoided his eyes as he walked into the miniature store whose sign declared it to be a "numismatic and philatelic emporium."

Sandi bent over as though to look more closely at the merchandise in the window. The man was arguing with the shopkeeper. He looked out at the street and towards the door, as the argument seemed to heat up.

"He's moved across the street to the stamp and coin shop and it looks like there's trouble," she reported.

"Stay put. Back-up is half a block away," said the earpiece.

Her slight motion must have caught the man's attention because he noticed her now and stared. In the split second that they held each other's eyes she noticed a few things about him. He definitely appeared to be *mestizo*, but quite tall—about an even two meters. In spite of his flight jacket she could see he was a body builder. There was something funny about his left eye, which had a noticeable tic.

She blinked and in the next instant he had drawn a pistol from under his jacket. As she dropped to the sidewalk she yelled, "He's armed," pulled out her own 45-caliber automatic, and rolled as glass exploded all around her and lead started to rain around her. As she looked up, her target disappeared into the rear of the store.

She jumped up without brushing herself off and pushed through the intact glass door. "Suspect making for the alley," she called into her microphone.

"Wait for back-up," came the reply, but the earphone dangled at her waist.

Cautiously, she eased into the dark back room and nearly shot a young girl sitting at a small corner desk. The girl covered her face with her hands. Sandi asked gruffly, "Where?" and the girl pointed to a rear door before her hands returned to her mouth. The policewoman dropped down by the door and pushed it open and crouched low as she went through. A bullet whizzed over her left shoulder and she twisted towards the sound of the concussions, but kept moving down the alley. Finding cover behind an overflowing trash bin, she spotted her quarry behind another trashcan.

"Police," she yelled, "you are under arrest! Put down your gun!" Another bullet hit the cover of the trash bin only centimeters from her head. Before thinking it through, she leapt forward and rolled onto her side, pumping three or four rounds from her 1910 Colt into the trash can hiding her prey and then waited for return fire. It never came.

The part German, part English Argentine federal detective lay quietly for a few seconds without moving, eyes wide open, feeling and sensing her body for serious damage. She blinked when the reports came in nominal and slowly pushed herself up onto her hands and knees. She inspected her gold Federal Police Academy ring for damage, too, but it was also untarnished.

"Jesus, that was close," she said to herself. Years of studying criminology and five years on the force and this was her first serious firefight.

"Sandi are you alright? Holy Jesus, what did you do to his face?"

She stood up shakily to see a small stream of blood running into the middle of the alley. Her loyal five-year partner, Raul, was standing over the man they had been following for the last two days. Her life wasn't over and it also looked like her aim was still good. She took one look at what was left of his face, leaned against the wall, and threw up.

Washington, D.C. (1230 EDT)

Karen entered the Hoover Building at 12:30, went through security, and up to the International Division on the sixth floor. The assistant director's receptionist greeted her.

"Welcome back Agent St. Cloud. The assistant director wanted to see you as soon as you arrived. He's not left yet for lunch— just a second, please." She pushed a button and announced her. "You may go right in."

"Thanks Natalie. Good to be back." She smiled at her and walked through the door.

"Come in, come in." Assistant Director Williams stood and met her halfway across the obscenely neat office. "Good to have you back, St. Cloud. Have a seat." Williams came out from behind his desk, and they sat down together in plush chairs to the side of William's desk.

24

"You have been doing good work in Europe. I am going to miss you." Karen raised an eyebrow in question. Williams chuckled to himself. "Looks like you're going to get promoted and a lot less sleep for awhile." His good humor changed to a look of concern and then he frowned as he pulled a folder off of his desk.

"Here is more intel on your new case and some of the details you have undoubtedly been missing. You are being attached to the Domestic Terrorism Division, assigned Special Agent status, and given special travel authorization for the duration of the situation. We won't call it a crisis yet, but this will put the National Threat Level up to red by tomorrow, unless I'm grossly mistaken.

"Due to the interagency aspects of this new threat, we're going to find office space here on the sixth floor for the duration, but you will report to Deputy Director Hale of Domestic Terrorism. I want you back when this is all over, if I have anything to say about it. We are all scheduled for a meeting at 1500 today to assess the situation—there should be an agenda in the file."

"We?" Karen asked.

"Homeland Security, CIA, NSA, a number of the military intelligence agencies, and Justice and us. FBI will be represented by Hale, someone from the Region Six field office you, and me. We've swapped him for Alex."

"Natalie will show you to your office. Go ahead and get settled in, but be prepared to report on the Lackland interviews, and we'll see you upstairs at three." Williams stood up and put out his hand. Karen took it.

As Williams walked her to the door he said, "Homeland Security has given this investigation a code name: Hot pants." He paused, "Go figure."

He looked a little embarrassed, but Karen just smiled. In her sweetest faux Texas drawl, she replied.

"Ya'll know there'll be hot seats where them hot pants been sittin'!"

He chuckled pleasantly, but not too loudly. Somehow she managed to get away with her always slightly bemusing atypical behavior at FBI. Maybe because her good looks made it easier, or maybe her military background, or her worldly experience? She didn't really care, because she really thought life was mostly a big joke, bent and cruel at times, but mainly just absurd. She wore a permanent half smile.

"Hot seats at Lackland, for now," she said in her normal Long Island voice. "See you this afternoon, sir."

He smiled and shook her hand again at the door.

"Again, good to have you back."

Buenos Aires (1400 ADT)

Sandi Gusman sat at her desk in the Peron Federal Building when one of the pool secretaries came up to her.

"You are wanted in the director's office. They are waiting for you."

Sandi thanked her and sat for a few seconds. The incident report sat ready to go. A webpage was open to the section on administrative review, which she closed. She shut down her computer, fearing the worse. A worried look crossed her face.

The door to the office of her immediate superior Captain Manuel Saavedra had been closed since she returned, so she figured that her troubles would begin in the late afternoon. There already seemed to be a cloud over the new silver on black placard on her desk that read Investigator Gusman. But she put on a happy face, picked up the report, and straightened her desk before leaving.

A written memo from Saavedra sat in her inbox ordering her to turn over all her active cases files to the staff rookie, Corporal Flores. She walked over to Flores desk and dropped one last folder on top of the files she stacked there earlier. Her face looked like she thought her career was about to go up in flames.

"Good luck Flores," she muttered to his empty seat.

She took the elevator to the eleventh floor and was immediately ushered by a secretary into the penthouse office. The occupants were the Federal Police Director, whom everyone called Doctor Vargas, her boss Captain Saavedra, and Raul. The captain introduced her to the director. They shook hands.

"I knew your father well. A good man."

"Thank you, sir," She smiled brightly.

"Please have a seat." He motioned to all of them and they complied.

She nodded and smiled a crooked grin at Raul. They had been kept apart since the Avenida Florida chase and shooting. He looked even more nervous than she felt.

"As you have undoubtedly guessed, there is a criminal conspiracy underway which may have serious consequences for the security and health of the Motherland. Moreover it has international ramifications and consequences if what we are being told by foreign sources is true." He swiveled around to look to his side where floor-to-ceiling windows opened up on the port area of the city. He took off his glasses and pinched the bridge of his nose as though his head hurt. He gestured at Captain Saavedra to continue.

"We all know that the individual you so successfully dispatched this morning was Alejandro Vera, an enforcer for the Bolivian drug organization around Santa Cruz. The mystery surrounding his arrival and business here in the capital is still obscure. We have been questioning the shop owner who is himself Bolivian and have asked the federal district court to allow us to keep him... for his own protection." He winked at the three and paused to light a cigarette.

Raul and Sandi exchanged relieved glances at each other and Raul even smiled.

"He is cooperating with us and was apparently part of a support network here in the capital for Peruvian terrorists. The shopkeeper claims that they were heading to Santiago—and that he knows little else beyond that. We are also holding his daughter—the one you ran into during the chase—so we have reason to think he is telling us the truth. He's very scared."

He turned to his boss, "Doctor?"

"Thank you Captain. This would have all been interesting enough, but late this morning after your adventures downtown, we sent inquiries to INTERPOL—once we had fingerprints and DNA samples. Apparently what we have come across is only 'the tip of the iceberg.'" He laughed to himself. Captain Saavedra began smiling. Sandi looked inquiringly at Raul who shrugged his shoulders and shook his head. Doctor Vargas sobered and handed a file to Raul and then an identical one to her.

"It is more that just narco-terrorists; something far grander. We are sending you both down to Punta Arenas and then to the Chilean base in Antarctica. Ever been there before?"

Raul nodded his head while Sandi shook hers.

"Yes and no, eh? Ha! Well, the files will tell you what we know at present. It appears to have something to do with drug money and the international environmental movement—a bizarre combination it would seem, but nonetheless dangerous. You two are going to help us find out what it is all about. Most of what you need to know is in the files, but we have arranged for backup support at our own Antarctic station and for travel authority to any of the other international scientific stations on the continent. That is where we think the terrorists are."

"I want to stress the importance of this mission and the danger to the Motherland. There is still much mystery surrounding these events, but there may be a threat to the nation. We will rely on the two of you to help us get to the bottom of it. I spoke with the president about the operation this morning, so you should know that it originates at the highest level. After you have been through the files, Captain Saavedra will provide further operational instructions, travel arrangements, and anything else you feel you need."

The phone on the director's desk rang.

"I am sorry to be rude, but I must take this call and send you on your way. Good luck and God bless you."

Before they had even stood up to leave, Doctor Vargas was on the phone and intensely concentrated on his conversation. They hurried out of the room and followed Saavedra to the elevators. He looked them both in the eye.

"I will give you two an hour to go over the material in those folders and then I want you to join me in my office."

The elevator doors opened. Raul and Sandi got in, but the Captain did not.

"See you later," he told them.

As the elevator doors closed on the two of them, Raul looked at Sandi and said, "I hate snow."

Hoover Building, Washington, D.C. (1500 EST)

Karen sat in her new "office," a no-frills cubicle, and struggled to get the new computer on the desk to interface with her voice controls. She uploaded her PDA files, and began a report on the Lackland interviews. She opened a small web window to RSS stream Reuters and the *New York Times* and listened to the headlines while she worked on her report.

The Baton Rouge evacuation was still the lead story. Folks from eastern counties were being allowed back, but river traffic was blocked and an area north of the city was now evacuated. The CNN reporter sounded skeptical, noting that the evacuation was not consistent with the current westerly winds.

The FBI online divisional summary report was much more illuminating. It reported that the huge rear door of the C-5 had been blown open at 20,000 feet and the rear pallets had been sucked, blown, or dropped out northeast of Baton Rouge. The plane landed safely in spite of extensive damage. Airman Jones' replacement, ironically named Smith, was in serious condition with massive ear damage and two other crewmen were also hospitalized. The pilot and copilot were credited with saving the plane and crew with some fast thinking. Karen hurriedly scanned through the rest of the file and requested a meeting with Hale.

At 2:50 P.M. Karen entered the ninth floor conference room following in the footsteps of Deputy Director Roger Hale. A young FBI agent in a dark blue Brooks Brothers suit checked his list against Karen's nametag, nodded at her and pointed her to a chair behind Hale's. They both sat and then he turned to her.

"Thanks for coming over to see me when you did. That was helpful."

"My pleasure," she said and her crooked grin passed across her face.

Karen scanned the room and at the same time reflected on their meeting over the previous thirty minutes. Hale was an intense New Englander who sounded like an earthy Jack Kennedy. Initially, they had good rapport and Karen started to like her new boss until she learned that he knew her father well. She asked herself: Why would Hale want to take an interest in her career? She wanted to be flattered, but she hated the old-boy politics of this town and really wanted to be appreciated for her own talents. At first it felt a bit creepy, but Karen warmed to Hale's sometimes self-deprecating humor and strategic approach to the fallout he expected from this incident.

Karen noted that the situation had changed dramatically in her assessment of the layout for the meeting. The principals were the National Security Council lineup, and Homeland Security. The FBI was the host of the meeting but the chair was Vice President Albert Gold. Representatives from all agencies organized under the pre-existing Nuclear Threat Response Taskforce were also present. "This is a first," Karen thought, seeing that the room was populated with some of the most powerful egos inside the Beltway.

While the others filed in, she pulled out her report, looked over a short agenda, which had been placed on her chair, and collected her thoughts. She pulled out her PDA and stylus and started jotting down the header info for this meeting: time, date, and participants.

The vice president cleared his throat and began the meeting.

"We don't have time today for lengthy introductions. Instead I will just read the following message from the president:

We are confronted with one of the greatest domestic threats that the United States has ever faced. I hereby order convened a meeting of the NSC and Nuclear Threat Response Taskforce to explore strategies to cope with this new threat to the U.S. and/or the international community. I am placing our armed forces on DEFCON 3 and in consultation with Homeland Security have raised the Threat Level to Red effective 3 P.M. EST. Furthermore, your Taskforce is granted the highest priority in terms of resource allocations and manpower to meet this crisis head on. I will be meeting later today with senior members of Congressional Intelligence committees who will be briefed here at the White House.

The Office of the Vice President will coordinate the activities of your Taskforce.

Godspeed in your work.

The VP continued, "Let's go down the agenda and hear agency reports. Any additions to the agenda at this point?"

There was no response other than a few who shook their heads. "Admiral Brown?"

Admiral Donald Brown, Vice Chairman of the Joint Chiefs of Staff and war hero, looked all around and made eye contact with nearly everyone in the inner and outer rows of seats.

"We have abandoned the Baton Rouge subterfuge. Navy divers found the weapons pallets in the river. No warheads, but they did find crates of rebar. Ballast. NSA was right about this from the beginning."

Karen shook her head ever so slightly. A few other people on the opposite side looked confused or blank. That made her nervous.

"Civilian evacuation was called off at noon. The fog is helping to obscure the real reason for the evacuation." He frowned, and then added, "At least for the time being. I seriously doubt that there is any way to hide the river search given the heavy traffic on that part of the river."

"We already face a credibility problem on this, and the Pentagon will not take further responsibility for lying about it—national security notwithstanding. It is already too big a story. Please convey our concerns to the president." He stared straight into the eyes of the vice president, who nodded.

"Message understood. We may want to return to this point before the end of the meeting," he said. "Go on."

"No radiation has been detected anywhere inside the debris field, even by sensors designed specifically by DoD for antiterrorism surveillance. The weapons were never on the plane.

"We've turned service record information over to the FBI as well as DoD subunits. The Pentagon would also like to have the DIA to have a second seat on the Task Force. I will have Deputy Director Helen Coleman give their report."

Brown was a large, barrel-chested man with silver-gray hair. He looked haggard and had obviously been awake for a while. Karen felt her own jet lag subside a bit. In contrast, Helen Coleman was a dynamic if physically diminutive woman at 5 foot 2 inches. She suffered no fools and her impatience with her superior was almost palpable. She didn't seem to like the vice president either, but not because she thought him a fool. Probably something to do with the presidential primaries heating up, Karen thought to herself.

"Mr. Vice President, friends, this is what DIA has. Two servicemen from the armory crew at Lackland are AWOL—somewhere in South America we think—and Airman Jones has just turned up dead in New Orleans. In the last few minutes we have learned that Airman Smith died from complications in Alabama. The kicker is that we found that he was wearing a parachute at the time of the C-5 explosion. Not standard procedure. That makes him a suspect, alive or dead. We will be working with the FBI to check out his family and friends." She impassively locked eyes with the VP until he nodded slightly. "Let me continue with the details."

"What we are missing are exactly one dozen cruise missile warheads. They are ten years old and have never been armed. They are not attached to missiles—their launchers. During their entire tenure at Lackland, they were kept in a high security area under three layers of defense barriers. The nuclear munitions bunker is physically inside a warehouse. The active electronic and human fences meant that any loading or unloading, entry and exit to the building was monitored and logged. The bunker itself has always had two armed

31

guards outside with electronic badges to open the bunker and internal lockers. The security system is complex and redundant. Any entry to the bunker has to be authorized by the base commander or executive officer. Warehouse video monitors cover the bunker entrance, loading dock, and warehouse office gate (where most of the traffic is located). The security system is interlocked with the base security which received a hardware upgrade and computer system last summer.

"We have not yet found any evidence of tampering with the bunker and storage system, but are reviewing logs and video archives—just to be thorough. One problem may be that those tapes are reused after six months, so a breach before July 1 may be impossible to verify. We are also investigating the possibility of a computer system break-in and cover up.

"What has provoked us to take this tack is the fact that two of the munitions staff have disappeared overnight, although they were restricted to quarters. Airman First Class Wallenstein and Airman Second Class Barnes managed to leave the base undetected and caught a commercial air flight to South America—Santiago, Chile. We have All Points' Bulletins out for them in Chile and other South American capitals. I understand one of the FBI investigators who spoke with them is here in the room." She looked right at her, without a flicker of emotion, but with an incredibly deep penetrating stare. "Perhaps she could enlighten us about them." But before she put Karen on the spot—and she was already in a sweat—Colman continued without hesitation.

"Airman Jones was found dead in a back alley behind a tavern on Bourbon Street in New Orleans. He was shot three times in the head with a small caliber handgun and dumped in a garbage bin. His body was found naked. That's still about all we know. His wife has not been notified, although the FBI was already in touch with her about his disappearance. I guess DoD gets the fun job."

Nobody smiled.

"Smith died in Huntsville about twenty-five minutes ago of internal bleeding. He was caught by the blast and may have had his chest crushed by something. He never regained consciousness. After the landing he was found near the hole in the tail of the plane with a parachute and heavy clothing on. This was not SOP, as I have said, which clearly suggests that he was planning to jump, or some monkey-business." She looked at the VP, who nodded more forcefully this time.

"So there you have it. We will continue to pursue our leads at Lackland and elsewhere. We're keeping the FBI Taskforce coordinator's office informed and will report hourly to the White House Situation Room." Karen caught her wink at the VP and nearly fell off her chair. No one else appeared to notice or care, but Karen kept looking furtively at the older woman, who paid her no mind.

She tried to recall what she knew about Wallenstein and Barnes: that both had been undistinguished in their military careers and were otherwise average middle class young men. What did set them apart and had actually caught her attention was that both had college degrees when they enlisted. She turned her attention back to the meeting.

Her new boss reported how little the FBI actually knew at this point, but had created a special crisis management team to be lead by one of the FBI's "best and brightest." She could feel the attention shift to her even before the words left his mouth.

"Based on what you will be hearing from NSA, I thought it prudent to bring on board one of our rising stars as FBI representative to the Task Force. Special Agent St. Cloud has considerable international experience, is a twelve-year Navy veteran, former DARPA employee, and was raised in the diplomatic community. Her understanding of *vodun* and a decade of living in Haiti as a young woman make her an ideal choice."

Her mouth dropped open and then as she realized it, she closed it again and the vice president spoke.

"Good to have you with us back in the States," and nodded at her.

"Thank you, sir" came out of her mouth before she even knew it. Thoughts flooded her head and a few more answers popped into place.

She focused on a spot on the wall on the other side of the room to stop from breaking out in her usual lop-sided smile.

"B.W." Erikson of the National Security Agency was the last of the senior officials to speak. Karen didn't need to remind herself that Erikson was the most enigmatic of the group, which was to be expected after decades at NSA. As a math genius and crack cryptographer, Erikson had always been on the leading edge not only of his profession, but also on the edge of the information revolution. He was one of the most powerful behind-the-scenes figures in international and domestic intelligence.

He gruffly began, "We would not be so blind now if NASA had been more competent." The VP looked at him sharply and frowned. Erikson pressed ahead without looking up. "Even though many of our capabilities have been served by the Air Force, our global reach and penetration has been compromised by continued low earth orbit transportation problems. If we get through this one intact, maybe Congress and the White House will see the light."

The VP was unruffled and replied, "I will convey your sentiments to the president. Beyond that, what does NSA have to report?"

Erikson seemed to go into a trance. There was dead silence for nearly fifteen seconds. As eyes began turning back and forth, Erikson seemed to snap out of it.

"After running traffic density analyses from the last year and turning loose our newest Internet AI agents, we've discovered some interesting anomalies. We strongly suspect either the warheads were stolen last summer or some major activity revolving around the missing warheads occurred then. We will be able to shed more light on this as the details become available, but there are high statistical correlations with Hispaniola, New Orleans, Ann Arbor, and South America.

"We can share lists of individuals and groups that we suspect have some involvement in this, based on traffic between some environmental groups, *Macumba* and *vodun* web sites, and South American narco-political groups.

"It will help our analysis if you can feed us more of the case parameters and geographical priorities when available and we will concentrate our resources on the problem. There are even more technical tools at our disposal, which can be brought to bear when we get more details. We are already plugged into the Sit Room Com interface and will, of course, help." He sounded apologetic.

After the reports were all given, the VP led a short brainstorming session to which Karen paid half-hearted attention. Her mind was racing trying to imagine what kind of domestic group would have the means or motive to steal nuclear warheads from a secure military base. On her PDA, she listed: the Mafia, former military personnel—maybe paramilitary survivalists, foreign terrorist groups, or…? While she was focused on the question "who?," the inner circle began exploring "what": generating possible scenarios for the president. There was now furious note passing from the aides and backbenchers. Then the word *vodun* registered and she smiled.

The vice president summarized.

"So, the consensus is that the most likely scenario is some kind of nuclear extortion. The second scenario is that they have been stolen for sale on the international black market. The third scenario is that they are actually intended for use on American or foreign soil. Okay, that seems good enough for now given how little information we have yet."

Each agency then highlighted its plan of action and agreed to meet the next afternoon at the White House. During the final few minutes of their discussion an aide rushed in to pass a note to Admiral Brown. He looked shaken.

"Just what we didn't need. A severe winter storm warning has been posted. On that note, I move we adjourn, Mr. Vice President."

Phoenix, Arizona (1400 MST)

Peter Wilde arrived at the TV station just as the day's heat was peaking.

The guard at the door greeted him.

"Earlier than usual, Mr. Wilde?" The guard waved him into and through the metal detectors.

"Have any of the evening crew come in yet John?"

"No sir, you're it."

Peter nodded, smiled, and headed down the hallway. Co-anchor for the 5:30 and 11:00 news on KPHX, he always came into the studios ahead of the rest of the crew to look at the wire reports that day. He took the box of loose reports into his office and fired up his espresso machine. The pictures on his vanity wall showed the usual pictures with celebrities and politicians, but also from Italy and Europe where he grew up as a military brat, and pictures from college days. Many pictures were taken in coffee houses. An ex-girlfriend had bought him a miniature espresso and coffee steaming machine a few Christmases ago and he used it religiously.

He needed it too, because he had only been up for an hour or so. It took him so long to wind down from the 11:00 P.M. show that he was rarely in bed until 5:00 A.M. and rarely out of bed before noon the next day. Today he got up at 1 P.M. and came straight into work after dressing.

He picked up one of his desk toys, a 9 inch Tyrannosaurus Rex, and began talking to it.

"T-Rex, I told you that 2012 was going to be another weird year!"

Each report he skimmed looked stranger until the following one. Item 1: twelve members of a Pentecostal religious sect jumped together to their deaths from the Golden Gate Bridge this morning. Item 2: in New Mexico, zealots were already gathering in the desert near the New Mexico Space Port to await the Second Coming/alien flying saucer "rapture." Item 3: dozens of reports of spontaneous combustion were reported in Colombia and Ecuador. Item 4: scientists with the US Geological Survey raised the level of alert for the slopes of Mt. Hood near Portland, Oregon, as steam venting and increased seismic activity under the [formerly] dormant volcano heightened concerns of a possible eruption. Fruit farmers on the slopes of Mt. Hood have been forced to evacuate. The lodge at 10,000 feet has been closed since December and the whole mountain is off-limits to climbers and skiers. Item 6: Saltwater intrusion up the Mississippi Delta has caused water rationing in New Orleans, and today the Governor declared six Mississippi Delta counties disaster areas. Item 7: Cargo cultists in the South Pacific have mobilized in the thousands for the expected return of John Frum. In a related item (#8), the Melanesian War escalated as 5000 more French Foreign Legionnaires arrived in Honiara, Solomon Islands. The UN Security Council was once again thwarted from taking action by a French veto. Papua New Guinea sent appeals for outside help to stop Indonesian incursions from Irian Jaya and skirmishes with the Kanak Communist Party (KCP) on New Britain and New Ireland. Singapore, Malaysia, and Australia were reportedly in discussions to find a collective common front in their conflict with the French and Indonesians.

Closer to home, and perhaps more mundane, Pete thought, was the Baton Rouge evacuation, now canceled, with emerging allegations of a government cover-up. Oh, and the government's decision to raise the Terrorist Threat Level to Red.

"More false alarms?" he wondered aloud to T Rex.

Baton Rouge was likely to be the lead story tonight. He punched up his computer to see what video was available. His machine warmed up and came awake and after a minute loaded his mail program to reveal scores of email messages. He minimized the window and instead pulled up the daily video log of available footage for the nightly news.

One piece was from an independent stringer in Honolulu of an interview with the PNG UN Ambassador on his way to New York. That might have potential. Ambassador Walker was a very colorful, Oxford-educated woman who gave great sound bites.

A video log entry titled, "Menlo Park gun battle" caught his eye. He punched up the full header info and read:

1/12/12AV09X. Security camera captures the murder of a security guard outside a USGS facility south of San Francisco early last evening. Two persons were found dead at the scene—the security guard and a USGS scientist. Investigator's hinted at an "inside job" since the robbers had a key. More than a million dollars of brand-new seismic and magnetic sensing equipment was reported missing from the USGS facility. Time: 5:11. Cross-ref: Stanford Univ. security vidlog ID 1/12/12AV12X. See Reuters same date 101.13. Copyright © 2012 KNXS San Jose, CA.

Peter knew that the story would not be big news to Sun Valley folks and that his news director would probably nix it, although it might fit into the 11:00 P.M. report if the network didn't pick it up. They would have the network's story list within the half hour. What was it about that story that intrigued him so much?

He phoned Jennie the station video archivist. "Hello Jennie? Peter here. What did you make of that Menlo Park download?"

"Oh, I dunno. The feed has that scratchy industrial camera look and its black and white, of course. It's a single angle but the security guy had the good sense to bleed to death in the middle of the shot."

"PG-13?"

"The stuff is pretty gritty but no more so than anything else from LA on a Friday or Saturday night. The black and white isn't vivid, but a pool of blood is a pool of blood. Want me to send it up?"

"Sure, that would be great. No hurry, I just got in, but when you have a chance, thanks," and he hung up.

A half hour later there was a knock at the door of his office and he looked up. It was a courier.

"Delivery for you, Mr. Wilde."

He thanked the kid as he took the thumbnail disk, popped it into the digital editing computer on his desk. He clicked through the color bars and punched up the audio.

The video feed sure was scratchy and blurry—about as low rez as it could legally be. Nothing happened at first. The black and white image showed a loading dock and a double doorway on the right.

"Could be any commercial facility out of a zillion or so," he told T Rex.

On the bottom left corner of the view camera, a pickup truck backed up into the nearest loading bay... Dark forms stood up in the back of the truck and emerged from the cab—four in all. The two in the back of the truck jumped up on the loading dock and the two from inside the cab walked up the stairs immediately below the camera. At first they appeared to be shadows and then he realized that they were dressed in black with ski masks covering their heads. One of the figures approached the door, looked inside the small inset window and motioned the others forward.

One of the other figures slipped a card key through the security lock and keyed in an entry code. The door popped open and the figures rushed inside. There was no action for minutes, so he fast forwarded the action. Then he caught a slight movement in the far left hand corner. It was a security guard, from the looks of his hat, with a raised revolver. Ever so slowly, the guard inched his way up the stairs while checking out the truck. Just as he arrived at the door, it burst open. There were muzzle flashes and the security man fell onto the loading dock. The men then jumped into their respective places in the truck—the two in the back sat with their backs to the cab. Just as the truck started up and drove off, the two in the back took off their masks. The video ended shortly after that as the security guard's blood began to pool upon the floor.

Something nagged at Pete. He backed up the video to the point at which the bandits took off their masks. The shooter on the right, furthest away, was not a man. More troubling was that, although the haircut was different, shorter, it looked very familiar. The lighting was very bad. Pete backed his way through the data again, pulled up one of the better frames, and dragged it into his enhancement software. After tweaking the contrast and sharpening the image, it hit him. He knew her! It was Danielle Thomas, the animal rights activist from his college chemistry class! He had gone out with her a few times. He simply could not believe it—the girl had been such a sissy back then. Well, you just couldn't tell about some people, he thought to himself. Then he picked up the phone and asked for the Menlo Park police department.

Karen stayed in agency meetings going over details and new evidence until 2 A.M. when the deputy director told her go home. She was bushed and put up no argument. But while winding her way home a number of issues surrounding the case continued to haunt her. While at a stoplight in Alexandria after exiting the beltway and up to Rose Hill, the reality of going home hit her like a brick. A honk from behind startled her, and she put the car in gear and sped away.

She was still on Central European time; her internal clock was working just a bit too well tonight. Maybe she should pick up some melatonin and a set of bright lights to help her reset that damn circadian clock. Getting up in a few hours would be an adventure.

Karen was home. Exhausted, but awake, she popped a frozen pizza into the microwave, and opened a beer. She walked into the bathroom and thought of a bath. "No, only time for a shower." The timer rang, and out came the pizza. She was beginning to realize that it had been hours since she'd eaten, as she alternatively burned her tongue and then soothed it with a bland beer. She smiled and thought, "Home sweet home."

Karen slept only a few hours, propped up in bed, surrounded by papers and files.

"Coffee would be good," she thought as she started to read through some of the files with details on the top four individuals under investigation.

She had set loose search bots to scour Internet records, credit bureaus, and bank archives; had dumped files from FBI databases, military service records, and IRS files—armed with a classified Homeland Security virtual search warrant and a new tool: a federal decryption key developed by the NSA. True, public encryption had made electronic privacy almost a reality, but this new codec worked wonders. There was a lot of information, especially consumer records, on each of the four airmen. All were in their mid-twenties and, except for Barnes, all had some brushes with the law while in their teens.

None had any problems while in the service as far as she could tell, and remarkably, all had recently re-enlisted for second tours of duty. Smith and Jones had wives, but no kids. Neither the missing

Randy Barnes nor Alex Wallenstein was married. The evidence suggested that the backgrounds of Barnes and Wallenstein diverged from the other two. Jones and Smith came from inner city neighborhoods on opposite coasts; Barnes and Wallenstein came from the same university town, Ann Arbor, Michigan. They had enlisted together, as well. Both had graduated from Michigan State University. Both were children of doctors: Wallenstein, a psychiatrist, Barnes, a cardiologist. It began looking more and more like the two dead guys had been set up and that the AWOL Air Force buddies were a part of a conspiracy.

Sleep returned to Karen after she called her secretary's voice mail to request an early-afternoon flight to Michigan and to ask for the local FBI office in Ann Arbor to arrange to have the parents of those boys brought in for questioning later in the afternoon. She pictured herself taking a nap on the plane and laughed herself to sleep. She slept like a baby for another hour.

Eastern French Polynesia (1100 HST)

Marge Davis finished the dirty breakfast dishes and cleaned up the galley. She carefully put the dishtowel on the rack to dry, stepped into the head, and put her hair up into a bun. It was a warm, languid morning and Marge looked like she felt great. She admired herself in the mirror, with rosy cheeks and a glimmer in her eye. She was in great shape for a sixty-year-old: athletic and trim, her naturally blonde hair was only slightly gray, and despite her three decades in the subtropics, she had taken good care of her skin. This trip would probably take its toll, she thought to herself. She had enjoyed the sun on this trip with almost reckless abandon. Live a little, she told herself. Besides, she very carefully covered every inch of exposed skin with sun block.

She went up on deck to join husband Brad and to write in her journal. Marge and Brad's 40 foot ketch was named *Mana Kai,* roughly meaning "the spiritual power of the sea"—not terribly original as boat names go, but it worked for them. Brad's early retirement was what they had been waiting for to set loose and sail the seas—a dream they had both had since their youth.

The *Mana Kai* was now somewhere between French Polynesia and the Cook Islands. Marge reminisced about the trip so far: They started their ocean trek by sailing first to the Marquesas, then through the Tuamotus on the way to Pitcairn, a place Brad had always been fascinated with and had long wanted to visit. The trip had been for the most part pleasant and enjoyable. Marge had fallen in love with the beauty and remoteness of the Marquesas, and Brad had to admit that Hivaoa and Uapou, the two islands they visited, truly fit his notion of what South Pacific islands should look like.

The more cosmopolitan Society Islands—Papeete and Moorea—were a different story. Both islands had become armed camps with thousands of metropolitan French soldiers and Melanesian refugees crowding the streets and shops. The Davises stayed in Tahiti long enough to refuel and take on water before they left for Moorea. Moorea, once called "unspoiled Polynesia," was now tarnished by a large military presence that outnumbered the local residents by two- or three-to-one. The French Foreign Legion had commandeered the famous Bali Hai Hotel and troop encampments surrounded the airport. Brad and Marge had been unable to rent a car, and even a taxi drive around the island was about all they could stomach. After topping off the boat's water tanks and taking on some additional provisions—mainly fruit and flour—they were once again on their way.

Marge entered in her diary:

Dear Betsy (as she called her diary),
We're a day out of Moorea and glad to be on our way to the Cooks. The weather is fair today with scattered clouds and 10 to 12 knot trade winds. The Mana Kai has been an absolute dream and seems to be as happy as we are to be back out on the open seas. There is just a slight chop today—the waves are only one to two feet. We are catching very irregular sets of four to five foot waves coming from a big storm to the south. Those are mean enough to have to keep an eye out for them, but she handles them very well. I'm glad they're coming in from the port side though.

I sure didn't get much of a chance to brush up on my French, but I guess I'm more disappointed that we didn't see more of Tahiti (dare I say do more shopping?). I could not believe the prices either, even with a favorable exchange rate these days! Maybe they're just trying to take advantage of all those Francophone New Caledonian refugees... although why more of those people don't just go back to France amazes me. On the other hand, I can relate: if you've spent all or most of your life in the Pacific, how could you stand the hectic pace of the EU?

Being south of the equator has been a kick. I've enjoyed picking out the Southern Cross each evening and am learning some of the other southern constellations. I'm finally getting the hang of using the astrolabe, too. Even though we have state-of-the-art GPS, Brad has been making a daily game of fixing our position manually before we take the NAVSTAR fix. I'm learning how to use the charts now—at least better than in Hawai`i, since I have more time to mess with that stuff. I'm actually enjoying it. Brad has taken to calling me "navigator" which wouldn't be so bad if he would get off his high horse about being called "captain" at least once an hour. I can tell it's just a joke, but it is wearing a bit thin... Maybe if the galley crew mutinied for a meal or two he'd change his tune...nah, things are going too well to play games with him. Besides, he makes such a sharp picture of a captain...

The one thing that still bothers me after the Moorea/Papeete stops is the warning we got from the Cook's Bay harbormaster about avoiding boat people, pirates, and steering clear of warships. I got the feeling that he was not just making a joke.

Bye bye, Betsy, write to you tomorrow.

Marge looked up from her diary. Her favorite writing spot, weather and seas permitting, was out on the forecastle, but today she curled up on the ample stern bench with her back up against the cabin wall. She looked up at Brad, who was in his favorite spot at the helm. They had installed an automatic steering device for nighttime and meals, but otherwise one of the two of them was there at the helm. Especially when there were strange wave sets coming at them.

"What did you make of the harbormaster's warning, Brad?" she asked.

"Aw, don't take it too seriously. On the other hand, maybe we should break out the shotgun." They had a rack for it just inside the cabin. "Would that make you nervous?" She did not like guns.

"Actually, it would. But Tahiti spooked me, for sure. Submachine guns just don't seem right in Paradise."

Brad seemed to ponder that. After a silence of a couple of minutes he spoke. "You know, we might do well to take some other precautions. For one thing, I'd like you to learn the GPS system better. And it may be paranoid, but maybe we should lock the cabin door at night, too."

Marge frowned but didn't say anything.

"Well?" asked Brad, expecting a response.

"Sure," she said, "but this is not exactly what I had expected for our South Pacific vacation."

Brad grinned at her.

"You have such a wonderful smile." She set down her diary and got up and gave him a bear hug. "I love you."

"I love you, too. Besides, this has been a great tip so far, eh? Fair weather, good surf, and lots of sun. What more could we ask for? And you've saved us a bundle not shopping for French perfume!" He chuckled.

She jabbed him in the ribs. "You old salt! How 'bout I not shower for a week? Then you'll wish I had Chanel!"

"You always smell good to me," he returned.

They stood side by side quietly for a while feeling the sun and the breeze in their faces.

San Francisco (1715 PST)

Jake unlocked the apartment door and told himself that at least the place looked better after he cleaned up this morning. Feeling inspired, he dropped his bag on the kitchen table and immediately began to put away clean dishes. He looked proud of himself.

His heart skipped a beat when a knock came at the door. He shook his head and dismissed the idea that it could be Leah. But he was eager as he opened the door, only to see a blur come out of the darkness. As quickly as the handkerchief covered his face, Jake collapsed as hands eased him to the ground. All he remembered later was the feeling of being smothered, a searing pain in his forehead, and then oblivion.

Karen awoke as the jet began to descend to Ann Arbor, the bags under her eyes now less obvious. She stretched, caught the flight attendant's eye, asked for water and turned on the in-flight satellite news feed. The headlines scrolled on the bottom: Melanesian genocide, mass suicides, religious furors, and high tech robberies. The last item caught her attention. The USGS sounded like the last agency to have problems with eco-terrorists or thievery. Who could possibly use the equipment unless it was another research group? It seemed to go against the scientific culture. She probably would not have paid much attention to the report if it hadn't been for her years with DARPA, but now was riveted to the grainy video footage. High tech industrial sabotage and industrial espionage had been one of her portfolios during her first few years with the Bureau, and she had no doubt that the FBI was already involved since the USGS was a federal agency.

The latest update on the Baton Rouge evacuation aired next.

"CNN is reporting that the Baton Rouge evacuation may have been a hoax. Sources in the Congress have implicated the number-two man in the military services, Admiral Donald Brown, as the person responsible for the recent evacuation of some 50,000 people from the area around Baton Rouge. Originally ordered due to a toxic gas leak, the evacuation is being questioned by politicians in the state capital. A report in the *New York Times* suggested this morning that a military accident is to blame and not an industrial one. The Pentagon has stonewalled questions and claims that this is a national security matter. A press conference was rumored sometime in the next 24 hours.

"For some political analysis, here is our senior White House correspondent Dane Williams. Dane?"

"Despite a façade of normalcy, the president's schedule has been altered and White House officials are tight-lipped about the president's activities—usually a sign of some international crisis. Nevertheless, officials say that the president is furious about recent leaks that appear to be coming from high levels inside the Pentagon. The clamp down follows an apparent leak within the Department of Defense about a government cover-up of a fake evacuation in Baton

Rouge yesterday. Eyewitnesses and sources close to the DOD investigation reported that the accident involved a C-5 Air Force cargo jet flying at 18,000 feet, not a chemical spill at the refinery. The latest breach in security appears to have rattled civilian officials. Fingers are being pointed at the office of Joint Chiefs Vice Chairman, Don Brown.

"Brown has been privately battling restructuring of the armed services and is often at odds, even publicly, with the Secretary of Defense. Political pundits are speculating that Brown is in big trouble and likely to take the fall for this latest embarrassment, even if it was not his doing. There has been no comment from the Admiral's office.

"This is Dane Williams at the White House."

Karen immediately recognized the Michigan agent waiting for her at the gate.

"Special Agent St. Cloud," intoned her friend Gilda Goldsmith with a huge grin, "it's been too long!"

"Oy! Gilda."

They gave each other a European kiss on each cheek and then pivoted almost in unison and made their way out of the terminal.

"I haven't seen you since our graduation at Quantico, but have heard you were vacationing in Hungary for the last year," said Gilda, "and it's only because some of the group at DARPA ratted on you."

"How did they get wind... no, wait, Steven." Karen frowned, never forgetting for a minute that Gilda had introduced them.

Gilda's face got serious, "I am sorry about the two of you. Yes, we still talk. He's not bitter or anything, moving on." She smiled. "I never could lie to you. But I am in touch with some of the old team."

Karen patted her on the back.

"We'll have to catch up over beers, eh?" Gilda said and the changed the subject. "We have a car waiting on the curb. Any luggage?"

Karen shook her head.

"Great. I am pretty much at your disposal while you are up here."

Karen looked grateful.

They were on the road within two minutes. Close to the airport, the Ann Arbor field office was on the second floor of a shabby looking little strip mall over a Radio Shack. Gilda guided her into a large, uncomfortably cool conference room.

Karen had no trouble identifying the two sets of parents from photographs. The psychiatrist, Dr. Wallenstein, was a short, bearded man in his mid-forties. His wife was well dressed, but an otherwise average-looking woman wearing a brunette wig. By contrast, the Barneses both looked like they belonged in Beverly Hills. Mrs. Barnes was a striking blonde who looked ten years younger than the Wallensteins. The cardiologist was tall, dark and handsome and had an aloof attitude that Karen immediately disliked. The two mothers looked pale and nervous; the fathers looked grim and tight-lipped.

Karen introduced herself.

"We're not saying anything until our attorneys are here," announced Dr. Barnes.

Karen looked at Agent Goldsmith, who replied, "… on their way."

"Fine, then. Please just wait here," said Karen and then she and Gilda left the room.

"Cooperative bunch, aren't they?" She muttered almost under her breath when they were in the hallway.

Gilda was quiet. After a few seconds she ventured, "Their attorneys were both supposed to be here fifteen minutes ago. Sorry."

"It's okay, hardly your fault. Anyone you know?"

"No, they're general practice, medical malpractice types. A bit out of their league here... Could help matters or could be a problem."

"Coffee machine?" asked Karen. Gilda pointed the way.

Ten minutes later they were back in the conference room. The attorneys turned out to be only one—a senior partner of the local firm of which the doctors were clients. Attorney Leibowitz took five minutes with his clients alone and then invited the agents back into the room. Leibowitz looked decidedly uncomfortable. Dr. Barnes was the first to speak.

"The Army called us yesterday to inform us that both of our sons were AWOL and all we can tell you is what we told them on the phone: we have no idea where they are. Furthermore, you are doing a disservice to the patients of both Dr. Wallenstein and myself. I am scheduled to be in surgery within minutes, so..."

Karen cut him off abruptly.

"I have neither the time nor inclination to indulge your indignation, sir. You are obviously—presumably—unaware of the

46

seriousness of this matter. Otherwise," she said with some degree of irony, "you would not be in such a big hurry. To be extremely blunt, your sons are suspects in very serious crimes against the state—at the very least, criminal conspiracy—involving robbery of nuclear weapons and murder. These are federal crimes that call for the death penalty.

"Furthermore, pursuant to Executive Order 12-875, signed this morning by the president, you may not communicate with any outside party regarding this situation on national security grounds. That includes you, too, Mr. Leibowitz." Karen pushed a copy of the Executive Order and the court order for the search of their homes to the lawyer.

"To reinforce this latter point, Judge Thomas, who issued the search order has also imposed a gag rule regarding the search itself under the Homeland Security Act. This is very serious business."

"We will begin with some questions about your two sons."

Dr. Wallenstein appeared to faint, slumping in his chair, and Mrs. Barnes burst into tears. Leibowitz kept silently reading up and down the Executive Order and opened his mouth a few times, but nothing came out.

Wallenstein slowly picked his head up, looking confused, and a young agent came in to whisper in Agent Goldsmith's ear.

Mrs. Barnes began to compose herself. She began.

"I knew those two were up to no good when they came back to visit the last time when they were on leave. They hardly visited with us at all and spent a lot of time in the yard talking to each other. They have always been close," she emphasized *always*, "but they hardly spent a minute apart during the ten days that they were here. They were inseparable." Mrs. Wallenstein was looking at her reproachfully.

"Just because you were unhappy with them joining the Air Force doesn't mean..." But her husband cut her off.

"I think maybe we should start at the beginning."

From the interview that followed, and from high school yearbooks, family photos, boxes full of memorabilia, and the parents' at first reluctant, and then earnest recollections, the story of the two young men's relationship emerged.

Alex Wallenstein and Randy Barnes had been friends since they were old enough to begin exploring their neighborhood together. Alexander was born half a year before Randy, but was a smaller child. As they grew up together, Randy was always bigger and stronger while Alex was the smarter of the two. There had been numerous instances where Randy stuck up for his runt of a friend. They seldom disagreed or argued. Mrs. Barnes recounted a story of one summer during grade school when the two boys had been at odds over some obscure issue. For weeks the boys did not speak to each other and were so sullen that the mothers both conferred over the phone about what to do. Then, one hot August afternoon, Alex got into a scrap with some older boys at a nearby playground. Apparently they taunted him for being a Jew and called him names. Just as one of the boys started to beat him, Randy appeared out of nowhere on his bike, slammed into the attackers and wailed on the boys until they took off bleeding and broken. After the incident, Alex and Randy were fast friends; the event seems to have sealed their friendship.

As the boys grew older and entered high school, they could only be called an "odd couple:" Randy grew tall, handsome, and popular; Alex short and plain, but very smart and bookish. The jock and the nerd stayed close through high school. There was reciprocity in the relationship: while Randy retained his role as protector, Alex helped Randy in his studies. As the two mothers recounted this period of their lives, Karen could sense their pain and even see sadness in their eyes. Whether or not each felt sad for the other, or for their collective fate, it was unclear. That became a little clearer when they haltingly told the story of Alex's arrest during his senior year in high school.

Alex was an "A" student, but ran into trouble with Mr. Hughes, his History teacher. While Hughes was not overtly anti-Semitic, his U.S. History class definitely—according to Alex—glorified "Aryan assholes." Mrs. Wallenstein reddened when she quoted him, but was apparently still upset about it herself. The Barneses looked embarrassed during this part of the interview.

"Alex broke into tears one evening during dinner. Mr. Hughes was covering World War II that week and had been saying sympathetic things about Hitler and the Third Reich, according to Alex. They got into an argument in class and Hughes apparently said something to make the class laugh at Alex. We were worried; he never cried and was rarely if ever angry, and never that angry. His father offered to call the principal, but Alex just shook his head and said he'd deal with it."

The Wallensteins continued to relate the story. Apparently, the next day, Hughes and Alex argued in class again, but this time Alex was sent to the principal's office. His parents were told that as he left class he threatened his teacher, and said something to the effect that 'he'd regret it.' Alex returned to class the next day, but by all accounts remained silent and cooperative. A week after the episode, the teacher was burned to death at his home in an overnight fire. Though his wife escaped, she was unable to awaken him. The fire was determined to be arson and there were numerous gas cans found in the backyard. Hughes' charred body was found to contain traces of an over-the-counter sleep medication that his wife denied that he ever used. Exactly how he was poisoned was never established, but the death was ruled murder and Alex was indicted by the grand jury few weeks later.

Alex maintained his innocence, but was formally arrested. The District Attorney made a big deal of the matter and even went so far as to have Alex picked up by officers during class and handcuffed—and on a Friday afternoon, so that he would be stuck in jail over the weekend. In a bizarre twist, the case was dropped a week later. They had a weak case. Although there was a motive, there was no evidence that absolutely connected Alex to the murder, and Alex had a strong alibi the afternoon and evening of the fire. The twist was that Hughes turned out to be a member of the Michigan KKK.

The DA had apparently felt that pursuing the case would be bad for his own political career. As it was near the end of the winter school term, Alex was allowed to finish up his classes and graduate early. He was easily admitted to MSU that spring and started college classes that summer. The Barnes boy joined him there in the fall.

Alex and Randy each continued to live at home through their first year of college. Alex got straight A's and Randy managed to get B's and C's. That was before they took a philosophy class and got involved with a student club. The philosophy professor, Dr. Stuart Adams, was the faculty advisor for the Green Alliance, a student group that organized the campus Earth Day activities and organized recycling efforts both on and off campus. Red flags went up and warning bells went off in Karen's head when she heard this.

The two spent less time at home studying together, and more time at meetings and working on club activities. When Randy ended up on academic probation and even Alex's grades began slipping, the two sets of parents conferred and there was a joint family meeting—a showdown. It did not go well. Randy announced that he was dropping out of school and Alex informed his parents that he was looking for

49

an off-campus apartment. He would be able to do that with a small inheritance he'd received the year before from his maternal grandmother. Both fathers had threatened and cajoled, but something fundamental had changed in the boys—now young men—and in their families. The parents had chalked it up to adolescent resistance to authority. But over the ensuing year, the situation did not improve. Randy, not surprisingly, moved in with Alex. They lived together in a house near campus with some of the other Green Alliance students.

Karen asked the parents what they knew about Stuart Adams. Not very much, it turned out, except what they occasionally read in the paper about environmental protests and activities around town. Adams had been instrumental in getting the city council to declare Ann Arbor a nuclear free zone in the late 1990s, said Dr. Barnes. He said that he had contacted the professor shortly after the boys had moved off campus, to express his concerns. Adams had been disinterested and said that it was none of his business—end of conversation. The parents obviously didn't care much for the professor.

Abruptly, after little more than two years in school, Alex and Randy enlisted in the Air Force and requested billets in Germany. Their parents indicated to Karen their great confusion and alarm at that turn of events. And yet during the first year of their enlistment, both communicated more with their parents. And both finished college by attending night classes. Both moms had shoeboxes with their letters and cards from boot camp and then Germany—now in the FBI vans outside.

The airmen had been home numerous times since their enlistment and had stayed with their families. Both sets of parents had been surprised that neither young men had shown any interest in getting together with their former friends. Mrs. Wallenstein said that she assumed it was because of the anti-military attitude of the environmentalists. The other parents nodded their heads in agreement. Alex and Randy had both called home religiously, too—about twice a month.

When both men were finished with their tours of duty, they both re-enlisted and were transferred—together, again, to Texas. After their last visit, which had been two months before, the families had neither mail nor phone calls from San Antonio.

Karen told them that their phones would be tapped and informed them that until further notice, an agent would be stationed

24 hours a day outside each of their homes. Karen apologized, but said that there was no choice given the gravity of the situation. Her intuition told her that the two sets of parents were totally in the dark about what their sons were doing.

After they returned to the office with the boxes of evidence, Karen asked Gilda to have Stuart Adams brought in for questioning, and also for someone to locate the files on the Hughes murder. She opened her laptop to review her research database on the radical environmental movement. But, her mind drifted back to the conversation the day before in Hale's office.

She looked up as understanding came over her.

"Greens," she said simply.

The discussion of her environmental research with Hale had seemed pretty irrelevant at the time. She was distracted when he asked how she had become involved in eco-terrorist work. She replied that the Green Party and other mainstream groups, as well as several eco-terrorist groups, had interested her for years, intellectually. She explained that DARPA had been rather dry and then intelligence analysis even worse, so she had requested fieldwork.

Internationally, various anti-globalization, anarchist, and green eco-tage groups had been getting more and more intelligence and law enforcement attention as confrontations between industrial development and anti-development forces heated up. The FBI provided some of the US muscle overseas in collaborative and bi-lateral personnel exchanges. There was a whole sub-unit in Washington that followed anti-vivisection and animal liberation activists. Some of her official work in her first few years at the FBI, and then on assignment in Europe, focused on animal rights attacks on science laboratories.

Hale changed the subject after that, and Karen had mostly forgotten the conversation until now. "How had he known?" she asked herself. He did tell her that one of her analytical reports on the various fringe environmental groups in Europe and the Russian "near abroad" had been circulated in the FBI and at State, but he didn't say by whom. Nor did she ask. There weren't that many fringe groups, so it was easy for her to emerge as an expert, he reassured her. She looked stunned to hear of her notoriety, nevertheless.

She scribbled onto her PDA: "Green Alliance" and "S. America connection" and then absently chewed on the tip of her stylus. She turned to the laptop and did an Internet search first for environmental student organizations and then for Green Alliance. She watched patterns emerge. One realization was that these were mostly membership organizations. She scratched her head.

The more radical groups, like the Animal Liberation Front, were not membership organizations. Rather, they were organized clandestinely in classic cell structures, like al Qaida and many anarchist groups. However, Green Alliance and similar groups were fertile ground for recruiting to more radical activities. Karen was becoming more and more interested in meeting Professor Adams.

She checked her email and reports from the Interagency Task Force. Things appeared to be in bad shape in Washington and the news media were like sharks in a feeding frenzy as the Baton Rouge cover-up unraveled further. The White House was not giving Admiral Brown any cover. That could only mean that they were looking for a scapegoat. God, I hate politics, she thought.

"Agent St. Cloud?" interrupted a young agent. Karen looked at him inquiringly without answering.

"Dr. Adams' university secretary reports that he is at an academic conference in Santiago, Chile, and has been gone for over a week. He was supposed to have been back yesterday, but his office hasn't heard from him."

Karen's eyebrows went up, but just slightly.

San Francisco (0600 PST)

Jake looked very bad. His eyes were almost welded shut with crud and his throat and mouth were drier than the sands of the Kalahari. His face was wrinkled in a grimace of pain. Unbearably loud yelling made his head hurt even more with each volley of sound. Then it stopped. Relief flooded his face. He managed to pry one eye open to see that he was bound, gagged, and blindfolded—the blindfold askew enough for him to see light coming from underneath a door. The voices began again and his head exploded with pain. He passed out.

It was quiet when he next awoke, and his hands were loose so he kneaded his temples. He had wet and soiled himself and smelled bad.

"Jesus Christ, what is this place?" he managed.

The sound of a foghorn answered and the room rocked slightly.

He fell asleep again. The yelling stopped, at least.

Boulder (0700 MST)

Leah woke up with worry written on her face and in her eyes. Her emails to Jake went unanswered as did her phone calls to the apartment and to his cell. The "wait" tone on their home answering machine was very long, as though a week's worth of messages had accumulated. She considered calling their nosy San Francisco neighbor, Mrs. Edwards, and then thought better of it. Leah wrung her hands. 7 A.M.—the time they often talked—came and went.

She ran a toothbrush once lightly over her teeth and brewed a cup of green tea, sat down and punched in their home number. After four rings, the message came on as usual. This time she did not leave a message. She grabbed her car keys.

She looked around her small dormitory-style apartment. It was neat and tidy as always. The plants by the window would need someone to look after them, so she made a mental note to call her friend Max to water them if she wasn't back by Monday, and to use the milk and anything else in her small refrigerator that might spoil. She sat down at her desk and shot off an email to her supervisor to tell him that she would be going home for the weekend and would be in touch, then unplugged her laptop. She quickly showered and packed a small bag. She always traveled light to begin with, and since she was going home, she'd have plenty of clean stuff there anyway.

She stuffed some papers in her briefcase along with her laptop and looked over the small apartment once again. As an afterthought, she opened up the fridge and grabbed the nectarine and a couple of apples and some sodas and stuck them in the top of her travel bag. Out the door she went, not even bothering to see if it was locked.

In the garage, she piled her bag, thermos, and backpack on the passenger side floor and gunned the engine. Then she gathered herself up and let the motor idle to warm up. She pulled out her cell phone and dialed her landlord's phone number, but thought better of the idea and closed the call.

She practiced her next call: "Max, sorry to call so early I need to ask a favor. I am worried about Jake... No. Shit..."

"Max, I need to go home for a few days..." No, that sounded hollow.

She spun out of the garage into the street with a bit too much foot on the gas pedal and redialed her cell phone.

"Hi Max. Sorry to call so early, but I need a favor."

"Anything, Leah." He was always chipper, even at 8 A.M.

"I'm heading back to the City for the weekend. Would you mind terribly watering the plants on Sunday or Monday if I'm not back and eating up anything that will go bad? Help yourself to the beer, too."

"Sure, no problem. Anything wrong?"

"No. Yes. Well, maybe… I don't know. I haven't been able to reach Jake for two days. He probably just got called out of town for some reason and hasn't been able to reach me, but it's not like him and I'm worried."

"Are you sure you're not overreacting, Leah?" He tried to reassure her, "I'm sure everything is fine."

"I can't work. Besides, you know me when I make up my mind about something. Listen, just be a pal and water my friends. I'll send you an email or check in with you early in the week and fill you in. Okay?" She made it sound like the conversation was over.

" Sure. I hope everything is okay. If there's anything else I can do, just let me know."

They said goodbye and Leah hit the Interstate going 90.

Phoenix (1000 MST)

Peter Wilde awoke midmorning from a nightmare. He couldn't recall the details, which faded faster than he could reach them, but the outlines of the dream were clear enough. He'd been back in classes at MSU and Danielle Thomas was there. The images from the USGS video were unfortunately still very vivid in his mind. The blood drained from his face again as it had when he first saw the video. Yesterday's experience had been very personal—especially after looping the last minute of Danielle's "terrorist footage."

"Danielle the nerd" fit his concept of her, but "Danielle the terrorist?"

"I guess I figured her wrong," he said to the mirror. There had been more in that dream, too, about strangeness in the world, a faceless throng that seemed to be standing around on the edges of his dream, lurking, observing… there, but not there. The dream faded quickly.

He visited the regional FBI offices the day before after talking to the police in California. The agent who met him was very serious, but somewhat distracted almost disinterested as Pete explained what he knew about Danielle. The agent showed him to an interview room, called in an additional agent in a dark suit. Neither FBI agent batted an eye during Pete's description of his revelation with the video. Downright blasé, they were. He mentioned that they had been classmates at MSU (but not that they'd slept together). Both agents sat up straighter and they glanced at each other for just a second. One of the agents apologized and left the room.

He finished his oral statement, and the agent thanked him. He said they might have more questions for him later and had him leave his business card. He made it back to the station in plenty of time for the 11 o'clock news, although his mind was definitely distracted. His co-anchor looked at him strangely a number of times, but Pete kept quiet. He read the teleprompter without any particular enthusiasm.

The snooze alarm startled Pete awake again. He looked at business card for the FBI regional office that he had left on the nightstand and realized that was what he went to sleep thinking about. He rolled out of bed and straight into the shower. He nicked himself numerous times and then ran out of toilet paper while sitting on the commode. He put coffee in the machine, but realized twenty minutes later that he hadn't turned the switch on.

He returned to the bathroom mirror and inspected the bleeding ear lobe now clotting on a nubbin of paper tissue. His short-cropped brown, naturally curly hair was getting a tad raggedy, even though it was cut on Monday.

He told the face in the mirror, "You are a good-looking boy." And smiled at his own vanity. He finished getting ready for work and headed out the door without any more absent-minded incidents.

By 3 P.M. Pete had been in the newsroom for two hours and was on his fourth cup of coffee. The phone rang.

"Turn on CNN."

He turned up the audio on a small monitor in a bank of four above his desk. It was Bret Forman—the famous network news anchor—and the front of the White House in the background. It was snowing lightly.

"...grave situation, according to White House officials.

"All signs seem to indicate that these developments are related to the Baton Rouge evacuation. The residents of northern Baton Rouge have now all returned to their homes, but questions remain why some 50,000 people were forced to evacuate. Opposition party leaders on Capitol Hill have been calling for an investigation of the actions of Admiral Donald Brown, former Chief of Naval Operations and the current Vice Chairman of the Joint Chiefs of Staff, who allegedly convinced the state's governor to issue the evacuation order. Evidence from Louisiana suggests that there may not have been an actual release of toxic gas and that there is a government cover-up of the actual reasons for the evacuation. Back to you Bob."

The image switched to the studio news anchor Bob Miles. "Thank you for the update, Bret Foreman—at the White House."

Miles continued. "For those of you who are just tuning in, the White House has announced that the president will be addressing the nation within a few minutes for what they are calling 'an emergency situation.' Bret, have officials there given any clue as to what this is all about?"

"No, Bob, they have been very secretive and indicated that the president's speech will be related to Homeland Security. White House officials have apparently contacted officials at all the major television and cable networks to ensure that the president's speech will be covered. This is unusual given the president's recent low profile and the upcoming primaries and caucuses. I can tell you that a number of the president's scheduled appointments in the last two days have been rescheduled or postponed. There has been a flurry of activity in and around the White House and the Executive Office Building across the street. Lights in the White House have also been burning late over the last two nights and..."

"I'm sorry to interrupt, Bret. We have the White House feed..."

The Presidential Seal flashed on the screen and slowly dissolved into a tight shot of the still-boyish face of the President of the United States. His mouth was drawn into what was almost a scowl. The family pictures and other cozy elements from his usual Oval Office props were missing—this was serious business.

"My fellow citizens, I am speaking to you today from the White House on a matter of the utmost seriousness. It is my belief, and the counsel of my closest advisors, that we are facing the most serious domestic crisis that this nation has faced since the terrorist attacks in 2001.

"Yesterday, federal investigators discovered that a dozen tactical nuclear missile warheads are missing from a storage depot in Texas. These weapons were among the last of our tactical arsenal protected under the terms of the START III treaty, recently approved by the U.S. Senate. The whereabouts of the warheads is unknown and

56

an intensive national and international search is now underway to locate them and the persons responsible for this theft.

"As the nation responsible for those weapons, we will be taking the lead in a massive search to find the weapons and the criminals who have stolen them. I have taken the following actions, as of 3 P.M. Eastern Standard Time: the U.S. Armed Forces have been placed on a high state of alert both at home and abroad, and the Homeland Security Threat level has been raised to Red. The White House Situation Room is operational and under the authority of an Interagency Task Force chaired by my National Security Advisor, and we have mobilized an emergency Nuclear Threat Task Force to investigate all aspects of the theft of the weapons and their recovery.

"The next series of actions which I am announcing trouble me deeply, but as the person ultimately responsible for the security and welfare of the people of the United States, and for those people in other countries who may be affected by this extreme act of global terrorism, I feel I have no choice. Under my executive powers as President, under the Emergency Powers Act, pursuant to Executive Order 723-65, travel into and out of the United States will be restricted immediately for a period of 30 days. Similarly, air and sea shipping shall be severely restricted. All air and sea transportation into and out of the country—including Canada and Mexico—will be suspended immediately. Within three days, limited shipment of goods will be allowed, but only under strict surveillance and inspection by agencies of the Homeland Security Department including U.S. Customs, U.S. Immigration and Naturalization, and selected units of the U.S. Coast Guard and the National Guard. These are extreme measures and will have serious economic and political consequences, but I believe that until we find these weapons there is no alternative. I ask you, the American people, for your support and cooperation through this time of crisis.

"I am also activating all National Guard units in all 50 states and territories. While I will not restrict travel within the United States at this time, National Guard and Armed Forces units will be setting up check points on Interstate Highways and near major cities and crossroads across the country. This will undoubtedly cause great inconvenience and hardship for some, so I am asking all Americans to stay at home as much as possible.

"I will be meeting with business leaders and groups today to look for ways to minimize travel to work, such as travel pools, staggered schedules, and telecommuting. After consultation with several Congressional leaders, all businesses will be closed on Monday and Tuesday. Federal and state government offices will remain closed except for those agencies related to Homeland Security and first responders. Certain federal, state, and local government workers will be called on to serve in emergency management capacities until the crisis is over.

"Further information regarding the restrictions on foreign travel and domestic conditions will be communicated through public radio and television channels on an hourly basis.

"At the bottom of the screen you will see two 1-800 numbers to call for any information that the public may have about the missing weapons or persons related to their theft. You can also get information and contact the FBI through their website at www.fbi.gov.

"Finally, I ask you all to help in this dark hour for America, for we must all pull together to avoid calamity. There is no reason for panic or worry if we all cooperate together to find that inner strength that has helped us get through previous threats to the nation. I am counting on the Homeland Security agencies and on you to see us through this crisis. Thank you and God Bless America."

The president dissolved back into the presidential seal.

"This is Bob Edwards at the CNN Center in New York. Well, there you have it. The President of the United States has just announced what amounts to a state of emergency for the next 30 days, precipitated by the disappearance of a dozen nuclear warheads in Texas. Details are sketchy at this point, but other senior White House officials are telling the press that the weapons have actually left US territory. But until that is confirmed the government is taking no chances, in case the weapons are intended for use in American cities or against targets here.

"For further analysis of the president's announcement and the strategy behind this mobilization, we have with us a former national security expert from the Clinton Administration, Dr. Arthur McMadden. Professor McMadden..."

The volume was lowered on the TV set in the Ann Arbor FBI office and Karen heard a male voice distinctly say, "good God," softly under his breath. The background noise in the office resumed. Her eyes glazed over with a wave of fatigue for a few seconds, but she was brought back to attention by the change of energy in the room. She looked around the room at the half dozen people who'd just watched the presidential telecast and although everyone has turned back to work, they all appeared blank, stunned. Karen shook her head as though to clear it, but was still surprised that things were moving so quickly. Was the president over-reacting? Maybe things were more serious than she'd thought.

She opened up her laptop and plugged in the data cable. She skimmed the morning's Inter-agency meeting notes for developments. Helen Colman reported that the DOD had isolated information indicating the most likely time the nukes were actually taken— sometime late last summer, between the 18th and 25th of August—the apparent window of opportunity. Suspects Wallenstein and Barnes had somehow managed to circumvent the three security layers around those weapons. The first layer was accessible to them because they were assigned to weapons loading and unloading—they were both gunnery technicians. Their access to the outer layer was within their security clearances and a matter-of-fact business; however, leaving the base with several tons of stolen equipment was not matter-of-fact business. Orders or official documents would have been required for any large commercial or military vehicles to leave the base.

The two also had clearance for the second security layer for the same reason; they were in fact responsible for loading warheads on Tomahawk or other cruise missiles. However, they did not have access to the inner fence (the "inner sanctum") that was manned by Special Forces MPs, except during drills. There had been three loading and unloading—and arming—training exercises that week as part of an overall readiness campaign for Rapid Deployment exercises that summer. The actual warhead arming was done virtually, through a VR computer simulation, but the rest was real enough. The Tomahawks themselves were ferried across base and "dressed up" (as in "dressed up, no place to go") in the covered loading dock of the building. They were required in the drill to load two warheads before pulling them back out of the missiles and retiring them to their bays inside the steel bunker, inside the munitions dump.

There were no apparent anomalies involving the Special Forces MPs, the base sentries, or other base personnel—they were coming up clean. The only exception was the inner sanctum logbook, which indicated that alarms had gone off repeatedly during that week.

A small wildfire near the base had caused smoke to intrude into the building and set off automatic alarms. Somehow, the two airmen managed to move one dozen steel cases weighing close to three hundred pounds each into the loading dock. That might have been the easy part, since Navy divers in the Mississippi River near Baton Rouge had confirmed that the two had replaced those bombs with nearly two tons of rebar. And they managed to do this under the noses of MPs, sometime before 25 August. That was the last opportunity that Wallenstein and Barnes had in the previous six months.

Coleman's report indicated Jones' story was still a mystery. Apparently, he had very little interaction with the other airmen. He'd only been in San Antonio a couple of months after a transfer from Ellington Field in Houston. There was no evidence to connect him to either Wallenstein or Barnes.

FBI and CIA officials in Latin America reported that the two had left a warm trail to a cold place. Wallenstein and Barnes had changed planes in Santiago and flown to Punta Arenas. Indications were they'd taken a charter flight from there to Antarctica. The money trail was not something they seemed concerned about, as even the charter to the Chilean Base camp in the Antarctic Peninsula had been charged to Barnes' credit card. By the time the FBI had contacted Chilean authorities in Antarctica, the two had disappeared, perhaps with a group of Greenpeace activists down on the Peninsula for the summer. They had moved fast in a span of less than two days since Karen interviewed them. Karen whistled and everyone ignored her.

FBI reports suggested that Wallenstein and Barnes' off-base apartment had been picked clean by the forensics team. The two had left in a hurry, but had left little helpful evidence. One piece of financial evidence was compelling: both young men had previously donated large chunks of their paychecks to the radical environmental group EPG*.

Karen's eyes lit up in recognition and she toggled back to her personal database on EPG* which was extensive. EPG* was an enigma. It was a "network" rather that a membership-based organization. It was more of a deep ecology movement and collection of official and "unofficial" groups that increasingly had referred to themselves as EPG*—not one acronym, but many: Earth People Group, EcoPlanetary Greens, Earth Planet Gaia, and various other combinations of the EPG acronym. One "branch" even added an asterisk (EPG*) to indicate a pro-space, "we are star stuff," post-millennial cosmic agenda. While most of the groups were more inward than outward looking, the asterisk became part of the culture.

Karen was often at pains with her FBI colleagues in arguing that only the fringes of the movement were inclined to violence, much of it small-scale and dramatic: widespread firebombing of logging trucks; ramming and sabotage of long-line and drift net fishing boats; raids on animal research laboratories; and, increasingly, attacks on personnel who worked for nanotechnology firms. EPG* had attracted remnants of the first wave of deep ecology direct-action groups that lost their appeal after the turn of the century: Earth First!, Sea Shepherd Society, the Animal Liberation Front. It also attracted other eco-lefties who were fed up with piecemeal direct action, and connected with some of the anarchist groups active in the anti-globalization actions in the first decade of the new century. EPG* also responded to a growing sense of alienation and apocalyptic sentiment among young people and the disenfranchised college-educated who faced minimum wage jobs, or no jobs at all, in the jobless economic recoveries of the early 21st century.

The EPG* message was: development and so-called "progress" are leading us down the path to destruction. Technological change makes the rich richer and the poor poorer. Everything changes but everything remains the same.

Karen pulled up an EPG* website. The banner at the top read: Bring back the Ice Age!

AP Newswire (00:30 14 January) Jerusalem
Church of the Prophet leaders came out of two weeks of seclusion and fasting. In a short news conference, all twelve "Apostles of the Prophet" claimed to have had a group vision of the Apocalypse, expected to occur on or before December 27, 2012—the end of the millennium for Prophet believers. The date is loosely based on the end of the Mayan calendar. Coincidentally, the date falls at the peak of sunspot activity—already seriously disrupting telecommunications around the globe. A major planetary alignment also falls close to that date.

The ritual fast, which they called "The Great Desert Meditation," took place in a small resort on the Sea of Galilee. The meditating apostles were monitored nearly the entire time by global news net cameras and observers. The apostles shared a light soup to break their fast before they spoke to reporters.

On December 31st, the twelve Church leaders led a New

Year's "Pray In" for the Rapture from Jerusalem's Peace Park. An estimated 20 million people, world wide, participated in the simulcast from such places as Madison Square Garden in New York and the Dorothy Chandler Pavilion in Los Angeles. Five million members of the Church live in the Southwest United States. The Church of the Prophet is a millennial group that believes in the Second Coming of Christ and that the next Dalai Lama will embody the Christ. A substantial number of adherents claim to have a shared vision of the coming of Godhead. The New Age branch of the group believes that the "reckoning" will be triggered by a reversal of the Earth's axis, followed by earthquakes, floods, and tides of "biblical proportions."

The Church of the Prophet follows the teaching of its late founder, Michael Ambrose, who lived his life by the Mayan calendar. While many groups and individuals celebrated the new millennium in 2000, Ambrose disciples believe that the millennium actually starts December 27—a central tenet of the Church of the Prophet. Continued economic decline and skyrocketing oil prices are fueling speculation that the Church of the Prophet and other millenarian groups will grow in numbers through the end of the year as hundreds of thousands continue to be laid off in industrialized countries.

National Weather Service. Atlanta, 1500 13 January 2012. Forecast alert.

A large trough has developed for the third time this season along the Eastern seaboard. A large mass of air from the Gulf of Mexico is being drawn north, which has set up conditions for another strong Nor'easter. Level three storm warnings (tropical storm to hurricane-force winds) are now in effect for most of the eastern seaboard from Cape Fear to Northern Maine. Most barrier island communities are asked to evacuate to higher ground or designated emergency shelter areas. Heavy snows are expected inland from as far south as central Alabama and Georgia. This storm is expected to be unusually severe due to a convergence of high lunar and solar tides.

Everyone from southern Georgia to Maine should stay tuned to weather reports and local forecasts.

This storm is already the third this winter, surpassing an all-time record for Nor'easters this early in the season. This will also set a record for the third worst winter storm season on the East Coast. All three record years have occurred in the last decade-and-a-half.

62

Central Nevada (1515 PST)

A large pile of rubbish accumulated on her bags and the seat of the passenger side of Leah's Corvette. Soda cans and snack food wrappers and some candy wrappers and Styrofoam coffee cups. The car was now dirty and dusty from the drive over the mountains and from braving a few stretches of snow and ice. Leah's eyes were blood-shot and dry. She reapplied lip balm and searched the AM radio for country music stations.

An hour west of Elko, the car was doing 95 down a stretch of desert highway where it paralleled the Interstate. She eyed the radar detector, then took in the darkening clouds to the west and squinted and frowned. The horizon was threatening and there had already been a few flurries as she passed through Elko. All the passes had been open through the Rockies, but it was getting colder. She reached down and felt for the bag of snow chains under the pile of rubbish to reassure herself that she could get over the Sierras tonight.

"Let's see if I can break a few more nails," she accused the bag of chains as she held out the fingerless nail, a victim of her hurried packing. She wrinkled her face and examined the rest of her nails—long overdue for a manicure and polish. She saw another cell tower pass by, so picked up her phone and tried Jake again. No answer, again, and the knot in her stomach grew tighter. Staring ahead at the weather, the large, tall white cloud in front of the storm reminded her of one of the first icebergs she saw during her research trip to Antarctica. The image lingered.

She pulled down the visor mirror and briefly inspected her face. She was shocked how haggard she appeared! What happened to the effervescent, bouncy, and happy Leah? She reflected on what had started it all a week before…

The insights she had about accelerated warming and cataclysmic sea level rise were potentially profound. Naturally, she'd gotten depressed considering the implications: New Orleans, Miami, and Manhattan under water! She played the movie in her head: continuing sea level rise would pull the Ross Ice Shelf apart.

She had worked out a PowerPoint presentation in her head showing how it all worked:

First, the most startling discovery was that the entire Ross Ice Shelf had lost 50% of its summer mass compared to 1990 sea ice coverage. The "before and after" aerial satellite view was unimpressive. However, in relation to the ocean bottom, the lateral

63

representation shows significant thinning. In her mind's eye she illustrated the second surprise: pictures of the undersea mountains showed that there was minimal contact remaining with the ice shelf and little anchoring left for much of the Ross ice sheet. Third surprise: there was growing seismic and thermal activity in more than half of the seamounts in the Ross Sea.

Leah got the shivers recalling how this had all come together for her in the past few weeks, but at the same time a growing disease. Earlier in the week at the NCAR central library, she'd had the uncanny feeling that she was being watched. It was an eerie feeling—as though Dr. Doom was looking over her shoulder. She'd had some large cartographic files spread out before her in a small nook. Thinking that someone was standing there, she had looked up, but no one was there. After the third or fourth time the feeling washed over her, she'd gotten spooked. She stuffed the maps back in their drawer and left. The event had actually been a catalyst of sorts.

Her thoughts were brought abruptly back to the present as she came up behind a large semi winding up and around a curve. It was now snowing lightly, but steadily, so she considered driving a bit slower for safety's sake anyway. After cresting the hill she passed the truck and looked down on a barren, sage-covered valley. The ribbon of road stretched straight out for twenty miles up to the next hill. Without another car in sight, Leah pushed the sports car back up to 90 mph.

Her motto of late at NCAR was to "hear, see, and speak no evil." As an ocean modeling expert, not a glaciologist or geologist, Leah was worried about serious accusations of poaching or charges of stepping outside her own discipline. She looked in the rear view mirror for anyone behind her.

The research implications were troubling and the changes could well be catastrophic, sooner than perhaps anyone had thought. Places like Bangladesh and Florida would cease to exist. New Orleans, Venice, Tokyo, and New York gone! Might not be much of a world to raise kids in, she'd thought to herself.

Leah had definitely had been spooked that night at the library. First the distinct feeling that she was being watched, then self-doubt and worry about her research, about the future, and ultimately about her own life with Jake. But when the runs of her model were complete and the results downloaded on her PC, she had an unexpected surprise—not all the runs showed ice breakup. She breathed a sigh of relief, until she looked more carefully. What she saw was that the only runs which did not lead to breakup and melting were the ones with outlier variables: greater ocean salinity, more or less land surface reflectivity, the percentage of cloud cover, and fluctuating ocean current pressures. It always came down to two critical variables: sea level rise and mean ocean temperature. As long as those continued to go up, the ice shelves invariably crashed. To account for the effect of sea level rise, it had to have something to do with the morphology of the shelf basins themselves. She was sure of it now. That was why she was looking at the bathymetric maps earlier. One thing that the simulations and models had not been able to account for yet was the historical pattern. For example, running the simulations backwards should match the historical patterns based on ice core samples. But the models did not yet match the historical record. There had been periods of accelerated sea level rise and shirking of ice shelves during the previous interglacial periods. There was some connection there with the arrangement of the sea floor bottom near Antarctica—she could feel it in her gut. Her intuition never lied.

Once again, Leah came back to reality. The snow let up as she crossed the valley floor, but as she neared the top of the pass, she came up behind yet another truck and into more serious snowfall. It was beginning to stick to the ground. She wasn't even halfway across Nevada, and snow already. Not a good sign, she thought... and then she said it out loud for good measure.

"You can say that again!" and laughed for the first time in days.

She turned on the radio and spun the dial until she came across a news station. After a half-dozen rural Nevada commercials, she caught the headlines: a national State of Crisis is announced by the president; the French Foreign Legion forces Kanak separatists from New Caledonia; UN Security Council action is blocked by France's veto; the General Assembly calls for collective security actions against France; a Nor'easter moves up the East Coast; and, Prophet Ministries charge IRS persecution in a case accepted by Supreme Court. She switched it off and watched the snow fly past her windshield.

En route to Punta Arenas

Sandi Gusman and Raul Dias were both rumpled and bleary-eyed. The Argentine Air Force plane delayed for six hours in Santiago due to engine problems, had them shuttling back and forth between the Argentine Embassy and the International Airport twice before the plane was finally ready to take off for Tierra del Fuego. On the last call, they were put on immediately ahead of a combined team of intelligence professionals from the U.S. and Chile. Already sitting in the back of the plane was a company of Special Forces soldiers who were very, very quiet.

The flight south took three hours. As soon as they were in the air, the dozen or so detectives were called into conference by the head Yankee. In flawless Castilian Spanish he introduced himself and got right to the point.

"I am Carlos Muñiz from the FBI's Puerto Rico regional office. The President of the United States, and the presidents of Argentina and Chile have assigned us to assist in a terrorist investigation. As soon as we reach cruising altitude I will pass out files to each of you detailing the facts as we know them. In the meantime you may wish to know what the broad parameters and orders are for us.

"We are looking for twelve nuclear weapons and the persons who have them in their possession. You should all be aware by now of the unprecedented state of emergency now in effect in my country... We have reason to believe that the parties we seek have been—at least at one time—here in the Southern Cone, most likely in either or both southern Chile and Argentina. This will be a fact-finding mission in Punta Arenas as we suspect that they have left.

"We will be landing in roughly three hours. Our headquarters are the Hotel Rio Seco. Accommodations are, for some, the hotel, and for others, the Officer's Quarters at the barracks with our companions." He motioned back at the soldiers. Muñiz picked up the files and began distributing them.

"Given the national security nature of this operation, we will work apart from local authorities. No disrespect is intended towards our Chilean hosts." He smiled at the two Chileans in front of him. They didn't smile back, but there were snickers from the Argentines in the group.

"Please get familiar with the information being supplied to you. After you are settled into your rooms, please meet me for dinner at the Seco. At that time we will review tomorrow's strategy."

"Questions?" he asked and looked around.

"Agent Muñiz?" asked Raul. He motioned with his thumb back towards the military. "Aren't we out-gunned?"

Muñiz frowned as though he was puzzling out the meaning of Raul's question, and then laughed as if Raul had been trying to make a joke—which wasn't clear at all.

"Ha! Well, we do not really believe that the nukes are actually down here anymore. It is hard to imagine what possible use they would have in one of the least populated, least important parts of the world." His face reddened as he thought about the comment.

"What I mean to say is 'strategic *military* area'—no offense intended." The Chileans, especially, managed to look hurt. He shook his head. "No, no, no," he insisted quickly, "we are concerned that anyone who *would* steal such warheads would probably not give them up without a fight. To be clear, our orders are *not* to recapture the warheads, but to locate them. Should conditions warrant any offensive action, we've been ordered to wait for serious backup. However, the Special Forces team is along for added security in case we get in 'over our heads.' We may need to rely on their tactical knowledge. You will be introduced tonight to the company commander and the squad leaders.

"In addition, each of you will be equipped with an Uzi and any backup hardware you reasonably require for this operation. We have some other gadgets we will be asking you to carry once we arrive in Punta Arenas." He raised his eyebrows and waited for any other questions. There were none.

Almost everybody settled back into their seats and each was going over the documents. Sandi heard light snoring coming from one of her Argentine associates. She watched Muñiz carefully the whole time. He looked at her from time to time, trying to hold her gaze. "A non-gringo Yankee," she thought, vaguely amused. She ignored him, his smug superior attitude, and his wedding band.

The deeper she read into the file, the more intrigued she was. For starters, she and Raul were being ordered down to Darwin, over on the Argentine side. Others in the team were being sent to Rio Gallegos, further north, back on the mainland. Half of the file was in English, good practice for the part-English, UK college educated detective. This was some serious stuff. Holy smokes, Batman, missing warheads! There was no indication what the intentions of these monstrous killers might be, but they had come this way. She had a feeling things would get worse.

Ann Arbor (2200 CST)

Karen was feeling ragged around her edges after a long day and suspected that her circadian rhythms were still seriously out of whack. She gave out a satisfied breath inspecting the day's accomplishments. Her afternoon was spent catching up on e-mail and "traffic" reports on the widening investigation and then she'd moved to an office they had commandeered from MSU. MSU's telecommunications and IT centers had also been cooperative in helping set up a secure satellite up-link for her. The early evening Task Force meeting was expecting a live report from her directly to the Situation Room in the White House. She decided to spend the remainder of her time in the MSU library, and Goldsmith shadowed her... now her bodyguard. Karen was impressed with the woman's coverage and had never had anyone watch her back quite so well ever before. During the afternoon, the assignment came directly from D.C.—it wasn't her idea, but she didn't mind.

The trip to the library helped even more than she'd imagined. The outlines of a conspiracy could be seen from a studied reading of radical environmental literature in print on the shelves, on microfiche, and archives from Internet newsgroups, blogs, and podcasts. The library had quite a large depository of transient and temporary digital archives that were protected behind security firewalls and on non-web connected hard drives. The more Karen looked at it, the harder it was to believe this sort of incident had not happened more often—except for a few individual sociopaths like Ted Kaczynski. What she was looking for were environmental or social action groups who were so angry that they would be willing to sully their image in the broader environmental movement. Only certain groups were driven to the extremes of "direct action". In Karen's experience, virtually all of the radical direct action groups on the fringe of the environmental movement were Gandhi pacifists or non-violent in orientation. This seemed counter-intuitive, but "ecotage" activists had no ethical trouble with property damage, would damage equipment or laboratories, but avoided hurting people. Only a much more violent group would fit the bill. EPG* looked like it fit.

Well, EPG*, but not EPG. It was becoming clearer that the group at MSU was a part of the broader EPG movement, but also a core of the pro-space apocalyptic wing. Abe Miller was one of their spokespersons; he called himself a *rapporteur*, and was a driving force within the movement. He had attended graduate school at MSU.

One of his books was actually on the library shelves and Karen had Gilda check it out. *Cosmic Green: Reporting on the Movement* was a collection of poetry and polemics and had a collection of EPG bumper sticker one-liners (note the asterisks):

*NOW!

Think Like a Mountain*

Gaia* First!

Neither Right nor Left; EPG* is Beyond!

There was also a curious list of phrases that began in this book and had then spread to other EPG* literature, which Miller called the "Element Cycle Series": Io or Bust (sulphur); Buckyball Blues (carbon); Nitrorgasm (nitrogen); and, IO2U (oxygen) among the thirty or so elements considered necessary for the existence of terrestrial plants and animals. These ended up in a variety of haikus and lyrics in Earth First! and EPG* folk songs. The most twisted part of *Cosmic Green*—and arguably what had made it a best-seller in the Millennial and New Age market—was the "end of the earth" section which detailed seven environmental catastrophes to befall civilization, prophesied by a Lakota medicine man.

According to FBI and national police databases, there were a number of groups supported by or identified with EPG*. The most prominent of these included: Earth Action, Forests Forever, Ocean Advocacy, and Save Antarctica—all legal non-profits. Karen was familiar with all of them. She had not known how closely linked they were. Abe Miller was on the board of directors of three. She couldn't find much in the way of financial information, so Karen sent off a request for a court order for a virtual search party to obtain the groups' IRS and financial records.

The teleconference went without a hitch, technically, in encrypted high definition video. They had flown in a technician from D.C. to ensure that the transmissions were ultra-secure. There were so many administration heavy-hitters at the other end that Karen really wasn't sorry that she was at a distance. And she got an earful before it was her turn. She sat next to a half-dozen senior Michigan FBI officials, most of them with earphones on and listening in.

Vice President Gold started the meeting. Karen observed that the man was posturing and being political—just what you'd expect from a man gearing up for the primaries and beginning to distance himself a bit from his boss, a lame-duck president.

Vice President Gold's preamble was about the political and tactical challenges posed by an extremely angry Constitutional rights lobby, which had formed overnight comprised by civil liberty groups, journalists, and political party activists on both the left and the right. A few challenges to the president's actions were already being heard in federal District court and would quickly be passed to the Supreme Court, likely on a "fast track," given the emergency. The High Court would be drawn in with the next 24 hours. The most serious challenge was coming from a few freshmen Republican House members who had asked for a restraining order on the commercial blockade action based on the commerce clause (Article 1, Section 8) of the Constitution.

After indicating that this issue was one for the lawyers and the legal scholars, the vice president went around the table for a progress reports.

Admiral Brown began with a short report on the Baton Rouge cleanup. There was no evidence of radioactive materials in the debris—further confirmation that the warheads had never been on the flight. He reported that the Russians had again expressed their concern to the Pentagon about the continued high alert status of U.S. military forces. Russian forces had also been placed on alert after the president's announcement. The VP acknowledged that the president had spoken with Russian president a few hours before the speech—so it should not have come as a surprise to the Russian leadership.

Brown reported a contingency plan for assignment of regular U.S. Army forces inside any of 200 large U.S. cities and in some strategic rural areas. He noted that this would need specific approval of the president and emergency congressional action to repeal the Posse Comitatus Act, to allow the Army to arrest civilians. Someone outside of camera range—Karen couldn't be sure who it was—asked him how much time they would need to fully deploy this scenario. According to Brown, the best estimate was 24 to 36 hours for a large force (for evacuation primarily), and a few hours for the Delta Force teams stationed in California, Colorado, Texas, and Virginia. Of course, there were SWAT teams and local Nuclear Emergency teams on standby status now across the country.

Helen Colman spoke next. She reported that the DIA had been following leads all over South America but had come up short of any good information. Some anecdotal evidence suggested that the weapons might have been shipped by boat through New Orleans. The only place outside of Texas that either Airman Wallenstein or Airman Barnes had visited during their stint at Lackland was New Orleans. They had spent a total of ten days on Canal Street. Paid for by credit card. They rented a car and had some meals near the port area. That was all they could find out so far.

The swap of warheads for scrap steel was still a major mystery that investigators were working on, Colman reported. There was obviously some sort of bait-and-switch operation the previous summer, but the "when" and "how" were largely unanswered. Part of the problem was that some of the personnel had been transferred to other posts or in one case, had left the service. All those individuals had been located and were being questioned, or would be soon.

Sam Nelson, the National Security Advisor, spoke in a sugary drawl about the intelligence-gathering shift to the Southern Cone and about the Joint Chilean-Argentine-FBI effort spreading out over Tierra del Fuego and down to Antarctica. There was a silence after the last word.

"Antarctica?" repeated Gold—apparently incredulous, judging from both the sound of his voice and a dumbfounded look on his face. Nelson asserted that there was no direct evidence that the weapons had been taken that far south, but that it was a possibility to explore. The evidence pointed south.

Nelson continued, detailing activities on the diplomatic front with U.S. allies, the U.N. and INTERPOL. No international organization had yet been contacted, threatened, or otherwise implicated in the saga thus far. He indicated that the NSA and FBI would have updates on specifics coming from those agencies. He also obliquely reminded everyone of the growing unhappiness among trade partners with the border closure and quarantine.

After the VP thanked him, NSA Director Erikson took his turn, and noted several anomalies. The first, a statistical anomaly, indicated a heightened level of activity on French governmental and commercial telecommunications channels, both domestic and international. While this might be explained by a number of factors—not the least of which was a civil war going in some of the French Overseas Territories—the activity had peaked about the time of the C-5 explosion over Baton Rouge. Those international messages that had been successfully decrypted revealed no relationship to the "Lackland event" (the phrase that had become the shorthand for the incident in the Task Force meetings).

The second anomaly was a statistically significant *decrease* in international voice and data traffic between large numbers of environmental organizations. This one caught Karen by surprise. Apparently others at the meeting in Washington reacted similarly. "W.B." went on to note that, although the NSA was not permitted to directly monitor domestic telecommunications traffic, they did have gateway sig-intel monitors for data packets moving internationally in and out of US web servers showing a marked decline in green traffic. He further noted that if additional algorithms were employed, they could determine whether or not the same phenomenon was true inside the US. The VP asked the Attorney General, who had become a part of the Task Force, to see that a court order be obtained for NSA for that purpose.

The third anomaly, continued "W.B." smoothly, was a large solar flare, which, although obviously not connected with the crisis, would not make matters any easier. It might even make the situation more dangerous as communications were disrupted. He said sarcastically, in his classic acerbic way, that "grandfather nature" could not have picked a worse time for the demonstration of HIS power. The vice president visibly glowered at the NSA chief, to Karen's amusement. She almost lost it and bit her lip.

Erikson reported that the full force of the solar storm would take roughly another six hours to reach Earth and that NSA was already powering down some instruments where there was the potential for long-term damage. Advisories were going out to military and other government agencies to switch to terrestrial cable and fiber links.

Erikson's announcement seemed to have a sobering effect on the meeting from that point. All attention now focused on the FBI's report.

Roger, Karen's new boss did most of the talking. He summarized the work of the Ann Arbor team and the other investigators across the country. The evidence pointed toward a radical environmental group which he identified as "Earth Planet Gaia*—also known as EPG*—and a national student organization called the "Green Alliance." He announced that the FBI would be staging a nation-wide raid early the next morning on all the offices of the two organizations. A list had been drawn up of over two hundred people who would be questioned about the two suspects, the missing Ann Arbor professor, and their connection to the Lackland event. He noted that court orders had been obtained for the search and seizure of EPG* and GA records. Furthermore, the FBI was also going to question leaders of the broader radical environmental movement and had asked for wiretaps on more than three dozen activists. Roger then brought Karen on the line to say a bit more about EPG* and the possible Ann Arbor connection.

"EPG* is not a membership organization," she began, "but a loose network. That makes it the most dangerous of the groups because it has the classic revolutionary cell structure embedded within a larger social network. What the background documents and interviews now suggest is that its leaders are passionate, visionary, and convinced the world is 'going to hell in a hand basket.'"

Her audience was riveted to her image on a monitor in Washington.

"One key missing EPG* leader styles himself as a 'rapporteur.' We are convinced that this is a clear case of psychological distancing and an attempt to deflect attention from his actions—direct acts of terrorism. He doesn't take responsibility, he sees himself as a conduit of environmental messages of doom and gloom. He is now implicated in a number of animal liberation attacks on research labs in the last decade.

"We have clear evidence that there is a connection between the missing professor here in Ann Arbor and others across the country in the EPG* movement who have gone missing. Ann Arbor may be just the tip of the iceberg. So to speak." She caught a couple of small smiles from around the room.

"Of considerable interest is a content analysis of some of key EPG* newsletters and web sites recently. For example, one dominant theme over the last six months is that the planetary 'body politic' is getting ready to reject the parasite species (read: us humans) and that someone needs to help Her (that is, Mother Nature) give us a little push over the precipice."

She briefly summarized the Barnes and Wallenstein developments and turned it back over to her boss.

After Karen's report, the meeting wound down quickly. Not only was it getting late but a blizzard was expected in the D.C. area and the entire East Coast was expected to get another heavy blanket of Nor'easter snow. After two of these already in December, people were taking it seriously.

International waters off Half Moon Bay, California (1715 PST)

The submarine drifted with the California Current and the sun set, pale and yellow to the southwest. Captain Derek Wilson's weathered, rustic face peered into the periscope.

"We'll surface an hour after sunset," he ordered. He pulled back from the 'scope, brought it down, and then looked for a reaction.

"Aye, aye," came from a diminutive twenty-year-old woman in shorts and a tank top who sat at the depth station in the control room. With a crew of eighteen they were "undermanned," but room was still cramped on the vessel. Women made up the majority of the crew, so they were undermanned in that sense, too. It was a tight and highly motivated crew—all university graduates and fierce environmentalists. The control room's staff was all women—except for the Captain.

Though militant millennialists made up much of the crew, they were not fatalists. They would give their lives for the cause, but saw that each of their roles was part of what the leadership called The Great Conundrum—a scheme for the salvation of the planet. They believed in Abe and the power of Gaia.

Captain Wilson picked up a microphone and turned on the PA system.

"The smoking lamp is out until further notice," he announced. There were only a few tobacco smokers on board, but many cannabis lovers, especially the majority of this crew who had been recruited from the Pacific Northwest. He wanted everyone alert and ready for action during the pickup. "We will be picking up passengers and cargo in about an hour then underway immediately."

"If things go smoothly, I will have Kitty open up the galley after 2200 hours."

He heard a few hoots down the passageway to the radio room and smiled. Those two were always hungry. On a memory wall inside the radio room, laminated and some yellowing paper and photos sketched her story.

Originally commissioned as the US Navy *Dolphin* (AGSS-555), the boat was now called the *Nemo*. It was one of the very last non-nuclear submarines built in the USA, constructed specifically for deep-diving operations. Manufactured in the late 1960s, it was designed with a 15-foot constant-diameter hull of advanced steel capped at both ends. Its design was also unique because the low length-to-beam ratio allowed it to travel underwater at speeds in excess of 30 knots.

The *Dolphin* was mothballed in the late 1970s, but after some US Navy downsizing, she was re-commissioned and transferred to the National Science Foundation and the University of California for polar research. Nearly a dozen ocean cruises and ten years of wear later it was put up for sale. International Nautronics, a marine robotics research and development company, purchased the boat some time later. International Nautronics had leased it to Ocean Advocacy New Zealand the year before. It was now effectively an EPG* boat because it had an EPG* captain and crew. Ocean Advocacy and the *Dolphin,* renamed the *Nemo,* had been together now for a year, with no crew changes, monitoring blue whale migration, not bothering anyone. No one bothered them.

Until now, that is. Captain Wilson was rather bothered by the unexpected quarantine of the U.S. mainland. Their original intention had been to cruise directly into San Francisco Bay and dock at the Alameda shipyards. But the tight border control had necessitated a change in plans. Now they were going to pick up their freight offshore and beat a quick path south. A medium-size deep sea fishing boat was on the way to rendezvous with them with a delivery for their cohorts far to the south.

The plan for friendly persuasion had turned into kidnapping. Other parts of the Northern California operation had turned sour, too. But that wasn't his concern at the moment.

He took the periscope up again as darkness took over. This time he saw signal lights to the east.

KPHX News Studio, Phoenix (2200 MST)

[Flyby] Continuous shot: Earth from space and zoom down through wispy clouds over the Mogollon Rim into the Valley of the Sun and then to the downtown tower of KPHX News and into the KPHX news studio.

[Voice over] The Valley's number one news source, from the universe of news to you: KPHX, Phoenix.

[Cut] [Close up: Evans and Wilde] "This is Will Evans."

"And this is Pete Wilde."

[Cut] [Close up: Evans] "The top story today is the Elevated Terrorism Threat Level to Red and what amounts to a national State of Emergency declared by President Clark. While there has been airport disruption particularly for international departures, the nation as a whole has taken the announcement in stride. For an update we take you to Bret Foreman at the White House."

[Cut to video] [Mid shot of Foreman with White House west entrance in the background.]

[Close up: Bret Foreman] "White House sources have confirmed that there is strong evidence that twelve missing nuclear warheads, stolen from an Air Force base somewhere in the US, are no longer inside the United States. Officials also insist that there is no evidence, as yet, that the devices are intended for use directly against this country or its citizens. There was no comment as to the identity of the suspected terrorists, although clearly some were US citizens. Senior administration officials admitted earlier that US servicemen were involved and that there had been two fatalities. The names of those killed in the incident will be announced pending notification of next of kin."

[Cut to stock video of Port of Long Beach, California]

[Voice over: Bret Foreman] The president ordered US borders sealed to shipments of goods, large and small, which brought gridlock to shipping facilities on both coasts. Across global stock markets today, shipping stocks took a beating, especially in Japanese and European markets. Some Asian and Pacific markets are open on Saturday, and nearly all that are trading today are lower. Volumes are low, as well."

[Cut to Bret Foreman] "The president, with the cooperation of Congress, has declared a state of emergency. Monday and Tuesday all banks and stock and commodities markets will be closed. After hours markets have also been suspended by a presidential order through the start of the business day on Wednesday. White House officials are confident that the weekend closures will save the stock market from panic selling.

"European allies have expressed some displeasure with the US response to the crisis, given the already unsteady stock and commodities markets, but the events of this weekend have given policy-makers on both sides of the Atlantic a little breathing room. The president has been in direct contact with the Russian president with regards to the heightened military alert levels. NATO forces are also on a heightened state of alert.

"This is Bret Foreman at the White House."

[Cut to Wilde] "In a bizarre development—on the same day as the State of Emergency—is the probable first contact with ET, that's right, extraterrestrials."

[Cut to Very Large Array in New Mexico; pan across dishes]. "In what may well be one of the most important scientific discoveries ever, first contact with another intelligent extraterrestrial species was acknowledged today, of all places, coming out of federal court. The scientific community has been in an uproar all day."

[Cut to Menlo Park high tech campus] "Papers filed by the well-funded and high profile SETI Foundation of Menlo Park accuse two smaller organizations of keeping the discovery a secret for as long as a year. Defendants are the SETI League and SETI@Home. Both deny the charges, through their attorneys, but have not revealed what they know about the signals from space."

[Cut to desktop computer] "SETI@Home has been networking home computers of tens of thousands of volunteers for decades, to share processing power for sky searches. The SETI Institute is seeking the 9th Circuit Court to force the other two groups to release radio wave monitoring data and what they claim are transmissions of data to SETI@Home computers.

[Cut to close up: Wilde] "Scientists involved, mainly astrophysicists, are being very evasive according to the SETI Institute and a few other science professional organizations associated with Stanford University. Those groups have also referred us to their attorneys."

"Legal briefs from the two smaller groups did not directly respond to the SETI Institute charges, but addressed privacy issues involving thousands of their network volunteers. Attorneys now also are raising concerns about national security considerations after this afternoon's domestic developments."

[Cut to close up of the UN Secretary General] "Media reports brought a quick response from the UN Secretary General, who stated that official communications should be opened through the UN Secretariat. The Vatican and several of the new micro-states took exception, saying that they would open spiritual channels of communication on their own initiative.

[Cut to close up: Wilde] "The Circuit Court is likely to give the plaintiffs 24 hours to respond. Among the few details released so far, the alien signals are said to originate about 20 light years away."

"We will return to more on this story and a look at weekend weather after this..."

After the News at 10, Pete was exhausted. He was usually pumped up after being under the spotlight for a half hour, but was dragging tonight. He meandered to his dressing room/office, gathered up his things, and managed to slip into the elevator and out of the parking garage without running into anyone.

Pete was in a daze most of the way home. But when he arrived in front of his stylish ranch-style house, the remote would not open the garage door. He left the car idling in the driveway and walked to the front door of his smart house.

"Good evening. Please identify yourself."

Pete cleared his scratchy, thick throat. "Peter Wilde. Apple pie."

"I'm sorry, you don't appear to be on the house list. One moment please for the doorbell to ring." Peter cleared his throat again.

"Pete Wilde," he said evenly.

"Welcome home Peter." The door clicked open.

"Unlock garage door." "Open garage door." "Unlock kitchen door." Peter returned to the car and parked it in the garage. As he entered the kitchen, he rearmed the security panel for the night. He house spoke again.

"Voice and email boxes have new messages. Do you want me to play them?"

"No thanks Mabel. Flag for later."

As he began to get ready for bed, that image of Danielle flashed again through his mind. What began as a nagging feeling had become a drum beat of impending doom. It felt very personal. He felt that he was more involved, somehow. An intuition became a certainty. He didn't know how or why, but knew—the more he thought about it—that Danielle Thomas and her comrades were a part the bigger terrorism picture. Surely the FBI was aware—he had, after all, suggested that to them, right? Hadn't he? Pete had an instinctive dislike for FBI and police that he recognized as an occupational hazard. This went deeper. There'd some run-ins with the police during his teen years; he had a "smart mouth" and often made matters worse with his attitude. Though never convicted of anything, Pete had spent more than a night or two in jail by the time his 18th birthday.

He could hardly go back to the FBI with vague suspicions, he thought gloomily to himself. Pete needed evidence. Dropping off to sleep, he tried to put together a set of logical connections worthy of mention to anyone in authority. His sleep was disturbed.

...and he dreamed of an alien invasion right out of *War of the Worlds*.

In one part of his nightmare, an alien turned out to be Danielle Thomas, or took over her body. At first it was the same old Danielle from college, but then she slowly morphed into an older and older woman, and finally into a pile of flesh that shape-shifted into a green alien blob with tentacles. This last transformation jolted Pete awake, drenched with sweat. Danielle Thomas was back in his life. And the news of the day had given Pete Bug Eyed Monster dreams, along with countless other millions of people across the planet.

Queen Maud Range, Antarctica (2300 GMT)

The chamber glowed with intense aquamarine light. It was like a small bubble in the ice, a kind of igloo, 30 feet in diameter, with a tunnel of light beaming down an empty column in the very top from which dropped cables and ropes. The cables connected to the nuclear warhead lying on a simple wooden cradle that it shared with a rubberized laptop computer.

A man in a heavy parka with a glove in one hand stood in front of the machinery where he examined all of the cables and indicator lights, tracing them with his bare index finger. He slowly and carefully closed the laptop and pushed a button on the warhead that turned from amber to green. A soft beep accompanied the change of state.

He surveyed the space, looking for anything left behind. Satisfied, he pulled the walkie-talkie from his belt.

"Haul me up," he said and clipped the radio back on his belt, replaced the glove, and slipped his foot into the loop at the end of a climbing rope.

"Ready?" from the radio.

"Pull," he yelled and was quickly pulled the first 20 feet.

"Easy," he said needlessly, for the thousandth time. His head and then torso disappeared up the round hole in the ice.

On the surface, he was assisted by two heavily dressed figures up into a large canvass tent full of tanks and hoses and drilling equipment. The hole down into the ice was crowned with a titanium tripod that pulleyed the man the rest of the way up. He climbed up as one of the assistants pulled the rope from his feet.

"Thanks menagerie." The two nodded silently—or perhaps reverently.

The two followed behind, out of the tent, into a light snowfall and then 20 feet toward an inflatable habitat airlock. They removed their overcoats and boots in the large habitat entrance, and then entered the inner envelope.

The leader, Abe Miller, was an older, grizzled man. He waved absently at the handful of his people inside the habitat occupied packing, sorting, and loading equipment and supplies into boxes. He sat down in front of a small portable satellite radio sitting on a folding table and pulled off the push-to-talk handset. He then set a couple of switches and cleared his throat.

"This is Buster Ten for Beluga, over," he croaked.

After a few seconds came the reply.

"Beluga here." The *Beluga* (formerly the US *Albacore* [AGSS-569]) was actually half a continent away, on the edge of the Ross Ice Shelf.

"Buster Ten is in the bag and we are ready to come home. Over."

"Affirmative. Buster Ten is a go. Await your return, over.

"Over. Out."

"Okay people! Listen up! Helicopters are on the way. Time to pack up and pull out!"

There was general pandemonium. Hoots and hollers and monkey screams and laughter erupted. Then came a hip-hip-hooray. And as enthusiastic and quickly as it came, the energy returned to their tasks quietly. It was a sober atmosphere.

He had to rally the team's confidence that they would get out of Antarctica alive. Many of them wanted to know that their plans would work and that the dream would be realized. The crazy scheme was, at the same time, both one of the most obscene acts of Man against Mother Nature and a gift from a man to Her.

Their two-year effort had not come without cost given that the interior spaces of Antarctic ice are among the most hostile places on Earth. The team had already confronted that reality in the planning stages two years before, and then the near-tragedy of placing Buster Four. And at this very moment a huge storm was bearing down on them.

Abe put his arm around Angel Stills, his second-in-command, and asked her to get the crew to stow gear in the tents, secure all their loose equipment, and make sure the dogs were fed. It was snowing still and the visibility was poor. Although it was the land of midnight sun, at midnight the sun was low in the sky. They had eight to ten hours to weather the storm and then get most of the remaining crew ferried back to the submarine for their getaway.

San Francisco (2300 PST)

    Just outside of Reno Leah came up behind a line of cars that she could see backed up at least a mile or more behind a serious roadblock on Interstate 80. At least a dozen emergency vehicles strobed and flashed their lights. She maneuvered the Corvette into the fast lane, did a 180 in the median, and headed back east. The police did not go after her. She got off the interstate in eastern Reno and worked her way down to US Highway 50. She stopped on the grade and put chains on her car with about a half-dozen truckers. There was little traffic and the snow was steadily falling. She made it through Lake Tahoe and over the mountains. There were no roadblocks on the state highway, but the detour added nearly two hours to her long trip. Tired and vaguely glad that she'd ended up on the back roads, she neared the Bay Area and hopped back on the Interstate.

    Once again she phoned home. There still was no answer.

    Leah felt very strange as she arrived in her old neighborhood. She'd been away too long, and had an eerie feeling that something bad was about to happen. She could feel it in her bones. Stepping over an enormous pile of mail inside the front door, Leah wrinkled her nose at the smell of the place—stale, acrid as if something had died. Rushing from room to room, she finally concluded that the odor was neither Jake nor the goldfish. There were no notes left anywhere. His suitcases and clothes were in the closet. Everything else was uncharacteristically neat and tidy.

    The worst smell was traced to the garbage pail under the sink. Two goldfish were missing, but otherwise the rest of the fish were okay. She fed them immediately—before any more disappeared. After dragging in her bags, she sat down on the sofa, leaned back her head and was out like a light. She'd been asleep an hour when the phone rang. Sitting straight up and totally disoriented, she picked up the phone on the end table next to her.

    "Hello?" she asked.

    "Leah, baby, it's me," she heard Jake's shaky voice.

    "Are you all right?" she responded softly, quickly.

"No," he answered, "please do as you are told." He sounded plaintive—not a Jake kind of sound. He really worried her.

Another voice—a male voice—came on the line.

"Dr. Wilson, if you wish to see Dr. Meadows alive, listen carefully and do as I ask. Turn off all of the lights and the TV. Bring a change of clothes, your suitcase, and purse downstairs to the street. Do not call the police. Do not call anyone, or leave any note. You have exactly two minutes or we will kill your husband." And the caller hung up.

Her head was suddenly very clear. Now she knew—at least in a general sense—that her intuition had been right. Jake was alive at least. She quickly grabbed a change of clothes and scribbled a note, which she left on the kitchen table: "Jake and I are being abducted by strangers." She put down the time and date. Quickly she turned off the lights, locked the door, and hurried down the stairs.

After waiting on the curb for a couple of minutes she began to worry anew. Could they have known she had written a note? But before her thoughts went much further, a dark van appeared at the top of the street from out of the fog, with only its running lights on. The side door slid open in front of her and hands grabbed her and pulled her inside. Before she could even struggle, she felt her mouth being covered and caught the overwhelming smell of chloroform as she passed out.

Dear Betsy,

We're about two days out from our next port of call in the Cook Islands—Rarotonga. It's barely past eight this morning. It's already pretty hot, but calm. Today the South Pacific appears calmer on the surface. That's the good news. The bad news is that the ocean is gray with an ominous little chop. These little waves are coming from big storms—close ones—large convection cells maybe 20 to 40 miles away. They show up on radar and the satellite weather display. We appear to be drifting along in the middle of a large disturbed air mass. The sun is bright, but there's a lot of haze—unusual for this part of the Pacific. It's just weird. Needless to say, we're 'battening down the hatches.' After I help haul in sails, I'll run down and make some sandwiches and secure the kitchen. The weather threat mirrors the political climate down here. My motion-sickness patch helps, but I sure hate storms. I said a blessing for Mana Kai—I have been through a hurricane in her, so I know she can take a beating.

And I was SO looking forward to the weekend! ☺
Talk to you later babe.

January 14
Saturday

Ann Arbor, Michigan (0600 CST)

Karen awoke in her hotel room near the airport and flipped on CNN. The East Coast was now in the grip of a major Weather Emergency. Most major airports were closed, and it became obvious that she was not going home. The Boston-Washington corridor was paralyzed—not the sort of circumstance you would wish for in the middle of a major terrorist crisis. CNN framed the news with the political fallout from the Nuclear Emergency. There was nothing in the news that she hadn't already heard. She left the TV on in the background while she got ready for the day.

After plodding through her morning routine, shower and room service breakfast, Karen checked her e-mail and messages. One item caught her attention, the USGS robbery. The robbery had been cross-listed to this investigation. Someone had been paying attention. She pulled up as much information as she could get and the more she read, the more she could sense a connection between the robbery and EPG*. What made the Palo Alto incident even more compelling was the lack of developments in other areas—no direct, hot leads in this country except for a growing list of people either missing or "incommunicado."

Given the likelihood that weather could only get worse, and the obvious shift in focus and FBI energy to California and Oregon, Karen decided to catch a flight to the West Coat while the airport was still open. She opened her laptop and found the first available flight to the San Francisco Bay Area. Throwing her equipment and baggage together she swept out of the room like a whirlwind. At least there'd be a good half of a business day left once she got to Oakland.

Two hours later, Karen settled into her business class seat, and used the time before the cabin doors closed to download USGS files sent to her by the San Francisco FBI office. The more she read, the more convinced she became that EPG* was behind the USGS theft. But why would they want seismic equipment? The connection to large explosives was easy enough to grasp, but why measure something that would be patently obvious? In spite of the lack of answers, a large wave of realization swept over Karen and literally made her face flush: the weapons were meant to be used, as in "used

84

up." Not for blackmail.

While she had already been forced to admit that the situation was overtly dangerous—the State of Emergency was no small matter—she had no obvious indication that the persons who had managed to steal the warheads were planning to use them. No phone calls or announcements taking credit. She'd imagined blackmail or threats, but exploding all of them? She could not imagine why or where.

The cabin doors closed and she shut off the laptop. She settled back and let sleep take over again. Sleeping in planes was becoming her art. Once again she was asleep before the jet had pushed away from the building. She dreamt that she was sailing through the clouds, large fluffy white clouds, and passing through their tops, as if in a glider, alternatively cool and damp and then warm and bright. This continued and she felt as if she was lighter and lighter, flying now all by herself—as long as she kept her arms extended. This was easy at first, effortless as the wind seemed to help keep her up. Then she tired and her arms started to feel heavier and she began to fall.

A cloud began to form in front of her, rising to form a large thunderhead with an anvil shape. The cloud twisted and became a distinctly human face.

It whispered to her in low rumbles like distant thunder, "*Shango! Shango* will save you." The cloud formed pursed lips that began to blow in her direction and she felt a cool, dry breeze help push her arms back and she stopped falling.

There they were, the human face of a cloud top and the flying woman, bound together by breath. Karen was again at peace and happy.

"Who are you? She asked the cloud.

"Why you know me, little girl, I am *Shango*, the *Loa* of wind and storms. I am your *Met Tet*, your guardian angel.

"And very bad storms 'a brewin'… You best be careful, little one."

The cloud dissipated and Karen continued to find the wind blowing to keep her afloat, but the landscape below changed. The fields below turned color, alternating patches of green and brown became a solid white, like new-fallen snow. The air turned colder and then there were flashes of bright light. The billowing cumulous clouds that had populated her universe, now took the form of rapidly rising mushroom clouds, dark and foreboding, black and sickly. They crackled with lightning and cast ugly shadows across the white snowscape below. Buffeting winds now began to tear at her, tossing her around like a rag doll.

The plane reached cruising altitude and the ping of the Fasten Safety Belts light going out woke her up. The word *Shango* formed on her lips.

Pete Wilde awoke to the shriek of his alarm with a start, having had some of the worst nightmares that he'd had in years. They evaporated as soon as he awoke, but he was left with a horrible feeling of dread and apprehension. He could hardly bring himself to get out of bed and face the day. There were vague recollections of alien invaders, mass killing, and planet spanning storms—the sort of dreams, which are uncomfortably real in the midst of them, but unreal by morning light. Getting out of bed made the night terrors dissipate.

He halfheartedly started on his daily routine. At least he only had one newscast on Saturday. He needed his rest and already looked tired. But after dragging his sorry ass out of bed and brewing a double espresso, he perked up. But then nagging recollections, ghosts of the dream began to intrude.

Getting on with Phoenix life was all that mattered, he thought. Then he immediately felt guilty that he was no longer worried so much about the environment—lost in his career—not like when he was in the Green Alliance back in college in Michigan. The Southwest desert environment always seemed more hostile than friendly and saving the environment seemed less important. Ozone degradation had made being outside in the sun dangerous and now the sun was an enemy, too. He had cultivated a slight Southwestern twang and left his Midwest life behind. But, shit, those were all just rationalizations.

Until yesterday... His life was narrow and shallow. He basically went through the motions of having a life, but not too deep beneath the surface he wasn't any happier than he was back in Michigan. No lasting relationships, no commitment except to being a rising star TV personality, and no connection to anything very real. The reality of the murders yesterday began to sink in.

Peter shook his head at himself in the bathroom mirror, focusing on not cutting himself shaving. It was just that he'd given up really caring about anything except his expensive house in Scottsdale and his BMW. While that superficiality may have made him a natural for

TV, for that "and now this" detachment from the pain, suffering, and degradation which he covered everyday, it made him care less for himself, too. He was appalled at his own reaction to seeing Danielle Thomas and her brutality in the Palo Alto killing. How could he not be horrified?

How could it be that he'd turned into this callous, uncaring bastard? He was looking objectively at his own detachment, and that was gnawing at his conscience. What were his true inner feelings? Surprise at seeing Danielle? Shocked at the brutal acts of violence? Regret at having left behind his freedom, commitment to some ideal, or love for and commitment to another person?

The video clip and the events of the previous two days touched something deep within that he had cut off and left to wither away. He stared at himself in the mirror and willed himself to get back his resolve. He had to get ready for the day, for work, and get on with his life. There was no going back. He couldn't afford to let this get to him. He straightened his shoulders and stood tall.

He would spend some time trying to find out more about what had happened in the Palo Alto robbery and maybe look into what Green Alliance was up to. Maybe he should track down other classmates? But by the time Pete got to work, the National Emergency, the East Coast weather story, and other news of the day absorbed all his attention.

Sandi had put her long hair up into a tight bun and donned her Argentine National Police uniform. She frowned at the tie, but it would discourage more leers from the gringo. With her backup already strapped to her ankle, she strapped on her Colt in the external holster, far more comfortable than in its usual hidden spot. She met up with Raul after breakfast and they joined the rest of the Darwin team for the ride to the Punta Arenas airport. Arriving at the airport, the team was driven straight to a runway where a large transport plane was waiting. As soon as the team and a couple of large satchels were loaded and strapped in, the plane took off for the short hop to Darwin in southernmost Argentina.

On the flight, Sandi and Raul compared plans and strategies for this operation. They had been given general orders to search for twenty persons and were supplied with pictures for each; they were mostly American men and women, the women outnumbering the men two to one and a few New Zealanders. They were also given very sophisticated computer radiation detectors that looked rather like a tricorder from Star Trek and instructed, oh by the way, to look for stolen nuclear weapons. The team was issued radiophone headsets and more automatic weapons, Uzis in lightweight Special Forces harnesses

The eight agents were met at the small, dusty Darwin airport by two Argentine Army sergeants, each with a large sedan. One team would cover the Army barracks and airport, and the other the business district. She and Raul headed for town. And as ranking agent in her team, she suggested that they might get further asking shopkeepers questions if they left their heavy weapons behind. Expecting an argument, she was surprised that there was ready agreement. The four split up to cover both sides of Darwin's main drag, Avenida Sarmiento.

It didn't take long to discover that two of the twenty had spent quite a bit of time in and around Darwin. While the photos identified the two as Marshall Steen and Angela Stills, shop owners knew them as Rolf Rasmussen and Gustava Nansen. Curiously, the townspeople believed these people were part of a Norwegian Antarctic expedition that arrived the previous summer and wintered over until the spring. The group had leased a small, empty church on the north side of town, had arrived in small groups throughout the year, but mostly kept to themselves. The two, Rasmussen and Nansen, had bought ample supplies in town during their "winter over." But they clearly had brought most of their own provisions. They had spent a lot on wine. Stores had sold out their entire wine stock in July and again in August.

The other group of agents discovered that the "Norwegian" group had rented a small storage shed at the airport. It was empty now and there was virtually no trace left. Hair samples were retrieved for DNA testing, but there were no fingerprints, and no radiation abnormalities. Midday, the group headed for the church—Iglesia Primavera, in foothills on the outskirts of town.

They were told in town that the church had been deserted since November, but the group took no chances. Even though the eight civilian agents were armed to the teeth, the Special Forces unit took the lead when they entered the property on foot. At the entrance, there was a boarded up, rustic cabin with a small crucifix painted on the front door. A dirt lane lined with pine trees ran down a slight incline toward a small creek. Across the steam was a rather good-sized rectangular building with a small bell tower. A lone chicken scratched at the ground in a gravel parking lot in front of the sanctuary.

Carlos Muñoz, the Puerto Rican, ordered everyone to spread out and to make the "microphones hot." Sandi and Raul went to the rear door of the church while others in the team went around to the front. They found doors unlocked, and the church and adjoining few rooms empty. The pews in the sanctuary had all been stacked and piled in one corner of the large room. A few of the pews still stood in the middle of the room covered with 4 X 8 sheets of plywood. They had apparently been used as tables.

A number of "all clear" yells went out from the soldiers who fanned out to check outlying buildings. Then quickly, the police began taking pictures of everything, dusted for fingerprints, and tagged and bagged what little evidence was left behind. Others scanned walls and corners with specialized radiation detectors.

One of the radios squawked.

"Perez here, I've found a radiation anomaly in one of the outbuildings immediately behind the church. Agent Muñoz, I think you should come see this."

"On my way," he said and motioned for Raul and her to follow.

They made their way out the back door and saw Perez in the threshold of the doorway to what appeared to be a kitchen area—a small covered area abutting the side of the hillside behind the church. As they approached the double-door, they could see behind what looked like a mineshaft.

"The radiation meter shows above background levels of alpha particles," volunteered Perez.

They found what they'd come for as far as Muñoz was concerned. He had everyone stand down and holster weapons. He ordered the Special Forces sergeant to cover the periphery and gathered the agents.

"I want pictures of everything and then a thorough radiological survey on a surface grid. Tag and bag everything that looks like evidence. Dust for prints after the radiation survey. Any questions?"

"Okay, let's do it." The last sentence he spoke in perfect American English.

They went to work.

The terrorists did not leave anything large behind. There were no obvious attempts to hide things or sanitize the evidence. There were abundant fingerprints here, hair for DNA analysis, and other trace physical evidence that was quickly on its way back to the mobile crime laboratory being set up at the airport. As eco-outlaws it was only fitting that most of what they left behind was biological detritus: hair, nail clippings, and other human leavings on the floors and walls. They left some small evidence of their high tech clothes and equipment. Fibers from new insulation and covering materials— spandex, wool composites, artificial down, and lots of cotton—the kind specifically used in T-shirts. The DNA and fingerprints coincided with the data they had on the fugitives, some thirty people from North America, New Zealand, and the Caribbean. And a few sets of prints and DNA that did not match any of the records.

Most revealing of all was a strong alpha particle signature detected in the cave behind the church. The culprits left a pair of common wood shipping pallets that picked up stray radiation from whatever had been on top of them. Further up the stream, agents discovered fresh piles of dirt and rock—presumably the tailings from the tunnel construction. Had the terrorists worried about radiation leakage or trying to keep the weapons hidden?

After five hours at Iglesia Primavera, Muñoz ordered Raul and Sandi to accompany the pallets and collected evidence back to the airport. The soldiers were ordered to keep the church site secure. The cabin had already been converted to a sentry post and a Sony generator powered bright searchlights. Agents would continue searching the area for hours, since luckily, the nights were very short this time of year.

Darwin was usually a sleepy little town near the bottom of the world, distant from the circles of money and power far to the north, east, and west. But Darwin was already being thrust into the limelight and under the global media microscope. Not only had military satellite dishes and other antenna sprouted around one end of the Darwin airstrip, but now global media teams were also arriving, with smaller portable satellite dishes. A media tent city was growing at the other end of the airstrip.

Leah's head did not hurt—it ached. Then it throbbed. Her arm hurt, too, where apparently she'd laid on it too long. She couldn't seem to move anything except her eyes in their sockets. Her eyes were glued shut. She let them relax and listened for a while. There was a thrumming sound of some kind of engine. Then she had a very strange sensation. She seemed to roll slightly to one side and then, barely, gradually to the other side. Like in an airplane. But it didn't feel like an airplane.

Her senses were waking up. She smelled stale, body odor smells: urine, vomit, and excrement. And she caught an antiseptic smell, too, and ammonia. She felt weak, bruised, thirsty, and a very full bladder. Then she heard raspy breathing. She stopped breathing for a few seconds to make sure it wasn't herself. She struggled again to open her eyes. There was a diffused red light and she seemed to be tied down to a rough bed. Awake now, she realized she was on a bunk bed, a small one, on a ship.

Then coughing, from below her, and a long low moan. It sounded like Jake!

"Jake, is that you?" she whispered. There was no response.

Louder. "Jake, Jake. Wake up."

"Huh?" he responded dully, and then coughed again—this time harder.

"Jake, is that you?"

"Jesus. Oh shit, Leah, they got you," he said sadly and softly.

"Are you all right? Where are we?"

"I dunno," he came back slowly, "on either count. They moved me last night, but I've been drugged since they kidnapped me. I feel pretty messed up." He coughed long, and hard.

"What is this all about?"

"Do you have any rich relatives you never told me about?" Jake asked.

"Not that I know of. What happened?" No response.

"Jake?"

She thought she heard him crying. He had to be in considerable pain. Jake was a classic stoic, and she'd never seen nor heard him cry during their entire relationship. The whimper became a loud, miserable wail.

She waited a few minutes until the sobbing subsided.

"Where does it hurt the most?" she asked.

"You don't understand," he moaned.

That really got her attention and worried her more than ever.

"What do you mean?"

Silence again, but she decided to wait him out. She knew him well enough to know when he was holding back and that he would eventually spit it out—whatever it was. What he said next she was unprepared for.

"Angel, I lied to you. I think this is my fault!"

She waited some more.

"Jesus Christ. It is my fault. I have been telling some friends about your work…" He stopped.

"Go on, please," she urged him.

"Environmentalist friends, radicals, but friends since college. They take action and I send them money, that sort of thing. I did not expect this to happen or get so out of hand."

Leah hardly knew what to say. She was shocked, speechless. She had never considered that Jake might be political. He just did not seem, well, that way. He was always more interested in basketball and football on TV… She gave up—it was just too much on top of everything else in the last 24 hours. He'd lied to her, he'd said. But he hadn't really lied, had he?

"I don't follow you at all. First of all, what has happened to us? Who are your so-called friends?" she yelled with one eye still glued shut.

"I should have been totally honest with you, but it was so incremental and secretive. Long before I met you I helped spike trees and destroy heavy equipment of developers up in the Sierra. I was a hobbyist and a weekend warrior until I went back East for grad school. Since then, I have sent them money, more or less anonymously." He coughed and readjusted himself under his restraints.

"Only a few years ago Abe, one of the old friends, called out of the blue and asked what I knew about Antarctica. I told him all about your work—he was extremely interested—and then he asked for papers and asked questions…"

"You have got to be kidding me. You never said a word to me."

"Well, yes, because he is more-or-less underground and I didn't want to implicate you any more than I had to."

"Jeese, Jake, that's really sweet of you," she managed sarcastically. "I just wished you'd been honest with me about this earlier so I could make up my own mind about it," she said quietly. Then she yelled louder.

"Just what the fuck does this have to do with being tied up and having to PEE SO BAD!"

That was for a broader audience—if anyone was listening. No one was, apparently. The fact that she was really pissed off did take

92

some of the focus off her bladder and back to Jake. He began the story of his connections to EPG* and communications with Abe Miller and some of the others in the so-called Menagerie until six months before when they stopped calling.

"I just know it is them. Something big has happened or is happening."

"Well you got that right smarty-pants. There is a bloody State of Emergency because of some stolen nuclear warheads!" her voice was a little shrill.

"Oh my god, you don't think…" his voice trailed off.

"Where are we?

He cleared his throat. "Not sure. I was first held in a ship somewhere, in a small cabin, bound and gagged. They fed me granola bars, pop tarts, and peanut butter sandwiches. I could hear foghorns, but not now. The pitch and yaw aren't the same. This feels like a bigger boat maybe?" He coughed again.

"So, they wanted me not you," she mused. "Any idea why?"

"No. I asked repeatedly what was going on, but nothing. I did hear some arguing at one point on the other side of the door, but who or what it was about escaped me. They must have moved me after I was sedated. I'm not even sure this is a different place, although definitely a different cabin."

"Then you think we are on some kind of ship?"

The light came on, bright and blinding.

"You are on a submarine," came a female voice, "the *Nemo*." A tall brunette with short-cropped hair in a smock came into view. "I am Myra Collins, First Mate and Medical Officer. I apologize for the restraints and utter lack of hospitality. Furthermore, it should be the captain greeting you, but regrettably, he is preoccupied at the moment."

Before either Jake or Leah could protest, she continued.

"You have a right to be indignant about such hostile treatment—especially you, Dr. Meadows. We will inform you of your role in this saga, but in due time. For now we will continue to keep you restrained until the captain can interview you."

"If you will cooperate with me, Dr. Wilson, I will take you to the head." When Leah failed to react, Myra added, "the rest room, you know."

"Of course. The bladder torture works every time."

Myra did not smile. She immediately unlocked the leather

medical restraints that had kept Leah pinned to the bunk. Leah was shaky, but let the woman support her elbow. The woman was very strong.

"We're going down the corridor to the left," the First Mate informed her.

After they turned the corner, Myra gestured to the left again. "In here," she said. "Watch your head." This time she smiled at her own joke.

"There is soap, washcloth, toothbrush and paste, and a change of clothing in there for you. You have ten minutes." She locked the door behind Leah with a key and actually gave her fifteen minutes, exactly when Leah was ready.

Somewhere over the Rockies, Karen was waiting to be briefed by a liaison the Bureau had assigned to her in the San Francisco field office. Karen made arrangements to take the call in the cockpit at the navigator's station through her laptop for encryption. The flight crew was all very deferential to her and passengers had been moved around so that she was in the first row of business class with the whole row all to herself.

Earlier, when one of the flight attendants, Suzie, brought her coffee, she thanked Karen with a "You're welcome, Agent St. Cloud."

Karen quickly grabbed the woman's arm and gently pulled her closer.

"How did you know who I am?"

The flight attendant looked her directly in the eyes and cocked her head. Her face carried a curious look.

"Why, the pilot and gate crew both told us an FBI Special Agent was on board. It was unusual. We're usually the last to know. We were told to give you lots of room and anything you want, you know, before you even have to ask?"

Karen nodded, but was shaken. There was no way they should have received that kind of information unless she had an angel in the Bureau looking out for her. She didn't particularly like that either.

When she asked to speak to the captain, Suzie arranged it quickly.

Karen asked him to use the radio for the encrypted call and then how he had learned she was aboard. He also looked back at her curiously.

"It's funny that you ask, it came in a memo with the flight departure paperwork. That comes from the tower, so it is FAA. It was unusual, but official, so I informed the senior flight attendant."

"May I have that please?" She asked, but it was command in her voice.

As the copilot dug out the memo from a binder, Karen pulled a latex glove out of an inside pocket where she always carried them. When he handed it to her, she took it pinched between latex.

"I'll be back in a few minutes to make the call if that's okay?" She asked this time as a question.

Back at her seat she pulled out a plastic bag to stick the curious memo. The small event seemed so far out of the realm of proper protocol that it unsettled her. The memo itself looked innocuous enough, but the implications were bothersome.

Soon she was back on the flight deck and adjusting the headset.

After exchanging a password sequence and two keywords, she was talking to someone.

"St. Cloud here," she said professionally. She was getting a little edgy, maybe due to being cooped up in an airplane again and drinking coffee instead of alcohol. Getting up and coming to the flight deck cleared her head and made her feel better.

"This is Brenda Chavez, your liaison, Agent St. Cloud. At your service, sir." Sass and inside information—from someone she didn't know? Or did she? Brenda Chavez, Brenda Chavez... Then it came to her.

"That wouldn't be the former Brenda Schwartz, would it?"

Laughter came from the other end of the line. "You never miss a jab Lieutenant Commander. Yeah, I got married last year."

"Are we secure?"

"All the lights are green at this end. I can go ahead with my report, if you are ready."

"Go ahead, please."

"There is now confirmation that the nukes were in Tierra del Fuego perhaps as late as October. The radionuclide forensics people will be on the ground by tomorrow, but the readings were high enough to establish that they were sitting there for several months. The trail leads to the tip of the cone of South America and probably on to Antarctica, of all places."

Chavez covered the highlights of investigations in various Green Alliance/EPG* strongholds and discussed some logistical matters. She said that she had hardcopies of all the reports that were coming in, unless Karen needed any sent ahead to her electronically. Brenda showing a lot more leadership than Karen remembered of her from training together at Quantico. Brenda agreed to email a digest of investigation highlights for her to read outbound from Denver.

"Very thorough, Agent Chavez. It is good working with you again."

"I have been pulled off of all my other cases indefinitely."

"Just your luck," she said jokingly. "Chavez, find out what you can about who informed the FAA or the FAA tower in Ann Arbor that I was VIP on this flight. The flight crew knew I was on board. Something is not right with that."

Chavez agreed to look into it.

"Things have been happening pretty fast..." she offered.

Karen's intuition about heading west was making even more sense given that the lion's share of EPG* activities were on the West Coast, and especially in the San Francisco Bay Area. No wonder, she thought to herself, the word Berkeley rolling over her tongue. She noted that the digest Brenda had created for her was already in her email inbox. Brenda was nimble. She also sent a proposed agenda for Karen's afternoon.

Karen scanned the page and then said, "Okay, we're in good shape. Let me get caught up on some of these files and I'll see you at the office."

"Sooner than that," Brenda responded, "A driver and I will be waiting for you on the tarmac. Headquarters has made it clear that your have the Highest Priority and carte blanche. They even have a helicopter coming up from San Jose just for you. I have never seen anything like it."

"My, my." Even Karen was impressed.

"Also, something else just came over the Bureau wire. Get this: despite the mess on the East Coast, the Task Force is working with the Pentagon to organize a polar strike team. Ever been to Antarctica?"

1300 EST
[CNN logo]
[Scroll down: "Winter Emergency"]
[Scroll down: "Special Report"]
[Cut to news center][Close up: Erik Thomas] "This is Erik Thomas at CNN Center in Atlanta. A severe winter storm has paralyzed most of the East Coast of the United States in what may well become one of the worst winter storms in US history.

[Cut to: animated weather map of Northeastern US] "A large mass of Arctic air is moving into the mid-Atlantic behind a nearly stationary low pressure system. Contact with warmer, moist Gulf Stream air is causing some violent weather along the front, primarily high winds and significant amounts of snow.

[Cut to video: JFK Airport terminal, stranded passengers] "Airports in Washington, Baltimore, New York, and Boston have been closed since midnight and the Pittsburgh Airport is reporting two to three hour delays. Many major carriers managed to move airplanes out of these airports before the storm hit, but cancellations and delays are plaguing most major airports across the country. Ironically, airline schedules had only recently returned to normal after the winter storm two weeks ago."

[Cut to video: New York City street scene] "The biggest saving grace of the storm was that it waited for the weekend. New York's governor appealed to the public to stay at home."

[Cut to video: Governor Castello] "I am asking the citizens of the state to stay off the streets—emergency vehicles and road clearing equipment must have priority. Emergency shelters have been set up for out-of-state visitors or New York City workers caught in the city."

[Cut to: Erik Thomas] "Washington, D.C. itself has only received four inches of snow, but at least another eight to ten inches are expected. New York and Boston have already received nine inches each. Snowfall in the Appalachian Mountains has been as much as four feet in some locations.

"The storm front is expected to move further south today. Currently, both Nashville and Charlotte are experiencing rain and some sleet, but will see snow in the next few hours. By later this evening, snow is expected as far south as Birmingham and Atlanta.

"Severe storm warnings are in effect from northern New England to Jacksonville, Florida on the coast. The Great Lakes area is in the grip of extremely cold air, but minimal snow at this point except in Buffalo and other lake effect snow-prone areas. Storm watches are now being posted for northern New York state and the Ohio valley.

"For a report on the ground, we take you to John Simmons in Roanoke, Virginia."

[Cut to: Simmons] "Erik, the mayor of Roanoke, Charlene Wesley, declared a city emergency last night at 9 P.M., even though the storm had barely begun. In the last twelve hours, Roanoke has had a record 27 inches of snow. This morning, we asked Mayor Wesley, how she knew it would be so bad."

[Cut to: Wesley] "John, I really didn't know it would be this bad. It was not woman's intuition, or anything like that," she drawled. "The storm two weeks ago caught us mostly by surprise, and when the weather reports indicated another serious storm, I thought it would be better to be safe than sorry."

"So you don't regret your decision?"

"No, not at all. We rarely need snow plows in this town, so I mobilized city and county crews and all available vehicles. The only problem right now is finding places to put this much snow."

[Cut to: Simmons] "The city is virtually at a standstill. We are located at the Holiday Inn near the center of town, and as you can see behind me, the streets are deserted except for road crews and emergency vehicles. With at least another foot of snow expected today, the road crews will continue to stay busy.

"From Roanoke, this is John Simmons."

"Thank you John. In related news, the Commissioner of the New York Port Authority has asked that shippers refrain from sending any more goods to the New York area. Due to the president's Emergency Order, off loading of cargo from foreign vessels has been reduced to a trickle.

[Cut to: harbor aerial video] "Container ships by the dozens have begun to pile up in New York Harbor and Long Island Sound waiting their turn. Many shipping company owners, and some foreign governments, are already complaining about the loss of revenue and cost of delays of off loading container ships.

"The Commissioner expressed concerns this morning that the bad weather would only make matters worse and said that he was concerned about the safety of ships and their crews. He urged ship owners and captains not to leave their ports of debarkation until further notice."

[Cut to: Thomas] "We will return to our coverage of the Winter Storm Emergency after this short break."
[Cut to: overhead cam, pan newsroom]
[Scroll down: "Winter Emergency"]
[Scroll down: "Special Report"]
[Cut to: commercial] "Hawaiian Getaway Tours"

Karen's plane began its descent into the San Francisco Bay Area. It seemed she'd been in the air more lately than she'd been on the ground, but her jet lag was tempered by a night in D.C. and then another in Michigan.

Operation Hot Pants was moving fast now. Deputy Director Hale spent 20 minutes on the phone with her after a plane change in Denver. There had been some progress in the case and some frustrations, too. Hale's call had been intriguing, mainly because it was more political than professional. He was blunt about the vice president's pressure to show some results, but conciliatory about the brisk pace of the investigation so far. He acknowledged that there was considerable confusion within the Bureau and on the Task Force about what they thought EPG* would actually do with nuclear weapons. It was totally out of character for most environmentalists, mostly a nonviolent and anti-nuclear bunch. Hale noted that FBI psychologists were doing profile work ups on Abe Miller, Stewart Adams, and few of Miller's lieutenants that would be forwarded to her when the work-ups were more complete.

The State of Emergency was more and more problematic for President Clark. China, France, Germany, and Canada had lodged serious diplomatic complaints. US ports were suffering already. Labor unions were extremely unhappy, too. The decision was not going to reflect well on the VP's presidential bid, Karen thought. Ultimately, it had been the president's decision to act, but Karen had little doubt as to who had pushed the idea. Hale indirectly touched on the subject by noting that there was an absence of evidence that the nukes were intended for the US mainland. After fifteen minutes of beating around the bush, it became clear that what Hale—and by extension the Administration—wanted, was evidence that the nukes were not a domestic threat so that they could call off the ill-conceived border closure. Karen said she'd pursue that line of inquiry, although for the life of her she couldn't imagine what kind of proof that would be.

Now as the rooftops of San Jose were coming into view, Karen tried to ignore the political ramifications of the operation and concentrate on the tactical. By now FBI agents from the San Francisco and LA offices should have completed a search of the Miller compound near Big Sur on California's central coast. Simultaneous early-morning searches had also taken place in EPG*-affiliated offices in Berkeley and Santa Cruz. In addition to the general interlocking relationships between a number of Green Alliance/EPG* groups, research into Miller's activities revealed that he held positions on the boards of directors of a number of these groups. Two of those he was most active in—and in close proximity to his Big Sur ranch were Earth Action in Berkeley and Ocean Advocacy in Santa Cruz. Additional raids were also taking place at a score of radical environmental groups across the Golden State. Karen was very curious what would turn up.

First off the plane, Karen was led down a set of jet way stairs to a waiting sedan. Brenda was there to meet her, as expected. They shook hands formally, and then Brenda gave her a big hug, unexpectedly.

"Welcome to California," she mugged. A young agent in an uncharacteristic turtleneck and sports jacket took her carry-on bag and put it in the open trunk. Brenda introduced him as Mark Tucker. He nodded to Karen and slipped behind the wheel. Brenda opened the back door for Karen and then sat herself in the front passenger seat. Tucker reached out the window and put a portable emergency strobe light on the car and turned it on. As soon as they started off across the taxiway Brenda spoke again.

"I have good news and bad news," she intoned with a twinkle in her eyes. She'd always been a joker and advancement in the Bureau had obviously not cramped her style.

Karen stretched her tired legs out across the back seat. "Okay, let me have it."

"The good news is that all the raids came off smoothly, with no injuries and no snafus. No small accomplishment since there were some twenty separate locations slated for searches and logistically awkward.

"The bad news is that we've come up with very little so far. We did seize a couple of tons of records and computer equipment, but made no arrests and located none of the people on the interrogation list."

"What?" Karen was incredulous. They had drawn up arrest

100

warrants for at least two-dozen EPG* members including Abe Miller. Twice as many others were identified for questioning.

"Brenda, this is not funny."

"No joke, Agent St. Cloud," she replied soberly.

"No joke, sir," echoed Tucker, who looked at her levelly through the rear view mirror. Must be another Navy veteran.

Brenda went on. "Get this: many of the tree-huggers have been missing for months. There was actually quite a stir when we realized how many Missing Persons reports centered on EPG*—amazing that hadn't correlated in any FBI or even state law enforcement statistical reports."

"It's like much of the radical environmental movement has gone underground, but no one noticed. It's bad enough that local and federal law enforcement didn't notice, but it's worse when you figure that they're up to something and we're just now starting to play catch up."

"Sweet Jesus," said Karen. "We are missing a whole bunch of angry, committed eco-freaks with nuclear weapons. This does not sound good at all." She pondered for a minute.

"These folks absolutely love publicity... I can't believe we haven't heard from them yet." She pondered whether that might be a good sign or not. "I hope no news is good news," she added, with a tone of skepticism in her voice.

Brenda looked back like she didn't think so either.

Sandi had prevailed upon Raul to accompany her on an after-dinner walk to the top on one of the bluffs overlooking Punta Arenas above their hotel. Partly she wanted to avoid the Puerto Rican who kept looking her over like she was a piece of meat. He really gave her the willies. But she was also concerned about the turn of events in her professional life. This certainly was the most serious case she'd ever been on, as well as the first international one. It wasn't that she really wanted Raul's company; she didn't want to be alone.

Raul had turned out to be the best partner she could ever have asked for. He had never come on to her—unlike most of the men in her division. All the more amazing because she knew that his marriage was unraveling. There was an unspoken understanding that as partners they should not be romantically involved. Well, that was her rationalization—she couldn't be sure of the reason, but he treated her always in a respectful, professional manner. She might not have lasted in the national police if it hadn't been for his support and solidarity.

"Scary business, isn't it?" he prompted.

"Yeah, you can say that again."

"Are you scared?"

"Who me? Iron Sandi?" She laughed. "No, not really, at least, not so far. Should I be?"

"Maybe."

"Well, I got a good rush of adrenaline when we drove into the compound today, but not expecting to see anyone there, I wasn't really, personally, afraid. Strength in numbers, I guess. How about you, how are you taking all this?"

"Getting in these old military airplanes scares me more than bad guys," he joked.

"There's that," she acknowledged.

"What I meant was: are you scared of radiation? You know, of confronting nuclear terrorists?"

"I don't know. I hadn't thought of it that way. I guess I'm more worried about guns and bullets. It is hard for me to be afraid of something that I can't see—like radiation." Then she changed the subject.

"Raul, are they going to send us south do you think? Or send us back?"

"Since I've been once to Esperanza and to San Martin, there's a good chance now that they may send me. Do you want me to ask to have you sent back?" He squinted at her.

"What, you never told me you'd been to Antarctica!" She punched him playfully in the arm. Then she hotly retorted, "No, you will not send me back!"

"When were you down there? Why didn't you ever tell me?"

"It was no big deal. When I was just a kid in the Army I went down one summer on a supply mission. At the time I hated it. I wish I'd paid more attention. Actually, Esperanza was nothing back then. Now there's a school, a movie theater, hotel, and hordes of people during the summer. The science base at San Martin was actually pretty impressive from what I can remember. I really hate the cold, so this is not a trip I look forward to."

"So, you really think we'll be sent, eh?"

"Well, we've come this far. Your English is good and my experience probably counts for something." He physically shivered.

102

"Crap, I'm cold already just thinking about it. Do you mind if we go back?"

"Actually. You can go. I want to stay and watch the sunset, but go ahead, I'll be okay."

"You sure?"

She pulled back her jacket, exposed her .45, and nodded her head.

He grinned and hurried back down the path.

She sat down on a patch of dry grass. The wind died down as if it had waited for her cue. Sandi wrapped her arms around herself and settled in for what might be her last sunset on the continent of her birth.

The late night Task Force meeting went poorly. Half the Washington participants were absent due to the blizzard and the other half stranded at the J. Edgar Hoover Building. A record two feet of snow had fallen in downtown Washington since morning. Those attending the meeting looked drawn and haggard. Fortunately for Karen, it was still early on the West Coast and she was glad once again that she was only there on video.

The VP was at the Naval Observatory across town, hooked up by videophone. Deputy Director Williams chaired the status review and reported that neither the Pentagon nor the NSA had made much progress. Evidence pointed to the nukes being transshipped out of Chile to Antarctica. Investigators were on the scene in southern Chile.

The mystery of how the weapons were swapped for scrap iron was still unsolved. There were discrepancies in the guard's logbooks, but the implications were still unclear. The MPs involved had all been questioned, but there was no answer to the obvious question: what had actually happened? This was a particularly vexing situation and the officers in charge were now on the hot seat, too. The DIA's prognosis was that it might take anywhere from a couple of days to weeks to get close to the bottom of the heist itself. As it stood, the impossible had somehow happened. The vice president was obviously unhappy and said so.

The FBI report was nearly as unfathomable. While there seemed to be little doubt that EPG* was either directly or indirectly involved with the missing weapons, there were now even more questions raised than there were answers.

At least sixty people related to the organization were missing. Some were now missing for six months or more. Letters from some of them had been mailed from more than a dozen places across the country to their friends and families. But the stories and locations were apparently faked. There was a grand conspiracy that linked all or most of these people.

Other anomalies also cropped up. Money and other securities had been withdrawn by some of the missing from banks and savings institutions—both institutional and personal funds. Personal items and material possessions had been taken, as well, like favorite books, computers, and cameras. It was as though these people thought that they'd never be back. They had somehow not let on to friends and family. Some vague hints, or apprehensions, could be had from some family members, but rather few considering the large number of people involved.

The FBI was entertaining the idea that there was also a conspiracy of silence—which they would continue to explore. The lack of evidence was unnerving—EPG* had certainly covered their tracks well. It spoke of extremely good planning and lots of money. It was a very troubling development indeed.

A blanket of dismay fell over the Task Force meeting that was thicker than the snowfall outside. National Security Advisor Nelson spoke for all of them when he asked, "Where in the hell is this going?"

Dear Betsy,

Whew, what a day! There is nothing more frightening than experiencing a tropical storm on the open ocean. The Mana Kai sure weathered it well though—thank the goddess Pakeva for a stout, well-built boat! We are now back in fairly calm seas and are getting a picture-postcard sunset to boot! We are still near some incredibly large cloud formations that look as though they extend all the way into the stratosphere.

The morning began with ominous dark clouds and a strange wave pattern, more like a small chop. But we could tell from radar that we might be in for some serious weather. Fortunately, we had Mana Kai batten down tightly and Brad and I managed to get the jib tied down before the rains came. We have hardly used the diesel engine on the trip so far, so the gas tank was full when Brad powered up her up. That was a reassuring sound and feeling, let me tell you!

By the time we were secure and under power we were really starting to feel a serious swell building—not like from a local storm but as though from a monster storm hundreds of miles away? Anyway, it was worrisome. It was the light in mid-morning that was the most dramatic. There was some blue sky above, but very dark clouds otherwise surrounded us, and the ocean was a deep, deep blue—almost black itself. It seemed like what it might feel like in the eye of a hurricane—surrounded by a circular wall of clouds. The difference was that there was no illusion that the storm was over—it was clearly building. The cloud walls looked impenetrable. There was also a steady northeasterly wind at 15 to 20 knots so Brad aligned our Mana Kai so we were driving with the storm.

Brad had me run down to double check the charts to make sure our heading would not take us smack into some island or reef. As I reported back to him, I handed him his rain gear that he accepted and donned without comment (I had already changed into mine). Since I'd made coffee earlier with the sandwiches, I offered him some. While below to fetch his mug, I heard the thunder and was alarmed for a minute. As I came up on deck I could see Brad staring at the dark wall of clouds coming up behind us. There were almost continuous streaks of lightning in the upper cloud deck.

The thunder started to roll over us in waves and got closer by the second. The rain fell steadily and the drops were getting big and fat and cold. Not a good sign. Moreover, the waves were getting higher as the wind picked up.

Brad yelled at me to put on my life jacket and to tie on a safety line and I quickly obliged with a curt "aye, aye Captain." Ironic, since it was Brad who went overboard around midday. For two hours we struggled with the boat and the weather. The boat—she was fine. The worst of the waves—the biggest sets—were coming on a southeasterly heading. Mana Kai seemed the most stable on an oblique tack to the north (actually we had the diesel pushing us at 4-5 knots). A huge wave struck us from behind. Brad struggled to keep his balance but slipped and then was hit by the backwash and went over the side. I quickly lashed the wheel down, throttled back the engine and grabbed his line. Somehow he found the rail and we got him aboard. He was sputtering and choking on the combination of salt water and the torrential rain coming down on us.

I ordered him down to get dry and into a change of clothes and a cup of coffee (I'd left the thermos below deck). The Captain did not *object.*

Then I had my turn at the wheel. What a ride! Almost within seconds after he disappeared down the hatch I sensed another wave coming and as I looked over my shoulder I saw I was right. I throttled poor little Mana Kai's oversized engine and took the 30-foot wave just right—without its breaking right over us and then slide down this huge hill of water. It was exhilarating and scary at the same time. There was a break in the rain and I could look down on hundreds of miles of ocean as though on an island mountaintop.

That's when I saw the other boat. It was an oversized lifeboat, but crammed with what looked like a swarming mass—maybe fifty to a hundred people. My god! We had all heard the stories about Melanesian boat people, but a thousand miles away, not here. They looked like they were drifting, too. I'm not sure if anyone could have seen me, but then I saw the flare—a parachute flare—rocket up and then begin to sink ahead towards the northeast. Abruptly, it went out.

Without thinking of the potential danger to us, I turned the rudder slightly toward the northeast as we sank into the next big through—and I moved us toward where I thought I'd seen them. Again, another large wave swept in from the south and I tackled it as I had the one before. This time cresting the wave, I saw nothing. Then the rain picked up and visibility began to get worse. When Brad came back on deck I yelled at him to get the binoculars. After he took the wheel I scanned the horizon and continued to look for the boat, but it had sunk or moved further away—I had no explanation other than it being an illusion and was not ready to accept that conclusion. It was spooky and unsettling. I wanted to help them, but now realize that trying to do so might very well have been extremely perilous for us. We could not have picked up that many people without jeopardizing our own survival. I did radio authorities in Fiji as soon as I could go below. I was informed that there are some Korean fishing boats in the area and a French frigate on the way. I feel badly now—partly from guilt because of my strong sense of relief...

The storm did pass. Brad and I traded off a few hours ago, and then around dusk things settled down enough for us to turn on the autopilot and set the main sail. We had some hot soup for dinner— first time that's sounded good in a while! Brad was exhausted and after cleaning up below deck (there were some things thrown about), I thought I'd get caught up with you. So, your tired confidant needs to get ready for bed now, too. Good night sweetie.

January 15
Sunday

(AP) 0900 EST

"The National Weather Service reports that record amounts of snow have fallen across the East Coast of the United States paralyzing air and ground transportation. At least fifty deaths have been blamed on storm-related accidents, falling trees and downed power lines. Officials are expressing concern that the high tides expected for later today will make matters worse for barrier islands and low-lying coastal areas. Flood watches are anticipated from Cape Hatteras to Northern Maine and the Maritime Provinces of Canada. Evacuation orders are anticipated for some areas, but officials express concerns about impassable roads blocked by snow and fallen trees.

"President Clark has declared parts of New York, Pennsylvania, Maryland, New Jersey, Northern and Western Virginia disaster areas. The Washington, D.C. area has received more that three feet of snow since the storm began yesterday morning.

"All major airports in Boston, New York, Philadelphia, Baltimore, and Washington, D.C. remain closed. Airports in Chicago, Atlanta, and St. Louis all report up to six to eight hour delays on west-bound flights. Airports in Europe and on the US West Coast are also reporting crippling system delays.

"An arctic air mass continues to move toward the southeast while a nearly stationary upper-level low pressure system over Pennsylvania draws warmer, Gulf Stream air over the coast and into New England. Some parts of the Appalachian Mountains have received as much as twenty feet of snow.

San Francisco, CA (0600 PST)

Karen's hotel room phone rang insistently. Even though it was only the third or forth ring, she could have sworn that it had been twenty times. She'd slept well enough, but not nearly long enough.

"St. Cloud," she said roughly.

"Sorry to call so early," said Brenda apologetically. She didn't sound very perky yet herself.

"What's up?"

"Get into the office ASAP. Big development." That was all she said.

Karen decided to keep her humor and not over-react, as everything seemed to be a crisis right now. She purposely did not hurry through her bathroom routine, and ordered room service coffee, granola, and a newspaper. It was Sunday, after all, she laughed to herself.

Yet she did not dawdle. She had been through enough crises to know that rushing around didn't solve anything, that one had to take time to do things right. Being in a hurry was a prescription for trouble: not being conscious of one's actions left one open to missteps and mistakes. She learned the hard way; she was one of those people who wasn't keen on repeating mistakes. The other reason she was not in a hurry was that the *Loa* had returned to her dreams and she was trying to stay unfocused for a few minutes, not to wake up too fast, so she could recapture more of that dream.

She recalled dreaming of a place she had been often as a child growing up in Haiti, high up in the rainforest above Port-au-Prince where her family went to picnic and escape from hot summer days. It was always cool and breezy, and sometimes the clouds would build above the ridgeline and send light rain down. That was usually when her mom would pull out the food and the family would eat under their canopy.

In her dream she was at that spot, but offered no protection from the rain or family to protect her from the evil of the world. She was grown up, not a child, but recalled that the *Loa, Shango*, had a message for her. Now that she was awake it faded from memory. Karen struggled to access the dream, but the harder she tried the more elusive it became. She finally gave up and started pulling out a set of clean clothes. Since it was Sunday and San Francisco, she decided to wear jeans and a denim jacket.

She hopped in and out of the shower, started her make-up and waited for room service. The cold bathroom mirror was heavily misted over and the steam from the shower lingered even after she opened the door.

She flipped on the fan switch by the door and felt cool air come in.

While she waited for the condensation to dissipate, Karen's mind wandered. The *Loa* appeared in the mirror as a wispy condensate on the mirror. The face was clear, but speechless, and had a worried look. When a draft came through the door, the face vanished. Karen looked herself in the eyes, not really believing what she saw, but at the same wanting to.

The FBI offices on Van Ness were noisy and busy already. Karen's basic nervous energy had already burned through the first cup of coffee and morning cereal, and she made a beeline for the coffee room. Someone with brains had brought in cheese croissants and sweet rolls—if it had been within her power, she'd have given that person a field promotion.

Brenda was at her elbow.

"Sit down?" Brenda asked and passed Karen a sheet of paper as soon as she had set down her coffee cup. She sat with the paper in one hand while the other fed croissant to her face.

"Before you read it you should know that about three hours ago this was delivered simultaneously by e-mail to the UN Secretariat, the thirty member states of the Alliance of Small Island States, and to the major news services.

"The Task Force had scheduled a meeting for noon Eastern time—but the president has called a National Security Council meeting and you were specifically invited. That will start in fifteen minutes."

"Oh, great." She meant to sound sarcastic, but failed given what she was now reading. She looked up gratefully, "Thanks."

AOSIS ALERT
To: The island nations of AOSIS and particularly the low islands of the Maldives, Tuvalu, Kiribati, and the Marshall Islands.
From: EPG* Kali Action

Be advised that one week from today, at 1200 GMT on 22 January, a cataclysmic event will take place in the waters of the Great Southern Ocean. The event will By Necessity imperil your various Nations and the health and safety of Your Populations. While not the intention of EPG* to hurt or endanger your lives or livelihoods, this will be the Effect of our Planetary Action. BRING BACK THE MEGAFAUNA!

On 22 January, 2012, EPG* will launch an Action intended to improve the Planetary Condition, but which will undoubtedly make much of AOSIS territory uninhabitable over the near and long term. The EPG* Kali Action, engineered to free a significant percentage of Antarctic Ice Cap, will have serious immediate as well as long-term consequences for your Nations and Peoples. BRING BACK THE ICE AGE!

ALERT: Within hours of the planned Kali Action, serious ocean tsunamis will be generated within the Pacific and Indian Ocean basins. Ocean tides of Lesser Magnitudes are anticipated in the Atlantic Ocean. AOSIS members in the Caribbean will not be affected by these tsunamis.

WARNING: Within some days to weeks following the Kali Action, sea levels are expected to rise from one to five feet above normal. This Planetary Change will make low islands uninhabitable.

Within some months to a few years, sea levels are expected to rise from ten to twenty feet above the average "normal" sea level. The Kali Action will have Global Consequences including: altered ocean currents and shifting weather patterns. These planetary changes will not only affect the AOSIS nations, but the United Nations and Planet Earth as a whole. THE FINAL OUTCOME WILL BE A NEW ICE AGE and LOWER SEA LEVELS.

EPG* is concerned with the health of Gaia, our Mother Earth, as a whole. It is not our intention to hurt People, but a consequence of this Gaia Therapy. We are particularly concerned for People of the South, and thus urge your countries to Act in accordance with this Action Alert. With this in mind, we offer the following Recommendations to Island Peoples of the Indian and Pacific Oceans:

1) High Islands — relocate to higher ground (defined as at least 100 feet above sea level) and northern sides of islands

2) Low Islands — relocate to high islands, or move aboard ships or boats to ocean waters at least 200 feet deep.

Tsunamis are not expected to be higher than 100 feet, but geomorphic conditions may result in locally higher tides, particularly near continental shelves. In all coastal areas, stay tuned to the tsunami warning radio frequencies.

There will be a Demonstration of EPG* Power in 24 hours to convince World Leaders of our Intentions. The Demonstration will be followed by the distribution of the EPG* Kali Action Manifesto.

Phoenix (0730 MST)

Pete slept poorly for a second straight night, with even stranger dreams than the night before. Perhaps a blessing to interrupt the thick, heavy dreams, his attorney called unusually early, to inform him that the FBI had asked politely but firmly that he come back for another interview.

"Jesus, Jerry," he started and cleared his throat, "what is this all about?"

"I was hoping you could tell me. Are you in trouble?"

He shook his head too fast. "No, I don't think so. But it does have to do with a federal case on the coast and someone I used to know. Listen, I'd rather not discuss this on the phone."

Pete hesitated. "When, where?"

"They'd like you in their office, or here, this morning, quote as early as possible, unquote. How about here in my office downtown at 9:30?"

"Yes sir." He smiled wanly. Jerry was one of his few Phoenix friends and a poker buddy.

He arrived at the attorney's downtown office in a high rise on Central Avenue, the FBI agents were there and Jerry introduced them.

"Peter Wilde, this is Agent Bill Miles from the San Francisco office, and I believe you have already met Agent Scott from the Bureau here in Phoenix."

"Mr. Wilde, we would like to tape record this conversation, if there are no objections?"

Jerry raised his eyebrows but said nothing. He simply nodded at Pete.

"Yes, I understand," he said, although he didn't really.

Agent Miles continued. "To be as straight as possible with you—you are indirectly involved, by your own admission, with two homicides and a robbery in Palo Alto which we now believe are connected to the piracy of nuclear weapons." Miles watched him for a reaction. Pete wore his poker face, but nodded his head. Jerry clearly was shocked, but before he could say anything, Miles went on.

"Given the gravity of the situation, we would like to ask your cooperation in answering some further questions. We have no reason to believe that you were involved with the Palo Alto crimes, but we have a growing need to get information on the Green Alliance and EPG*. Do you understand?"

Now it was his turn to look shocked as the realization of his situation dawned on him. It was his EPG* friends, "fronds" he had once called them, who snatched the Air Force warheads. He had left Ann Arbor in disgust, but did he want to rat on his old friends? The FBI had once been their enemy—the long arm of Big Brother, the national government. Now he was being asked to inform on his former brothers and sisters.

"What is it that you want to know?"

They asked him questions for two hours, spent looking over photos and literature from Ann Arbor and the broader EPG* movement. Agents brought with them both hard copies and showed him documents on a laptop computer. He was asked to confirm who certain people were, how he had known them, what their relationships were among the group, and their capacity for violence—as he evaluated their personalities. His own role in nearly three years of active EPG* politics became apparent. He had been a meeting organizer, mediator, and observer of the various collections of people and projects of the movement. They spent considerable time probing whatever he knew about Abe Miller, Professor Adams, Angel Stills, and few of the other leaders.

He admitted to becoming disillusioned after three years in the group in his senior year, due to the maniacal attention being devoted to the Green Man Miller and his teachings. Pete was basically cast out of the movement for not embracing Miller's teaching and the emerging personality cult growing up around him. Pete had only seen Miller up close a couple of times—his base of operations was in California—but had taken a personal dislike to him.

He explained to the agents that he was eventually banished from meetings for being "prone to violence" and "obstructionist." He told the agents how the fact that he had Kung Fu movie posters on the walls of his apartment was the basis for one of their last confrontations.

In his final comments, Pete said, "I left the group for good. Six months later, I graduated *cum laude* with a dual major in Journalism and Communications, and moved to the Southwest and took up a career in television. I thought I'd left the Green Alliance and all my green 'fronds' behind." He used his fingers to make quote marks.

One last component of the interview was photo identification. There were only a few of the people's photos he didn't recognize. Snapshot-size photos were now laid out on one end of the conference room table adjoining Jerry's office. As he looked at the array he noticed that local, quiet FBI agent, Scott had laid out nearly two dozen photos, eighteen of which he recognized, and a handful to one side, now, which he couldn't identify.

Agent Miles flipped a tape over in the recorder and asked Pete to look at the group of "unknowns."

"Can you say anything else at all about these people?"

"Well, as I said, they are familiar. I have seen them or maybe their pictures somewhere, but can't place them."

"You may as well know that the two dozen people in both groups of photos and probably more have disappeared from sight over the last six months, gone underground. Do you know where any of them might be? Except, of course, for Danielle and her friends in Palo Alto…"

Pete said that he didn't have a clue.

President Clark was definitely having a bad day. He had taken advantage of the snowstorm's disruption to his schedule by sleeping an extra hour, until 6 A.M. He awoke to the snowstorm greeting him darkly through the White House second floor East Wing window. Even before he'd finished shaving, the private phone flashed at him. That was Chief of Staff Craft telling him that there had been a breaking development in Operation Hot Pants. Clark said he'd be right down.

In the Situation Room the scope of developments abroad and the snowstorm gave a sense of monumental emergency. The Washington-Baltimore area was covered under a heavy blanket of wet Atlantic snow that continued to fall. Outer western suburbs in Northern Virginia and Maryland were now covered in six to seven feet of snow with blowing snow making drifts twice as high. It was a mess. Despite all this Clark called for a meeting with senior members of both the National Security Council and the Nuclear Emergency Task Force. Nearly all were brought in by Special Forces teams equipped with heavy-duty snowmobiles and Snow Cats.

The snowstorm had become a major headache. It was making an already bad situation even more dangerous and unwieldy. Many of the regular White House staff were trapped in their homes and apartments and were being brought in by the Special Forces teams. The underground tunnel between The White House and the Executive Office building was a real help and the General Services Administration with Secret Service oversight built a snow tunnel to Blair House across the street where some Task Force members would have to stay for a while. Some senior staff members were assigned rooms in the East Wing.

Before the meeting, the president scanned through his national security briefing file and read the staff summaries of other developments related to the EPG* communiqué. He read the verbatim text of the AOSIS Alert and shook his head in wonderment.

"I have a lot of questions. I would like ya'll to answer three questions: Is this legitimate? If so, can they do what they threaten? Can we stop them?" He pealed off his fingers at each question.

"First off, who are these people? I assume we're talking about this because some of you believe this is genuine."

Helen Colman spoke first. "Encryption key. They left us one of their computer encryption keys and sent us a scrambled copy of this AOSIS Alert. It's them alright."

Roger Hale went next. "We know that they are dangerous. There are at least three dozen or more U.S. nationals involved in EPG* and an unknown number of supporters in other countries. We are beginning to suspect a Bolivian political connection. The EPG* leader is Abe Miller who has a long history of activities federal authorities have been following. He basically 'dropped off the radar' some months ago and everyone thought that he had just gone to Jackson Hole, Wyoming to be in seclusion."

"Although we have known of the group for some time, they appeared to be 'all talk and no action'. That is to say, their political and philosophical values were mostly opposed to U.S. political and social culture. Yet, they seemed not so much interested in the overthrow of the government, but in the overthrow 'of the American worldview.'" He made quotes in the air. "So we have monitored their newsletters and literature for some time. Our review found no significant clues nor have yesterday's searches produced much. Bottom line: we have found few clues in this country of EPG* planning efforts. The South Americans have uncovered far more with some arrests in Argentina and the base camp in Tierra del Fuego. We have people on the scene there working 24/7."

"Basically we don't know how they've been able to do this, but what we have found in spades is motive and a lot of circumstantial evidence. They want to save the Earth and have some cockamamie theory about putting humans back 'in their place.' I can say more about Miller himself if you want."

The president held up his hand.

114

"Maybe we can return to that." He looked in turn at Admiral Brown and General Smart and asked, "Can they actually detonate those weapons?"

General Smart frowned just slightly. "In theory, no. There is a fail safe code required to arm each of them. In practice, I guess we'll know tomorrow."

Admiral Brown leaned forward and added, "If they pull this off, it suggests a very high level of technological sophistication."

"Can they do what they threaten? Crack the ice and start an Ice Age? Eliot?" Eliot Majors was the president's science advisor.

"Setting off the nukes is one thing, sir. Damaging the ice pack is another thing—I don't think they can do it. It is just too far-fetched. Besides, this is totally at odds with environmental thinking. If I follow their logic, they believe polluting the Antarctic with radiation is acceptable if the result is some sort of ice age? Their mainstream environmental friends will not be happy with this idea. This is lunatic fringe as far as I can tell.

"The tsunami warning sounds rather far-fetched to me as well. The sea level rise claim is absolutely over the top. It just appears ridiculous. But, I will consult with others in the scientific community. The science of this idea is certainly cataclysmic by definition, but not plausible to me. Maybe their so-called 'demonstration' and manifesto will tell us more."

The president asked, "Dr. Erikson?" Erikson was on a video feed from Ft. Meade at National Security Agency headquarters.

"We think these folks are what they claim to be. The AOSIS alert was accompanied by a validation signature— a mathematic code matching a corresponding 'key' on the laptop computer found by the FBI in Big Sur. There was no question that it was intentionally left by Abe Miller or one of his associates for the FBI, as his signature, and as a taunt, we think—showing their awareness of how we would respond. It was a message for you, essentially. So, yes, the threat is legitimate and is connected to a radical underground group. Their SIGINT is sophisticated.

"Their electronic points of presence come from three sources: web sites in Amsterdam, Haiti, and Bolivia. We have monitored those for years. There was a spike in bandwidth use in the last few days. We will have analysts working on the significance data around the clock. I will contact the Situation Room operator as soon as we have any actionable intelligence."

When it was obvious that the NSA Director was finished, the president thanked him.

Admiral Brown had been quiet, but seemed determined now to make his presence felt.

"There appears to be little doubt that EPG* is a revolutionary organization intent on destroying the United States government. The fact that they do not appear to be on US soil should be welcome news. However, it is the Joint Chiefs' position that before we open our airports, ports, and borders that we make sure that some EPG* members are not still hiding out here in the US, that we know where the others went, and the location of our warheads."

The president raised his hand up again.

"Admiral, you are getting ahead of us. I want Roger to tell me more about the FBI investigation. Roger?"

"We continue to look for and interview friends and families of the missing EPG* members. There are lots of interviews going on more broadly with former members and the larger environmental community. We have identified roughly fifty people who we believe are directly involved in the conspiracy in one way or another. They have all been issued state, federal, and INTERPOL arrest warrants. There are likely to be more US citizens involved, but these are the most obvious individuals connected to EPG*—who have disappeared."

"The missing conspirators are mostly college educated. The average age is 27, the oldest is 62, and the youngest is 18. There are some highly technical people involved, it appears. Nearly a dozen have advanced degrees in computer science, MIS, and software development. A dozen are biochemists, ecologists, or biologists. The rest are mostly full-time environmental activists."

"There is good reason to believe that this is a real threat, and not just a bluff or a publicity stunt. There are no nuclear scientists in the group, but there are some rather interesting skills represented which give some credence that they are at least trying to do what they claim. We have identified two certified helicopter pilots, two transport plane pilots, a master mechanic, two engineers, an expert in hydraulics, and two doctors. Everyone on the list either was a skier, or had taken up skiing in the last few years. They have been planning this for some time.

"My last thought is that if they were able to pull off the Lackland heist, they undoubtedly have given considerable thought to detonating those bombs."

Secretary of Defense Brown (no relation to the Vice Chair of the Joint Chiefs) had been quiet during the first part of the meeting.

"Mr. President?"

"Yes, Mark. Go ahead."

"I'm concerned with the both intended and unintended consequences of this threat. If we take this seriously, then we have naval and shipping assets to consider, and the Antarctic science bases. Then there's the public panic, the stock and securities markets, flood control, and lord knows where it'll stop. Sir."

"Go on."

"Not to change the subject, but the solar storm is getting worse and shows no sign of letting up anytime soon." He paused for a few seconds and considered how to say what was obviously coming with some difficulty. He was a multiple Gulf War veteran whose claim to fame was a "MacArthur pipe and pragmatism" that had endeared him to junior officers and enlisted alike. For reasons not entirely clear, Brown resigned early in his career and went into politics. First elected to the U.S. House from California's First District, then appointed to Under Secretary of Defense for Appropriations, and then Secretary by the new President, Brown was considered by the Washington news media to be a political rising star. He and the president worked well together and even enjoyed a few evenings of Tennessee whiskey together earlier in their relationship.

"While I am deeply concerned about Antarctica, I am also mindful of the US strategic interests. My recommendations are the following: First, reduce the alert levels for the Armed Forces. It is clear that the Chinese and Russians are very nervous about this situation and worried we are over-reacting. The solar storm in itself is enough reason to back off given the strain on our C-cubed-I systems.

"Second, order most of the Navy fleet to sea as soon as possible. I know this will be expensive, but our coasts are being threatened militarily."

"There is also the possibility of electromagnetic pulse radiation in addition to the solar storm, if any of the weapons are exploded in the air. No one can say definitively what the effect of the storm might have on EMP propagation, but the general consensus is that is probably an enhancing variable. That is, the solar storm could make EMP worse. If we are to believe their timetable, all commercial and military aircraft should be grounded south of the Tropic of Capricorn during the blasts. The UN and our allies should be informed.

"We have NEST teams on their way to Antarctica by the direction of the Task Force. Those are two of the nearest Nuclear Emergency Strike Teams—from bases in Panama and Florida. They will join an FBI team already en route to Esperanza Station operated by the Argentines. Lt. Commander Roth of the 12th Fleet Intelligence Systems Office who has spent more than five years on Antarctica assignments will command the teams. He has impeccable credentials and was the Heisman trophy winning running back at the Naval Academy in 1990."

"Chain of command?" asked the president.

The president's chief of staff answered. "There's another issue, sir, given the delicate international nature of the situation. The terrorists have broken U.S. law and the senior law enforcement agent we send would technically have jurisdiction. Given the military crimes involved, the military has jurisdiction as well. However, since there are a lot of civilians involved, and since the Antarctic is ostensibly 'demilitarized' it makes political sense to have someone from the Justice Department in charge. I spoke with the Attorney General in New York earlier this morning and, at your request, she will direct the FBI to take charge. FBI Special Agent St. Cloud will head down later today."

"Are you ready?" asked the president.

Karen had just been taking all this in over the monitor, so the question caught her slightly by surprise, but she recovered quickly.

"Yes sir, I am. The San Francisco office is pulling out all the stops to assemble a team. We will stay in contact with the Situation Room operator."

"Thank you. Good luck. I suggest you get going." She had obviously just been dismissed.

The president held up his hand before anyone else could speak. "Policy decisions? Support for Secretary Brown's recommend-ations?"

There were nods all around the room. But Helen Colman had to be devil's advocate.

"I suggest we stay on high alert. This is a serious threat to the country and perhaps we should be even more cautious."

118

The Secretary of Defense said, "Helen has a point, but this threat is turning out to be a different kind of military threat. It is limited: there are no foreign powers or military forces involved as far as I can see. Lowering the threat level may contribute more to our overall security so that we can focus on asset integrity. We have a major storm that has degraded some capacity to organize, even move assets. The solar storm worries me more than foreign powers trying to take advantage of our situation. Hell, winter is bad in most of Europe and Asia this year, too."

The conversation turned to public reactions and damage control. The group speculated wildly about the possible implications of a nuclear burst on Sunday. The president was getting impatient.

"For the most part, all I have heard from you people is either doubt that EPG* can pull this off or what will happen if they do. What I want to know is whether we can stop them."

General Smart spoke first. "Sir, I do think it is implausible that a dozen relatively low-yield weapons could so dramatically alter global climate. It just seems absurd."

The Science Advisor nodded his head.

The president turned to him. "Eliot, I want you to get a panel of NSF scientists convened to explore the matter, okay?"

"Yes sir."

"Mr. President?" asked Defense Secretary Brown.

"Yes?"

"We have roughly 200 military personnel on the ground in Antarctica, mainly Navy logistical support. We do have our own communications and weather monitoring systems in place and connected to the Pentagon. The solar storm has degraded that somewhat, but we are in fairly good shape. For example, the space segment of the GPS system is fine due to its low orbit. The earth's magnetosphere protects it through most of its orbit. The closer you get to the poles the more interference there is. Five to ten degrees north of the pole should be nominal. Other systems are in worse shape, but we can manage."

"In terms of human resources, the strike force teams on the way comprise another 80 military Special Forces and the Justice Department group adds another 20 or so. We have a few hundred other civilians-scientists and contractors—who can be drafted to help us. We can get a segment of our Delta Force down there in three or

119

four days. The bad weather is our biggest problem here, since Fort Bragg is caught on the edge of the blizzard.

"Sending a couple of carrier groups south would seem in order, as well. Air support may be a critical factor in dealing with these lunatics. We have a dozens of planes in the Antarctic, but they are relatively slow workhorses. We could ask the Brits for some help as they have a small squadron of Harriers in the Falkland Islands.

"It will take four to five days to get the carriers close enough to give their planes nominal operating ranges. We can also get some limited support from the Argentines and the Chileans. The FBI has been coordinating their investigation and we might ask for back-up military support. We recently graduated a dozen Chilean Air Force officers through the Air Defense School in New Mexico. Although range is still a problem, they do have the capability to cover much of East Antarctica."

After some additional back-and-forth between the president, the Secretary of Defense and the VP of the Joint Chiefs present, President Clark drew himself up and asked if there was any opposition to the general thrust of the military option. There was agreement all around the table.

He gave the orders: the U.S. Armed Forces were placed on the lowest alert level, the Fleet was ordered to sea ASAP, and the rest of the National Guard was ordered to mobilize. In addition, he ordered aircraft carrier USS Enterprise to the South Atlantic and the aging USS Coral Sea, already off New Zealand, south toward Antarctica. He scheduled a television address for Sunday evening.

It was in the final few minutes of the meeting that matters got psychologically worse. The chief of staff asked, "Mr. President, remember what is supposed to happen on the 22nd?"

The president frowned and then saw the light. "The State of the Union, of course. Jesus H. Christ, what a mess... Did they time that deliberately?"

Abe Miller knew he had a problem the first time he heard the *Loa* in his head. Then when they didn't stop talking to him, he was certain. It didn't take a genius to figure out if he told people that they might think he was crazy, so he didn't. On the other hand, he *was* a certified MENSA genius, which made him even more cautious. Abe first reacted as though it was real, yet being a skeptic he began to doubt the origin of the experience. He was a trained scientist, so even when he believed it was a valid experience, he couldn't be sure it was a metaphysical thing, his hypothalamus making it up for him, or the drugs.

The two voices were *Ezili* and *Ogun* and the whole adventure started as an argument over who could possess him. In retrospect, taking the mescaline that weekend years before in Belize had probably not been the best idea, but now he was stuck with the flashbacks, or possession, but definitely *Ogun*-in-the-head. *Ezili* was there somewhere, too, but *Ogun* had silenced her mostly. She spoke to Abe in a muted, irregular way.

The first time in the Yucatan was followed a few months later in the Philippines where he was working with a consortium of aid agencies. At first they came to him while he was awaking up in the morning. A couple of minutes before his alarm went off, he heard *Ezili* calling his name—as though from a distance, many miles away, very faintly. She was the strongest presence in the very beginning, there in the Northern Islands where he saw the vast clear cuts in the forest. Her song was strong in the telling of the savior of the spirit of the forest in melodious repetition. It was then that he knew he had to do something to help save the Planet. The teeming hordes of Filipino kids that seemed to follow him wherever he went, the festering garbage dumps up and down the coast, the immense Japanese and American corporate billboards—all those things and more finally pushed him over the edge. Maybe that was it—maybe it was the stress, the rage, and the frustration that triggered the visions...

His growing anger seemed to feed *Ogun*. *Ezili's* plaintive sweet songs were seductive and Abe listened to her as though they were just songs in his head. The chants that he began hearing from *Ogun* were much more visceral, a gut-wrenching response to emotions that seemed to be washing over him more frequently as he saw what was happening to the Philippine forests. It reminded him all too well of what he experienced in the Peace Corps in Hispaniola.

He'd been working in Northern Luzon for a couple of environmental NGOs, as an observer, and had also reported to the UN Environmental Programme on reforestation. Mainly he'd just ended up watching chunks of the forest finding their way into the maw of a system that transported tropical hardwoods to Japan and increasingly to China. He was grew more and more concerned for the Philippines. But one morning, a year into his contract, it had come to him on an unexpected trip south through Subic Bay Naval Station—a place he normally avoided like the plague.

Driving through the outskirts of the city, on his way back to Manila, Abe was overcome with a wave of emotional intensity. He was first sad and then angry, not really being able to identify over whom or what. He had an epiphany that someone needed to level the playing field. Third World countries needed an economic and political break from the rapacious hunger of the factories in the North. That someone would have to be himself—but how? It was then that an American Navy truck swerved out in front of him, honking its horn as though he was in the way. He followed the truck towards the base, with half a mind to report the driver's ill manners to the Base Commander. By the time Abe arrived at the base gate he had lost interest in the driver; instead his interest in the base grew.

He wasn't really sure where he was going. The MP at the gate looked carefully at his UN ID card and then waved him through. Abe wound his way around the sprawling Naval facility as though he belonged there. He gradually worked his way closer and closer to the dock area. He eased slowly through one chain link fence gate. An MP appeared out of nowhere. He was in a restricted weapons storage area.

That day had been pivotal. *Ogun* spoke clearly to him that day.

Abe shook his head to clear the memory.

He looked at the blue-white walls of the shaft in the ice and tried to mentally pull himself together. Abe had been so focused on the Antarctic undertaking, but the lack of sleep and deep exhaustion was beginning to take its toll, and he didn't have the luxury of getting too lost in reverie.

He engaged the winch and dropped the last hundred feet to the bottom of a large ice cavern. He was in the midst of a huge natural cavern formed in the Lambert Glacier above the Amery Ice Shelf in East Antarctica. The light from his headlamp and the lantern beside him set the ice off in both bright reflective white and smoothly cool blue tones. It was cold, but never quiet with the ice making cracking and hissing sounds from time to time. He glanced over at the bomb. It was cigar shaped originally but now sat in two pieces, side by side looking somewhat like fancy medical monitoring equipment.

It had turned out to be incredibly convenient for the team to have hit bedrock so close to the surface. And the ice cave was a blessing, hiding their activities so well and also exposing the bedrock for them to begin destruction. The contraption that they made for

122

digging shafts across the continent, the melting tube, had traveled only a few hundred feet down in this spot when it struck bedrock. Actually, it had given way when it opened up the ice cavern and crashed into bedrock. They had mangled a few melting tubes, but the loss of the last one could not have been timed better.

The last placement was actually the easiest. It took a bit of the pressure off thinking about all the things that could go wrong. In many ways this first test device was a reality check on all their activities for the last two years and hopefully a validation. What was so incredible throughout the operation of laying bombs across the continent was the fact that the spots they had chosen for their structural weaknesses and strategic geographic locations had nearly all ended up with anomalous features: caverns, tunnels, ice falls, and crevasses. These occasionally complicated their work, but in most cases had made things enormously easier.

The crew had been in here already, but by now had cleared out and was waiting with the helicopter ready to leave. His job was last. He could have as easily have done it from the surface, but this seemed the appropriate thing to do. The device here was different from the others though. This one was not part of a radio and computer network. This was the one they called "the Stand Alone"—the one that would be a warning to the world, the harbinger of things to come.

Abe had a special feeling about the Stand Alone, as the last device placement and the first one to be detonated. There was an actual affection—which the others wouldn't understand, so he made the final pilgrimage down by himself. It seemed only appropriate that he should give the last sequence of initiation commands here. It was the beginning of the end of the world, as they knew it.

Then the *Ogun* spoke.

"This is it, dude. No turning back now."

"I have been having second thoughts."

"Well of course you have. 'To err is human.'"

"Go away. I have work to do." The *Loa* complied, but hummed softly, deeply in the background.

Abe pulled out the small PDA, pulled a hand out of a glove and pushed two buttons in succession as he held the PDA against the laptop. It made a small satisfied "beep." Putting back the PDA, he stuck his hand back into its glove, pivoted, and made his way back to the rope and harness and buckled up. He radioed above for them to pull him up. He began his way back up to the surface.

Ogun said, "This will be one monster blast! And the volcano will blow!"

Abe didn't answer back, but instead concentrated on working his way back up through the narrowing tunnel in the ice above him.

"We'll see," he finally retorted.

"No you won't." *Ogun* was right about that.

They all returned safely to the submarine, Abe in the last transfer flight almost 24 hours later. The transfer of equipment and personnel back into the submarine should have gone smoothly, but the weather was not cooperating. The temperature had dropped to -20° and 30 mph winds made the landing and outside activity dangerous. The crew struggled for three hours to get the helicopter refueled even though it was only fifty feet from the submarine. Moreover, the 'copter was getting buried in snowdrifts piled up against the sub.

Abe sent out a relief group to help pull in the fuel hoses and had the helicopter crews down in the sub to warm up before departure. The pilot looked worried, but the meteorologist reported that the storm blowing off of Wilkes Land was ending.

The crew leaving on the copter was headed for their base in the Admiralty Mountains to the east. They were all volunteers who were planning to stay behind and monitor the progress of the Ross Ice fall. Martyrs all. They were all stanch "eco-warriors" and proud of it and, moreover, dedicated scientists, observers, and activists. They self-identified as "the Menagerie", a name they'd adopted after participating in their first "Council of All Beings". In that role-playing ritual each had "represented" a species or an ecosystem. They had faced the species homo sapiens and confronted it with its shortcomings and destructive tendencies. They had basically experienced a "distancing" with their own essential humanity and had—by psychological projection—identified with Otherness. Ironically, it was their intense human bonding through those eco-warrior experiences that held them together like glue. They had become a community over the years: in conferences, at rallies, over the 'Net... Now to confront their mortality together was the ultimate extreme experience.

The Menagerie, Bear, Owl, Sparrow, and Angel (also known as Worm) braced themselves for the cold, hoisted up their backpacks through the submarine hatch and cheerily bade their comrades "farewell." The atmosphere was rather sober and the crew did not return the goodbyes with equal fervor. The Menagerie as a group had always been an exclusive club and had set themselves apart within this otherwise close-knit environmental community. But they were admired and loved, even begrudgingly from their various colleagues with personality conflicts. Though sober and somber, the atmosphere was still intensely charged.

"Good luck," came Abe's voice, and then the rest of the crew chimed in as one, "Goodbye!" Then additional "Goddess be with you!" blessings were added.

The boatswains helped the group and the flight crew out to the helicopter. The wind was picking up, but the visibility was improving. The jet engines throttled up slowly and gained in intensity just as a break came in the storm. The main blades were brought up to lift off speed and held for a good two minutes. Then the helicopter rose slowly and picked up speed and rose over the crest of the glacier some 500 feet above.

Angel settled in to her now familiar seat on the bird. She rearranged her protective clothing and loosened her gear. She switched her headset from SSB radio to an Aretha mix on her handheld. Flying south again, she thought to herself. The whole mission was near suicidal, and that was *before* the Kali Action. They were flying the 'copters to the limits of their range under less-than-optimal weather conditions. Testing the Fates, for sure. But it was all in the interest of the planet and humanity. "Human beans," she said to herself and chuckled at her sad joke.

She rubbed her frostbite-scarred and near-frostbitten extremities. For all the care and attention to their health and physical wellbeing, the Antarctic had taken its toll on her—heck, on all of them. But no one had complained, no one had groused. Two years before, Angel would have been called pretty. Now, as Worm, she looked weather-beaten. She smiled to herself. Bruised, not beaten, she told herself. She felt a warm glow grow inside her and she relaxed into the comfort of doing something for which she had a calling. She was on a Mission for the Goddess. Satisfied that she'd come a long way from her upbringing in Shaker Heights, Ohio, Worm basked in the adrenaline thrill of racing over the frozen landscapes of the Ross Ice Shelf en route to the Latady Mountains. She could feel the heaters kicking in and loosened her parka more.

The copilot caught her attention and pointed to his headphones. Worm gave thumbs up and flicked off Aretha. She plugged her 'phones back into her radio.

"Worm, over."

"Thanks. A last few details before we lose contact." The single side-band radio would normally have been more reliable, but the solar storms had made a mess of their communications. The static was already degrading the signal badly.

"We've been underway for a couple of minutes and things seem to be on track." This was followed by a sharp screech.

"Worm. We have krill, over." Worm's ears prickled to the invocation of the alarm signal for intruders or cops.

"Yes. The krill... Bleaching seems to be continuing at approximately a 5 percent per annum rate." She tried to make it sound convincing to anyone listening in. "It seems like a kind of red bloom, only the algae is in the krill shell. We've never seen anything like it before—except in corals, of course, over to you base."

"Good luck Menagerie. We look forward to your next report, over. Out."

"Thank you, base. Break a leg. Over and out." She couldn't help herself somehow from trying to wish Abe luck. Was that a serious breach... a small theatrical phrase? It was out of the ordinary and clearly a mistake. Shit. Now she really started to worry. What an asshole she was. The Menagerie had an important job to do and she may have screwed it up. She may even have opened a hole in the whole Kali operation. Shit. Now she couldn't go back on the radio to warn Abe. Had Abe caught her booboo? Of course he had. But at least he was heading out to sea. Worm touched her damaged ears.

San Francisco (2300 PST)

Karen was exhausted. The first half of the day had been spent sifting through evidence in the central office, a diversion in the afternoon to Stanford, and a frantic afternoon getting equipped for the sudden, but not unexpected orders to Antarctica. She had had only a few hours of sleep the night before, and now another long airplane ride. This one promised to be one of the longest she'd taken. No frequent flier miles this time.

Thoughts of Antarctica began to loom large in her consciousness, cutting through the "lag" like a hot knife. Standing there in stark relief. The ice continent and the place of her dreams for the past few nights! Hardly surprising since she'd always had a fascination with the southern continent, ever since doing a sixth grade research report, Perry, Scott, Amudsen, Shackleton, and the high tech adventures and research of the latter half of the 20th century. While in the Navy, she'd requested a posting there, but it never happened.

After returning to her hotel room and preparing for bed, she mentally reviewed the highlights of the day. The EPG* AOSIS warning, videoconference with the president and the Task Force, the blizzard in the East, and the bizarre warm weather here in California. The solar cycle peaking with auroral displays as far south as Mexico, communications disruptions, and incredible pictures on the nightly news of the most spectacular sunspots in recorded history.

"Who'd a thought it?" Karen asked herself. As a person with a skeptical, scientific mind, and as an agnostic in general, Karen continued to hold disbelief that this disaster was "for real." Couldn't happen. Then the existential side of her kicked in and she laughed out loud.

"Oh yes it could, children," she said to herself in the mirror and shook her head in mock amazement.

The mounting evidence of the morning and afternoon pointed to terrorists with capabilities that no previous non-state group had even come close to possessing. The scale and power of the operation they were following south was unprecedented. It appeared that EPG*s level of sophistication and planning was as good as any professional organization on the planet. The afternoon had taken her and a team down the peninsula to a facility near Stanford in the heart of the Silicon Valley. They uncovered a warehouse-sized facility that was now nearly empty, but contained evidence of a very large production facility—at one time in the recent past—and a very impressive parallel super computer system. It would take FBI computer experts some time to assess what they'd found.

The paper left behind was very disconcerting, and there hadn't been much paper left behind. Recycling might be great for environmentalists, but it was hell on evidence collection. What was found was that which "fell between the cracks" when a place is totally torn apart. Stuff behind the filing cabinets, a few pieces left in files and drawers by mistake, a couple of trash cans that for some mysterious reason never got emptied/recycled, and one bag of shredded paper that never made it to the recycling pickup.

From what could be pieced together, the EPG* had used this place as a trans-shipment point to somewhere in the Pacific Islands called Kiribati. The trail appeared to be about three months old. The lease on the building had been paid up for a two-year contract that was just half way through. The corporate owners of the building and the local property management were clean. They said that the lessees had impeccable credentials and the lease payments—the most recent at the first of the year—were paid out of a corporate account at Chemical Bank in New York. Nothing suspicious had drawn their attention. Inquiries to Chemical Bank revealed that the accounts involved were tied to two organizations, Photonics, Inc., and Pacific Central Enterprises, S.A., Panama-registered corporations. Both were in evidence on some of the material found in the warehouse. Photonics was tied to the supercomputer. PCE was the logo on some of the shipping invoices and labels that had fallen through the cracks when the EPG* people cleared out.

The fragments of Phonotics' work suggested some rather serious computing power. One memo they discovered discussed some very technical programming issues, the right formulae—the mathematical algorithm—for systems modeling. The modeling equations, still on the computer, were for ocean currents and specifically involved an algorithm for the El Nino-Southern Oscillation cycle of ocean currents and warming. All very interesting, but what did it have to do with nuclear terrorism? Why were they interested in putting their energies into a scientific research project? It matched the incongruity of the raid on the USGS lab. It just didn't quite add up.

Pacific Central's role seemed clearer. There were clearly signs of some serious purchasing and shipping activity. One invoice they found beneath a wooden pallet listed nearly half a million dollars worth of high tech camping and expedition gear. Interesting items included: three stainless steel high pressure steam cleaners at $75,000 a pop; $25,000 worth of specialty high fiber energy protein bars; and, double-walled aluminum 55 gallon drums. What for? Karen wondered. Water? Fuel? Their discoveries in the warehouse seemed to conjure up more questions than answers. But it was progress of sorts.

Another wrinkle in the day was the case of Peter Wilde. He was a young television news personality in Phoenix, who seemed to be the only person the FBI could lay its hands on who knew much about the EPG* organization—even though it was five-year-old information. He was to be interviewed in the morning before they flew south. She'd have to handle this one very carefully. Her orders were to charge Wilde as a combatant unless he cooperated. Karen was a little unnerved by the strong-arm tactics, by the suspension of suspect's rights, but the ongoing war on terrorism had opened that door.

It was hot in the hotel room, and after Karen had undressed, washed her face, and brushed her teeth and hair, she turned down the lights and slid open the room's window and was refreshed by the cool evening air. Far away to the north she could she the fog making its way into the Bay. Tomorrow would be cooler. She almost fell asleep there standing by the window.

She crawled into bed. But she wasn't alone. *Shango* came in on the breeze.

Karen was once again quickly asleep and then flying above the clouds. This time she felt herself to be thousands of feet above the ocean. It was shallow because she could see light colors of sand bars and darker coral reefs. It was warm and she was headed into a steady trade wind.

She felt *Shango* this time. She wasn't scared. She just calmly rode the wind and waited for him to speak.

"You must know the storm of war is approaching, do you not?" The voice rang loud, and clear as a bell, no whisper. And it was audible, not a voice in her head. "Can you feel it?"

She could. "Yes, I can feel a presentiment. Why?"

A rich, deep Caribbean laugh seemed to shake the world.

"You truly a fine soul to ask the right question. But the answer... must discover yourself."

"Are you *Shango*?"

"That is my name in your language. I am of the *Loa*, the guardians of Earth and her people."

"There's more, isn't there?"

"Yes, my dear, there is always more..." The *Loa* actually sounded wistful.

"What do I need to know?"

"All that will come in time, not in dreams. However, some light may come through messages I bring you from *Aida Wedo*."

Aida Wedo! A name she hadn't heard since she was a small child in Haiti. She had often heard the name invoked, muttered more

129

accurately, by Haitian women who worked in the ambassador's house—her nanny and the cooks.

Surely she isn't real. She's a fantasy from a rural religion.

"You may not understand what I am about to say to you, but you will remember it when you awaken."

The voice in the sky rumbled on, "The three messages from *Aida Wedo* are: 'Lead from your heart, not from your head.' 'Remember Nature bats last.' 'Even *baka* have free will.' Again: Lead from your heart, not from your head. Remember Nature bats last. Even *baka* have free will. Lead from your heart, not from your head. Remember Nature bats last. Even *baka* have free will. You will be reminded of these lessons in the coming days."

She had heard that word, *baka*, before but couldn't for the life of her remember what it is. She asked.

"Who or what are *baka*?"

"Okay last question. The *Loa* would be guiding spirits, or guardian angels, but the *baka* would be evil spirits to take the form of an animal. To my Masters, the *baka* are you humans. Not so happy with homo sapiens. The *Loa* have their opinion, but those usually don't amount to much. I think that *Aida Wedo* actually likes you, so that's a point in your personal favor. Fortunately for you, you are not representative of your species.

"You have a big day tomorrow. You go girl."

Karen, in her dreamy state, floated on the wind and tried to absorb what she had experienced. What a crazy dream. Deep sleep took over and the dream faded away.

Pete Wilde did not have a very good evening. After leaving the FBI office mid-morning, the day had gone by fairly uneventfully—at least at a personal, if not international level. He had even managed to do a reasonable job of walling off thoughts about the whole matter while back at work at KPHX studios. With the new week ahead and a day off, he'd have plenty of time to reflect. The busy news day took care of his attention. But a nagging worry followed him all day, beyond the crisis in Washington, the unfolding news of alien First Contact, wild reports of humanity's reaction to that, and the relative calm of the newsroom at KPHX. Moreover, the weather was unsettling with a record 93°F and Arizona monsoon conditions more typical for August. Thank god for the routine he'd established. He muddled through. Then the other shoe dropped.

130

The FBI met him at home as he pulled his car into the driveway.

"Mr. Wilde." The agent stated. He read from a 3 by 5 card. "You are hereby placed under detention as specified by Presidential Order 2012-14." He did not look very comfortable. But Pete was already in shock as though all his pent up thoughts cascaded through his brain at once.

"Huh?" was all he could manage.

The FBI man gently said, "If you come quietly we won't have to handcuff you." He didn't smile.

Pete figured he must be in some serious trouble when the agents refused to say a word as they drove him to the Phoenix Airport freight terminal. The only response he got was when he asked to call his attorney.

"The way I understand it, under this specific Presidential Order, your status is like that of an enemy combatant and you have no legal rights, period. You are now under the jurisdiction of the Special Military Tribunal that sits in northern Virginia."

Pete was stunned. But he felt too guilty to argue with any of this at the moment, He was definitely in shock. He still wanted to avoid handcuffs, too.

"So, is that where I am going?"

"They'll tell you in San Francisco, I imagine."

"San Francisco?" he asked incredulously. They didn't answer him.

He was the only passenger on a small unmarked Leer jet. The agents handcuffed him to a seat and gave the keys to the copilot who came back to join them.

"Mr. Wilde, we don't consider you dangerous, but want to have your assurance that you will cooperate at this point and not create any problems?"

Pete nodded and stammered, "Yeah, sure."

Agent Scott, explained the service arrangements, "Once airborne the copilot will get you a drink. Or anything else you need during the flight to California."

"At least we won't bore you with a safety lecture."

The FBI agents got off the plane and before he knew it the engines started and they taxied down the runway, and were soon in the air. He'd hardly had time to catch his breath when the copilot came back. He eyed Pete over as though he was as big a threat as a puppy.

"I am taking those handcuffs off of you. Are you okay?"

Pete must have really looked relieved, because the copilot laughed.

"Those cowboys are clueless." And winked at Pete. "I watch your show all the time. What can I get you? We have a full bar."

"Gin. Please make it a double." Pete immediately looked better.

The uniform went back to the galley and came back with two cups of ice and three shot bottles of Beefeater. "Hope this helps, whatever trouble you're in." He added, "If you want anything else, just push the attendant button up here. We'll be at SFO in an hour—around midnight."

Dear Betsy,

We both slept in this morning on calm seas, and didn't get up until nearly 8 o'clock. After rolling out of bed, we began the regular routine: I stayed in the cabin and worked on breakfast while Brad checked the autopilot and the rigging. I rarely eat much in the morning, but today I made a hearty breakfast for both of us—and I could have eaten more! Besides, we had good fresh eggs from Tahiti. Brad lingered over his meal—he usually wolfs it down—and I asked him if there was anything wrong. He smiled and said that, except for being sore all over, he was fine. He also said something about feeling very mortal and held my hand in a very tender way. He put his hand on my thigh and then I figured out what was on his mind. We went back to bed and made love for the first time in a week. He really felt good and I had the best orgasm I've had in ages. He paid a lot of attention. Wow. Maybe we should look for storms and not avoid them.

I couldn't wait to get back up on deck and a get little sun, but I had my chores to do: clean up the galley, check the radar and weather report, and take a navigation fix. The galley and cabinets aren't in very bad shape. The guys who built this boat designed her very well. The cabinets were built tight and have nifty dividers to keep things from moving around too much, even in a storm. The one exception was the one of the utensil drawers that ended up on the floor. The drawer itself seems okay and all I had to do was wash the half of its contents that had ended up on the deck. Some water had leaked through a portal in the head, too. I wrote a note to Brad to fix the leak. My favorite plant, the geranium, had worked its way loose somehow and had made a mess. I doubt the poor thing will make it, but I got most of the potting soil back into the pot.

Weather reports and radar are nominal although the same storm we experienced yesterday is still pretty well organized and behind us to the east. You'd never know it outside, though. There are lazy sets of 2-3 foot waves from the southeast and the temperature at 1000 hrs was 83° F. Partly cloudy with the usual fair-weather fluffy white ones. Relative humidity is 40 percent.

What was not nominal was the GPS. It took five minutes to get a reading. Usually takes a minute to locate the satellites. The weather report did say that there is a solar flare, so that is probably the reason. The weather report itself was hard to hear over the static. Might be a good time to practice my navigation with the sextant. I wonder if we'll be able to pick up BBC tonight.

The thought of news did sober me as I went up on deck. I remembered dreaming about seeing another boat—this one full of women and children—screaming for help as it sank beneath a monster wave. I can still see their anguish and fear. If there had been Melanesian boat people out in the storm yesterday, there was no sign of them today. I don't know if I would have felt better or worse seeing flotsam—knowing that what I had seen was not a figment of my imagination, or knowing for sure that fifty-odd people had drowned in the storm. The thought gives me the shivers.

I talked to Brad about it and he hugged me hard and told me that we had done all we could. I think he was a little worried that I would have tried to bring them all aboard. Sheesh—what a dilemma!

I reported our position and told him about the solar flare. He reminded me to put on extra sunscreen. I fell for that one and he laughed—hey, what do I know about astrophysics? It messed up my GPS, so why not my skin? He agreed to give me another sextant lesson. I couldn't believe that he was hungry already, but this he was serious about. Brad does not joke about food.

Another bonus from yesterday's storm was a good push towards our destination, Pitcairn. By my estimate we are about five days out at our present speed. The storm had in effect cut a halfday off the projected travel time. We aren't in any hurry, but after the fiasco in French Polynesia, I am truly looking forward to Pitcairn.

Well, that's it, enough for today.

January 16
Monday

San Francisco International Airport (0008 PST)

Drinking all that gin so fast had been a big mistake. As the plane touched down in thick fog, Pete's head was swimming. That's great, he thought to himself, swimming through fog... What a mess. Who was going to feed his cat?

Two new quiet FBI guys took him from the plane and escorted him to a sedan. The cool damp breeze helped clear his head a bit but the alcohol in his system was just enough to keep him loose. The car took quite a long time to thread its way along a row of hangers, closed and deserted at this late hour. Eventually they stopped in front of a tall set of stairs that led up to what looked in the fog like an Airbus A380; it was so big that the tail was obscured by fog. This must be a corporate jet, Pete thought. The jet was like no other super jumbo jet he'd ever seen. He was led to a relatively large compartment equipped with plush couches and its own lavatory.

After unlocking his cuffs, one of the agents said, "Special agent St. Cloud will be on board in a few hours. Meantime, make yourself comfortable. There are blankets and pillows in the cabinet below the couch. You are welcome to use the TV, but don't try to use the phone. There is an intercom by the door if you need anything else." They locked him in.

Pete fumed for a minute but then settled down. There was no point in getting all worked up when clearly he had been swept up in events beyond his control. He walked into the lavatory and saw gold-plated fixtures and a small shower. He turned on the shower, even though all he had to change into were the dirty clothes that he had on. After showering, he stretched, pulled out some blankets and a pillow, and lay down. They weren't the typical airline-issue coach articles, but high-quality 280 line-weave fabrics. He put his head down and was out like a light.

He was awakened by loud thump and clunking sounds some hours later, coming from below. Cargo was being loaded. There was a veritable light show of green, yellow, blue, and red lights projected on the cabin walls coming through the windows. He leaned over to look through one of the small windows and saw a cordon of police vans with flashing red and blue lights surrounding the baggage loading

134

ramp and baggage carts. At that instant, someone knocked at the door and then slowly eased it open.

"Mr. Wilde?" inquired a new face—this one a good-looking, muscular, short Vietnamese-American with a crew cut. He came on inside the small cabin.

"I'm agent Brian Minh, your shadow, at least for the short term."

He smiled pleasantly and held out his hand. Pete took it and they shook hands.

"For now you are a prisoner, and yet, there is a Zen riddle: for you are also to be our guest on this secret mission. Quite a conundrum." He winked at Pete as though he was having fun.

"Come on, you get to meet the boss. Follow me. Please."

Having taken off his coat and tie, Pete grabbed his jacket and followed the agent into the airplane's main corridor. He shot a quick glance right towards the cockpit and saw a half dozen technicians working on a large array of computers, display panels, and what was clearly telecommunications equipment. The exit he had come in through was yawning open but not particularly inviting. He could feel the cold of the fog nipping at his ankles. He shivered involuntarily.

Agent Minh looked back and motioned for Pete to catch up.

"This is actually an Airbus A380 corporate jet that the FBI requisitioned for the emergency. It may take us another couple of hours to get prepped and loaded."

"Where are we going?" He asked innocently.

"I will leave the telling to Special Agent St. Cloud."

They passed a small suite of first class seats that appeared to be set on swivels. Coming up on the left was a bar and kitchenette, then more lavatories. Next came a large conference room complete with an oblong oak table and captain's chairs circling the table. They skirted the table. It was stacked with boxes of maps and other piles of papers, books, atlases, and paper and plastic tubes.

"What a mess," Pete remarked.

"You get to clean it up," Minh replied. He looked back with a serious face and raised his eyebrows.

It dawned on Pete that this time Minh might not be kidding. Now his brain went into overdrive. What the hell was going on here? He was more confused than ever. The residual fog of gin didn't help much.

They moved through a narrow corridor with rows of cabins on both sides. He was led into a right-hand side cabin that was even more luxurious than the room he'd been in. There was a small bed built into the bulkhead with storage above it. There was a couch, a small bar with microwave, and fridge. A large high definition plasma screen was the focal point of the room. A computer workstation was set into the wall next to the couch. A couple of laptop computers sat on substantial round oak table in the middle of the room. Piles of boxes and luggage were everywhere. The place was such a disaster area that it was almost hard to tell that it was a nicely appointed room. The design was a combination of modern aerospace and Danish modern. The colors were pleasing pastels with bold primary color accents. The upholstery was plush and very expensive-looking. Then he focused on the woman hooking up a laptop computer to some wires leading to a black metal box on the table. Pete had assumed she was a technician. Not. Minh spoke first. She turned around to look at him and when she stood up straight, Pete saw that she was his height.

"Agent St. Cloud, Pete Wilde."

She didn't offer him her hand, but instead motioned for him to sit at the end of the table. He was a bit taken aback when the first thing she asked was, "Is that your given name? Sounds like the stage name of a porn star."

He answered very slowly, trying to gauge her, sensing humor behind the question. "I go by Pete. My parents were Pentecostal, so I doubt they realized what they did to me." And added sarcastically, "But you are the first person to ever ask me that question."

"Mr. Wilde, do you realize that it's a federal offense to lie to the FBI?"

As the color evaporated from his face, Karen watched his reaction and her face broke out into the widest smile she'd had in weeks and then laughed… laughed so hard she was almost hysterical. She caught herself as Agent Minh started to look worried. She quickly changed gears.

"Sorry, it was a short night. Coffee, or tea? I'm needing more caffeine myself."

Before he could even answer, she pushed an intercom button set into the table.

"Could someone bring us a coffee service for three?" She looked at Minh who nodded.

Pete sighed, then seemed to squirrel up his courage to get indignant.

"I..."

Agent St. Cloud put her hands up.

"I know, I know. You've been practically kidnapped and imprisoned, but I'd like you to listen to me first okay?"

He was so tired and worn out from the adrenaline rush of the last five hours that the wind was knocked out of the sails of his indignation.

A steward showed up with a fancy tray and a gold-plated thermos of coffee, sugar, cream—the works. He sat it down on the end of the table, poured them each a cup and left. St. Cloud continued.

"This may sound corny, but we need you to help us get to the bottom of an immanent, sorry..., imminent, threat to the nation's security. And if you'll excuse the cliché, we are on a mission to avert the end of the world. That may sound melodramatic, but we believe that some of your former friends and acquaintances are precipitating one of the most serious crises in the nation's history.

"This evening, an Executive Order was issued that expanded federal jurisdiction into several areas, including transportation and public movement, and under the Homeland Security Act, the president has designated members of certain environmental groups as enemy combatants, until the end of this emergency. That should be a sign of how serious this has become.

"The deeper we get into this crisis, the more I am persuaded that it is perhaps even bigger than I, or we, imagined; potentially this is a crisis of global proportions." She paused and looked up in the air for a second.

"I can't say that I am happy to be kidnapping a member of the Fourth Estate, but I am acting under direct orders from the president."

She shot a dangerous look at Minh, who sat impassively between them.

"The point is that the White House has ordered us to Antarctica to help find your friends and disarm them."

"What? You can't be serious!" Pete's anger was rising above his astonishment.

"Well, there we are... I was hoping we could make you a deal that you can't refuse."

He stared straight into her eyes.

"You are a reporter, right? If you will cooperate with us fully, we'll give you a grant of immunity, and exclusive story rights to this operation."

The dumb-founded look was now more than gin and fog. But he then appeared very attentive.

"Go on," he said.

St. Cloud continued, "In exchange for information from you, we will give you unlimited access to our files on the case and opportunity on the ground in Antarctica to record and report what you learn."

"And an interview with the president," he interjected. Karen's suspicions about Pete were right on the money.

"Don't push your luck. This is not the time. Listen to me... these lunatic friends of yours seem prepared to destroy humanity. At the very least, they are a threat to international peace and security. Your options are to stay here in custody until the end of the crisis, or you can cooperate fully and come with us to Antarctica. Your choice, but you don't have long to decide."

She appraised him slowly, as though seeing him for the first time.

"I have lots to do as you can see from the mess, but if you decide to join the team, once we're underway we'll talk further. Brian will show you to your room and brief you on much of what has happened. Think it over, but we leave in a hour, and the clock's running."

Brian wasted no time in finding his arm and escorted him— more physically this time—to a room a few doors further down the corridor. It was much smaller than the one he'd just been in, but just as richly appointed. It was a more impressive room because it was clean. He heard the door click locked, and sure enough when he tried, it was. He sat down and tried to think. Then he made up his mind. He banged on the door, hard.

Almost immediately, the door opened and Minh's face appeared.

"What is it?" he asked frowning.

"I'll go. Tell St. Cloud that I agree to the deal."

Brian Minh actually looked relieved. "Good, I'll tell her." He considered Pete for a minute. "We need to get some of this stuff stowed, but if you can stay out of the way for a while, I'll come back and then put you to work after we take off, okay?"

What were his options, he wondered? "Okay. Could I get some more coffee?"

Minh grinned at him. "Sure, no problem."

This time he did not hear the sound of the door lock. While he was waiting, he checked out the room. It was quite a deal: gold-plated fixtures in a small bathroom, an extremely comfortable Pullman-type sofa that pulled down into a bed. There was even a single rose in a vase that was fastened to a couch-side tray. The storage compartments were basically empty, but he did find pillows and some blankets. To his delight the blankets were silk and down comforters. This was all very elegant and very expensive. It appeared that guests of the largest computer software company in the world were treated well.

Pete gazed out the window. The activity outside was riveting. The light show was now replaced, overshadowed, as it were, by some portable high intensity lights that had been set up to illuminate a large area where gear was being deposited and then inventoried. There were some large boxes being unloaded and he could see a Food Service Inc., truck being unloaded directly onto the loading ramp. It was surreal: a dense fog punctuated by bright lights and scores of red, blue and yellow pulses from a dozen security vehicles. Intense, he mused to himself. He found a letter-sized notebook in the desktop and he began writing down questions and summary list of what he knew. Two days of dramatic political crises had resulted in his entanglement with some of the actors, weird and fantastic weather-solar-climate changes, the pre-apocalyptic background noise, aliens, and now a borrowed super jumbo jet headed for Antarctica.

Avoiding going to jail was a strong incentive to go with the flow, he thought to himself. Besides, this was an opportunity of a lifetime—assuming of course that he wasn't killed in the process. He recorded the scene outside and tried to identify what was being loaded onto the plane. Most of it looked heavy and nondescript.

A knock came on the door. It was Agent Minh who came in with packages in his hands.

"For me?"

"Jump suits, in a few sizes and colors. Until your clothes catch up."

"Would you clarify that?" Pete raised his eyebrows for emphasis.

"With your permission, we will have our Phoenix office pick up anything you might want out of your residence. Actually, we don't even need your permission." He smiled at himself as though he was amusing. Pete ignored it, as Minh's sense of humor was already getting on his nerves. Minh continued.

"Other than clothes, passport, and toiletries, is there anything special—anything in particular— you want us to collect for you? We've already made arrangements for your cat. We'll be refueling and picking up additional materials in Panama." He motioned at the boxes. "These should suffice for the time being. I expect we'll be fairly informal during the flight south."

"How long is this flight? Where are we going?"

"Last question, first?" He paused. "We're heading for the US McMurdo base, Antarctica. Ever been there?" When Pete continued to ignore him he went on.

"It's roughly a 10,000-mile trip. We'll make two stops, one in Panama and the other in Santiago, Chile—20 to 22 hours we figure. Refueling time along the way is uncertain at this point. Oh and by the way, the trip might take us a full 24 hours if there are any weather problems. You get motion sick?"

He shook his head minutely, trying his best to be oblivious.

"They are supposed to lengthen the airstrip there just for us, too. Let's hope they finish in time."

Pete formed a question but didn't utter a sound. Pete closed his mouth.

"So… you still with the program now?" Minh was all business.

"Yes, I think so."

"I'll give you a few minutes to think about your clothes and personal items in Phoenix."

"Do I need my coats?" He looked uncertain.

"A couple for indoors I'm told, but we'll provide all the gear that you might need, boots and outer wear, goggles for outside weather wear. Much of that is coming aboard now, expedition grade gear… great stuff. It shouldn't take much longer to get everything aboard.

"Sorry about the delay on the coffee. I'll get it for you now."

"Please." He said reasonably. "Meanwhile, I'll change clothes."

Minh left to get coffee and returned within a couple of minutes.

"We are almost squared away and will be taking off shortly. Make yourself comfortable. I'm sure that once we're underway, Special Agent St. Cloud will want to talk more with you."

After he left, Pete locked the door from the inside and tried on a couple of pairs of coveralls until he found one in a size that actually felt and looked good. He wasn't especially pleased with the peach color, but it was a grand step up from the lavender. This must be more Microsoft fluff. He also found two pairs of new boxer shorts. Not his style, but they were clean.

The coffee helped. It was good strong Peet's Coffee. He smiled at the coincidence of names. The engines started up one by one. He couldn't recall ever having heard the turbines of a jet airplane start up from a dead silence. It seemed to take a long time, as though the engines were cold. Then a frightening thought came to him. What if the engines froze once they reached Antarctica? Would he ever get home? He shook off the thought as a childish worry. But vague doubts lingered.

Outside, the vans pulled away and ground crews yelled and motioned at each other. The last of the gear moved into the hold of the plane. A couple of dull thuds and vibrations were followed by the last of the support equipment being pulled away. The engines reached a steady whine, within a minute there was a small movement and then the plane began to move deliberately down the taxiway. The slow trip to the runway seemed to take hours. He buckled himself in and pulled one of the comforters up over his legs. The plane pivoted slowly to the right, the engines throttled up, and they were headed down the runway south.

Foot of Lambert Glacier (70° W, 72° S) (0500 GMT)

Deep in the bowels of the glacier, the extreme cold was a concern for the Device, which had to be kept warm. Small ceramic heaters and fans periodically came to life and pumped their heat into the cold silicon and metal mechanisms. Finally, a confirmation code came into the radio receiver on an open Ka band frequency beamed down from a polar orbiting NPOESS weather satellite. The Device emitted a return sequence of codes on an even higher frequency and even tighter beam due north. Then a second Ka signal was received —the long cryptographic key developed by the Department of Defense and NSA to thwart any unauthorized triggering of the weapon. That hadn't stopped Abe's team from replicating it and coming up with an alternative method of arming the Devices. The key opened the inner mechanisms to remote access. Within two minutes, the Device was armed and ready. The modified laptop computer strapped to it sent the command for the two-minute countdown.

Things moved very slowly. The Device continued to warm up during the countdown. It was getting downright hot inside its foam insulation. Small gears turned and the chemical explosive bolts were armed and ready. The inner shielding between the two halves of the uranium was mechanically pulled away to open up a small space in the core. The explosive bolts ignited, which in turn triggered the sphere of explosions directed inward at the core. The uranium halves jammed together and instantaneously they reached critical mass. The 50-kiloton Device blazed like the sun.

Within 40 milliseconds, the Device was itself vaporized. The fireball expanded to room size in the next 80 milliseconds. The 40,000° cloud of plasma and steam made contact with bedrock. Ice and snow in the surrounding bubble joined the fury of the heat and light. But the shockwave soon encountered the bedrock of the Antarctic's American Highland. The fission process itself now complete for over 150 milliseconds, a ball of plasma expanded—at the temperature of the surface of the sun—at 50 meters per second vaporizing rock as well as ice. Within a half second of fission, the bubble of expanding gases and debris broke the surface of the glacier above. The fireball emerged and rose into the sky over the southern end of the Amery Ice Shelf. At ground level, the heat and blast wave pushed their way down assisted by the cold dense air above, north onto Amery Ice and up, south into Lambert. Placed at the boundary between Earth and ice, the Device did exactly as planned.

The energy of the blast was contained primarily inside the soil and ice. The thick mantle of the ice cap held much of the energy from the blast. The ice even served to contain and concentrate the energy under the ice, particularly at the ice/bedrock boundary. The air and loose snow inside of the caverns forced a wall of compressed air ahead of the blast front throwing a wedge underneath the ice and lifting it away from the bedrock that had been taking its own good time to grind to dust. Within a quarter of mile of ground zero the snow and ice was turned into a hellish mix of water vapor, steam, fog, and radioactive soil now beginning to fall around the outlines of a large crater. Peak static overpressure above the glacier was 10 pounds per square inch creating fierce winds with nothing in the way particularly to slow them down. Due to the effects of the thick cold air, the blast wave dissipated more quickly than it would have at the equator, but still blew 100 miles an hour five miles from the epicenter.

Almost a third of the Device's energy was given off as thermal radiation. This heat vaporized 700 cubic meters of ice, most of which was sucked up underneath the rising fireball. As it rose and cooled, the column of water vapor turned to liquid water droplets that coalesced into a fog. As the frigid surrounding air sucked the energy out of the water and fog, it settled quickly back to the ground. A huge cloud formed over the cooling crater. It mixed within the first few minutes with the falling particles of rock and soil kicked up by the explosion. The ice fog was like no other ever seen before on earth. This was a radioactive frozen soup. It drifted with the prevailing wind over the frozen landscape.

Underneath the ice the pressures were contained, but transferred to the fairly inelastic sheets of ice. The shock wave's main energy pushed north toward the Amery Ice Shelf mostly on the waters of the Southern Ocean. The Lambert Glacier, a grounded glacier moving from the south, was more stable and effectively directed the blast even more toward the north. After two minutes, the shock wave reached the tip of the Amery Ice Shelf and immediately caused tens of thousands of cubic feet of icebergs to calve into the sea.

The flash came instantaneously, but the blast wave didn't reach the Australian research station Emily II for a full two minutes after the detonation. Emily II was a couple of Quonset-type huts out on the tip of the exposed mainland at Cape Darnley overlooking MacKenzie Bay. The crew had all been indoors luckily—they could have easily been blinded had any of them been looking to the southeast.

Cook and part-time meteorologist Mark Humphries saw the flash reflected off of the galley wall.

"Wow. What was that?" It was so bright that it hurt. His first thought was a meteorite. He blinked and his vision returned, though there were lingering bright spots.

"Did anybody else see that?" was accompanied by yells from several of the half dozen other scientists in the common area. Suddenly the structures shook and rattled for what seemed to be a half a minute. No windows broke. A dull roar accompanied the shaking.

"Christ on a cracker… What the fuck was that?" asked Chief Scientist and expedition leader Charles Waverly. He was literally thrown out of his bunk where he was reading a cookbook. The team in the commons was running to get outdoor gear on and suit up for the outside. Waverly raised his voice.

"Hold on, hold on. I want the engineering and logistics personnel to go out and survey for damage. Science and professional personnel stay inside and do a damage assessment of your area. Do we have communications?"

His young radio person, Margaret Symes, asked, "Dr. Waverly?"

"Get the Navy on the horn, ASAP." He did not smile at her as usual.

"Yes sir." She walked back toward the radio room.

Seconds later a 60-mile an hour wind whipped across the station. Radiation monitors intended for quite different scientific tasks suddenly went off their scales and warning lights flashed.

The fireball rose to 8,000 feet in three minutes before the cold thin Antarctic air snuffed out the ruby glow. The hot cloud raised high into the clear air and began to drift to the east and to the Antarctic highlands, Enderby Land. Ever so slowly, it climbed and glided up into high country, the forbidding glaciers of the Antarctic plateau. Enderby Land and the more distant Queen Maud Land would have a layer of radioactive snow to serve as a historical marker for some later generation of scientists. As steam condensed and then turned into rain and snow it precipitated back down—a radioactive rain of 100,000-year-old frozen water and shale. The Amery Ice Shelf rocked back and forth against its confines—the Grove Mountains to the west and MacRobertson Land to the east.

Washington, D.C. (0600 EST)

A phone call woke the president.

"Something's happened." It was the voice of his chief of staff. "We have confirmed a nuclear detonation in Antarctica… the explosion was about five minutes ago… think you better come down, sir."

By 6:30 the president was behind his desk in the Oval Office with a mug of coffee in his hands. He listened intently to his advisors bring him up-to-date.

"We lucked out this time. A real-time imaging polar satellite of NASA's and a NOAA weather satellite were both overhead and we caught the flash of the detonation."

The president responded, "And you are absolutely sure?"

"There's no doubt, sir." This was the Chairman of the Joint Chiefs. "It correlates with seismic devices in Australia, Argentina, and South Africa. We would like closer first-hand corroboration, but the flash and the seismic data are pointing to a 40 to 50 kiloton explosion. That is the expected yield for one of these warheads. Unfortunately, it's right on the money."

"Sweet Jesus." The president stared into his coffee cup.

The FBI Director began. "The evidence we have uncovered in California suggests that they do know what they're doing. They have technical abilities. Nevertheless, they are amateurs—from a military standpoint. Even from a criminal standpoint. These people are radicals, but they have not been violent before." He didn't look too sure of himself all of a sudden.

The president obviously had other things on his mind. There was an uncomfortable silence that blanketed the room.

"So they detonated one of our bombs. Now maybe we can find them?" He was clearly angry and sarcastic.

"We have NESTs and the FBI on their way down there. One of our aircraft carrier groups is preparing for a flyover of western Antarctica."

"Sir," he added.

The president was still thoughtful—or maybe just waking up. "What makes you think that these kooks can actually bring the world to an end?" Everyone in the room looked at him, like, how could *he* be serious?

"Can they keep the other devices hidden? Can they really melt that much ice? Can they really bring on an ice age? I just have a hard time seeing all these things happen." He shook his head in disbelief. "This is nuts." It was becoming his favorite refrain.

Then he said clearly to himself, and no one else, "And I thought the last few reports about possible aliens were strange."

"The British Prime Minister is on the line for you, Mr. President."

"Thanks, Greg." He'd included his press secretary in all of the high-level meetings recently on the Nuclear Crisis. He'd become a very useful facilitator, a Bill Moyers type. He was easy-going and was not easily ruffled—an important element to have in a crisis management team.

This was becoming a real mother.

"Mr. Prime Minister?"

"Mr. President? I've been informed that a joint British-German Antarctic research team has been killed in an explosion in Antarctica. What in god's name is going on President Clark?"

Clark was slow to answer. "You surely must know much of what's going on, yes? I had not heard about the loss of any research team."

"Yes; the stolen weapons… the Tierra del Fuego hideout… the Antarctic deception… and now this, surely, an atomic blast. A team of about thirty people is missing and believed dead. We have a squadron of Harriers en route from the Falklands and twelve Royal Navy vessels in the Southern Ocean region. We have already been coordinating at high levels with the Pentagon and the U.S. Naval commander at McMurdo. They have been good enough to run interference with the Argentines—an inconvenient traditional rivalry under the circumstances.

"The point I'm trying to make is that we are engaged, no... Implicated is a better word. But now British citizens have been killed and there are clearly many more potential victims of this lunacy. I think we need to work together more closely. I have spoken with most of my colleagues in the EU this morning and while I do not share this view, they asked me to express their concern that the U.S. may have gone 'too far' this time."

"Too far? I don't follow your meaning?" Clark was stunned.

"The State of Emergency."

"Go on..."

"Well, the closing of borders has been nothing short of an economic disaster. In case you haven't been paying attention, the Asian and European stock markets have been in a tailspin since they opened this morning. UN Security Council members are uniformly upset that we are unable to physically convene in New York. Between the storm and the flight delays, State Department delays, it has been impossible to convene in New York. We will meet in Geneva today with or without the U.S. You must have heard all of this from your Ambassador Moore or Secretary Adams?"

"No, quite honestly, I have not. Both have been requesting meetings, but we have been distracted."

"You have my sympathies, Mr. President, but under the circumstances, you must realize that this is more than just a U.S. problem. The German Chancellor and I have agreed to send additional expeditionary forces to the South. We also believe that our Scandinavian friends should be included." The U.S. had been having problems with the Norwegians over fishing conflicts in the North Atlantic.

"I need to consider our options and speak with my advisors. I hear what you are saying, and understand the EU and UN positions. I don't believe the Geneva meeting is a problem. I will inform our ambassador."

The president paused and an awkward silence grew. He then continued.

"I am sure that there is strength in numbers. Given the constraints of the Antarctic Treaty, we should perhaps proceed as an international force." He paused again and the PM waited him out.

"Okay. I will speak with my advisors and get back to you later today. You may convey my apologies and concerns to the Chancellor and other leaders in Europe. My only concern has been for a resolution of this crisis and the terrorists... as a national security threat. But there are obviously larger issues here to consider. I will get back to you."

"And, Mr. Prime Minister?

"Yes?"

"Thank you." He said warmly.

Then he got off the phone, walked over to the coffee tray to warm up his mug. Everyone in the room was waiting for him to speak.

"What do we know about a British and German team of scientists near the explosion?"

Don Brown walked in as the president was asking the question. He was carrying a large map that he laid out on the coffee table in the middle of the Oval Office.

It was a large color satellite image of the area around the Amery Ice Shelf.

"This is the Amery Shelf which, as you can see from this line of dark spots, is surrounded by a mountain range. Actually, a set of mountain ranges which flank the bay. According to scientists I spoke with from the NSF, the bay was ice-free during the last interglacial warm period about 90,000 years ago. There is apparently general consensus that the Amery is vulnerable to global warming and sea level rise. During the last few Southern summers, the face of the Amery has retreated 20 kilometers—that's about 18 miles—per year.

"This is an image from last week, one of the best images in terms of percentage of cloud cover in the recent few weeks." He pointed to the top, middle part of the picture. "This is the approximate spot of the explosion. The research team was out in the middle of the ice shelf." He circled his index finger in the middle. "We should get new imaging after the bird passes over in about 90 minutes. It will not be as good an angle, but good high rez images."

"We also heard through the Australians that they witnessed the blast from their summer research station on Cape Darnley—which is here," he jabbed his finger at the sharp outlines of a peninsula on the 70° East meridian.

"We have confirmed visuals of the nuclear fireball. They were about 200 miles away—pretty shaken up, but no serious damage."

"And, Mr. President?"

"Go ahead, Mr. Secretary."

"May we move this meeting down to the Situation Room? We need the displays and maps." The president was already nodding his head. He pushed a button on his phone.

"Joyce? We're moving to the Situation Room. We're going to need a brunch setup, too. Will you see what the kitchen can do? What is the staff situation?" One of the few people on his staff who ever gave him any static was his personal secretary Joyce Garcia. He had insisted on it. Joyce had been with him back in Tennessee when he had first run for the state senate. She had been his sounding board then, and she was still. She never called him Mr. President, either. All his other friends refused to call him by his first name, but to Joyce in private he was always "Raymond," in public he was "Sir."

"We're in luck. The kitchen staff is almost all here. Maintenance is slightly undermanned, but we have a surfeit of extra security. The Secret Service is doing a double shift and we are up to our eyeballs in FBI."

"Great. Find a couple of them to come in and give us a hand. Thanks Joyce."

"We're on it sir."

148

"Please get Secretary Adams and the UN Ambassador on the phone. Make it a conference call, if possible. If not, I'll talk to whomever you get first."

The fighter tore across the deck. The fact that the deck was 8,000 feet above sea level to begin with, and one of the coldest spots on earth, hadn't even fazed the young pilot.

"Sending headings," he said into the radio as he pushed a button on the computer.

"Roger. Stand by... Headings received. Over"

They didn't want to rely on instruments too much given the horrible solar storm. Doppler telemetry was the only way to go. Clear weather ahead, but a storm over the horizon. He and his mate were near the edge of their range and would have to return to the carrier soon.

He wasn't fazed by the cold, but was definitely in awe of the terrain. Skirting the Transantarctic Mountains was not an average day's patrol. Lt. Danny Monroe was exhilarated.

"Time to turn back, Mack." He always called his wingman Mack. It was annoying, but Danny was so easy-going most of his mates just let it go.

"Roger, Danny boy."

"Pretty amazing landscape."

"You got that right."

"Look at the size of that glacier."

"Hate to tell you this, but most everything down there is a glacier."

"No shit?" He played dumb. "Just looks like a lot of snow to me."

"Like I said, ya got that right."

Dan got serious. "No company, so let's get back. On my mark." The two F-18s banked together and headed back north. They would over fly McMurdo on the way back home, the USS Coral Sea, still a good 1000 nautical miles north of McMurdo. There had never before been an attempt to take a carrier group so close to the pack ice, but this was not a normal set of circumstances. The pilots had been glad to get off of the ship given the gnawing nervousness of the crew about being in iceberg country. The pilots were generally oblivious to the mundane concerns of the ship's sailors, but this time it was starting to get to them. Being in the air was a great elixir.

For some reason flying over the icy terrain was a real turn-on for Danny. It was so smooth, so plastic. Except for the distant mountains, the passage over the ice was unmarred by human or biological disturbance. Flying over water was like that, but, well boring. This over-the-ice flying had a depth and fascination that the water did not hold for him. It was mesmerizing—and then there would be some subtle shift in the pattern of the flows below... a set of crevasses, or an icefall, the very subtle shift in patterns of color and reflection. He had been tempted at first to think that it was all the same, but now the differences were crystallizing.

He radioed Command. "This is Beaver One. Returning to base."

"Coral Command. Acknowledged. Any radar?" They were asking for what should be obvious—he would have reported any unusual EMF or radar activity.

"Negative, Command." He wouldn't let his voice show his irritation given the likelihood that their conversations were being monitored by the Admiral and probably recorded for the Pentagon, to boot.

"Fuel status?"

"Looks nominal. Sixty percent. Mack?"

"Same here. Nominal at slightly under sixty."

They were now flying over a pass in the Queen Maud Mountains.

"Sending another set of headings. We're right on top of the Queen Maud Mountains and have a clear view of the Ross Ice straight ahead. How's our weather report?"

"McMurdo reports a storm building near the coast. You should be fine at 20,000 feet. The Man requests that you shoot wide of McMurdo."

"What no fun?" The pre-flight briefing earlier had gone over some of the finer points of the Antarctic Treaty that they would be technically violating. No point in annoying the civilians if it could be avoided. Even with the minimal amount of information that Danny was operating, he could see that military involvement in this affair was inevitable. So why worry about sensibilities? Scientists were the worst, too. So sanctimonious and full of shit, he thought. They didn't know shit, either. He'd just love to give them a little of his exhaust.

"Roger, steer clear of the coastal activity. We're back over glacial ice. More headings coming... Transmitting."

"Received. Thanks Beaver."

Danny wondered which joker picked that moniker for the mission. He stared down at ice that looked like it had been there forever.

Karen anchored her coffee mug as the plane hit a spot of rough air. The Fasten Seat belt sign came on, but there was no accompanying announcement. That is eerie, she thought to himself, unused to the comforts of corporate class service. The workday had started early. Dealing with her young journalist guest had been awkward, but resolved, it seemed, to everyone's mutual satisfaction— so far. While Pete caught up on his sleep, the news of the Antarctic explosion had come across to them on a secure channel. Karen was neither surprised nor shocked. She was just more determined. The plane hit a pocket of air and her stomach lurched.

She picked up a phone and reached the galley. After ordering breakfast, she got back to work, quickly skimming an inch of reports accumulating around her. She picked up a file that someone in the San Francisco office had flagged with a red tab. She read what looked like a poem.

Freya, Goddess of the Southern Continent

As weeks passed by
Freya found rapprochement with Gaia
An uneasy truce—an accommodation
Gaia let Freya's icy tendrils caress her body politic
Hot core tempered by a cold heart

Freya, once a young warm continent, bathed in the tropics
Until she found her lot in life—a cold heartlessness
Numb to the world but essential to it
A balance between heat and quiet
A role she grew into, to support her sisters

For weeks she found her place as the seeker of cold
Pulling around her the shroud of ice and snow
Basking in the mantle of frozen water
Only letting go
From time to time as the sun and stars would have it

151

A pretty lonely vigil for a goddess, but hey, it was
Her job
No one else's
And things were working out
The weeks of a mature cycle
Frigid, desolate, bleak—punctuated
By a weekend of warmth

A refrigerator goddess, relegated to the end of the Earth
To balance the life forces of Gaia—her Mother
Key to Her healthy circulation, moderating the bastard Sun
An answer to Cosmic forces and dirt
Hiding her secrets with icing

The eons became weeks of cleansing
Scouring a continent for the Ocean god Agwe
Pumping the blood of Gaia
Powering the four Winds
And now mortals thought they were gods, too.

Not

The scribbling in the margins in pencil appeared to be corrections and editorial marks. Stapled to the poem was a handwritten memo from one of the analysts in California.

"The poem was one of a small number of documents found of Abe Miller's—this one from his sister in San Jose. She alleges that he left this by accident in her spare bedroom after a short visit in 2010. Partial fingerprints were found to match his. The laser printout is similar to the output from a machine found at his abandoned office.

"Keyword searches of online and academic databases have uncovered about a dozen similar poems of varying length. None of them bear his name, but what appears to be a pseudonym, Keva Kelly. They appeared in environmental and other new age publications, and a couple of webzines.

"A preliminary analysis shows a common theme. There is the mythical goddess *Freya*, the Earth Mother goddess Gaia, and other pagan and *Vodun* gods and goddess, like *Yemanja*, *Agwe*, and *Pele*— the Hawaiian goddess of volcanoes. Yet, interwoven into this theme is the contemporary Gaia theory that the Earth is like a living organism. The poems suggest that the author believes that there is a millennium-old goddess of the Antarctic continent, *Freya*.

"There is a traditional goddess from Scandinavia by the same name, a fertility goddess associated with a winter solstice celebration (through her consort *Frey*). There is no evidence of anyone previously linking this particular goddess to the Antarctic. Yet the poetry clearly subscribes to this notion.

"Our forensic psychologist noted that if Miller really believes the Antarctic to be female, or like a female, that his hatred toward his mother may be a reason for this act of terrorism. The evidence gathered from family sources indicate that the Miller children were physically and psychologically abused by their mother—she is reported to have humiliated them in public.

"While the poetry appears on the surface to be loving and respectful, the psychologist has pointed out that there are violent undertones throughout the poetry. See the Clinical Evaluation Report, 15 January 2012."

Karen frowned at the notion of the Antarctic as goddess. She'd have to find that Clinical Evaluation. Karen was still having a hard time seeing how someone could, on the one hand, elevate a piece of real estate to godhead, and then on the other, want to blow it to smithereens. She dug through the piles of files to no avail. The report was here somewhere—it was on her list of documents. Maybe she'd better eat first. At that instant, there was a knock on the door. Her food arrived. She ate and worked at the same time.

Searching for the Clinical Evaluation, Karen discovered one small file that had been put together for the FBI by the Science Advisor and the National Science Foundation. There were some statistical summaries of climate, geography, and Antarctic flora and fauna, and rather beautiful maps, almost art. She then skimmed two short papers that assessed the probability that EPG* could actually bring on a new ice age. They were written pro and con style. Both papers reflected a view of the continent that was new to Karen. She had always assumed that Antarctica was isolated at the end of the world and while an interesting place, not germane to what was going on to the north.

Maybe not quite *Freya*, the continent was becoming understood by a certain sub-set of young scientists as a dynamic, integrated system. These young scientists called themselves geophysiologists—those who studied the health of the planet reconciling Gaia theory and natural selection. While not a new field, inspired in the last century by the work of maverick scientist and father of environmental monitoring James Lovelock, it had blossomed into a respectable although still marginal subfield of planetary and ecological studies. Some scientific fields such as microbiology had been totally taken over by the Gaia theory.

The geophysiologists it turned out had published extensively on the Antarctic connection over the last decade as the research mounted on the relationship between the icy continent and global climate change and sea level rise. No doubt, a motivation behind Abe Miller's poetry, but the geophysiologists, being scientists, would scoff at the anthropomorphism of Miller's *Freya*. Antarctica was Gaian, not because it was a deity, but because it was a cybernetic subsystem whose purpose was to sustain the optimal conditions for life on the planet. Sure, Antarctica looked dead, but the appearance was only skin-deep. Bacterium had been found alive and growing in all but the least hospitable places. The surrounding seas were rich with nutrients and teemed with life.

Both papers argued that in the planetary scheme of things, Antarctica was a fundamental regulatory subsystem of the global cybernetic whole. In other words, the continent had evolved into an essential temperature regulation mechanism. Without it, the Earth would have already jumped to a higher temperature equilibrium state. Perhaps still below the boiling point of water, but certainly above the tolerance levels of humans and most other land-based mammals. This was complex—the planetary temperature—regulatory system, integrating not only the southern continent, but the oceans as well. Circulation and feedback loops involving the atmosphere were other key elements, but Antarctica, in a sense, drove it all, as the great "heat sink" intrinsic to the planetary cooling system. Humans, so preoccupied with heating things up, had failed for the most part to recognize that Gaian systems involved mitigating Sol's tendency to heat up a biological system one byproduct of which was a dangerous greenhouse gas called carbon dioxide.

Antarctica's influences had extended far beyond the understanding of Enlightenment science, and only recently had the holistic study of geophysiology uncovered the depth that "all things are interconnected"—especially when it comes to climatic control and Gaian regulatory processes. Fortunately, the system is robust, with

154

ample parallel and redundant feedback loops. However, humans have been degrading those, one after another. And the Antarctic, as a relatively fragile complex of systems, is in trouble, according to geophysiology. In trouble in Gaian terms—cut off from its ability to naturally recreate cyclical ice cycles to the north.

For the last two million years, Gaia has become dependent on 100,000-year cycles of ice ages. While humans opportunistically evolved a technological civilization during a warm period, the norm was 5-10° cooler. 90,000 years of ice followed regularly by a 15-20,000 year interglacial period. Ice ages served as important periods of mineral and nutrient transport to the middle and low latitudes when overall biomass production was at a maximum. Geophysiologists had discovered that the relationship between Earth's temperature, carbon dioxide production, and solar radiation was also tied to two other systems: ocean morphology (current patterns) and hemispheric albedo—the reflectivity of clouds and ice sheets. Scientists for a long time had assumed that the Antarctic ice cover was a result of a cooling climate cycle. It was beginning to look to geophysiologists like the Antarctic controlled the cycles!

That was where the two papers diverged. One argued fairly forcefully that the cycles were extrinsic and related to the orbital forcing (planetary orbital eccentricities and wobble). The other argued that intrinsic forces such as volcanism and carbon dioxide cycles could just as easily tip the balance to a new ice age. In the end, Karen was overwhelmed and didn't know what to think. However, the uncertainties made her very nervous.

Leah and Jake were hungry again, too. They were cuffed to their bunks and except for some soda crackers and water bottles had nothing to eat since their arrival. Some crewmember looked in on them from time-to-time, but no one spoke to them.

Leah was quiet and still mulling over what Jake said many fitful hours before. She slept on and off since she and Jake were allowed to change clothes. They were moved to new, clean bunks in what seemed to be an officer's room, with its own desk and drawers. The lights were off and they couldn't see much. Jake tried to reach the drawers; but he was handcuffed too close to the far wall. Exhausted he eventually gave up. He then fell into a deep sleep and was snoring. She could almost feel his heat in the bunk above. The drumming of the engines and the constant vibration—she adjusted to those quickly.

The tightness in her chest and a sense of claustrophobia had grown over the hours. It was now a palpable terror, but she worked up a frenzy of rationalizations and responses to her fear. She was calm—terrorized, but calm. It had a lot to do with her loss of control.

She had absolutely no idea what time it was. No idea where she was, where she was going or why this was happening. The "why" of it all really ate at her…This business of Jake's closet eco-radicalism, her ignorance of Jake and his past; and now, the drugs and kidnapping; what the hell was going on? Her wrist hurt where the steel cuffs pressed into her flesh and she was getting a cramp in her arm from the awkward position. It wasn't particularly a lot of information to assimilate, but there were only questions, no answers. As a person who had a high level of need for order and control, she was at a loss. That probably was the very worst of it, she thought to herself. The smoothly drumming of the engines put her back to sleep again. This time, at least, she was once more in control of her dreams.

"The Captain is ready to see you." The First Mate had returned, she switched on the light and began to unlock the hand restraints. "There is a head with a wash basin immediately across the corridor. After you have both washed, the woman outside will escort you to the galley." She left the room and said to someone out of sight to "watch out."

Jake eased himself up and very slowly off the upper bunk. Leah helped him get his feet onto the ladder and to get down. He hugged her with a sense of desperation. She loved him back, with just a bit of reserve. She wasn't quite sure about him anymore and he smelled bad. She did feel sorry for him. He was humiliated and it showed. Arm-in-arm they stumbled out into the narrow corridor and saw a young blonde woman in coveralls. She held what looked like a taser stun gun and she was not smiling. Leah opened the door to the head and said, "You go ahead first."

Jake just looked at her, but went ahead.

She steadied herself against the wall. It did feel good to stand, even though she felt weak.

"Hi," she offered to her guard.

The woman responded. "I am not your friend, so don't fuck with me."

"Right." Leah didn't see any point of striking up conversation either. Jake only took a few minutes and she traded places with him. He repeated her attempt at dialogue, to which the guard repeated herself exactly. Listening through the hatch, Leah decided that it was a practiced phrase, or the woman used it regularly. That was a sobering thought.

"My name is Bee, follow me. Time to meet the captain." Leah's first impression was that Bee's name didn't have anything to do with honey. After seeing the young woman's hair in various kinds of lighting, she decided it might be for the honey blonde hair. Leah would not ask.

Leah and Jake followed her down the corridor, through a hatch, and then past an area with bunks and lockers. A glance ahead showed Bee with her stinger held high, a not too subtle reminder. She had only briefly, casually looked back at them as they made their way through the ship. They walked through another hatch and into the kitchen and galley. Leah gasped because it was so large—relative to what she had been expecting. The decor was hardly what she expected either.

The port wall was covered in a large mural, a rain forest scene teeming with large insects and wild animals. The dominant colors were deep green and blue colors picked up by accents all over the room. She had actually been in a submarine in some museum exhibition as a child. The colors had been drab and neutral. The colors—she was just realizing—throughout the whole submarine were bright and primary. The galley was a blaze of brilliant earth and sky colors. She noticed that Jake was staring at the wall with his mouth open.

The sight of the captain and his retinue coming out of the galley itself brought them up quickly. Each had a mug in their hands.

The First Mate called out cheerfully, "Tea or coffee? There's vegetable soup for you if you'd like, too."

They both requested coffee as Bee led them over to the far end of the dining area.

"Milk, sugar?"

They both drank coffee black.

Bee introduced them. "Captain, Professor Jake Meadows, Dr. Leah Wilson." Leah looked at her funny, as though seeing her for the first time. "Professor... Doctor... Derek M. Wilson, Captain of the *Nemo*."

"Please sit down." He did not offer them his hand. Myra produced their coffees. Leah drank hers appreciatively. It was strong, too.

"What is this all about?" asked Jake.

"Regrettably, you are prisoners of war. We will notify the International Red Cross at the earliest possible opportunity," said the Captain.

He was a small man, but was ruggedly handsome. He sported muttonchops and looked to be in his mid 30s, with jet-black hair with a slight graying in the temples. He was the only one of the crew who actually dressed in a uniform—a white suit, but without any rank insignia. He did wear a black plastic nametag with "Captain Wilson" printed on it. He was almost a parody of a cruise ship captain.

Leah and Jake both looked uncertain and then skeptical.

Leah shot back, "We would have to be in the military to be prisoners of war. You can't be serious."

"We are obviously very serious. You are both receiving federal funds from NCAR, is that not so?"

"So what?" Leah responded tersely.

"That makes you agents of the U.S. government and from our standpoint, enemies of Mother Earth."

Leah snorted loudly and started to speak again, but hesitated long enough for the captain to continue.

"We are Rainbow Warriors embarked on a war for the soul of the planet... We have been called eco-terrorists, eco-Nazis, or freedom fighters... Or we are compassionate saviors. Yours, in this case..." He seemed to pause for effect.

Leah just sucked on her coffee. Jake coughed into his hand. He did not sound good. Leah looked behind her to see that Bee had taken up position on a table behind them with the taser poised and ready.

"It was either bring you here," he pointed a short stubby finger at Leah, "or kill you. That simple."

Leah gave him a cold hard stare. "I beg your pardon."

"You were getting too close to the collapse sequence."

"For West Antarctica," he offered as if that would explain it all.

Leah still didn't get it.

"Antarctica. Sure, I study it, but what does that have to do with this?" Her voice was getting shrill.

"We are about to destroy it. If you put your mind to it, you could figure out how, unless our informants were wrong about you."

All of a sudden it began to sink in. These people were going to destroy the ice cap. Float the Ross into the sea.

"You are planning to blast the Ross Ice Shelf." Jake looked stunned.

"Not bad. Very close," cheered the Captain.

Leah took an immediate dislike to the man. She did not share his obvious humor about the situation.

"You might as well kill me and get it over with. I am not a willing prisoner," she said as Jake looked at her in alarm.

"What do you want with us?" he asked the Captain.

"That part is complicated in the long run. In the short run, the situation is a bit more straightforward. But to deal first with Dr. Wilson's death wish... We are planetary patriots, but we do not consider ourselves wanton murderers. Basically, you are hostages. Consider yourselves our prisoners for the time being. We will treat you with respect and to the extent that you wish to be integrated with the crew and our daily chores; you may be treated with the privileges accorded the crew. That part of it is up to you."

"Nor do you need to make a decision now. You will have plenty of time to consider your options."

"Options?" asked Leah sarcastically, "You won't get any cooperation from me!"

The Captain ignored her and spoke directly to Jake.

"We are headed for the South Pacific. As we get closer, you will learn more about our destination and the prospects for your future. We will be underway for approximately ten days. We are sailing during the day under battery power and at night under diesel power. I am telling you this because we will be operating under 12 hour shifts—when major meals are served, important daily events aboard a sub.

"You will be allowed the freedom of this deck only. The crew quarters, lounge, laundry room, mess hall, observatory, library, and showers are on this level. You may not, unless accompanied by the First Officer, or me, go up to the command level or below to the research and engine levels.

"You will be locked into your quarters at night and during the day if you fail to cooperate. By cooperate, I mean, share in the labor. We each have kitchen and KP duty. According to the Geneva

159

Convention—as prisoners of war— you are not obliged to do these things, but if you do not, you will be confined to your quarters."

"Just so that you know, we have successfully detonated our first little surprise, and I expect that if the U.S. Navy finds us, they will try to sink us. I have no illusions about your motivations, but I would appreciate not getting static from either of you. I will have the science officer go over the duties with you if and when you are ready."

At that point, Leah lunged for the captain and grabbed him around the neck, sending their coffee flying. She was immediately pulled away from him and knocked to the ground. Bee stunned her for good measure.

Pete did manage to sleep, in the captain's chair that unfolded into a sleeping platform. The chair was plush and very comfortable. After a couple of hours of restless sleep he finally drifted off to a light sleep. He had a normal cycle of REM sleep. In the beginning of his next light sleep cycle, the dream began. It began the same way as the archetypal dream he often had since his college days, a mythic goddess romance at the Oracle.

Pete often had the dream when upset and uncertain. He'd had it the first time after experimenting with sex and drugs during his freshman year. The dream was always comforting and in retrospect influenced, he thought, by the mythology that he learned in English literature classes and philosophy.

This dream began, as usual, in a mythic Aegean setting, on Crete. He was at the place of the Oracle—an artesian well, a holy spring that surfaced from deep in the earth. A rippling face emerged from beneath the pool. But this time it wasn't the same face or feeling from previous dreams. This is no Grecian goddess, but an African one. It was a pretty, attractive face with a colorful scarf wrapped around a towering pile of hair.

The surprise must have shown on his face, because the goddess laughed with abandon. Then she smiled brightly and the sun sparkled on the edges of her snow-white teeth.

"Child, you look surprised to see *Yemanja*. Perhaps you were expecting *Osun*, the god of the healing spring?"

Pete stammered, "No *Yemanja*, I was expecting another."

"Of course, you are bound to *Aida Wedo*, who you want to see here."

160

Pete wasn't sure who *Aida Wedo* was, but he didn't want to contradict the goddess, especially if he wanted to get the Oracle's advice.

But before he could formulate a question, *Yemanja* spoke again.

"I know you have many questions, child. The uncertainties you face at the moment present more questions than answers. That is the nature of the forces swirling around you. Be strong. Your task is to be strong and an anchor for the warrior woman."

"So you know about her?"

"Of course, child. She is the *ti bon ange* of *Shango*. She is trying to save the world, as you are the *ti bon ange* of *Aida Wedo*. You must look over her."

"But I don't understand."

"In time, you may... or may not. There is no destiny in that. Tonight, I must leave you with a riddle: What goes up that must come down?"

She looked back into his face and the shimmering of the water seemed to slowly dissolve her face. As the face faded from view, another voice could be heard in the background, a high-pitched male voice.

"*Yemanja*, don't play with his head! Mr. Pete, she's no Oracle, just a messenger. There is no answer—only enigma."

Then the dream faded into a deep stage-four sleep, where Pete's fatigue took him for recharging.

Some hours later, Pete awoke to find the blankets around his ankles and the cold penetrating his bones. He shivered and pulled up the covers. Raising the window shade, he looked out the window—but could only see ocean below. Down came the curtain and back came sleep again. The goddess' laughing face haunted him even as he drifted through layers of consciousness. He let his mind drift back to his days at MSU and the times he'd basically buried over the past few years. Those memories seemed to interest certain people, so perhaps he'd better try to reconstruct some of them. Many were too painful. Talk about enigma. Maybe that's why they'd been easy to wall off, to put in small box, to bury in his subconscious. They hadn't been all bad, either. Just, well, disturbing.

Maybe that was also why his giving in to being a stoolie for the FBI hadn't bothered him much, a logical capitulation to his embarrassment and shame at ever having been mixed up with that green scum who obviously had no compunction about killing innocent people. Or worse…. The second voice jerked him back from sleep again—in one of those reflexive jerks his body often made while falling asleep. The disembodied voice repeated, "There is no answer, only enigma."

Pete slept again.

Dear Betsy,

We are heading east now at a good clip, sailing into the wind, tacking back and forth in long legs. Brad has developed a very relaxed cadence and the wind, waves, and weaving patterns are very soothing. We are obviously in the lee of some island. The more I sail, the more I am getting a feel for that. I brought the Micronesian wave maps, and even though they are not from any of these Polynesian islands, some of the patterns are recognizable at times. This morning we have a relatively calm ocean level with little wind chop—even with a good trade wind blowing today already—and these little ripples of waves crossing each other at an oblique angle. It sure feels like the lee of a good-sized island. There is nothing in sight—not even a cloud pattern on the horizon this early in the morning. But the charts show inhabited Raroia and Nihru a hundred miles north and scattered smaller islands even closer to the north.

The BBC reports overnight are not good. The events in Washington and even Antarctica seem pretty far away, but Brad is worried. The threat of tsunamis seems to have the Japanese disturbed and reports are that Hawai`i and Alaska are preparing for the worst. The official U.S. government position seems to be that there is no serious threat to coastal areas. More alarming is the report that U.S. allies are up in arms about U.S. travel and border restrictions. It's starting to sound very serious and scary. I am thinking maybe we'd best head for home, or port, but Brad thinks we should just stick to the plan and wait and see. We are safe on the open ocean he says. He's my practical engineer.

We'll have fresh fruit for a few more days and we have a ton of food, so I won't worry. I am keeping the distiller going and have pretty much kept the fresh water tanks topped off.

I spent part of last evening getting caught up on my card writing and will post them on Pitcairn next week.

There, Brad just tacked back to the southeast. I think I can see an island... Back in a minute...

162

Betsy, you wouldn't believe what just happened! What I thought was an island was a huge flock of birds! At first I thought that we saw a rocky shoal come up, but all of a sudden this huge black spot on the water, rose up, and then fragmented into thousands upon thousands of birds! I've never seen anything like it. And then, as we got closer, they settled back down and continued whatever it was that they were doing. I thought at first that maybe it was a reed island or some collection of flotsam that you sometimes come across.

Brad said they are following a school of tuna. It must have been one mother of a school, too, because suddenly we were in the midst of them and there were literally tens of thousands of sea birds. They were really interested in the fish below and seemed to be landing and then darting back into the air. Sometimes they appeared to have small bits of food, but clearly no tuna. Brad seems to think that the tuna school must have been feeding on a smaller school of something, like anchovy. He said it was the biggest school he'd ever seen. They were actually banging up against the sides and bottom of the boat as we passed over them. It was quite an experience. You could see the iridescent tuna near the surface-many of them four and five feet long. They were monsters.

Brad, who would usually have pulled out a fishing pole, just stared at the spectacle. They were vibrating the boat's fiberglass shell with the impacts of their bodies. And then as quickly as it began it was over. A few birds lingered up over the sails—coasting on the trade winds—but were gone in a few minutes. Brad and I looked at each other in awe. "Looks like some kind of Tahitian shorebird. Member of the tern family maybe... We must be near land," he said. Then we both said simultaneously that we should have grabbed a camera. Then we laughed. Talk about one of those once-in-a-lifetime experiences! The colors of those fish were indescribable — it was like an iridescent rainbow of blues and greens, a brilliant array of sparkles like a thousand prisms displaying the blue end of the spectrum. It was absolutely hypnotic.

But the excitement has sure made me hungry—and what do you want to bet Brad is hungry, too! Talk to you later!

Pete opened the window shutter. They were flying high over the Pacific sometime in the mid-afternoon. He had mostly slept through the Panama stopover, although he had been vaguely aware of the banging of doors, loading of more equipment, the starting of the engines, and the takeoff. He was pretty wasted and told himself to take advantage of the peace and quiet that he felt. This was the quiet before the storm.

His head hurt like hell, and he took a couple more aspirin with some cold leftover coffee. He pushed his seat forward and tried to get up, but stumbled and had to catch himself by grabbing the armrest. "Whoa!" he said to himself and then shook his head, also a mistake. He dragged herself into the small bathroom and was immediately grateful to the software folks for their luxurious allowances. His eyes fell on a familiar, but unexpected sight—one of his gym bags that lay on the counter top just outside the bathroom. A dawning recognition was followed by an involuntary series of motions that unzipped and opened the bag. He pulled out some of his own underwear—which must have come from his house in Phoenix. A shiver ran through him as he realized that FBI agents had been through all his drawers and closets, but then was gratified that he had left a clean drawer of underwear. He put on briefs and then put back on the corporate overalls, which were just fine for now and comfortable on the plane. His head hurt too much to figure out where all his other clothes were and to coordinate colors.

He washed his face and found his shaving kit—also part of the contents of the gym bag—and slowly shaved and washed his hair in the sink and then started to feel human again. He drained the cold coffee and then brushed his teeth and inspected himself in the mirror. The bags under his eyes were not going away, but who would care on this flight? He took a deep breath and stood up straight. All right, he told himself, "attitude!" He smiled back at the reflection, even laughed a small laugh at the absurdity of his situation, and prepared to go find his captors.

Pete tried the door and found it unlocked. A wave of dizziness came and went as he headed down the hallway to the conference room. He wasn't particularly surprised to find agent Minh sorting though piles of documents.

"Good afternoon, Mr. Wilde," he said without looking up.

"Good afternoon," Pete returned.

"I took the liberty of ordering you some breakfast," he pointed at a tray of food covered with a silver cover. "It should still be warm, but there's a microwave over there behind you." Pete turned to check out the small counter area, which was covered with cardboard filing boxes.

"And the coffee is still blistering hot. Help yourself."

"How did you know?" He pointed at the food.

"I'm your shadow, remember?" He was obviously going to be obtuse and Pete decided once again that he wouldn't give Minh the satisfaction.

"Whatever," he replied noncommittally. His attention turned to the food, which was still quite hot. He absolutely loved pancakes, and these were as good as if they had been hot off the griddle. The syrup was hot too. Good Vermont maple syrup. He devoured the sausages too; they were delicious. He hardly stopped to breathe.

"Hungry are we? You know it isn't good to eat so fast."

Pete ignored him. He slowed down after realizing that he had been wolfing down the food as if it were his last meal. He helped himself to coffee and after a few more mouthfuls started to get curious about what Minh was doing. Pete asked.

"I'm doing our job," he retorted. Then Agent St. Cloud's comments from the night before began to sink in. She actually had been serious about having him help. Slowly, as the sugars and nutrients started feeding his brain cells, Pete's mental gears went into action.

An hour later, Karen poked her head in the room and cleared her throat. Pete and the young FBI agent were well underway putting the various files, documents, and pictures in order. She raised her eyebrow at Agent Minh.

"Ready yet to tell me what we have here?"

"Aye aye, sir. We probably can have this presentable within the hour."

"Great, I'm about to start a conference call with the White House and we can brief each other when I'm done." She turned to leave and the caught herself. She looked at Pete carefully and asked, "Get anything to eat Mr. Wilde?"

"Thanks, yes, my compliments to the chef. Does he go with us to Antarctica, too?"

"As a matter of fact, yes. He's a Special Forces lieutenant, a Steven Segal type. Damn good Cajun cuisine, I'm told."

His look of disbelief made her laugh. That simple act actually made her feel good for the first time all day. Karen sensed there was more going on here, a certain attraction she felt to the news anchor, even though he looked like hell. He was quite pretty, she thought and smiled to herself. She had been so distracted earlier that she hadn't really noticed. He had just been one more problem. Now she began to wonder if she had misjudged the situation. She realized that having him around might make this a much more pleasant crisis; but, her appointment with Washington stole back her attention.

Pete said, "This is surreal." He laughed back at her.

"There's a lot of that going around, brother. You two keep at it." She tried to turn to go, but resisted. Yes, it was the slight dimples that got to her. Hmmm.

"How did you sleep? You look like hell."

He smiled back. "Oh thanks. Being in prison does that to you," he said and then realized he was flirting with her.

"The truth is I had strange dreams."

"I wouldn't wonder. And I'd love to hear them, but Washington is on the line waiting." Now she did turn and took a step through the door.

"See you *Loa*," Pete said, making a pun about his dream without thinking.

Karen whirled around and stared at him.

"What did you say?"

"I said see you later. Sorry." Pete's face reddened.

"No you didn't. You said the word '*Loa*.'"

"Okay."

"Why?"

"I had a strange dream about voodoo gods. It didn't make any sense, but I can still remember a lot of it."

The color drained from Karen's face as fast as Pete's blushed.

"Brian, get him a piece of paper. Mr. Wilde, this may sound strange, too, but I'd like you to write down as much of it as you can remember."

"Okay, but I don't understand…"

Karen was already gone.

This was no ordinary Nuclear Threat Task Force meeting. It was a National Security Council meeting if she'd ever seen one, so Karen took a deep breath. She was sitting before a rather large camera and set of built-in monitors in a small conference room in the forward section of the plane. The secure communications setup was one reason the plane had been borrowed by the FBI. The communications officer placed a lightweight headset and microphone over her head and then pointed out the volume control under the monitor.

"Push-to-talk is the nominal mode, so to engage the microphone push the green button here until it turns red. That is best when you are giving a report. When you are off the air temporarily, like in a discussion, you can switch to 'voice activation.' Got it?"

"Push here to talk; voice activation here; volume here."

Karen nodded and set her demeanor. She had a little mantra: "Time to report, time to sound knowledgeable." She didn't really know much more than yesterday. That comment about the *Loa* had rattled her. It was too bizarre.

The monitor showed the cabinet room and the Secretary of State and the UN Ambassador were arguing softly, but intensely. She saw her own face with two others in the monitors in the center of the room across from the president's seat. He wasn't there yet. Who were the other two remote participants? It was hard to make out.

The president came into the room quickly followed by a number of people. Everyone stood up and the president motioned everyone to sit back down.

"As I call this meeting of the NSC to order, I'd like to start by acknowledging three remote participants..." An aide gave him a sheet of paper. "Dr. Gerald West, the director of the National Center for Atmospheric Research; Navy Commander Randy Johnson, Navy liaison at McMurdo Station; and, Karen St. Cloud of the FBI joining us from somewhere over South America. I invite them to join the conversation at any point, although I do have some specific questions for each of them."

He motioned to one of his aides, and the young woman began passing out folders. He continued. "The agenda today basically revolves around two or three points, I believe. The first is the attempt to locate and disarm the remaining nuclear weapons in Antarctica; second, the broader issue of international involvement; and, perhaps the most critical problem of all: damage control, public and political."

"Dr. West, I think I'd like to hear from you first. I have asked you to coordinate with the folks in NOAA, NASA, and USGS to give us the best scientific data on this crisis. What can you report?"

"Mr. President, logistically we are in good shape here in Boulder. We have dedicated lines both to JPL in Pasadena and to the folks at UCLA for the seismic data links. We still have some trouble getting high-speed links to interface with the Space Command up at Cheyenne Mountain, and a similar problem with NOAA and Woods Hole, but the Colorado National Guard is setting up some microwave relays. That is the good news. We have also been linked to the NFS/Antarctica computer net; there the news is more troublesome."

The president looked over at the other monitor, "Mr. Johnson, what's going on?"

"Scientists here at McMurdo and at Cape Darnley have been analyzing seismic data following the explosion. We have a sophisticated array of seismic sensors across the continent and computer software here at McMurdo that is working to integrate data from a number of different research stations down here. The Cape Darnley station monitors ice flow at nearly two dozen sites across the Lambert Glacier and the Amery Ice Shelf and the readings from these various stations are troubling."

"What do you mean troubling?" The president asked impatiently. "Please get to the point."

"Sir, the first issue is the aftershocks. Nuclear explosions, even those carried out deep underground, rarely produce aftershocks. We have been recording repetitive aftershocks, earthquakes in other words, in the 2 to 3 point range on the Richter scale. The peculiarity goes even further, because the aftershocks appear to be propagating in a northern direction away from the original detonation.

There are now small swarms of aftershocks where the epicenter is correlated with movement of the ice shelf. About half of the motion sensors show that the ice movement has accelerated up to an order of magnitude in the past two hours. In real terms, the usual flow is about a meter an hour in the active central regions of the Amery. It is now about ten meters an hour."

"So, what does this mean?" asked the president, obviously not happy about the report and maybe even frustrated.

West answered from Colorado. "Sir, it looks the blast has accelerated the ice flow. The trouble is that this does not follow the assumptions of known physics. Actually, the energy release of the nuclear weapon should not be enough to move that amount of ice. The mass of the ice shelf is calculated to weigh as much as the entire Catskill Mountains—there is no way a small tactical nuclear weapon could budge it. The earthquake swarms argue for some kind of resonance. You might think of it as a sympathetic response. If the ice sheet is considered to be a plastic object, perhaps the vibrations unleashed by the weapon have caused it to wiggle, not exactly like Jello, but somewhat like a stiff plastic." He looked happy with his metaphor. He president looked at him as if he was crazy.

"So what is the big deal?" The president looked perturbed.

"There is the hint that the explosion may cause the Amery Ice Shelf to collapse, or even worse, take some of the Lambert Glacier with it. Such a collapse would liberate more energy than a hundred thousand bombs the size of the one that exploded today. There will be severe tsunamis in the Indian Ocean. Any ships at harbor in the Indian Ocean should head for open waters."

"How can this be happening?" His voice cracked and the president sounded almost hysterical. He bowed his head, hard in thought. There was a ten second silence in the room as he gathered his thoughts.

"Make this an international effort." He looked at the Secretary of State and the UN Ambassador. "Get to Geneva and get to work with our allies. We are now in over our heads gentlemen, and need help."

"Agent St. Cloud, you are to work with the Navy and the Argentines to organize a search for the terrorists and the weapons. Under the Antarctic Treaty, this will be a civilian-led operation under FBI jurisdiction. The Navy and armed forces of Chile and Britain will be participating with some logistical and supply support. You will work cooperatively with the Argentine Intelligence Service, and report daily to me or FBI Director Beal."

"Have you anything to report?"

Karen took a deep breath, pushed the microphone button, and plunged ahead.

"We are still collating information on the EPG* leadership, completing psychological profiles, and processing material from the raids of the last 48 hours. We'll have a more complete report later today. The team is either on this flight or scheduled to meet us in 24 hours once we are on the ground in Antarctica."

"Fine, Agent St. Cloud. Thanks. You are excused to go back to work. Commander Johnson, stay in touch with St. Cloud and keep her in the loop. You and Dr. West may break off now also. Thank you." Karen saw the other two images blink-out. As her image lingered, she watched the president watch her back. There was an eerie silence as the president just stared at her, and then she blinked out, too.

Sandi and Raul were ushered into "the mayor's" office. Jordi Hoffman greeted them. He was a tall wiry blond man with deep blue eyes. Graying in the temples, he had weathered skin that made him look ten years older than his mid-50s. Sandi's background report on him had been an interesting read. The administrative head of Chile's sprawling General Bernardo O'Higgins base, Hoffman got his start as an executive in Chile's export industry before being tapped as a trade negotiator and then Chile's UN Ambassador under the last center-left government. But instead of going back into business, Hoffman had somehow wrangled this post in Antarctica. Chile once had great plans for the economic exploitation of this part of the world, but was now satisfied with a serious quasi-military presence and a lucrative and growing tourist industry.

The base itself had grown to a permanent 2,000 year-round population, which expanded to over 12,000 during summer, of mainly tourists and some transiting scientists. The base also had grown thanks to the support of the USA's National Science Foundation that had invested hundreds of thousands of dollars in airport modernization, refueling, and shipping infrastructure. Much of the development was tied to the rebuilding of the new US South Pole station. His connections from his days in New York and Washington had paid off. Having earned a reputation for VIP introductions to Graham Land and the Antarctic continent, he also knew Sandi Gusman's father well from his days as a diplomat. He shook hands with each.

"I knew your father, Detective Gusman. He was a good man and always a pleasure to work with. I am truly sorry to hear of his death."

"Thank you, sir." Sandi smiled. She waited an appropriate two seconds and filled the silence with a comment. "That is an incredible view."

"One of the perks of my office," He pointed out the large triple-paned windows at a rocky outcropping in the distance. "This is the closest point in the settlement to the penguin rookery. I am indeed lucky." He snatched a pair of binoculars and offered them to Sandi while turning to continue to talk to Raul.

"Find some time to explore the beauty of this place while you are getting acclimated."

Raul shook his head and said; "I doubt we will have time for that, Ambassador Hoffman, under the circumstances..." He finished his sentence uncertainly, not knowing how much the Mayor of General Bernardo O'Higgins Base actually knew.

The mayor nodded knowingly, and straightened him out. "Yes, I have been briefed by the Americans and understand not only the urgency, but also... shall we say, the delicacy, of the matter."

Sandi was still enraptured by the window. Raul came up next to her and she turned over the field glasses to him. The mayor continued.

"Detectives, I have cleared out an office down the hallway next to the communications office. It should be large enough for a command center, but I will make additional space available as necessary. Fortunately, the warm weather will make getting around easier, but we are also full to the gills with tourists now. The crisis does mean we are sending people north as quickly as possible and turning groups back. In a day or two we should also be up to our necks in gringos and Limeys." He caught himself.

"My apologies, Detective Gusman," Hoffman had obviously known either about Sandi's British mother or of her birth in London while her father had been there on assignment.

"No offense taken... Remember the Malvinas!" She said clearly tongue-in-cheek. She'd developed a fairly thick skin growing up after the war with England, subjected to considerable taunting in school. Nevertheless, she rarely allowed her pedigree to cause her regret for being born on foreign soil. Her good looks and bilingualism helped her maintain an exotic air.

The mayor's continued discourse brought her back to attention.

"You have complete run of the base and will carry my authority. Furthermore, if there is anything I can do personally to help, just ask. We will be making helicopters and planes available to you. I will have the transportation liaison meet with you as soon as he's available. We are currently lengthening the airstrip so he's out on the peninsula."

"You will be housed at the Officer's Club, a reasonably comfortable barracks about four city blocks away. I regret it is not closer to this building, but it is the best we can do at this point. I can have food brought up here though." They were on the third floor of a large three-storied cinderblock building.

"That's fine." Raul and Sandi both said at once.

"I assume the Americans will want to visit the former Hungarian research site. Maria, my assistant, will be at your disposal while you get organized. She knows everyone and everything there is to know about this base and coordinating with the other Antarctic stations."

"You might want to find your rooms and grab a meal at the Officer's Club. I would like to have you join me in about two hours for a joint telephone conference call with all of the various station commanders—well, the more important ones. We will get an update from McMurdo and the Aussies on the Lambert Glacier and Amery Ice Shelf situation."

They both gave out puzzled looks, so he added, "The ice sheet is breaking away from the continent. We are also getting some unusual seismic readings... As I say, we will learn more in two hours. Back here, then?" It was more of an order than a question.

He introduced them to Maria and went back to work. If they had had any questions about how they were going to set about establishing a mega-sized investigation in one of the most hostile places on earth, Maria began to put them at ease. Not only was she talkative, she also was a fountain of knowledge and seemed to anticipate most of their questions. She showed them their office space, as technicians were already busy at work bringing in boxes of computers and communications equipment. She also indicated that a suite of offices across the hall was being cleaned out for the American FBI's usage.

Within five minutes, Maria was ushering them into a large van that whisked them to the Officer's Club. A young soldier had joined them who helped with their bags. They were issued room keys and towels at the front desk and take-charge Maria continued her tour by pointing out the amenities of the Club—the small 24 hour bar and grill, lavish entertainment room, swimming pool!, gym, and self-service laundry. She added hastily, that if they needed laundry service or toiletries—whatever—that she would see to it. The young soldier—the name embroidered on his breast said Lopez—Maria called him Juan—nodded. He was their orderly, apparently.

After showing them rooms, which shared a communal bathroom, they split a sandwich. Maria explained: that she needed some time to make further arrangements for them and that visitors and first-time scientists and researchers normally received an orientation briefing from station staff. Maria said that she would arrange one for them after lunch and a tour of the transportation sheds and logistics center. She promised them a chance to meet later in the day with the weather and communications department heads.

As she walked the two into the grill, Maria became very serious.

"Most important is your outfitting." She frowned and actually stopped talking for the first time in 20 minutes. She looked thoughtful and raised her left hand to show them she was missing part of her index finger. Then she rushed back into her stream of conversation.

"Small tiny mistakes here can have serious implications. Your clothing on the continent has been well designed and built after a century of trial and error. But errors in its use"—she stressed the word *use*—"can be disastrous, even fatal. I lost part of a finger because it stuck to a camera body during a late summer cold snap. You have to rethink your actions in a very unforgiving environment. You cannot take for granted many things that you do unconsciously up north down here—especially further south on the continent. Don't repeat my mistake."

"Mother Mary, what happened?" Sandi blurted out.

"Subzero metal sticks to bare flesh like super glue. One of my first years here, I made the mistake of trying to pick up a tourist's camera left on a shelf outside the hotel. Unfortunately, the camera was stuck to the shelf and I was stuck to it. Before my hand could get totally frostbitten I pulled free from the metal. Guess which gave first? I had to have the first knuckle amputated. They would have sent me to the mainland but I recovered quickly." She smiled.

"They were already dependent on me." Then she let out one of the most contagious laughs either of them ever heard.

Soberly, she pointed at the gun in Sandi's holster.

"From now on, put cotton gloves between you and your friend there."

Their early afternoon was spent digesting a greasy chorizo sandwich made with tasty, fresh sour dough bread. Meanwhile, Raul and Sandi attended a thorough introduction to Antarctic clothing, from head to toe. Sandi was surprised that except for the innermost layer of underwear, everything was supposed to be a loose fit. They were first outfitted with extremely comfortable white Lycra underwear—and a sports bra for her. Lycra was among the few newer developments in the basic gear; the US Navy had perfected all the other clothing components years before. The basic philosophy underlying the ensemble was to trap layers of air between the outermost layers and the skin. The human body radiates enough heat to maintain temperature equilibrium if the effective insulating can trap that heat layers of air. The outer layer cuts the coldest blasts of heat-robbing wind, but still has to be porous enough to breathe, to release perspiration.

The tutorial was so matter-of-fact that Sandi lost any self-consciousness about standing around only in her knickers. They were quickly instructed in the use of the pants and coat layers, and gloves. Their boots, surprisingly, were made of one piece. They were massive and solid compared to the upper layers. Two layers of wool socks were fitted snugly into large leather boots that they were told contained six separate layers of insulation. Lastly, they were given goggles and ski masks for extreme conditions. By the end of the survival lesson, Sandi was both tired and exhilarated at the same time. Their gear was stored in a set of lockers back in the Officer's Club and then they were escorted back to the base HQ.

Sandi's adrenalin rush waned at about the same time that they were served espresso and tea in a large conference room near their temporary office. They were introduced to nearly a dozen scientists, army officers, and administrators. Technicians were working on video monitors, computers, and audio gear and running sound checks and test patterns. A few more people trickled into the room right before Ambassador Hoffman entered with an aide. He nodded at the two of them while he began shuffling through a stack of papers in front of his spot at the head of a long conference table. At virtually the same moment four video monitors in the corner came to life showing similar scenes in other places. A large projection screen flipped from a test pattern to a shot of Hoffman. He looked up as a technician walked up behind him and held up a white piece of cardboard in front of his face. Hoffman looked oblivious as though this was routine for him.

Another tech, this one in the corner across from them with a headset on raised his arm and spoke toward the Ambassador.

"Sir, we are thirty seconds from airtime. Could you give us a sound check?" The Ambassador obliged. Then the room got quiet. The tech counted down with his fingers from ten.

"This is Commander Johnson at McMurdo Base Antarctica. Under the terms of Article 1 of the UN Charter and Article 4 of the Antarctic Treaty, I am calling this Extraordinary Session of the Antarctic Signatories to order. Representing Chile is Ambassador Hoffman, Great Britain by Dr. Lewis Mott, and Australia by Dr. Charles Waverly. I represent the United States of America. We have been granted extraordinary authority by the Security Council under Resolution 74-17 passed just a few hours ago in Geneva. Copies have been made available to all participants."

Sandi had not yet looked at the pile of documents in front of her, but her eyes were now drawn to the top sheet with a UN logo on it. It was short and to the point, which was what Johnson went on to note.

"Very simply, Treaty principals have been granted authority to protect the Antarctic Treaty area, the Southern Ocean, and human life by whatever means necessary from threats to same by the EPG* terrorists. Coordination of the overall effort is delegated to the representatives of the American FBI and the Argentine Federal Police. The American designee is Special Agent Karen St. Cloud."

One of the small monitors showed a clean-cut young woman raise her hand in acknowledgement, but didn't say anything.

"Argentine designees are Federal Agents Raul Dias and Sandi Gusman, who will have authority for all ground operations." They also waved their hands at the cameras.

"I am U.S. Navy Commander Johnson and will be serving as military liaison with the U.S., British, Australian, Chilean, and Argentine navies in the Southern Ocean until Admiral Brown arrives from Washington."

"First item on the agenda is the status of the Amery Ice Shelf and the fallout from the blast this morning. Dr. Waverly, please?"

Waverly cleared his voice and looked uncomfortable in front of the camera. His image was low quality and jerky, using a low-bandwidth connection. The solar storm was interfering with many satellite connections. It became even more obvious when he spoke. His movements lagged his audio.

"Seismic activity in the area is still more active than normal. By that, I mean that we normally have earthquakes from under Mount Menzies, an active volcano to the south of the Lambert Glacier. We are currently recording micro tremors that we believe are from the magma chamber there, which lies about 2 miles below the surface. There have also been cyclical tremors that would be defined as aftershocks from the explosion that seem to be coming from along the eastern edge of the Amery Ice Shelf. The shocks are slowly gaining in intensity, too, but fortunately not on a logarithmic scale like the ice movement.

"Most alarming is the movement of the Amery Ice itself. Our laser array in the central glacier area indicates that the rate of motion is now approximately 100 meters per day, or two orders of magnitude greater than normal. However, the most disturbing part is the rate of growth is itself increasing. Is seems to be doubling very two hours at the present rate.

"According to one of the visiting glaciologists from Canada, there appears to be a surge phenomenon developing. She bases this theory on the so-called running glaciers that periodically advance at great speeds in some parts of the world—especially Alaska and the Yukon. These glaciers have been witnessed to travel as fast as 10 km per hour. While this has never been seen before in the Antarctic, additional evidence has come to our attention that confirms this threat.

"One of our team members here has been researching great whale songs in the McKenzie Bay. He has hydrophones placed at half-a-dozen locations near our station here as well as a few across the face of the Amery. One of the difficulties that he has at this time of year is the noise generated by calving icebergs and the crackle of the summer ice as it moves. It took some sophisticated audio filtering techniques for him to get rid of the noise so he could hear his whales.

"The point of this is that his whales have disappeared and the noise has worsened. The whale pods which are nearly always in Bay waters—they were here yesterday—are now gone. Our young scientist believes that the explosion scared them to deeper waters. The more interesting aspect of this is the correspondence between the sonic and the seismic activity. When he brought up the sound interference earlier, we thought there was no correlation. The noise, we believe generated as ice deforms or compresses in the glacier, seemed to come when the seismic abated. A few hours ago, we fed the seismic and sonic data into a computer and then ran a time-series comparison. To our surprise, the sound and the earthquakes are inversely correlated.

"The conclusion we have come to is that the Amery Ice Shelf is slipping out of position and is becoming a running glacier. The behavior of the shelf suggests that it is vibrating like a large plastic plate. The seismic and sonic energies appear to be resonating with each other, but at different frequencies. They are vibrating at two harmonics, according to the Canadian researcher.

"As is true for many Antarctic ice shelves, the majority of the Amery is grounded. For the non-scientists, that means that the shelf rests on the ground anywhere from 200 meters to 1500 meters below sea level. Only the lower one third of the Shelf floats above seawater. The consequence of this is that—at least this is the current theory— ice is contained behind the glacier like a large dam. Amery Ice Shelf is particularly interesting—one reason there are so many of us here at McKenzie and across the bay at Davis station to study it. Lambert Glacier and some of the other main feeder glaciers—Kreitzer glacier, for example—feed into the Amery at 500 meters above sea level. They are held back, we think, because of the large grounded 'footprint,' as it is called, of the Amery. We are concerned now because it appears that the Amery is losing its footing.

"Planes sent over the site of the explosion have brought back images which show that the crater from the explosion has basically vanished, or at least been replaced by a large fracture zone. We believe that the terrorists purposely planted the device exactly where it would have the greatest effect, at the glacier boundary. It is not a coincidence that the boundary is also a dynamic fault zone. Thus, various energies were brought to bear on a natural pressure point in the Lambert-Amery system. We could not have planned a better science experiment ourselves." He caught himself and dampened his growing enthusiasm.

"In other words, this is even more serious than we had first thought."

Ogun spoke to Abe as he was easing into slumber. After being awake nearly two straight days, his exhaustion was bone deep. *Ogun* spoke in a reverberating voice that seemed to fill the small cabin.

"Events are proceeding on schedule. *Freya* is awakening." Abe waited for more. The *Loa* was rarely cryptic—*Ogun* just seemed to love to talk.

"The window of opportunity is over the next 2 to 4 hours with a 90 percent probability of an eruption on the central west fracture zone. The fault zone lies over a magma pool of moderate pressure. Chance of an explosive eruption is about 50 percent less likely than a fluid basalt flow. The more explosive, the more quickly the shelf transformation will occur. But probabilities always make the outcome of this sort of event so exciting!" The god hummed a soft tune to himself. He loved Gilbert and Sullivan musicals and hummed intricate melodies.

Abe struggled to formulate a question in his mind.

"Did this sort of thing happen at the end of the last glacial cycle?"

"It is interesting that you should ask. From a Gaian perspective, the carbon cycle on Terra has been getting a bit tricky to regulate over the last four of five cycles. This coincides nicely with recent human evolution. We are beginning to think that ice cycles have tested your species' mettle.

"To answer your question, no. Solar instabilities were the catalyst the last few times around for the ice-carbon coupling, most probably. The local arm of the Milky Way passed through a density field of virtual particles—an area of high quantum frequencies. This boosted solar output on the order of 5 to 10 percent. That helped melt the West Antarctic. Lower salinity of the Gulf Stream slowed the deep ocean currents to a standstill over the span of a few decades. That's how the last ice age appears to have started."

"Enough lecture, thank you. So what happens next?"

"The forces that you have helped set into motion have an 80 percent probability of collapsing the Amery Ice Shelf into the South Indian Ocean. It will have a 50 percent probability of creating some rather large tsunamis along the entire Indian Ocean Basin. Cleanse the bowl of some the human infestation."

"Yes, yes, I know. We've been over that hundreds of times. What I meant was what happens next to us?"

"The captain is on the right heading. We continue at a 45° angle from the coast. This is one of the few parts of East Antarctica with such an extensive offshore continental shelf. So, we have to maximize the depth of water between the sub and the ocean bottom and at the same time hold a decent course towards Pitcairn. When the tsunami hits us we should feel some acceleration and deceleration at about half the speed we are currently moving. Your sonar crew will clearly hear the sound of the ice fractures along the bay/shelf boundary. They may be loud enough for the crew's ears to hear above the engine noise.

"The captain should be alerted to turn to 60° East-Northeast and throttle back to half speed until the shock wave passes."

"As you wish." Abe picked up the phone and gave the captain those orders. *Ogun* continued to hum softly a Broadway show tune.

Karen had the geologist on the phone for fifteen minutes. After hearing an update about the seismic data, she asked how serious the Amery Ice Shelf collapse could really be.

"Ice shelves and glaciers in Antarctica are dynamic, moving structures. We use more familiar analogies, or metaphors, to explain those dynamics. The ice and snow are not as static as we once believed. The most active ice flows are actually called ice streams and rivers. That has become a critically important perspective. Yet understanding Antarctic dynamics from a geological standpoint requires seeing a more static model of surface morphology. The geology of Antarctica is active, too. In fact, the tectonic migration of the continent to the polar area has had a significant impact on global climate over the last few million years. Yet, the Pacific Ring of Fire runs right through the middle of the continent, essentially defining the East and West.

"Even though the ice is moving, it also acts as a weight, pushing on the mantle and compressing the underlying rock. There are plate boundaries, fracture zones, and upwelling magma zones throughout the entire continent and concentrated along the Transantarctic Mountains. There is another level, not common knowledge, and that is the deep lithosphere convection and upwelling of heat. We are fairly sure that there has been a cycle of convection every million years or so which is overdue.

"Recall also that East Antarctica is almost entirely above sea level, covered in another couple of kilometers of ice. The West is largely ice grounded below sea level. The West has the most volcanism and tectonic action. There are sizeable areas that have magma pools not too far below the surface. These are no different,

179

mind you, than magma chambers under Yellowstone or Hawai'i's Volcano National Park.

"By contrast, the Antarctic highlands in the East are a relatively stable area with its constant shroud of ice. One of the few exceptions, of course, is the American Highland above the Amery that does have evidence of recent magma pooling. There is no recent evidence of volcanism, but we suspect that it is a significant factor in uplift caused by magma swelling. There's evidence also of greater heat convection to the surface because of recent glacial speeds increasing into the Lambert Glacier and the eastern front of the Amery."

"So, okay. Are you ready for the next metaphor? The dam metaphor?"

Karen said, "Yeah, we're doing fine. I'm following you, continue."

"The Amery Ice Shelf is mainly created by monolithic granite outcroppings several hundred meters below sea level. Most of the ice mass floats on seawater, but now backed up behind these undersea mountains. The granite extrusion is massive in its own right, a veritable mountain range that once was among the highest peaks on the continent. Now a subsided and highly eroded remnant, it nevertheless has resisted the grinding action of the moving ice more than surrounding rock. Due to this great resistance, this has helped create the Amery Ice Shelf in four ice cycles over roughly half a million years.

"Now above the lines of resistance is a highly inclined mass of ice. The upper end of the ice stream is fed down from the American Highland. It passes through what is called the Mawson Escarpment to the Lambert, the primary feeder. Then other ice streams, Krietzer and Polar Record, come off the Highlands.

"Cumulatively they weigh literally trillions of tons of ice and ground rock. The Amery is both blocked and precariously balanced on this granite remnant and the shelf as a whole is inclined more than any other ice shelf on the Eastern side of the continent." He paused.

Karen asked, "So the Amery teeters on the brink anyway. How does the current situation bear on its stability? The explosion was nowhere near the fulcrum."

"This is where the discussion goes past my area of competence," the scientist said cautiously. "I think the blockage may no longer be an issue if the conditions have changed significantly. It seems clear that the ice shelf has been unstable for some time and recent warming trends have accelerated the instability. That's the current scuttlebutt."

Karen asked, "There's something else you haven't told me."

"The current level of seismic activity is totally inconsistent with any nuclear testing we have ever done. The reason I bring this up is that I had a post-doc with Livermore Labs on nuclear explosion modeling. I have seen most of the historical telemetry and seismic records for hundreds of monitored explosions. The aftershocks and swarms we are seeing are many hundreds of times stronger than any we've ever seen. Today shocks are more like the signature of Mount St. Helens before it exploded. In other words, there is a possibility of a volcanic eruption that might make the ice shelf collapse look insignificant.

"If the shelf slips off the fulcrum and away from the bay, the magma chamber may swell even more, releasing more heat and speed up the glacial ice streams even more. We'd get a set of running glaciers coming off of the American Highland."

Karen didn't like the sound of that at all.

Pete and Karen sat facing each other. They had moved much of their gear into the conference room and he and Agent Minh had settled down at the end of the room's long table and had been listening in on the conversation.

Karen thanked the scientist for his time and asked him to call her if there were any significant changes in the telemetry. All three pulled off their headphones at the same time.

"Agent St. Cloud? Connect the dots for me. Why are you concerned about the ice more than the terrorists?"

She looked at him as if he was a little stupid, or maybe she was just tired and impatient.

"Well, it's pretty straightforward. This is our warning, our test. Even if this event unfolds the way Dr. Lamm just described it, then the same technique, applied to the Ross, could mean a real catastrophe. I don't know about it triggering ice ages, but your friends could make a hell of a mess of the shipping lanes for decades or maybe centuries to come. It may or may not change the climate, but I'd wager that there will be some impact on the weather."

"Mother Nature taking her course, huh?" Pete asked before he really considered what he said.

Karen rebuked him sharply. "That's a rationalization if I ever heard one."

He didn't reply immediately, but tilted his head and said quietly, "We are a part of Nature, you know. I am not condoning the violence. What if they are only accelerating the inevitable? Mother Nature is violent, after all."

Karen appeared to chew on that for a minute and shuffled some of the papers in front of her. The phone chirped and she picked it up. After listening and nodding for a couple times, she turned to them.

"We're landing shortly in Punta Arenas. The Powers That Be have abandoned any thought of having the super jumbo take us all the way. This is the most southerly landing strip that can handle this size plane—and pilot is nervous about this landing. We have Hercules transports fueled and ready to take us on."

"You both go ahead and get ready for landing."

Minh got up quickly and asked, "You need anything Karen?"

"No, I am doing just fine." She smiled, but it was more wan than she intended.

"Brian, go… just give me a few minutes with Mr. Wilde."

Minh didn't bat an eye and was out the cabin door in a flash. Karen looked hesitant. Pete could see that she was trying to put something into words. Her question caught him off guard.

"May I call you Peter?"

He smiled and shook his head.

"No. My friends call me Pete. Pete, is fine."

"Karen." She put out her hand. They shook hands and both released very slowly. There was a blue spark of static electricity as they let go.

"Strange, that brings me to the question about your dream. Tell me everything that you remember. And let's keep this between us for now?"

"Okay." He pulled a slip of paper out of his jumper pocket.

He recounted the dream from what he recorded earlier. And while he did, the imagery returned fairly clearly.

She raised her eyebrows when he told her the part about his charge to look after her. She frowned when he related that she was the only one who could save the world. She frowned more deeply when he mentioned *Shango* by name, but still didn't say a word.

Then he repeated the echoing message about the enigma. At that, she shook her head slightly. He stopped.

"Did you skip anything? Anything else?"

"Well, basically that was it, except for a specific message to you from *Yemanja*. It doesn't make any sense really, since it was in a dream, but she told me to tell you to 'wake up.'" He paused to wait for her response, but none came so he continued.

"Surely you can't take my dream seriously? I really am a serious reporter and not into any new age thinking, despite this funny dream."

"Pete, sometimes life is stranger than fiction." She was speaking slowly, deliberately. "I have been dreaming about *Shango* myself. How is it possible that our dreams could be so entangled?"

He could only shake his head in puzzlement.

The "fasten seatbelt" lights came on.

"Go strap yourself in... Enigma indeed."

It was a threshold event; a discontinuity. The volcano exploded and the ice shelf was suddenly pushed north. It tipped like a 4000 square-mile Frisbee and began sliding down the continental shelf. The initial surge released energy equivalent to 1000 Hiroshima bombs and then the volcano continued to fountain. It broke above the ice and shot another thousand feet in the air. It looked like some National Geographic pictures from Iceland. The volcano was the eye-catcher, but the really significant event was the earthquake—actually ice quake—that first absorbed the initial burst of energy and then released its own energy. The Cape Danlay seismographs registered a massive 10-point event on the Richter scale—one of the largest quakes ever recorded.

From the polar orbiting spy satellites, it didn't look like much at first, except for the volcano, movement of the ice sheet itself was at first imperceptible. The military intelligence folks were lucky to have a bird exactly overhead at the time of the Amery collapse, but the initial images were in the visual spectrum—nice for the eyes, but missing some information. The radar data that came through a bit later told the tale. After computer enhancement, it was clearly discernable by image comparison where the ice shelf had moved hundreds of feet in a matter of minutes—representing a mass movement of significant geologic force.

The tsunamis that now worked their way along the continental shelf were mute testimony to the energy released. They stirred up the bottom mud, but mainly deformed and fractured sea ice and made large icebergs literally ring like bells. The first large wave passed around the submarine and gave it a healthy push. Alarms rang out all over the ship but there was no major damage and things settled down quickly, the captain was directed back to the earlier northeastern heading.

Ogun sounded absolutely giddy, like a schoolboy.

"Now that's the ticket! We work well together don't you think?"

"I don't really know what to think. Actually, I think I am very tired."

"Now Abe, don't go sentimental on me—you knew this was going to be a tough job."

He didn't answer.

Ogun was indefatigable. "Oh, it is so sweet when things work right. Ya know... in spite of Murphy's Law and all?"

"I thought you were infallible."

"If I were, I sure wouldn't have needed you would I?"

A very smug minor god, he reckoned. "Why don't you leave me to my own thoughts for now?"

"Because I worry about you."

"It seems rather unlikely that a voice in my head would seriously worry about my being depressed if that same voice is partly responsible for destroying my world."

"To save it we must destroy it. We've only said that a thousand times."

"Maybe I'm getting tired of hearing it."

Then the *Loa* was gone. The humming trailed off as though going down a tunnel.

Just as Abe was falling to sleep, *Ogun* was back.

"Quick, tell the captain to turn the boat's heading again. Another wave of energy is coming."

Abe picked up the phone and made the call. The ship began to make its turn, but this time was caught by a worse surge. Abe was thrown to the floor. Alarms went off. He opened the door and stumbled into the passageway. The submarine lurched to the side as Abe lost his balance and cracked his head against the metal bulkhead.

The lights went out.

184

January 17
Tuesday

The Western Pacific Tsunami Centre (WPTC) located in the small town of Cairns, Australia had a relatively quiet night. Except for the excitement of the nuclear explosion in Antarctica early the night before, regional seismic activity had been nil. The staff had all gone home late so many were sleeping late. A skeleton crew of two staffed the computers and monitors. At midmorning, all hell broke loose. The first shock was a staggering 9.1 Richter earthquake—extrapolated and triangulated from sister stations in Fiji and Hawai`i. The epicenter was in Antarctica, but this was vastly different from the nuclear detonation in intensity and aftershocks.

Centre personnel straggled in after they were rousted by emergency calls. Then the second event registered on the seismometers. The second earthquake was stronger than the first, and was larger than anyone there had ever seen firsthand. It was an immense series of readjustments in the Earth's crust that peaked in a jolt of around 9.5 on the Richter. The Hawai`i Pacific Tsunami Center then recorded seismic readings even stronger than those from Australia and Fiji suggesting a very focused direction to the compression energy. Twenty minutes later the third major quake came and by then the WPTC Director had arrived and was on the phone with Honolulu. His second-in-command was waving another phone with South Africa on the line. It looked like the conditions were right for a tsunami in the Indian Ocean, potentially orders of magnitude larger than the tsunami earlier in the century.

The tsunami forecast team had quickly spread out huge maps of the Indian Ocean Basin over a large conference table. It looked like the closest part of Australia facing the incoming energy was ironically the least vulnerable with a rugged coastline and sparse population. Perth, Dongara, and Geraldton on the west were likely to see only minor coastal damage due to the angle of the approaching energy. The towns along Spenser Gulf in South Australia were more problematic. The director FAXed signed evacuation notifications to the Prime Minister's office in Canberra.

The director held an impromptu staff meeting after the third major earthquake. "Looks to be perhaps 7-8 hours to Western Australia and then another hour to Kangaroo Island, maybe 13-15 hours to Bangladesh, and somewhere in between for Padang. This looks like a possibly big hit on Sumatra. Ten hours. We need to post hourly reports to the Indian Ocean network. I want the network team to see to that and to alert all the affiliate stations. See if we can get the Civil Defense staff in South Australia on line, they may see the worst of it."

"As soon as there are any readings from the tide gauges at Heard and McDonald Islands please let me know. Also, can we get any current ocean radar telemetry for Southern India?"

There was a lull in the pandemonium in the room.

The satellite tech, Robinson, replied after a few seconds, "We have the TOPEX right now about 140 degrees east and 20 degrees south. Almost right on top of us here, so the angle's wrong. The South Indian Ocean is not in its observation footprint. About 60 minutes will put it over Heard—well, a few degrees off and then every 90 minutes it will be back with about a 5 degree drift to the west. However, there is a four-hour lag for data recovery. It was not designed as a real-time bird. The onboard computer collects data and downloads it six times a day. We usually get it time-delayed from Hawai`i, but are in the telemetry footprint ourselves about 8 hours out of every 24.

"Bottom line: we can get a four to five hour turnaround on sea height data from TOPEX. I can get the last download batch from Hawai`i and get you baselines for Heard and McDonald Islands."

"Do so," replied the director. "Get to work people, and I'll call another meeting over lunch. Helen?" He looked at his secretary who had been taking notes. "Better order us pizzas, love."

Heard and McDonald Islands were the most far-flung territories of Australia, nearly 3000 miles southwest of the continent and only 1000 miles north of Antarctica. Along with Cocos and Christmas Islands far to the north, these islands comprised Australia's territorial claims in the Indian Ocean. They were strategic claims. This is one reason for Australia's physical presence here in one of the most remote, forbidding parts of the world. Australia's weather station on McDonald had been manned continuously for seventy-some years-since the end of WWII. The ten men stationed there led a pretty lonely existence, one reason for the six-month rotations. The wind-swept island was treeless and except for some hearty woody bushes and lichen it was a 3 square mile barren basalt outcropping.

The men stayed mostly in the military Quonset huts and took their weather readings, watched movies, read paperbacks, played chess, and ate. Eating was a major focus of their lives. The cook was the most popular man at the station. The Navy always sent the best. They had learned the lesson decades before.

Situated smack in the middle of the West Wind Drift and the Southern Ocean Current, McDonald was routinely buffeted with gale-force winds and heavy seas. Today was no different from most. What made McDonald inviting at all was the small portage provided on the eastern lee side of the horseshoe-shaped island—a small natural harbor that stayed ice-free in winter served to protect the monthly supply ships. There were no ships in port today, however. The automated tide gauge sat in a housing at the end of a small pier on the north side of the small bay. The winds lashed the bay and the sun shone weakly through low clouds.

The massive ocean waves traveled a thousand miles without losing much strength. If anything, the interaction between the three large releases of energy had consolidated their frequency harmonics and their interaction with the Southern Ocean morphology produced a "super set" of three waves of equal amplitude. In other words, the earthquake and ice shelf collapse produced pulses of energy whose sum was greater than the parts. As they traveled across the open ocean, the slower early waves were followed by larger, faster waves that packed them all tightly together.

As the energy waves moved towards McDonald the ocean floor got shallower. The toe of the wave slowed as it encountered more resistance. The upper column of water continued to pile up. Traveling at 500 miles per hour in the open ocean, the wave now slowed to 50 and then to 30 mph as it dragged on the bottom. The peak of the wave rose higher and higher. The wave peaked at over a thousand feet and washed over the island in seconds. The weather station, tide gauge, and a rookery of penguins were all swept away.

Had anyone been outside the Quonset hut, they might have heard the roar of the 1100-foot wave as it crested over the hill. The gale-force winds were pretty stiff competition, but the roar would have only lasted a few seconds. None of the ten men in the weather station had time to know what hit them. McDonald was a big enough island to cause the wave to break, and it did, dumping a million gallons of water right on top of the station. The water receded and then repeated the 1000-foot-plus breaking wave twice more. After the water receded less than 10 minutes later, the island was literally scoured clean. Only the lichen remained with an occasional fish or some other displaced sea creature dying in the weak summer sun.

Punta Arenas (0610 AST)

Pete was essentially under house arrest—a surreal concept since he was in an airplane. It was bordering on cruel and unusual treatment, he thought morosely, as the air in the cabin was getting stale and malodorous. The current situation took him back to the beginning of the trip in San Francisco, although this time the plane was being unloaded. The same banging sounds continued for some time and he drifted off to sleep, only to be bumped awake again and again.

They refueled the monster plane in Santiago and took a chance that the big plane could land in Punta Arenas. The airstrip here was rather long, since it doubled as a military base, and the plane had landed. Only trouble was that the airstrip wasn't long enough after all and the relatively smooth landing was followed by a nasty deceleration and an even bigger lurch when the plane overshot the end of the runway and traveled another few hundred yards into a bog at the end of the field. No one was hurt, but the plane was stuck and they had been there for hours dealing with the logistics of transferring materiel to smaller airplanes. The Hercules—their Antarctic transportation—were taxied down to the end of the tarmac and Pete was unceremoniously locked into his stateroom again while the FBI team went about whatever it was they were doing to transfer gear and do FBI work. It wasn't made clear to him why he was being excluded this time.

He was too tired and jet lagged by this point to care.

The noise abated for a while and he slept.

He drifted into a sound sleep and the dream returned.

A disembodied voice softly repeated. "Enigmas inside enigmas. Enigmas outside enigmas…" His vision cleared and he was on the edge of the sacred grove of his imagined Delphi and now the trees took up the refrain, "Enigmas upon enigmas," they seemed to be softly saying. He felt the early summer sun on his face and felt like he was at home. This was his place of sanctuary.

Not in any hurry, he wandered past ancient stone foundations, tall clumps of grass beginning to yellow and smelled saffron on the air. He could hear a gurgling of the artesian springs ahead and the soft voices seemed to follow him down the path.

He came to the familiar spot where he had his discussion with his Greek goddesses, but the place was deserted and there were no faces appearing in the water. In fact, the waters rippled with the light breeze.

Pete felt so warm and mellow that he lay down in a sandy spot next to the circular pond and closed his eyes.

Time stood still for a moment, but suddenly a cold wind whipped across the pond. He sat up, startled. The trees suddenly made a crackling sound and their leaves turned quickly brown and then they began to fall with gusts of wind. Curiously, Pete observed that the leaves blew all around him but did not touch the water as though there were a force field pushing them on their way.

The trees became bare and the sky turned gray and overcast. Yet at the same time, light began to emanate from the pool as it had in the past. Instead of a face, the surface became glassy and a distinct image formed. The light was almost blinding, but it was actually a reflection from a snowscape that was suddenly in motion. He was drawn in to what only could be described as a birds-eye view of glaciers, icefalls, and mountains covered in snow. Pete had always been fascinated with Antarctica and had read many of the classics of exploration and avidly watched National Geographic specials… But this was beyond his wildest imagination. It was beautiful and terrifying at the same time.

The brightness resolved as his irises adjusted and he seemed to be suspended, flying over the incredibly varied landscape below. He had assumed there would be some uniformity to the continent, but was overwhelmed at the range of textures, and then the colors. There were not only the blues and whites that he expected, but reds and yellows in the algae blooms, awesome greens and darker effects made by the fractures and patterns of crystallization, freezing and refreezing. It blew his mind. It was so incredibly beautiful that he was overcome with emotion and realized that he was quietly crying.

"Enough," said a voice and the vision in the water slowed and then faded. He looked up to see that it was still summer and felt the warmth of the sun again on his back. The tears kept coming, but also slowly dried.

A new face dissolved into view in front of him on the water. It was another African face, but this one was almost lizard-like, humanoid, but with what appeared to be fine scales that had an iridescent quality.

"Yes, my young friend," said the heavily-accented persona, "I am the *Loa* Rainbow Spirit, *Aida Wedo*, your guardian angel."

Pete was still stunned and could hardly get his voice box to work, but managed, "Did you do that?"

"Yes, my child. It is a foreshadowing of a possible future ahead of you. But it will never again appear to you with such beauty. In fact, it may be your mortal undoing."

Pete seemed to consider that and waited for the spirit to speak.

"You are wise for such a young creature. I can see that in your eyes. It was humanity's good fortune that *Ogou Balanjo* predicted your role in this adventure and that *Yemanja* arranged your involvement. Delicious complication, you are. Mythic quality stuff."

Pete was confused, but kept his counsel.

"I know you have a curious mind and many questions, but the enigmas are not to be trifled with, so we can only give you riddles to unravel."

"The first riddle: What happened to the animal that once was prey, but who vanquished all its monsters?

"The second: What happened to the same animal when it began to prey on its own, on its animal friends, and its planet?

"The third: Who cares?

"The first answer is humans, right?" Pete relied.

"Oh you are quick! Mr. Smarty Pants. Don't be so quick to answer the third as the answer may surprise you."

Pete thought he'd be sarcastic. "Well, it sure isn't likely to be *Loa* that care, so it would have to be aliens."

Aida Wedo began to gently chuckle and then roared into laughter and tears began to run down her eyes. The pool began to ripple and then small waves formed as the laughter deepened and faded.

A loud knock on the door woke Pete and Agent Minh poked his head though the door. "Time to go. Collect your stuff, we're leaving for Antarctica."

Back at WPTC, the loss of signal from the tide gauges and automated Heard and McDonald weather stations was not good news. Nor was the failure of the McDonald team to respond to satellite telephone or radio queries. Nor was the timing. The time duration between the quakes and the time the satellite lost the Heard and McDonald telemetry was too short. The short interval meant one thing, that the ocean wave was a strong one. The faster the wave came, the greater the energy would be. At nearly 600 miles per hour, these were unquestionably killer waves.

Tsunami warnings had already gone out all along the western and southern coasts, and for all of Tasmania. Advisories have been sent out to the entire network, but also to senior government ministries in New Zealand, Indonesia, and the rest of the Indian Ocean Rim countries. Estimates gave Western Australia around four hours warning and Southern Australia a little more than five hours. They had done their jobs superbly and now all they could do was wait. It would be a long four hours.

They began receiving reports from ships at sea off the southwest coast. While ships in the open ocean rarely were affected by tsunamis, the Navy cutter Livingston some 100 miles off Cape Leeuwin reported a dramatic swell of some 20 feet—a bad sign in relatively deep water. But the TOPEX satellite beamed down the worst news. The tide indicated by radar was in excess of 1000 feet at both Heard and McDonald.

The three tsunamis piled up their energy as they sped across the southern ocean but as they encountered the continental shelf of Australia, they slowed and pulled apart. The tsunami energies were directed northeast of the earthquake epicenters that focused the peak of wave energy toward Indonesia. Thus, Australia was catching only the weak edge of the tsunami energy. That was small consolation to the small coastal towns of Nornalup, Albany, Hopetown and Esperance.

Margaret Fisher was in her boat and worked as fast as she could to get the motor to catch so she could power her way out of Nornalup Bay. She had heard the sirens and had been out of the house in a flash. Her insurance was not paid up on the boat and she had poured her life savings into the stupid thing—no, no she loved the boat! At 20 feet, it was small. But it had been handcrafted nearly 30 years before in England, and she loved and hated every inch of it. But the 750cc gasoline engine was nearly as old as the boat and she cursed it and cursed it.

By now all the other small boats in the marina were either abandoned to fate or their owners/operators were well out past the breakwater. She knew she wouldn't make it, but she couldn't just give up now, either, could she?

She cleaned and gapped the spark plugs, blew out the fuel lines, but still for some reason the engine would not start. She gave the starter another half-hearted attempt and—lo and behold—the engine turned over, coughed, and then came to life. She mentally kicked herself for not having the damn thing overhauled ages ago.

Maggie jumped onto the pier and loosened the lines as fast as she could. She didn't even bother to coil the ropes, she just gunned the engine and pulled away from the dock and then left the marina as fast as she could. She noticed that she was not the only one getting a late start, a local fishing boat about twice the size of hers was paralleling her coming out from the commercial docks on the west side of the bay. She locked eyes with the captain for an instant before they both went back to work.

She tied down the wheel so she could pull in the ropes and organize the mess on the deck. It took only a few minutes and by that time she was halfway to the breakwater. Now she was only a few hundred feet away from the fishing boat although she was overtaking it slightly. She looked for the captain's eyes. The locked on each other again, but he pointed toward the mouth of the bay. She looked but could hardly believe her eyes. A gigantic wave was beginning to crest and then she noticed that it was at least twice the height of the bluffs overlooking the east end of the bay. The wave was five hundred feet tall.

Without even thinking she dropped down to the cabin of her small boat and bolted the hatch. That was the last thing she remembered before the wave caught her boat and rolled it end over end five miles up the Swan River. The wave pulled the small boat apart at the seams. But it also carried it to the leading edge of the wave and then unceremoniously deposited it on the edge of a gravel pit on the river's edge. Neither of the two subsequent waves came quite as far upriver, which probably saved her life. Miraculously, Maggie regained consciousness with pieces of her shattered boat lying around her.

Devin and the others had already been in the water for a couple of hours when the tsunami siren's song began. They were a motley crew, to be sure. They were among the rowdiest and raunchiest of the Australian professional surfing circuit. There were about three dozen or so of them—more if you counted all the girlfriends, boyfriends, and assorted groupies. But about a dozen were in the water this afternoon at Wooloowa Point.

The occasion was the southern swell. These waves only came up for a few short weeks every year—some freakish combination of regular summer storms that made the Wooloowa beach equal to Pipeline or Cape Town. Perfect tubes formed far out into the Bight. These waves could give some of the longest rides in the world. The waves were morphologically ideal: tall, slow and with curls that broke west to east in long smooth patterns. But Wooloowa was in one of the more deserted parts of eastern West Australia and you had to be truly courageous to leave the beaches of the Gold Coast to gamble on this place. But this time the trip paid off for the caravan of cars and vans and small trucks on their walkabout. The waves had been perfect and the weather glorious.

The party the night before had raged until the wee hours of the morning and most had slept late into the morning in sleeping bags, vans, and a few tents. By noon the party was back in swing for the hangers-on, many of the surfers were not quite warmed up enough for the cool waters. But the hard core, as usual, was doing what they loved best. Their enthusiasm was not dampened at all at first by the single siren at the parking lot.

Devin, as usual, was the first to taunt the group.

"Who's up for the ride of a lifetime?" The few levelheaded surfers in the group were already paddling for shore.

"I'm in," said his current girlfriend, Mary, a world-ranked long board surfer. She was still slightly wasted from the all-night party and too tired to be scared.

"Me, too," chimed in a couple of the others, Mike and Charley. Charley looks dubious and nervously looked at the others already halfway to shore. He asked, "Our approach?"

Harry yelled back at them, "Are you assholes serious? Come onshore or you'll get yourselves killed!"

"Never met a wave I couldn't handle," smirked Devin who was now paddling out to sea.

The four friends continued their progress until they were a good mile from the beach and stopped. All looked to the horizon, but there was nothing to be seen, yet.

Charley offered, "Maybe this wasn't such a hot idea."

Devin frowned. "Maybe. But think of the publicity if this is a big one that we can really ride. Your career is almost over anyway." Charley at 35 was the oldest of the group and took a lot of teasing.

"I would like to live a little longer, mate."

"So go back. Nobody's stopping you."

"He's right," said Mary, coming to her senses, "this is over the top, Dev."

"Fine, you chickens go on back. Mike will hang with me, eh?"

Mike, who was always easy to dare, took the bait.

"You bet. Ride of a lifetime. What's to lose?"

Charley and Mary looked at each other and started the return trip.

A few minutes later as they watched the progress of other two, Mike turned to Devin and asked, "So, should we go further out? Stay here? Whaddaya think, mate?"

Again Devin frowned and looked to the south.

"A truly large wave might break even further out. Been thinking about our chances. The Bight is pretty uniform and gradual even up to the foothills." He jerked his thumb back behind him. The siren periodically pierced the quiet lulls between the breakers a mile away.

Devin made a decision. "Let's go further out." As they began to paddle, both began to feel the surge beneath them.

"Holy shit, feel that?" came Mike.

"Must be a biggie. Put some muscle into it."

Both moved their arms furiously. Mike stole a glance back to look at Charley and Mary but discovered that he and Devin had fallen into a large trough. He turned his attention back to the building wave in front of him. There was no way to judge how far away it was, but it was a monster in anyone's book. The outgoing surge was moving them at least as fast as they themselves were paddling. They were now on the growing side of the trough and could feel themselves being lifted up. Both intuitively knew to reverse direction and to start paddling toward the beach. Mike started to swear to himself under his breath and wet himself. Now, he was scared.

Devin, by contrast, was calm and collected. One reason why he was the reigning world champion was that his nerves of steel were matched by an ability to find his center, his inner calm, when challenging the forces of nature. It was almost as though he could "psych out" the very waves that he rode. He had never tried to explain it to anyone, but it must be a kind of Zen thing—he simply became "one" with the wave. But this was different. This was definitely a level of natural energy beyond his experience. Still he concentrated on that center and focused his attention on the slope and feel of the growing wave.

"Faster, Mike," he admonished his friend.

"Right," Mike managed, but he had never been so frightened in his life. Somehow they found themselves on the ridge of the wave that had grown to some fifty feet. Almost in unison, the two surfers stood up on their boards. They could see cars and trucks a mile ahead of them fly across the dunes away from the oncoming tsunami. The bad news was that Mary and Charley were directly below them, stuck in the trough running before the huge wave.

Now at a hundred feet, the wave was slowing perceptively and both surfers turned slightly east as the crest started to form a frothy head. Devin led the way and pointed down the wave front. At two hundred feet the wave was moving twenty miles an hour, but the weight of the massive pile of water was now too much to sustain the height and it started to collapse. For Devin and Mike, though this was just a larger version of the waves they'd been surfing all morning. The curl was bigger, but the waveform was exquisite and they were riding the biggest tube anyone in the world had ever ridden.

Even Mike was exhilarated now. Then they swept over the parking lot and a couple of cars below and Mike lost his balance. He started to tumble and the wave swept him up and into the chaos of the crest. The forces of the wave tore at him and broke his back, killing him instantly.

Devin was concentrating on his progress, but could feel the growing instability of the tsunami wave as it worked its way inland. The water below was beginning to pick up debris, mainly sand and the sparse vegetation from this arid coastline. While the wave had slowed considerably, Devin was still traveling a good twenty miles an hour as the tube structure of the wave collapsed around him. Or so it seemed. The tube was still there—some ten or twelve feet in diameter, but filled with foam, spray, and chaos. He was upright for a few minutes and then felt the air sucked right out of his lungs. His feet lost contact with the board and he closed his eyes and prayed for the first time since Christmas Mass five years before. He was turned end over end for what seemed like an hour, but must have only been a minute or two. His shoulder hit something and then his head hit something and then it was all over.

Back at the WPTC, the news media began to descend. By late afternoon, there were a half dozen television vans and dozens of reporters milling around outside the front door. A couple of local police had been brought in to keep some semblance of order, but this was all just a bit much for Director Jones. This was his first experience with such a throng. His deputy, however, urged him on and helped him put together a statement. At 7 P.M. local time he went out to read the statement and answer questions. He brushed back his thinning sandy hair and pushed out the front door into the humid summer evening air. He stepped up to a podium that was now almost covered in microphones.

"I am Harold Jones, Director and Head of the Western Pacific Tsunami Centre. The WPTC is only one of nearly thirty tsunami centers located around the Pacific, in the Indian Ocean, and more recently, the Caribbean. I know that you are all very eager to hear news of today's Indian Ocean tsunami, but I must first make a few facts clear.

"The WPTC mandate is to monitor and record seismic and tsunami data that come either directly from our own domestic networks or indirectly from cooperating centers around the world. That means that some of the data that I will be sharing comes from other parts of the world. The lead is the Honolulu Pacific Tsunami Center and much of the credit rests with them for correlating data and coordinating the worldwide tsunami network. Furthermore, site-specific damage reports and disaster relief efforts are being coordinated through the Ministry of Defense. We are hoping to get a Ministry rep here soon, but as yet those reports are unavailable. I believe there will be a press conference in Canberra within the hour.

"Okay. So, here's what I can tell you. At 9:48 A.M. local time, that would be 0048 hours GMT, a massive earthquake at 9.1 on the open-ended Richter scale was detected and measured at this station. The epicenter is at approximately latitude 70 degrees South and longitude 72 degrees East. The initial seismic readings would place the epicenter about one kilometer below the ocean floor. It is important to note that while the actual epicenter was believed to be about two kilometers below sea level, it was directly underneath the Amery Ice Shelf.

"At 10:15 and then again at 10:42 local time, two additional seismic events were recorded each very near to 9.5 on the Richter scale. These are the largest recorded quakes since 1960 — the 8.9 earthquake in Afghanistan. Today's series of three quakes are unprecedented in their release of energy. The epicenters were not precisely in the same spot, but appear to have propagated along a volcanic rift zone underneath the Amery Ice Shelf. Other seismic data from today's events have been processed by the U.S. National Earthquake Center in Golden, Colorado and they indicate that all of the earthquakes today fell somewhere in the 9.0 to 9.5 range of the Richter open-ended scale. Those data also indicate that the quake was produced by an upward adjustment along a transform fault which was previously unknown. These are the first major earthquakes under an ice shelf known to produce tsunamis.

"The first waves came onshore at Point D'Entrecasteaux and at West Cape Howe at almost exactly 5 P.M. in Cairnes—which was 3 P.M. local time in Western Australia. The waves hit the Adelaide area about an hour later—about an hour ago. Tasmania had only minor tsunami activity about an hour ago. No subsequent waves are expected at this time.

"Wave heights were the greatest along the northern coast of Western Australia, along the Bight, and in interior waterways, such as the Spencer Gulf and Gulf St. Vincent. Those areas experienced waves in excess of 100 meters. Waves on headlands, such as Point D'Entrecasteaux and at West Cape Howe were recorded at some 30 meters above sea level. For clarification 'wave peaks' are actually calculated at maximum height above the average sea level, while wave reach—that is the distance inland—is calculated from the high tide mark.

"Reliable reports give maximum wave heights at the following locations in Western Australia: at Steep Point, 120 meters; Geraldon, 60 meters; Fremantle, 97 meters; Nornalup, 102 meters; Hopetown 99 meters; Esperance, 80 meters; and, Eyre, 102 meters. In Southern Australia: Point Fowler, 110 meters; Ceduna, 90 meters; inner eastern exposures of the Spencer Gulf near 90 meters; and inner portions of the Gulf of St. Vincent, including the Adelaide Harbor, 80 meters. Wave heights in Victoria fell off dramatically although some reports of damage were reported through the Bass Strait. As I indicated previously, no significant wave heights were reported in Tasmania.

"Given the incline of the coastal area of Western Australia, wave reach did not exceed predicted intrusion into the designated tsunami zones. Staff will be passing out these maps that will give you an idea of the extent. Again, I hasten to point out that we do not at this time have any damage reports—which should be issued by Defense. Unfortunately tsunami intrusion along the Great Australia Bight in the southern gulfs was far greater than ever anticipated. The large waves traveled inland as far as a kilometer along stretches of the Nullarbor Plain. The waves covered most of the small coast towns of Nornalup, Hopetown, Esperance, Eyre, Eucla, Penong, and Ceduna. Similarly, wave forcing, the effect of concentrating wave energy in confined harbors and gulfs—you could think of it as a funnel effect—was extensive. The towns of Whyalla and Port Pirie were inundated and waves washed as far as three kilometers up the river beyond Port Augusta. The coastal urban areas near Adelaide were flooded up to a kilometer inland.

"I will stop for questions now while I have my staff pass out some of the previously drafted maps and many of the summary statistics, such as those which I have just presented. The loss of life was, as you know, significant, but thanks to the warning systems and evacuations, far less than it might have been otherwise. Preliminary Defense estimates place the death toll near 10,000. We expect the losses in Indonesia to be several orders of magnitude greater. Your questions?"

There was a short lag, as the enormity of the event sank in. But being journalists, a tsunami of questions shouted at once. Director Jones waved them down and pointed to a woman in front.

"So you are saying there was more than one tsunami?"

"Oh, right, sorry I didn't make that clear. The three seismic events each produced a large wave. Now without getting too technical, these waves apparently bunched up and actually reinforced each other. They were more distinct on the eastern side and more clustered together in the west. They arrived about 20 minutes apart in the east and 12-15 minutes apart in the west. Also, the second wave appears to have been strongest and traveled the furthest inland. We believe that the focal point of the wave front is headed north from the epicenters. That probably means that Australia only caught the outer eastern edge of the wave front. Our models forecast that the brunt of the energy will be felt on the Indian subcontinent, or perhaps Indonesia. The waves should impact on Indonesia any time now, and

India in a few hours. Bangladesh should be another hour or hour and a half after that. Yes?" he pointed at another hand.

"What can you say about the connection between the nuclear blast yesterday and these seismic events? Are they not connected?"

Director Jones smiled and took a few seconds to answer. "I am not an expert on nuclear weapons so I will not speculate. You should refer that question to the Ministry of Defense. From a geological standpoint, it does seem rather unlikely that a small yield weapon could produce that sort of dramatic reaction, but from a layperson's standpoint, it is rather curious. I guess I'd like an answer to that question myself." Then the director looked embarrassed that he'd commented at all.

Leah woke up and immediately rubbed her temples with the palms of her hand and groaned. The dream faded. It was almost like the echo of voices in her head, but she shook her head vigorously and that seemed to clear it. Her eyes began to focus. She heard Jake moving around in the bunk above. She got up without disturbing him and tried the door. It was unlocked, so she opened it and went across to use the head. After splashing some water on her face she actually started to feel a bit better. There were basic toiletries on a small rack under the mirror so she helped herself to some aspirin and ran a brush through her hair. She looked a wreck. A couple of her fingernails were broken and she felt violated in body and soul. Taking a deep breath, she straightened and made a decision.

She was deeply disturbed by the revelations about Jake, but still loved him dearly. This was simply not the time to delve too deeply—they needed to pull together and support each other. Their survival might well depend upon it. She did need to head off any sympathies that he might have for their captors and keep him on her side. There was only one way to do that. She knew where his most of his weaknesses lay. After brushing her hair, she proceeded to give herself a sponge bath with a washcloth, powdered herself and brushed her teeth.

Leah made her way back into their cabin—she thought of it as their prison cell. She quietly took off her clothes and climbed up into the upper compartment with him. She worried at first if it would support the both of them, but the steel shelf beneath them seemed invulnerable. The little compartment was snug and she nestled up next to him and wrapped her legs around him. He was startled, but she nuzzled his neck and put her hand into his shorts. He responded to her immediately. She found his mouth and kissed him passionately. They made love without exchanging a word and he gave out a huge sigh when he came into her.

They lay together in a tight embrace for some time. Neither said a word for a long time. When Jake started to talk, she knew it would be another apology, so she put her fingers lightly over his mouth.

"Baby," she began, "don't say a word. I love you still and want to get through this horror alive. Maybe if we get out of this intact we can work through it, but for now just let it be."

He nodded his assent. She added, "Let's go clean up and get some breakfast? Okay?"

"You bet, precious." He murmured with tears in his eyes.

They squeezed into the small bathroom, washed, and dried each other. Their stomachs were growling, and when they returned to the cabin they found clean piles of clothing. Leah wondered if someone had eavesdropped on the lovemaking too. It didn't really matter to her and she shrugged the thought off.

The clean clothes did feel good, even if they didn't exactly fit. Both were now dressed in blue jeans and T-shirts. Hers a classic black Grateful Dead T-shirt, and his had a simple yin-yang design on the pocket. They inspected each other, embraced in a long bear hug, and went out the door into the corridor. They made their way down to the galley single-file. They encountered no one on the way, but the galley contained nearly a dozen people. Their tormentor, Bee sat alone and watched them intently as they entered. The others looked up at them, but quickly looked away. No one smiled or otherwise acknowledged them.

Bee arose and met them halfway to the buffet.

"Your timing is good today. The morning meal is still being served."

She pointed to one end of the serving line. "Utensils and trays are at that end, coffee at the far end." All this was fairly obvious, but as on edge as they both were, it was strangely comforting to be given directions.

"I will keep an eye on you two, but eat in peace."

"Thank you so much," Leah returned sarcastically, but Bee ignored her and went back to her seat, picked up a paperback book and nursed a teacup.

200

The others in the room had been quiet during this exchange, but now began to chatter, as they had been when the two came into the room, and then laughter from one table filled the room. The laughter was jarring to Leah, but she concentrated on investigating the various food trays in the steamer. One looked like eggs, another appeared to be breakfast patties. They didn't smell like sausage, so she guessed they were some kind of soy protein or veggie patties. One tray contained cottage fried potatoes, which she heaped on a plate. Another tray contained waffles. There was fruit off to the side along with cereals, juice, yogurt, and milk. She made a small bowl of yogurt. Jake, on the other hand, filled a plate with a little of everything. He had a ravenous look on his face. It made her laugh, and she felt a little better. She smiled at herself and told herself to relax. It helped, but eating helped even more.

After they finished and were both working on their second cups of coffee, Bee came over to them and laid down a piece of paper in the middle of the table. It was a diagram.

"Here's a little map I made for you of your area of liberty." She said this very matter-of-factly. "You will be allowed to roam freely on this deck only, and only in these rooms and corridors. You will be given a ship's tour if you behave yourselves."

Leah almost said something nasty, but Jake gave her a look and she kept quiet. She had a very strong dislike of this young woman and was about ready to tear her hair out. On the other hand, Bee looked very buff and taunt—obviously someone that could probably put Leah on the floor even without a stun gun—noticeably absent this morning.

Bee pointed across the mess hall. "That door over there leads to the library, where you will probably spend a good deal of your time while we are underway. Most all of the compartments between here and your stateroom are within your limits—but only those I've marked. I suggest that you behave."

"We'll be on our very best behavior," said Jake with a smile. It was Leah's turn to glare at him.

Bee continued. "The laundry room is next on your left—that's the port side. We have some of your clothing from the City already laundered, but from here on out, you are your own."

She pointed again at the map.

"Here is the stores room. From 10 A.M. to noon ship's time, the purser is there and will issue you any small items or dry goods you might need. There is a list of available items outside that room. Under the circumstances, I will review any requests you make. Understood?"

"The media room is next to that. There's a video library, but there is a signup sheet to schedule the DVD players. We regularly schedule an evening video here in the crew mess hall, as well. The media room has CDs and tape players that you can check out. Oh, and coffee mugs are allowed in the library, but not outside of these two rooms, like in the corridor or media room. Mainly a safety issue."

"Neither of you smoke, I understand?" They both shook their heads.

"Good, because the smoking room is upstairs near the crew quarters.

"There are communal showers down the corridor past your room. The purser can issue you soap and shampoo, but we usually just share what's in the shower—there's always some there. Suit yourselves. We will bring you shower slippers and towels later this morning... Next to the showers is the weight and exercise room. We use resistance machines rather than free weights which can be dangerous in a submarine." Leah guessed she spent a lot of time in that room.

"That's about it. Living in such close-quarters takes some getting used to, but we should be in port in five days."

Leah screwed up her courage. "Where are we now?"

"It won't hurt, I suppose, for you to know we are headed due south of the Bay Area and about a day north of the equator. Happy?"

"Not very, you..." Jake kicked her under the table so hard she had to catch her breath.

Bee stood up abruptly. "Watch your Ps & Qs, Dr. Wilson, or you will be confined to your room." She looked directly at Jake and asked, "Any questions?" He shook his head and Leah rubbed her shin. Bee left the mess hall, but Leah suspected that she would not be far away.

Leah said, "I'd really like to wash my hair."

"Okay, do you mind if I check out the library?"

"Why don't we stick together for now? We can come back afterwards. Even though we washed up, I still feel dirty."

"Sure, no problem. It sounds like we have plenty of time." He looked deeply and lovingly into her dark brown eyes and sighed slightly to himself. "One more cup of coffee?"

"Not for me, but go ahead." Jake went and warmed up his cup and came back and sat down with a more audible sigh this time.

"What is it Jake?"

"Oh, you know, getting us into this mess." He looked crestfallen.

"I am beginning to think that you had little to do with it. They would have found a way to get me, maybe without you. Let it go." Jake shook his head.

"The sedatives have worn off, but I sure had strange dreams last night." Leah raised an eyebrow but said nothing. She motioned with her hands for him to continue.

He furrowed his forehead and stared at his cup for a few seconds.

"You may remember that I was scared of the water when I was really small, until I had swimming lessons. Well, actually my first few times in a swimming pool were even scary. Anyway, I dreamed last night that I was floating inside that same pool. But the strange thing was that I was floating in the middle, not on the surface. But not holding my breath... I was just hanging there, feeling the coolness of the water, little currents tugging on my body."

Leah was looking at him kind of funny, but he continued.

"Then there are these voices, women's voices, I think, talking all around me. Not at me, but to each other? Then, I am not in that pool, but at these hot springs I went to once in Oregon called Medical Springs... I am on the edge of the pool now and it's night, but there's bright moonlight and everything is all misty from the steam and hot springs. There's a slight sulfur smell and the voices begin again, like a babbling, but there are deeper men's voices now, too." He paused to try and remember something.

"They were talking about me, but not to me? And I could pick out silhouettes across from me, but couldn't actually see them? One person was being addressed by name... it was, um... um... *Osun.* Maybe he was the hot springs owner, because they said these were his healing springs." With that, Leah grabbed his arm tightly. Jake looked around to see what had happened.

"What is it?" He asked worriedly.

"That was my dream."

"What? You are joking." His frown deepened.

"I can't remember much now, but it was very vivid when I got up. But in my dream there was a waterfall, like from our trip to

203

Hawai`i? Sacred Falls, I think. It was warm and sunny. A man comes up to me—a very dark-skinned man with a big toothy grin. He asks me if I know the way to *Osun*. I thought it was a place, but that is the same name that I dreamed. But that's all I remember. That can't just be a coincidence."

"Maybe I was talking in my sleep and you dreamed it?" Jake offered.

"Well, dreams are funny, and it might have been something else, but those dreams seem oddly similar. But I interrupted you. Was there more?"

"No, I don't think so. There were the warm healing waters and then I felt your hand in my shorts." He smiled sheepishly at her. "I could do that again."

Interestingly, for some reason, she wanted to, too. She took his hand and they dropped off their trays and headed back to their cabin.

Punta Arenas

It was late afternoon. The ancient Lockheed C-130BL Hercules had been ready to take off for hours, but was waiting for a clearing in the weather. A really nasty storm had blown in off the Southern Pacific and the plane was so heavily loaded that the pilot refused to leave. Weather reports did promise a clearing very soon, so Karen swore under her breath and she and the rest of the team took the time to try and make themselves comfortable—no mean feat in the cargo plane. They had abandoned any idea of taking the super jumbo jet south and had transferred their gear to the Hercules, one of the workhorses of Antarctica, affectionately called a "Herc." While the plane was extremely reliable and suited to foul weather, comfortable inside it was not. This was quite a contrast to their luxurious accommodations the day before. The team was sprawled out on what were basically not much more than padded benches surrounded by gear lashed down with netting.

The copilot leaned through the cockpit door. He had to raise his voice above the drumming of the engines.

"Okay, ladies and gentlemen, strap yourselves in, we're cleared to taxi out and get this show on the road. Expect some bumpy air on the way up to cruising altitude. We're looking at about a four hour flight this afternoon, but I'll come back and give you a report after we pass the half way point."

Pete was scribbling away on a notepad. A small digital video camera was now in his possession, but he didn't have the time yet to get to know it. They had been briefed earlier on the damage reports coming in from Australia and Indonesia, so he was determined to record how these FBI men and women were reacting to the news. He could see their determination and resolve written in the expressions. They continued to pour over documents and laptop computers. The forensic psychology team from Washington had joined them in Santiago and they had already had two lengthy meetings going over what they knew about the EPG* members who they identified as the core of the terrorist group.

Part of the problem was the large number of people who appeared to be involved. Pete wasn't totally surprised, in the sense that he had run across lots of people who were committed environmentalists. It was curious that so many could have been involved without more leakage from the organization. FBI experts had now identified over sixty people associated with EPG* who had more-or-less vanished over a two year period. These were considered "confirmed" terrorists while another twenty-five "missing persons" comprised a second-tier group. Of this group, none had had any direct connection to EPG* but been had been reported missing by friends, families, or businesses and had some affiliation with "eco-warrior" groups such as Earth First!, Sea Shepherd Society, or other fringe green groups.

The eighty-five had been sorted and cross-referenced by the usual demographic characteristics (age, sex, socio-economic status, level of education, etc.), their place of geographic origin, place last seen, psychological profile, and another dozen parameters. There were some interesting patterns emerging and some additional clues generated by the process. Karen took charge of what she called the "advance team" who all seemed especially interested in the likely composition of what they referred to as the likely "functional cadres." They seemed to have a good handle on the cadre which had come down through South America last year and whose trail they were following.

By eliminating those most likely to be in the first functional cadre—which they were now calling the "A" cadre, they were left with a pool of EPG* members which they were trying to puzzle into other discrete groups. Even the first "sort" of people into "A" cadre revealed some interesting facts. They knew directly of only a handful of the 12 to 15 members of "A" cadre. And they identified some of the others by having investigators show photos to witnesses in Darwin. Therefore, they had a fix on about a dozen EPG* in the group that passed through Tierra del Fuego. By using a functional analysis of the group they were making some conclusions about the cadre. And they made some assumptions about what functions were missing, to look for likely suspects both in the larger pool, or perhaps others who were not yet identified. They knew there had to be some of those. Pete was fascinated since he had never seen FBI profilers and forensics in action.

The first thing they noticed is that they could not identify anyone in the "A" cadre core who had medical experience nor a pilot's license. Thus, they made a short list of other "likely" candidates who might belong to "A" cadre. The advance team communicated with Washington the need to look for missing pilots, nurses, and medics, regardless of their environmental leanings. The "A" cadre identification produced some relevant information. It had some Antarctic veterans, including a European expert in ice-core drilling who had worked in Greenland, and two geologists, one a university researcher and the other an oil-company prospector. There was the professor, Stewart Adams, and the mastermind, Abe Miller. The remaining four or five people were being puzzled out. Where the two AWOL airmen fit in wasn't clear.

There was a shortage in the larger pool of some likely critical functional skills, especially mechanics and pilots. The larger pool appeared to contain many people with boating and ocean skills. That raised some interesting questions. The advance team was fairly certain that the EPG* escape route would not follow the same path out they took coming in. That supposition would be confirmed more solidly once they had found the base camp in Antarctica—their next goal. But the advance team was stymied about the sheer number of people involved at this point, since it appeared that the group they were following only numbered twenty or less. Where were the others? How were they involved? It seemed clear that at least some of the larger pool were involved in the Antarctic operations. But exactly how was still obscure. They hoped they would find some answers in Antarctica and that the investigations back in Michigan, California, and elsewhere would uncover more clues.

Everyone in the group was very tense, except for Karen. This was a revelation for Pete. He wrote that down, because he found it so very curious. Prior to the explosion and tsunamis, the agent had seemed uptight and stiff but now she was relaxed. The others seemed very serious and determined and she was smiling. The other change was that all of the advance team and even the forensics and support personnel from FBI headquarters were deferential to her in the extreme. Why? What had changed? Maybe he should ask Minh? Maybe later…

The team also consisted of a small crew of communications and computer geeks who were not having a very good time at all. Just when the reports were coming in on the destruction in the Indian Ocean, the radios went all haywire due to new solar flares. The techies even expressed some concern about flying, but the pilots said that was silly. The copilot seemed amused and told them that close to the poles, where the planet's magnetic force lines were nearly vertical, there was some reason for caution at high altitude, but this far north it wasn't a serious problem. He said they were far more worried about radio blackouts, the primary reason for waiting for better weather for taking off and landing since even the radar couldn't be totally trusted. The sun was mad.

As the plane finally took off, Pete put down his notepad and closed his eyes for a few minutes trying to recapture some of the wild dream that he'd had early in the morning. After the plane had climbed and leveled off, he found a document on his lap—a FAX summary of the destruction in Indonesia. The scale of the destruction was staggering. From Sumatra to Timor, the coast had been hit with 300 to 400 foot waves. Although most of the major cities along the Indian Ocean coast are well inland, with the exception of Padang, the loss of life had been massive. Up to five million people were dead in Indonesia alone. Hardest hit was the island of Java. The island lay perpendicular to the waves and the southern coast was highly populated. Dozens upon dozens of fishing villages were totally wiped out. Similarly hard-hit were the coastal islands of Sumatra such as Pagai Selatan, Pagai Utara, Serbut, and others. Some small coastal islands were wiped clean not only of human settlements but everything, trees, structures—everything.

Although they had not seen any reports yet from Sri Lanka, India, Bangladesh, or Burma, the projections for destruction in the central Bay of Bengal were also grim with as many as another ten million people threatened. Not only was Bangladesh near the focal point of the wave energy, but also experience with monsoon flooding suggested that the Ganges River delta would inundate hundreds of miles inland as least as far as the capital Dhaka, if not further. Over such a large area, evacuation attempts would largely be futile. The reports came in while they were waiting in Punta Arenas, when the FBI team had become particularly intent in their determination to apprehend the terrorists. There was also a certain measure of disbelief that this could all be happening. One agent even commented that it seemed like a bad dream.

Pete's impression was that they had for the most part nominally accepted the nuclear detonation. That, after all, was only a large explosion and the FBI had dealt with many an explosion— although never a radioactive one. Bomb threats they'd dealt with before, even often. But comprehending the consequences of such massive destruction was obviously not in their scenario planning. The scale was so far beyond what they had expected that they were still trying to adjust. Well, Pete was, too. As a journalist, he had already reported on massive earthquakes and other disasters of immense proportions, but this was a painfully human disaster. The idea that some people he used to know could intentionally cause the deaths of so many others was unfathomable.

Pete reflected on his interaction earlier with the forensic team. They asked him very specific questions about the mental disposition, backgrounds, motivations, and behaviors of Green Alliance and the extended EPG* "family" he'd known in Ann Arbor. They were not accusatory, just very thorough. They focused on three people, primarily, Stewart Adams, Abe Miller, and Angel Stills.

He had worked with Abe and Angel maybe a half-dozen times, during three or four trips to California during the height of his Green Alliance involvement, and as many times during conferences and meetings in the Midwest or on the East Coast. Angel had been Abe's right hand and a kind of bodyguard, he offered. They were always whispering together, Pete recalled. Whereas Abe always seemed relaxed and comfortable with himself, Angel was intense and nervous. Abe was an ideologue and Angel was a functionary. He gave the speeches and the inspirational messages; she kept him on schedule and took care of the details. Although they'd been together only a half-dozen times, Pete remembered many of the details fairly vividly. Perhaps Pete was already becoming a good, observant journalist back then. Perhaps it was because Miller was so charismatic and hypnotic. Perhaps it was because Pete had taken such a strong disliking to him early on. He couldn't be sure. The FBI did not really seem as interested in his story as in his impressions of Abe and Angel. He skirted the personal when possible and shut down introspection.

Abe's public persona was that of a green preacher, a "hellfire and brimstone" inspirational speaker, explained Pete. Miller was very successful in his evangelical style. The preamble was always the same: that the earth was going to hell in a hand basket. He painted a picture of the earth in decline, overpopulated, polluted, and thrashed by human development. He conveyed to the audience their own culpability—they were all sinners, no one was above reproach for either rampant consumerism or aiding and abetting the "system." He was *hard* on people. He beat on them psychologically, emotionally, and intellectually. He challenged his followers to see it any other way. And then he poured salt in their wounds. He questioned the very existence of the species, the reason for going on, suggesting that the entire human race had abrogated its rights and responsibilities.

Then he skillfully changed direction and tempo. He called the sinners to action and got them to commit to Alliance activities—protests, educational programs, or civil disobedience—so they could enter the Kingdom of Green Heaven. He made his parishioners feel guilty and then lifted their guilt through a cathartic call to action. Pete was moved the very first time he experienced this in a Southern California tent revival meeting. The second time, in Ann Arbor, it was different, maybe it because he was on the "home team" or because it was a verbatim, repeat performance, it didn't work the same magic. Pete recalled being disturbed, looking at the glazed, hypnotized eyes of the young students in the audience, who at the end of spring term were already sleep-deprived and susceptible to Abe's voice and rhythm. He had been appalled that next time.

In smaller, informal groups of organizers and staff, Abe was very personable and friendly, and yet there was an edge to him. This was something the forensics folks honed in on. They asked: what did he mean?

Pete said, "It's like he was distracted sometimes, or not always there." He considered how to put it.

"When he was on stage, he was always 'on,' always in a groove. He never hesitated. In person, there were times when people who talked to him had to repeat themselves because his attention drifted. It was subtle, but I almost wondered if he had narcolepsy or some sort of attention disorder. Sometimes it was more pronounced than others."

These behavioral quirks interested the FBI team intensely. They were looking for motivations, values, and beliefs, but foibles seemed to pique their curiosity. All the forensics folk would scribble furiously on their e-slates and electronic notebooks. They seemed to take turns automatically; one agent asking questions while the others scribbled notes. Two were psychologists; the other was identified as a psychiatric pathologist. They were meticulous and thorough. Pete felt like he'd been through an interrogation—which, of course, he had. They were cordial enough when they probed him, but were also very clinical about it. He was glad that he wasn't a criminal suspect.

He began to remember things he had long ago buried deep in his consciousness, about the Green Alliance, and about the individuals, especially. He had really believed in Alliance values, but had been discouraged and disillusioned about the lunatics that were attracted to the group: the fringe, the weirdoes, and the dogmatic. Pete, therefore, poured out a reasonably well-heeled analysis. Exactly what the FBI seemed to want. He was, after all, a journalist. The details he had simply filed away in the inner reaches of memory, but a lot was still there.

One visualization exercise that they put him through repeatedly was a regression technique. Although not precisely hypnosis, it proved highly effective for him to go back in time and visualize a particular situation, say an annual GA meeting. The team would then gently prompt him for memories of people, faces, smells, music, literature, personalities, and then specific behaviors, especially those quirks that bubbled to the surface. The memories were at first fractured, but as he revisited a few more meetings and events, he opened up and the memories crystallized. Pete would even have intense flashes of incongruous or bizarre experiences as the psychologists encouraged him to recall just such details.

For example, he recalled the time that Abe had been speaking to a group of students in Ann Arbor after a meeting. Pete was part of the clean up detail, stacking chairs and cleaning up the coffee and cookie table. As he skirted the group, who were generally enraptured with the green guru, Abe stopped talking in mid-sentence. Pete stopped in his tracks and looked at him. For five seconds he had this glazed look in his eyes, and then they unfocused.

He recalled that Abe said intensely, "That's not possible!" to no one in particular. It was so disconnected to the previous comment that all of the students looked stunned. Angel, who he had only met personally for the first time at that very meeting, grabbed Abe by the elbow and forcefully led him towards the door. She mumbled something about getting to the motel for his medicine, and almost to the door when Abe turned around and loudly, cheerfully said goodbye to everyone. Those around the room returned the salutation, combined with a few hoots and animal calls. Meanwhile the small circle of students just looked confused. One longhaired teenage boy shrugged his shoulders; a young college woman raised her eyebrows. But the stragglers left the meeting room and the incident faded away into the summer evening.

Pete had pondered that episode in the first few weeks after it happened. But nothing quite as strange happened again when he was around Abe. Sure, Abe was distracted and sometimes had strange pauses in his speeches, but only once did he seem to be hearing voices.

When Pete said it like that, all of the team looked up at him. He'd hit on something apparently that they must have heard before, given the shared looks between the forensic team. But they didn't pursue the point with Pete. Shortly after that, his interview was over.

Sandi and Raul spent the day getting organized and already planned to move their base of operations from the Peninsula into the interior. They spent the early morning settling into the space they have been given by the mayor, but then the evidence mounted pointed to EPG* Antarctic activities in an around the former Hungarian base on the edge of the Ronne Ice Shelf. That had partly been a process of elimination, since it was one of the few modern science bases on the continent that had been unoccupied for a while. It was also a stroke of luck, as tour operators in the area also reported activity there and in the nearby mountains over the early part of the season. Satellite imagery confirmed substantial goings-on as well. It was now uninhabited. The signs were strong. This had been enough evidence for Washington to decide to move the FBI-led operations there and Sandi had no reason to object.

The day went by quickly as she and Raul met members of the military contingent, inventoried supplies and equipment, sketched out plans to approach and secure the base, collect maps, aerial and satellite photographs, and so on. They seemed to have things well under control by late afternoon in preparation for departure early the next day. That was when the Mayor and a half-dozen staff paraded into the room.

"Detectives," he said and bowed.

They both looked up and smiled at his imposing figure taking such a low bend in their direction.

"Mr. Mayor," they acknowledged in union.

"My spies inform me that you are nearly complete in your work here."

Both raised their eyebrows and glanced at each other.

"I am here to relieve you of your duties and take you touring."

Sandi was about to object, but realized that under the circumstances, she was unlikely to get anywhere. Besides, they were both tired and a break would do them some good.

"It is settled, then. My staff will help you wind things up here and bring you to the helipad in thirty minutes. I have the honor of escorting you to one of the remaining Emperor Penguin rookeries." He bowed again and was quickly gone.

Exactly thirty minutes later they were hustled into a large, empty transport helicopter, except for the Mayor, one assistant, and themselves. For about another half hour the older man talked non-stop about the growing threats to the Emperor survival as a species, especially the rookery they were visiting, due to shifting sea ice and the fact that this particular rookery had suffered due to an ice jam for almost a decade that had blocked the parent's entrance to the ocean. The local population had declined by half and was threatened due to the weakened state of the population, egg predation by rats and other birds.

Sandi wondered whether coming was a good idea after all and started to feel depressed, but then they landed on the edge of what appeared to be a rocky coastline—except for the lack of a coast.

They got out and walked along a worn rocky path in a freezing wind, but in ten minutes came up to a low ridge. The Mayor motioned them to stop.

"The penguins are very tolerant of humans," he said, "but this is the end of the mating season and so the mothers can be very aggressive. Just walk around slowly and ignore the noise."

They walked around and in spite of the awful, fishy smell, the din of thousands of penguin conversations, and guano at every step,

Sandi fell in love with the beautiful birds. Knowing so few of this year's hatchlings would survive depressed her deeply, but she stayed out in the cold as long as she could stand.

As they flew back to Esperanza in silence, Sandi was dour, determined to find out why terrorists had the temerity to bring nuclear weapons to this pristine part of the world and kill such beautiful animals, as had clearly been the case on the Amery. She was pissed and perplexed at the same time.

Dear Betsy,

Old girl, we had another splendid day in the South Pacific! I did a little cabin cleaning and aired out the stateroom because of the glorious Trade Winds that blew all day. It was blustery at times, maybe up to 25 knots, but Brad kept the sails trim and I only lost my footing once when we lurched a little. It was even fun, except I'll probably have a bruise on my arm.

I took a few turns at the wheel, mainly because this kind of weather makes sailing so much fun. There was a lot of spray, but the waves were small almost all day.

The real excitement, of course, was when the tsunamis went past us. Fortunately, we had BBC World News on at breakfast and heard about the Indian Ocean disaster. I was concerned, at first, but Brad hauled out the atlas and showed me: first, that we would likely get only smaller side waves, and that second, we were in a deep section south of the Tuamotu Trench, so I relaxed. Imagine his surprise when they passed and turned out to be at least 2-3 foot swells traveling oblique to the background waves. I don't think that he even thought we could feel them here, but he whistled. There was not much doubt, because they came as discernable waves at about thirty minutes apart, late in the afternoon on top of a light chop.

But we both relaxed after that and broke open a bottle of brandy and each had a glass before dinner. I just rummaged together some leftovers and Brad seemed happy. He rubbed my feet after dinner; he was so sweet! He used to do that all the time, but has gotten lazy. Maybe we should drink more brandy! The winds calmed after dark and he set the autopilot a few minutes ago. Time to turn out the lights, soon.

Talk to you tomorrow!

January 18
Wednesday

The mood in the White House early the next morning was dismal but the tension of the previous days was gone—now replaced by a sense of foreboding. The storm outside howled with a ferocity that paralleled the destruction halfway across the planet. President Clark had not slept well which his staff could see in his face. That morning his senior staff gathered outside the Oval Office in the secretary's office soberly watching the CCN Tsunami Crisis coverage. The senior staff normally did not linger long there. Today was different, because even if the crisis had not resulted in cancelled meetings, the Nor'easter would have. Except for the occasional howling of the wind through the portico outside, the White House was relatively quiet.

The staff was then sent into the Oval Office where the president was also watching the television.

The president waved the TV remote control and muted the sound.

"What's next?" he asked to no one in particular.

A silence returned his question.

Chief of Staff Craft filled the void choosing his words slowly and carefully.

"The Security Council should convene a special War Crimes Tribunal to start its work prosecuting the lunatics responsible for this human disaster. Next, double or quadruple our efforts in Antarctica."

Press Secretary Bundt added, "You need to make a public statement. We need to evacuate coastal areas now."

Max Henderson, senior aide to the president, shook his head. "This could have been coincidence or dumb luck. Evacuation of 40 million people will only lead to panic and would be an over-reaction." The others in the room looked like they were trying to make up their own minds.

The president stood up and paced in front of the windows and looked out at the blizzard. "Come back in an hour and give me some options on a public statement. Greg, see if the networks will take pre-emption. Max and Greg give me a range of evacuation contingencies and the rest of you give them ideas. Max, I also want a statement of sympathy crafted. I am near tears about this and don't want a something that will make me well up, ah, look weak, you know... Something firm and strong."

"Yes, Mr. President."

"Also, Nelson, have Elliot and Sam get to work on a worst case estimate of actually how many would have to be evacuated, and from where... if the Ross Ice Shelf does collapse."

"Yes sir, Mr. President." Nelson looked grim but stood up and quickly left the room, and the others filed out quietly behind him.

"Joyce?" he pressed his intercom.

"Yes?"

"Get me Ambassador Moore on the phone, please."

The wind howled outside of the base in Antarctica no less ferociously than in Washington. Sandi gritted her teeth and braced herself for the bitter cold—made worse by the fury of helicopter backwash. Sandi and Raul dashed from the airlock across the concrete pad with technicians and marines taking up the rear. Everyone was armed to the teeth, which made the egress and boarding awkward and dangerous.

The pressure coming down on them was palpable. Between the CNN reports and repeated inquiries from government "higher ups," Sandi was getting really worried. The whole situation seemed totally out of control. Their mission's failure might literally mean the end of the world, and she was dogged by fatigue and the experience with the penguins depressed her. The thrumming of the chopper bothered her sinuses. She gritted her teeth and focused.

They were now mobilizing to occupy the abandoned Hungarian base several hundred kilometers to the southeast. Satellite imagery from a month prior showed considerable activity that was unquestionably their terrorist band. The images showed a beehive of coming and going, personnel and materiel. Some shots of the equipment matched what analysts also saw in satellite images from Punta Arenas. Sandi pulled out the 8 x 10 satellite images of the Hungarian Camp, near the base of the Latady Mountains that bordered the Ronne Ice Shelf. She studied them one after the other, intently focused on the out buildings and the layout of the compound. She tapped the marine captain on the shoulder and pointed to the picture.

"Tell the pilot we need to drop down well away from the side of the base—opposite from the fuel tanks."

He nodded. "Booby-trapped, you think?" He said it as a statement, not a question.

She continued. "Expect the worst. I'd worry about land mines, but they'd be too tricky to use down here. You think?"

He didn't look too sure.

"In any case, have your men secure the main building first so we can set up the forensics and communications equipment. I want an uplink as soon as we are off this bird."

"Yes ma'am," and he went back up to the cockpit.

The flight was long, but it gave her and Raul plenty of time to go over the plan of attack and to bounce some questions off the marine captain. There was some comfort in learning that the marine had earned medals in the Malvinas Islands War and had spent most of the last ten years in Antarctic duty, of his own choosing. He did not question Sandi's command in the slightest and even displayed diffidence more than the typical Argentine male. Sandi trusted him immediately.

The captain pointed out that the most likely booby-traps were in the main building, so he persuaded the two federal agents they should enter the compound in a two-step operation, by securing the motor pool shed first, then the main building. After some discussion the three agreed to let the helicopter return once the shed was "all clear." As cold as it was the helicopter had to keep its engines going, so it could not afford to stay long without running out of fuel. And there was no guarantee that there was any fuel left at the Hungarian base. A backup helicopter back at the Chilean base was standing by, and would take upwards of three hours to reach them. Of course serious weather could strand them indefinitely. More storms were in the forecast for the next few days. Sandi wondered: What else could hamper the investigation?

The first answer to that question was the burned out motor shed. The charred remains of several large snow cats and a dozen snowmobiles gave testimony to their enemy's cunning. The helicopter circled the base and then landed smoothly, without incident. The marines fanned out and the detectives and their team headed to the motor shed. Sandi put two young detectives to work to look for whatever evidence might be left. The marine commandoes encountered no booby-traps, but discovered that building after building had been torched. Sandi swore out loud at the spy satellite analysts who had obviously failed to note that the compound had been nearly burned to the ground. She then cursed herself with the realization that the terrorists had undoubtedly waited for one of the frequent summer storms to cover their handiwork.

Curiously, the communications shed—a small, well-insulated rectangular box—had been left untouched. It had been cleaned out: not a shred of paper could be seen, although a thin layer of dust covered everything. Sandi smiled. She knew two things: first, it was no accident that this building was still usable and someone might be returning. Second, she knew that she would squeeze some information out of that little building and its contents. That was her job, and she got started. She didn't even hear the helicopter take off.

The first thing, most obviously, was that a small solar-electric heater had been left on, and that all of the communications equipment appeared to be in 'standby' mode except for one computer. She put Raul to work to see what they might find on its hard drive. After ten minutes of dusting for fingerprints—there weren't any—she noticed one set of clocks that did not fit. There were, in fact, too many clocks. Most of the equipment in the room was German, Russian, or Hungarian. Above a German set of clocks sat the three Seiko digital LED readouts proclaimed local time, GMT, and a countdown. The latter announced 83 hours, 22 minutes, and a few seconds. Then it dawned on her: Omega time. She quickly got back to work.

Karen and her entourage landed late the night before at the US Palmer station on the Antarctic Peninsula, and were now on their way to the Hungarian outpost. No one had gotten much sleep so they were all drawn and haggard. Even Pete, who had the most even and balanced disposition, was grumpy. The big cargo plane had no passenger windows, so he invited himself up to the cockpit and spent some time meditating on the harsh surroundings. For a long time he sat next to the navigator in an extra seat, but finally the copilot got up for a stretch and offered Pete his seat. Pete couldn't stop himself from staring at the instruments and the pilot caught his eye.

"Looks ancient, right?"

"Yeah. Common reaction?"

"These planes are older than most of the crew, but still reliable. Sometimes the gauges stick a little, but manual manipulation usually does the trick." And to make his point he tapped lightly on one fuel gauge that moved closer to empty. He laughed at Pete's reaction.

"You're in good hands."

Pete laughed a little laugh, and turned his attention to the frozen land below. It was mesmerizing. He had thought that everything would be white, but the colors varied, shades of blue, a hint of green sometimes with flashes of dark, of brown, and glimpses of deep dark crevasses. Hardly the white sameness he'd expected. There were even suggestions of textures in the snow and ice—wavy forms, like sand dunes, streams of glaciers, and desiccated broken heaving forms of ice. No sameness, but lots of snow and ice. Then, slowly, the snowscape began to look familiar, and the dream came back to him, all at once. He shivered involuntarily.

The copilot tapped his shoulder and Pete got up and went back to his bench in the back. He realized how loud it was and put the mufflers he was issued back over his ears. That was fine because he really didn't want to talk to anyone. He was generally overwhelmed by the news of disaster in the Indian Ocean as the death toll mounted and more specifically by the dream. The words of the *Loa* now echoed in his head. He wrote them down.

And the images of disaster were equally as vivid. During their brief layover at Palmer Station, they were all riveted to CNN until solar storm activity wiped out the signal. Radio reports from Auckland continued through the night, of course. Their instructions also came in to proceed east to meet up with the Argentine team designated as lead. Army Rangers were also en route.

There was some concern about logistics and supplies for the effort, but Palmer, McMurdo, and all the other scientific bases were operating on a crisis footing, summer research was at a standstill for now as resources were marshaled for this battle for the future of the planet. Testament to the seriousness of the situation was the extent to which British and Argentine forces were cooperating, even though many of the Harriers and soldiers were coming from the Falkland Islands. But Pete had a bad feeling about it all, mainly because they had no clue where the enemy was at the moment. And the enemy was "armed and dangerous," very smart, and had a huge head start. Oh, and they were armed with nuclear weapons. And they proved that they were willing to use them. Oh boy. Not much room for negotiation, so all the military forces made sense—if they caught up with the terrorists in time.

Bear, Owl, Sparrow, and Angel arrived back at their original base, called "the Grotto," in the Admiralty Mountains just before a summer storm came up. It was a long flight and they were nearly out of fuel due to strong head winds. None of them expected to live out the week, but no one had any desire to die in a helicopter crash, either. Angel sent a short encrypted message to Abe that they arrived back safe and then made the rounds of the encampment before laying down to sleep. Cape Hungary at the base of the mountains was about 20 km away and they could trek down there to a supply cache to bring up fuel and other provisions as needed. They were well equipped, but to be on the safe side, had scattered their resources and established caches near their sites—to play it safe. As it turned out, they had had very little trouble and had not run into any official Antarctic scientific or tourist groups all summer. The Goddess was surely looking out for them. She could feel it in her bones. Her bones were also very tired, so she finished her rounds and crawled into her sleeping bag and soon was fast asleep.

Big old Bear, a gentle lumbering giant of a man with hair everywhere, cautiously roused her from her slumber. He did so at arms length since she had punched him a number of times at about this hour of the morning. She was definitely not a morning person to begin with and sleep deprivation made her dangerous—not intentionally, she just didn't like to wake up from her dreamtime.

"Worm, wake up, Abe's calling for you."

That woke her up instantly since they were supposedly under radio silence. She didn't even pull on her tunic, but stumbled over to the radio room in her sport's bra and sweat pants. She fumbled with the headset but got it in place and toggled on the single sideband radio.

"Good morning."

"We have a problem Houston." He loved NASA lingo.

"Well?"

"Number One is not responding. No signal, no response to inquires, nothing. You know that we have lots of redundancy, and the autopilot should work, but of all the devices, Numero Uno must work to start the cascade."

"I know, I know. What do you want us to do?"

"Well, I would hope that is obvious. Replace the transponder. If necessary detonate manually, I am sorry to ask. I was concerned that the device was discovered. No sign of any visitors there, I gather? Look around and let us know what to expect."

"Okay, okay." She paused a moment. "We'll get on it."

"You're wonderful, all of you. Of course use the satellite for further communications. Out." And the connection was cut.

Angel sat there for few minutes and went through a mental checklist of what was needed to carry out her orders. It was short list: a set of transponders—the last in their backup cache. Everyone was up and awake by this time and Bear put a cup of coffee in her hands and then went back to the galley where breakfast sounds were emerging.

She was tense, but shook out her shoulders and willed herself to relax. She told herself that everything would be all right. She went back to her bunk and quickly dressed. After checking the weather report off the satellite, Angel gathered up Bear, Owl, and Sparrow and faced them in the small kitchen.

"I know you guys are bone tired, but we have to do another heroic thing. The transponder on Device One is screwy and we are the ones to unscrew it. Here's the plan: first we go down to the Ronne cache and get spare transponders and then hightail it back up here, get to Numero Uno and make her behave.

"The industrial bees are all stirred up now, so we'll really have to watch our butts. The storm is weakening, but should give us cover for the trip down the mountain to Camp Hungry. Any questions?"

There weren't any—they all knew their jobs and had done this so many times before that they just fell into their places: Bear and Sparrow got the snowmobiles fueled and warmed up; Angel and Owl went down their usual departure checklist and powered down the equipment in the shed. In a half hour they were ready, on their snowmobiles and making progress down a narrow valley to the coast. It was going to be another long day.

Back on the ground at the former Hungarian station, the place was getting really busy. The storm had let up somewhat just before the Americans touched down. From that point things flipped into high gear. By default, this seemed like it would end up being base camp for the antiterrorist effort. More supplies and troops were on the way.

The crew disembarked and unloaded several tons of supplies and equipment. The Americans, too, were armed to the teeth. Support crews set up additional tents and inflatable habitats. Another Herc followed on the first's departure and disgorged a half dozen snow cats and fuel. Another plane followed with more communications gear, a dozen snowmobiles and sleds, dogs, and fuel. Another followed with a British marine platoon and lots of guns and food and fuel. And so it went into the late afternoon.

Little other evidence of the terrorists had emerged, except for two small discoveries, weeks-old high-altitude remote sensing imagery and the discovery of a religious shrine. The aerial images were a fluke—the discovery that Chinese scientists had been taking high altitude thermograph readings looking for under-glacier heat sources in the region. Their passes had taken them over the site a month earlier and the thermographs indicated both the fire and various active heat sources. It certainly wasn't news, but a confirmation. The religious artifacts were more unsettling for Karen.

One of the dogs had sniffed it out 200 meters north of the base nestled in the chunks of an icefall outcropping. The altar itself was a piece of shale. A geologist was being sent from McMurdo to look at it, but the Argentines said it resembled the rock around the Punta Arenas area. There was a feather tied to another rock — this one a round river rock. There was a large round piece of bleached bone, probably whale vertebrae. There was a large pink quartz crystal and finally a fairly good-sized iron meteorite. Traces of carbon and plant fiber had also been found in the snow caught under the leeward edge of the shale alter. A burnt offering—Karen suspected sage or some other smudge material—or incense, evidence of serious, practicing pagans. Earth, wind, fire, and ocean all represented. Political fanaticism tied with religion was a dangerous combination. These were not just a bunch of agnostic radicals, but deeply religious, or spiritual, zealots. Mother Earth jihadists.

The team of investigators met to discuss the day's developments and plan for the next steps in a large inflatable habitat. It was crowded, and the warmth and body odor verged on the unpleasant.

Sandi led the meeting in a matter-of-fact, no-nonsense fashion and moved them through an agenda briskly. A British corporal took notes. The most discussion was provoked by Karen's suggestion that they should take the religious artifacts seriously.

"These are valuable possessions," she said. "They might come back for them."

Most of the others looked at her dubiously.

"Maybe not consciously. What I mean is that while the plan may have been to never come back, someone, or two, left personal objects that they probably did not mean to leave behind."

"Why was the communications shack left intact?" she asked and no one had a good answer for that, either.

But all the other evidence pointed to the place having been abandoned.

Leah was fairly seething her way into trouble. She would have been rested, but the bunk was not very comfortable and she had even more disturbing dreams than the night before. They had been sitting in the mess for an hour or so during ship's "morning" making small talk and Leah seized her chance when the captain came in for a snack. Leah was in front of him quickly, before Bee could react this time. But Leah did not attack him physically.

She fumed at the captain "I want to talk to someone who *knows* something. I want to know why we're on this wretched submarine."

He raised his eyebrows. "Like you can make demands of me?" He looked incredulous.

"You people have been snooping on me, you stole my research, and you've kidnapped us. You have some hair-brained scheme to blow up part of Antarctica. What is the point? Why, why, why?" She was getting hysterical and Bee was close enough to restrain her.

He looked worried for a fraction of a second, looked quickly at Bee and shook his head at her, and then laughed hard and loud.

Leah backed up as if he'd hit her. He smiled at her as if she was a small child. He raised his hands as if in supplication.

"Chill lady. It doesn't really matter too much at this point, I think, to let you in on a few things." He scratched at his chin beneath his beard. "Okay, I'll have our Political Officer talk to you. Let me get a doughnut and coffee and I'll have her come down and talk to you in the library… or here, if you want." He smiled again, as if they were friends.

Jake went to get more for coffee them and Bee became inconspicuous again in the corner with a paperback novel. Jake could see that Leah was fuming. He had given up trying to calm her—at least for the moment. Maybe it was good to let her process it? He wasn't sure and actually getting a little restless himself.

222

"We have got to do something!" She whispered.

He wanted to please her, obviously, but not at the risk of getting them locked up or even killed.

"Sweetie, let's bide our time and see what they have to say." He tried to sound firm and resolute.

She looked up at him and he made motions with his eyes back at Bee. She appeared to catch his meaning and was quiet. She sipped her coffee and growled softly, which actually made Jake laugh softly. Leah actually smiled back. Jake remembered how much he loved her passion.

Jake faced the door and noticed the First Mate, Dr. Collins come in slowly but deliberately. He noticed this time that her willowy frame carried a subtle grace as she made her way to them, fetching a cup of hot water and a green tea bag on the way. She was even more attractive than he'd remembered from the first day they met. Leah had been deep in thought, but noticed that he was staring at the woman.

Jake acknowledged her. "Dr. Collins."

She held out her hand, but neither of them took it. She pulled it back without seeming to notice or care. She sat down.

"Call me Myra, please. I agree with the captain that it's time we talked." Bee moved closer to the group.

"We have run into a bit of a snag and need your help."

Leah ignored that and instead asked. "Why did you abduct us?"

"Because you have the key."

"What key?"

"The propagation key. The model for the most probable sequence of eruptions to loosen the Ross Ice Shelf."

Leah laughed but the doctor's face was passive and unmoved.

"You are joking, right? You can't really be serious! That's nuts! What makes you think I'd help you? Even if I had a clue what you meant?"

First Mate Myra steepled her fingers and took a moment to reply. "I hope that, once I explain the Big Picture and the rationale of what we are doing, the logic will convince you. Secondly, the veracity of my answers to your questions will confirm that your research is true and good. I know you are not a vain person, but surely you are at least a little curious why so many of us in EPG* are devotees of your work."

That took Leah totally off-guard. Then it dawned on her that these lunatics were hell-bent on destroying part of Antarctica, maybe even modern society—and her research might make it all happen!

EPG* Press Release
Days Before the End

Prepare for Magnetic Disruptions or Axis Reorientation

For eons, the Earth's history has been permeated with periods of disaster and destruction. In geological timeframes, Earth's history has been peppered with mass extinctions brought on by comets, volcanism, and the Ocean Herself. Most of the last million years, ice age conditions have predominated. It is ironic that our pathetic species has arisen to so-called civilization in a period of benign climate and geology. This is about to change.

EPG* is committed to help Gaia even the playing field once again and is prepared to unleash Hell on Earth for one reason—to bring industrial civilization to its knees. The EPG* Action in 85 hours—what we are calling the Omega Event—is anticipated to severely disrupt the Earth's magnetic field and may even bring about a shift in the polar axis. Either of these two secondary events will disrupt transportation and telecommunications.

Here's how it works: The Earth's magnetic field is influenced both by the Sun and internal Terrestrial dynamics. In other words, the solar wind and fluidity of the Planet's core make the magnetic field unstable from time to time. When first monitored, the Earth's magnetic poles moved slowly, around ten miles per year, within a few hundred mile-radius of the geographic poles. In the last decade, the magnetic poles have shifted even more erratically, hundreds of miles a year while the radius has expanded to five hundred miles. On top of that, we are currently experiencing one of the most active sun spot cycles on record. EPG* believes that our phased explosions over the South Pole are likely to affect the South Magnetic Pole in some way—to cause it to move abruptly or to oscillate. This is likely to disrupt air transportation, for example, in the Southern Hemisphere.

Further communiqués will advise peoples in low-lying areas and general Dos and Don'ts for All Concerned. Remember: We're Doing this for the Planet.

Bring Back the Ice Age!

Leah's rather long conversation with the EPG* Political Officer had answered most of Leah's initial questions, but raised many more. The worst part was that Leah was beginning to think that however ill advised, however radical the EPG* was, their scheme was plausible and scientific. Their passion was indisputable and determination clear. They were well organized and financed—that element PO Collins would not get into with them—as evidenced by the submarine that they were in. And it was far from "wretched," as Leah had described it earlier. There were no tell-tail leaks, or even, for that matter clear signs of aging. The sub had been refitted and appeared modern.

The most baffling element, however, was how they had stumbled on to her work because parts of their Omega Plan even suggested that some of their thinking was far ahead of hers, or at least others had been working on this effort long before she even made some of her discoveries and conclusions. It really bothered her that she had become an instrument for their design. Her work was an instrumental set of pieces in their End of the World puzzle.

Leah also began to think that they were not crazy either. That thought earlier had been a comfort—that these were a bunch of pot smoking, "bent" eco-freaks who were following some megalomaniacal guru into oblivion. The passion came through Collin's interaction with her, but the analysis was solid and the rationale was very logical and Leah had to admit, sophisticated. Where there were uncertainties, the PO admitted it. The scientific aspects, the geology, climatology, oceanography, glaciology, all had massive uncertainties, but the political and sociological implications of their plan had redundancies and intentions that sounded robust and calculated to achieve their goals.

She was still very angry that she and Jake had been caught up in the EPG* mischief, but Collins had deftly appealed to her analytical nature and had laid bare their vast scheme and even some of the technical aspects of the devices—yields, limitations, and how they were deliberately hoping to minimize fallout and adverse impacts on Antarctic wildlife. But where she really sucked Leah in was in the integration of her own theories of Ross Ice movement, grounding, and geological evolution. Moreover, their extension of her ideas to encompass the whole of West Antarctica—an area ten times larger— literally took her breath away. The plan was so preposterous, so bold and seemingly beyond human intervention, that she had sat quietly for almost an entire minute while the entire design was described to her.

Hours later, Leah luxuriated in a hot saltwater shower—they were restricted to one minute of fresh water to rinse, but could use all the salt water they wanted. Leah physically and metaphorically let it soak in. The briefing began to have a transformational effect on her. While she was still angry, some of her anger was already being displaced to those in her own scientific community who had ignored her or treated her like a child. She blamed them for not paying attention—it was their own damn fault if some fringe environmentalists paid her work more attention. But, she caught herself, reminding herself to continue to resist, and not fall victim to the Stockholm Syndrome.

Her eyes started playing a trick on her: a face seemed to appear as a void in the steam a few feet from her face at the edge of the shower cubicle. It was clearly a woman's face: an African face, round lips, a thin nose, and broad forehead. The lips moved and at first Leah could not hear words, but then she realized that there are words being whispered from the nozzle of the showerhead, and although soft, she began to clearly hear each softly-spoken word.

"Do not succumb to the lunacy," said the showerhead, but the lips were in sync.

"The End of the World is not predetermined. Your choices matter."

And then as Leah rubbed her eyes, not willing to believe one more insult and assault on her psyche, the face faded away. While Leah did not think that she was going crazy, the sleep deprivation and strange dreams were obviously getting to her. Obviously some part of her subconscious was trying to tell her something.

Leah soaped herself again and turned the heat up more and the room filled even more thickly with steam.

This time she heard a voice first, but it was a much deeper voice with a resonance that filled the cubicle. In the same place, a larger, rounded face appeared—a man's face this time.

"*Yemanja* is not your *Loa*, it is I, *Agwe*, who is your *Loa*."

The face was a bit harder to see, but also a void in the steam— kind of like a balloon, without the rubber skin. She looked away hoping it would disappear as the other one had.

"You cannot avoid me, Leah, any more than you can avoid your dreams." That got her attention, because there was something

226

familiar about the face—it was the man in her dream who asked her for *Osun.*

"There are troubles ahead, but *Agwe*, the *Loa* of the ocean will be by your side and be your protector. You have earth-shattering work to do. Don't ignore your obligation."

With that the void disappeared and the space filled with swirling steam. Leah pinched herself to make sure that she wasn't dreaming. She hurt herself so much that she actually let out a small yelp. Then she realized that she was naked, but had not tried to cover herself. The thought was such a contradiction: she took it that there was an actual man in her shower, but there wasn't really. It was only an apparition of some sort. Or a figment of her imagination...

Before other faces appeared, she quickly turned off the salt shower and turned on a spray of cool fresh water to rinse. She got out and started to dry herself. This development was so bizarre that she was working hard to convince herself that sleep deprivation was getting to her. Then she saw two words written on the condensed steam on the mirror in front of her: *Yemanja* had an X drawn through it; *AGWE* was below it. She was suddenly weak in the knees.

The rag-tag EPG* stragglers left their cavern base and started down the mountain. Angel and Owl took the lead on a two-man Yamaha snowmobile while the other two followed behind on smaller machines. Owl attended to the GPS and gave Angel course corrections when they were needed. They were lucky because the ice most of the way down was flat and smooth and because they had done this trip so many times it was as if they had a trail worn into the ice. There was, of course, no trail, but it was all familiar terrain.

Visibility waxed and waned, but Angel kept up a steady pace and depended on Sparrow and Bear to keep up. They made their way down the incline toward Camp Hungary in good time despite the weather, but then an airplane passed overhead and she forgot about the creeping chill working its way into her digits.

She knew they were getting close to the Ronne and all of a sudden realized that they were going to have company. She slowed the Yamaha and made a wavy course to get the attention of the other two. They pulled up along side her and all came to a stop.

The wind was blasting them with ice crystals and she motioned them together and they crouched in the lee of the larger snowmobile. Just then another plane—or was it the same one—passed

227

overhead to the west. Apparently the winds were mainly at the surface, confirmed by the breaks in blue sky that occurred every five or six minutes.

"Trouble in Hungry City."

Nobody said anything; they waited for her to lead. Angel had been in charge as long as any of them had been in EPG* and nothing had changed.

"I'd say we're maybe three or four miles out from camp. We'll put on skis and leave the snowmobiles here. We'll rendezvous at the bluff and scope out the supply dump."

When they abandoned the Ronne base many weeks before, they had buried some backup gear and fuel at the far end of the airstrip. The bluff was nothing more than a small rocky outcropping where Angel had made a pagan alter. But in a windstorm like this the bluff should be enough to provide them with cover.

"Bear'll take the lead and the 55mm cannon. Sparrow, please grab one of the AK-47s, and four walkie-talkies. Owl, an AK and the C4 pack. I'll bring the shovels." She looked them each deeply in the eyes and said to Sparrow, "In the worst case scenario, let Abe know that we failed." Sparrow shook her head slowly back and forth in silent denial.

"Okay then." Angel looked thoughtful. "Sparrow, break out a thermos of coffee—we may not have a chance to hydrate for a while. Everyone with me?" They all nodded at her. They shared coffee quietly in the lee of the machines.

"Okay, let's do it," she said after they took turns drinking.

It took them another five minutes to struggle into their skis while the wind picked up a little and the sun seemed to dip lower in the sky. Even though the sun did not set this time of year, when it was obscured by ice or clouds the temperature dropped. It was -20 degrees and they were slowing down despite having been on the continent over a year. Strapping on weapons was a daunting task with the bulky clothing and all three of them had to help Bear shoulder the large machine gun. But soon they leaned into the wind and headed north. Bear was in the lead but Angel barked at him every few hundred feet to make subtle changes in course after she looked at the GPS receiver. They heard no more planes come in or out. The rising storm had most likely made it too dangerous, even for hotshot Navy pilots.

Angel wondered to herself, why the Hungarians had chosen windswept Dodson Peninsula for their base. It was a mystery—maybe because no other national science establishment was brave enough to pick such a spot? And on a spot that caught the prevailing winds nearly 80% of the year. It was a brutal location, weather-wise. On the other hand, as a point of stability along the Ronne Ice Shelve, it did have its geological strong points. She chuckled to herself at her little joke. It had her rocky outcropping and her alter materials that she had left behind.

Then the small outcropping appeared. She motioned for all of them to drop their gear and they sank down behind the rocks where the wind wasn't so strong. She passed the satellite radio receiver and the GPS to Sparrow.

"You guys stay put. I'll get in close to see what we're up against." She knew that she couldn't leave them there long. Moving kept them warm and in this weather, staying still—exposed as they were—would be dangerous.

Angel quickly began to circle the old Hungarian Camp working clockwise, first to the fuel dump where she came up against a Herc with its engines running. There were no guards outside—a surprise, but not such a surprise, too. But it told her that the Marines were not expecting any visitors. Her sixth sense told her that there were Marines, or Special Forces here somewhere. Not exactly intuition, since she was ex-Marine herself. The last time she'd been with Marines was in the blistering desert of the Saudi Peninsula— quite a contrast.

She abandoned her planned circuit and doubled back around the fuel tanks and hit the ground when she saw movement near the burned out hanger and motor pool. She pulled out field glasses and focused on the surroundings. During brief breaks in the wind she saw that there were now a variety of tents and inflatable habitat units ringing the communications hut. Her heart sank. Somehow she needed to figure out a way to get to the far end of the airstrip without being seen. They had to make enough time to find the storage cache and dig out the spare transponders. Her own energy level was dropping—not a good thing. She swore under her breath. Then the plan came to her. When the next wave of wind came she pulled herself up and returned to her team. They did not look well, but she worked her magic on them with a pep talk.

"Guys, the whole Kali program depends on us now. If we can't do this then the bloody planet killers will have won. We have come too far to fail Abe and the rest of our brothers and sisters. *Freya* is truly with us at the moment—find your inner strength and ignore the cold!

"Bear I want you to take the C4 and set the timer for 2200— that is 20 minutes from now. Place it next to the fuel tanks and then get back up here. I want you to set up the 55mm right here and fire on that plane on the end of the runway, which you'll see from the fuel tanks. I don't care if you hit it. Give us another twenty minutes, get on your skis and meet us back at the snowmobiles. Think you can find your way back there?"

"Sure Angel," he said but without any conviction.

"You two, we're going to circle the long way around the airstrip to the cache. Grab a shovel and an AK." She waited while Bear dug out the C4 timer and fumbled with it. He had to take off his outer glove to punch in the elapsed time, but finally got the numbers to light up and then armed it. She aligned the bezel on her own watch and gave the thumbs up. They all stood up into the wind and she and Sparrow and Owl latched on their skis and picked up their guns and shovels. They traveled part way with Bear but then sped ahead and to the west to maneuver their way around the Herc at the end of the airstrip. Angel said a silent prayer to Gaia and *Freya*.

The storm kept howling and the three desperados silently skied around their old Ronne Base Camp. Frostbite was now a problem, but Angel pushed them, hoping they could find the cache quickly. The airstrip, established by orange-painted fifty-five gallon fuel drums, was pointing for the Herc—which they could hear over the wind. They could barely see the line of drums on the side of the airstrip opposite the camp itself. They followed the line of orange until they passed the last one. She aligned herself with the drums and at the same time referred to the GPS readout. About 100 meters from the last drum she motioned to the others to a small mound of snow that resembled a sand dune. They attacked the mound with their ice picks and snow shovels.

Meantime, in the Recon Hut, Sandi and Raul conferred with Karen while a dozen others looked on. They had just decided to let the Herc return to Esperanza as soon as the next break in the storm came their way. The pilot waited patiently on the end of the airfield, but was antsy as the onboard fuel dropped below 60% full and getting low for the flight back. It had been idling for nearly an hour waiting for a promised break in the weather and for the go-ahead from Sandi who called the shots.

Karen and Sandi liked each other immediately, so they had no trouble jumping into a broad-ranging discussion of logistics and points of investigation. Data still came in from a variety of fronts and they spent some time just working out the organizational framework of the command post—asking for more computers and personnel from McMurdo and the Brits. There had been some resistance from HQ to expend so much effort and resources and then to haul it to the even-more isolated Hungarian Base. But pressure came back quickly from Washington and Karen and Sandi delegated much of the data analysis and feedback responsibility to their seconds-in-command.

They had had some power problems during the first few hours, but now things settled down and were expected to improve considerably once the weather cleared when they could get more tents and generators up and running. They had shifted gears minutes before to a discussion of the possible locations of EPG* strongholds or hideouts in the Admiralty Mountains and had tasked some of the FBI-and-Intelligence folks who had arrived to work on the photo recon and satellite image analysis.

Logistics was the biggest immediate problem since they were located five hours by air from McMurdo—the South Pole was actually closer. So, they were relying heavily on Chilean and Argentine aircraft, fuel, and food.

The Argentine, Marine Captain Jones, reentered the hut with a British captain followed by a dozen soldiers carrying weapons and extra flak jackets. The Brit interrupted the conversation, although all eyes were already on him.

"It seems we have some visitors. Everyone put on a vest if you don't already have one on." He eyes the walls of the inflatable habitat. "These walls will not stop bullets."

Sandi quickly donned a vest and opened her mouth, but before she could say a word the captain spoke.

"We only left a couple of sentries on rotation outside in this mess..." His emphasis was clearly on the word mess. "... But we set up a perimeter of motion detectors and have detected a small group of intruders."

At that very instant the fuel depot exploded and the whole inflatable shook violently and some of the equipment crashed to the ground. Everyone instinctively dropped. The soldiers piled out of the airlock, which deflated the dome somewhat. Sandi felt like a sitting duck, but was not sure what the best move was. Raul, on the other hand, pulled out and chambered a round in his .45 and finished strapping on his own vest.

Raul took charge.

"Sandi, Agent St. Cloud, and your people—suit up and move over to the Communications Building. It offers the best protection and is more defensible. Go!"

Sandi and Karen did not hesitate, and Karen grabbed the shaken and visibly stunned Pete Wilde by the shoulder, led him to the pile of parkas near the airlock, put one in his hands, grabbed one for herself, but it was hardly on before she was outside in the cold and pulled him toward the small building 20 meters away. While the force of the storm clawed at her shirtsleeves, the cold did not penetrate the adrenaline that pumped through her. The –20° air burned her throat and hit her lungs like a fist. She gasped but kept on going until they were all inside the small building. As they pulled the door shut another explosion—this time a much deeper, duller detonation—shook the building. One of the older agents who Karen had only just met said simply, "The second fuel tank, I bet."

Shrapnel hit the communications hut and they heard a short burst from the machine gun on the outcropping. A volley of return fire from the Marines sounded closer, and then the firefight began in earnest.

The Herc's pilot could be heard on the console radio, "What the hell?"

Bear had only a few thousand rounds and knew he'd have to marshal his resources. He decided to wait a few minutes after the explosion—mainly to give his mates more time to reach their goal. The large man was shy, sensitive and normally wouldn't hurt a fly. His experiences in the Colombian drug wars and then his love and devotion to his friends in the Green Alliance had transformed his views. Accidentally hitting Angel, Sparrow, or Owl with "friendly fire" was not something he could contemplate. So he held off, which began to look like a mistake because the wind had dissipated and he could begin to see the Herc and dozens of figures winding their way around the end of the camp towards his position. He let out a stream of lead toward the burned out hanger in the middle of his field of view and then pulled back behind the center of the outcropping and pulled himself to the left side where he took aim at the Herc.

He gritted his teeth and readjusted the gun's tripod slightly in the snow. Then Bear dragged the amo bag closer to the machine so that the feeder belt wouldn't get hung up. He'd had that happen to him numerous times during his stint in the Marines in the jungles of Columbia. He ducked his head as bullets whizzed by both sides of the outcropping and dull thuds gave evidence to direct hits. A few ricocheted off the rock. Bear listened patiently to the sounds—far different from the sounds of battle back in the Amazon.

He took a deep breath and pulled back slowly on the trigger. As the wind died down again, he directed his fire at the middle of the plane's fuselage and the nearest wing. He stopped for a second to look at the plane as the smoke from the gun cleared. He couldn't see much and a gust of wind obscured his view again. He pulled the trigger and sent out a few hundred more bullets. Then the plane burst into flame. A couple of men piled out of the front hatch, but Bear ignored them.

He took advantage of the next gust of wind and pulled the gun further to the left so he could work over the approach of Argentine marines. Their arctic camouflage gear didn't prevent Bear from catching their movements on his flank to the right and coming up from the burned out hanger and motor pool buildings. He raked over both clusters of soldiers and then a grenade went off right on top of the rock. Hot metal pierced Bear in a number of places in his arms and legs and he unleashed a blood-curdling cry of anguish and anger. He wasn't able to move his right arm, but with his left he pulled the trigger on the Gatling gun and he held on tight to it until the gun was cycling on empty. Another grenade went off on top of him and took his consciousness with it.

A silence fell over the camp as the fuel dump made muffled, small secondary explosions and Herc put out huge clouds of billowing smoke. Then came the cries of the wounded.

While Sparrow crouched and kept a lookout, Angel and Owl dug vigorously and they finally reached the cover of the metal box containing their cache. At nearly the same moment the gunfire stopped.

"Uh oh," said Sparrow softly.

Angel looked up without stopping and spied figures between the runway and new tent encampment in the distance. She hauled up the electronics pack and stuffed it into her backpack.

"Sparrow, back into your skis. Owl, you'll have to cover us." She didn't sound apologetic, just the flat voice of command.

Argentine marines began to shoot at them and Angel and Sparrow quickly snapped into their skis while Owl dropped into the hole they'd dug and returned fire. Sparrow got off a few shots before Angel tugged her arm and they took off in an oblique direction.

Bullets whizzed by but they zigged and zagged and within two minutes they were well out of range. Owl slowed the soldiers advance and when he took a minute to look after his friends they were out of sight in the blowing snow. The wind picked up again. In another minute the windblown powdery snow cut visibility even further.

Owl emptied a clip from his Kalashnikov and then reloaded. The return fire was just as vigorous but wide of him—possibly because the wind had picked up again. The soldiers would move closer now, so wisely, Owl decided to move himself. He took the time to snap into his skis and then moved back toward the runway and toward the flickering lights of burning airplane and fuel. He dropped behind one of the empty fifty-five gallon drums that marked the runway and unloaded a clip in the direction of the new tents. Bullets flew by again, but this time a slug caught him on the side of his head. He passed out and crumpled into a ball.

Sparrow and Angel worked up a sweat and the wind buffeted them ferociously. It was a worse wind than before and this time they ran directly into the wind. Angel would have been more worried, but the GPS put them right on track and they would be back to the snowmobiles in minutes. She pushed thoughts out of her head of the loss of her two friends. Now was not the time to mourn.

Sandi and Karen slowly made their way along the line of burned out buildings towards the still burning fuel tanks and the wind blew the thick black smoke away from them. Ahead of them went one of the marines who Captain Jones had sent to get them. Sandi ordered Raul to get in touch with McMurdo on the Com Shack radio and they had left the other civilians huddled together there, too. Sandi discovered that the cold attacked a person in funny ways. Overall, the gear protected her well, but her feet grew cold and her nose and face burned. She tried to ignore the cold and focus on putting one foot ahead of the other. Karen grunted, so she assumed Sandi had similar trouble. Each breath was painful, too, like breathing icicles or needles.

The soldier ahead of them turned and said in Spanish to Sandi, "Follow closely, we're walking about 200 meters over to the rock outcropping."

Sandi translated and then they moved away from the security of the buildings, Karen followed two paces behind Sandi. They walked away from the wind, which eased the blasts of wind on their faces, but into a disconcerting maelstrom of blowing snow and whiteout. But the young soldier knew where he was going and by the time Sandi was getting really worried that they were lost in the blizzard, they came upon a familiar sight: a crime scene. At least that was what it felt like since the marines had somehow managed already to set up klieg lights and were photographing the intruder's body— what was left of it.

Capt. Jones grimaced.

He looked back at her. "Four of ours are dead, seven wounded. We have one other intruder, too. Wounded, but in fair condition."

"Okay," she replied, "And there were others?"

"Yes ma'am. They had a small supply depot buried at the end of the runway and removed something from it. We think there were two others and have search parties out looking for them, but they are gone."

"How?"

"On skis. The one we captured was on skis. He's being examined by the doctor."

"Okay, wrap it up out here. Collect his body and bring it down to the camp—wherever the other bodies are going for now. What a mess. Get everyone out of the cold, ASAP."

She explained briefly the situation to Karen.

"What about the plane?" she asked.

In fairly decent English, Jones replied, "A total loss and blocks the runway. Not so good."

Angel and Sparrow went way too fast. Although she knew it intellectually, Angel was not able to argue well with her adrenaline, so she simply didn't try. One thing she had learned about surviving in Antarctica was that balance was crucial: to keep your footing on the ice, for example, and especially, not to overheat. Overheating left you vulnerable to exposure. The new fabrics were great to wick moisture away from your body, but ice also tended to work its way into those fabrics from the frigid atmosphere and that cut down on efficiency and the cold worked its way closer to the body. Keeping those layers of air between you and the outside isolated was important—how you actually stayed warm in such an unforgiving climate. And the exertion itself was a factor. Replacing burned calories was another balancing act. She began to worry about how safe they would be once they reached the 'mobiles.

The thoughts finally manifest themselves to her.

"Sparrow, slow down. We are almost there."

Sparrow followed instructions, but Angel could tell that her friend suffered from fatigue and probably emotional shock.

The storm let up somewhat and Angel carefully surveyed the surroundings, but she saw nothing. She knew that the industrial bees swarmed behind them somewhere and was disinclined to give them an opportunity to sting. They came up quickly on the stash of machines. She briefly debated whether to torch Owl's bigger machine, but in the interest of time and to save vital energy, she quickly helped Sparrow out of her skis and once they both had stowed skis and the transponder, they powered up the two smaller snowmobiles and warmed them up for a scarce minute they didn't really have. Those 'mobiles would keep them alive a bit longer. She kept a sort of conversation going with Sparrow, "remember this, remember that" about the return trip as much to keep them both focused on the moment rather than from necessity. She knew that her friend was upset about the loss of their two male comrades.

Visibility continued to improve and they both revved their engines and headed back up the hill toward the base. The cold worked its way inexorably into her body and Sparrow's. She actually was worried more about the smaller woman—who had less of her own padding and who had also already lost a toe to frostbite in the early days of the expedition. Angel wanted to toggle on her radio and speak to her, but no, radio silence. She tried to left go and instead shifted her focus back to the trail ahead. Now the growing visibility could worry her since they would be sitting ducks in this wide-open landscape. They would have to wait until the very last possible minute to refuel and stop for food and water.

They continued to make their way up the ice massif. This slow-moving glacier was actually one of the oldest stretches of ice on the continent because it was mostly ice grown—deposited—on the leeward side of a mountain hundreds of miles to the west on the West Antarctic spine. The ice here—at the end of the flow—predated the last interglacial period, according to their research before they stumbled onto the Hungarian's abandoned site. In any case, the ice was dense and smooth for tens of miles up the slope. She half expected the Special Forces units on their tail, but there were still no sign of them. She reminded herself that she was a guerilla fighter. This was "her" terrain, not theirs. She had spent close to three years down here, so it stood to reason that she was the master of her space. Then she reminded herself not to get cocky.

She kept her eyes peeled for the ice falls about thirty klicks from the Hungarian base and hoped, now, that their gas would hold out that long. Her fuel indicator was teetering on empty, so she mentally prepared herself for a stop anytime. Besides, she was starving now and the adrenaline was definitely wearing off. At that very instant, she made out the ice falls coming up and waved a couple of times back at Sparrow who acknowledged with a wave back at Angel. They might make it.

Then, all hell broke loose in the form of the thumpa-thumpa-thumpa of large helicopters and the scream of jet planes: a swarm of them erupted around them. Angel's heart was in her throat and she throttled up to the max and shot even further ahead of Sparrow. Once she gathered her senses, however, and calmed down a bit she realized that while loud, the jets hadn't yet noticed the two snowmobiles. Even more jets arrived, maybe a half dozen, and the large 'copters thumped behind them. The storm had let up to allow the industrial bees to get closer. US advanced stealth fighters. They were flying slower and lower over the frozen terrain and made a considerable racket.

Finally, they were spotted as they made it over the ice falls, a small snowy hummock that indicated some obstruction deep beneath the surface of the glacier—an ancient mountain top, perhaps. The irregularity in the landscape there had camouflaged them from above, but no sooner had they passed through, when a jet quickly returned to their position and then another. Each got lower, in turn. In one last low pass, a third fighter shot by only a hundred feet above them. Both green warriors kept going but wobbled in their paths. The sounds of helicopters grew louder. A wall of snow loomed ahead. The noise peaked and faded as blowing snow surrounded the sound of the jets in icy fury. They pushed on, running on empty.

Sandi and Karen questioned their captive on and off for two hours, but they got little out of him. Both his legs were shattered and the morphine he'd been given hadn't helped. He drifted in and out of consciousness. They had the doctor follow the morphine with a sedative hypnotic, one of a new generation of "truth serums" and waited for him to come around again.

Sandi asked him gently where his friends were going. Very clearly, he said, "Mount Helix."

"Why? What is at Mount Helix?" she asked.

He would not or could not answer. His shoulders and face tightened up and he looked pained, then he passed out again.

Karen looked at Sandi, and she spoke into her headset. "Raul, find Mount Helix on the map."

They made their way out of the medical tent and over to the command center.

There was no Mount Helix on any of their maps. Karen got on the phone to Washington and within minutes had a small army within the intelligence community working on the problem. An hour later an answer came back from the CIA Photo Intelligence section. One possibility was a set of mountains directly to their west along the spine of the West Antarctic Mountains—a pair of conical peaks with summits approximately the same height. A quirk of geography drew the prevailing winds to the north of one and to the south of the other. From space the wind-blown snow patterns gave the mountain's morphology a distinctive "S" shape. That might be Mt. Helix. Unfortunately, it was nearly a thousand miles away.

They had to take some chances, so Karen ordered a mobilization of troops and planes to the area and set the team in motion. They would leave a contingent at the Hungarian base in case any of the terrorists returned again. They would continue to follow the two terrorists who had escaped, and assumed that they were headed west. Luck was on their side as the weather began to clear.

"Mr. President, we have an update from the FBI we'd like you to see." The chief of staff had been away from the Oval Office for hours and the president actually looked happy to see him.

"Lay it on me." The president looked up expectantly, but Craft shook his head.

"It's not good. This will go faster if you just read it, sir."

The president spent a good fifteen minutes reading through the slim volume, marked "Top Secret." His friend and top aide sat in a leather chair, and sipped coffee, and stared out the window at the snowstorm. The wind howled and rattled the windows slightly. The light faded into dusk, but the horizontal streaks of snow played a tiny symphony of off-white as they bumped into each other and the window. A small drift had gathered on the eastern exposure of the rounded window set. A pair of Secret Service agents in heavy parkas stood silent vigils outside the west door of the portico.

The president looked up.

"Let me get this straight. A graduate student, who likes fast cars and older men, knew that this Antarctic catastrophe was possible?"

"No sir. The way I read it, her research corroborates what they say they're going to do. The evidence points to her abduction as another act of EPG* in the execution of their plan. Wilson and her husband seem to have gotten in the way, or have information that the EPG* wants. Her research was very controversial—according to some of the wiser minds in that field—considered maverick and flakey. Earth sciences are poorly understood and the previous Administration and Congress reduced NSF funding in that area. It was too closely related to global warming research. In any case, her most recent research work seems to have disappeared and we have only found traces of it. But her work on undersea volcanoes and the West Antarctic rift zones has been published and the FBI, CIA, and the science people have put together a fairly alarming picture. Related work by her professor husband—point to periodic volcanism in the Antarctic geologic record that appears to be tied to sea levels over the last million years or so."

"So why has no one taken any of this seriously before?" The President looked incredulous.

"Mr. President, with the economy behaving the way it has most folks are focused on the very short term, no surprise to you I am sure. Even the scientists looking at climate change have been focused on the last ice age, which is a misnomer, they actually call them 'ice cycles' in scientific circles—the last 100 thousand or the last 200 thousand years. The ice cores from Greenland go back only that far. Only deep near the South Pole have ice cores been drilled that show older records. As I said, we don't really know much about our planet's history. Ironically, our species has been around for at least the last 10 or more ice cycles. Too bad they didn't take notes."

The president looked at him sharply and obviously did not like the joke.

"The point is sir, that even if this young woman's research had been considered more 'mainstream' it still would have been a fairly obscure set of discoveries. At least that's the way it seems. She's really young. Her work was so off-beat it was like the people promoting plate tectonics in the 1950s—no one was listening."

"Woe is us, then?" asked the president.

"I am not saying that. We have the best minds and the world's most powerful military and intelligence forces focused on the problem. Just because EPG* got this far doesn't mean that we can't stop them. We will. We must."

The president looked deflated. "The thing that worries me is that they have a huge head start." He paused. "How are we coming on contingencies for evacuation and protecting coastal infrastructure?"

The chief of staff looked at his watch. "We can pull together an update within an hour. Okay?"

The president nodded and his chief of staff stood up and walked toward the door.

"Thank you, Mr. President."

President Clark looked out the window at the deepening, darkening snow.

Dear Betsy:

I had another strange day. We both slept well after the weirdness of yesterday and awoke to a bright clear morning with gentle swells coming from the southeast. I fixed us a big breakfast— we were both hungry and so I took out some canned ham and made ham and eggs. We lounged around and Brad got a fix on our position and helped me wash and hang up some clothes.

By late morning it became very calm, with no wind at all and the sea surface became glassy and becalmed—nary a ripple. Although we are not in the doldrums, that was exactly what it felt like. We're in no particular hurry, but I could tell Brad was a bit bothered. You know him—he always likes being "on the go" so I suggested that he power up the diesel engine. He shook his head and went down to call up the weather on the satellite. We just drifted on the southwesterly current.

After a while I joined him below deck to get out of the blistering sun. I could have put up the canopy, but felt lazy and wanted to see what he was up to. He told me we were still making 8 to 10 knots—which I found hard to believe since we were totally still, but he turned the GPS to face me, and sure enough, we were. A strong current, so at least we were making some headway. Brad looked puzzled and I asked him what was going on. He showed me the radar. It looked like a huge island to our south—we were drifting to the northeast—but we were not supposed to be close to anything.

I went up on deck to look and see. At first all I could see was a line of clouds on the horizon. It seemed, well, strange because there were no other clouds in the sky except for this cluster low on the horizon. I just stared for the longest time before Brad joined me. Brad seemed worried—but that's just like him, so I made myself busy and went down and threw together a couple of sandwiches and brought him a beer, too. Once I got up on deck, the perspective changed and I realized that I was not looking at clouds. For one thing, rainbows appear below clouds, not above them! We were definitely seeing rainbows, or at least that is what I would call them... It was a shimmering dance of light across the spectrum, an intense dazzle of light. But the white was bright, too. The line of bluish white was not the fuzziness of clouds, but a very intense solid shape.

Neither one of us could figure out what it was. This has been a strange trip and we have seen many things, many haunting things. But this was different, in a way, very compelling. The closer we drifted, the brighter and whiter it got. Brad went below deck and checked the radar. The island, if that's what it was, was now within fifteen miles and it drew closer.

Brad exclaimed, "It's an iceberg!" I looked at him in disbelief. He nodded and repeated himself with even greater conviction and then swore under his breath. It was a goddamn BIG iceberg, too! Then we heard the explosions. At first it was a crackling sort of sound, maybe like the sound of a rifle shot from a distance. And viewing it with binoculars, we could see the face of the ice cliffs more clearly, huge portions of the ice crumbled and cascaded into the warm tropical waters. For some unexplained reason the splintering ice sent small chunks high into the air—the reason for the rainbows Brad thought. We drifted closer and closer and the sound became loud and punctuated with a hissing sound as well. Brad seems to have been mesmerized, in a trance watching this spectacle, but shook his head and reached over and turned over the engine.

We both seemed to realize at the same time that we might be in danger. We could see a swarm of smaller icebergs, many far larger than our boat, surrounding the island of ice. We could feel a cool breeze come at us from the island and saw that it was immense. Maybe five miles away, by that point, the island stretched to fill the horizon toward the south. The face of the ice cliffs looked to be hundreds of feet tall. Brad turned the boat to the east and asked me to monitor our distance so that we stayed well away from the halo of smaller bergs—we were now about three miles away. The sound of that exploding ice was like nothing I have ever heard. It reminded me of the sound of cracking ice cubes in warm water, but only deeper and more resonant, perhaps because it was relatively far away. The sound was enchanting, in a way, and seemed to echo—maybe echoing on itself? Très bizarre!

The ocean surface was now rippled with wavelets that came from the ice cascades. The heat of the day was held at bay for a time by the cold wind that picked up force as the afternoon wore on. We continued to parallel the "coast" of the island, a good ten miles wide, and who knew how many miles long? It was plain that the current we were caught in was not the same as some deeper current moving the ice island—perhaps the reason for the ablation going on in front of us and a reason to avoid the back side—another Brad speculation...

While we watched and tracked to the southeast, Brad got on the phone and called the U.S. Coast Guard in Honolulu, to see if they had heard of this 'berg. Much to our surprise, they had, but were astounded to hear that it had drifted so far north. It was a splinter of an even larger piece of the Ross Ice Shelf that had broken off Antarctica almost five years before.

Over the afternoon we pulled further away to the southeast, but continued to hear the noise of the disintegration echo across the still waters until well after dark. I am getting ready to get some sleep so I can relieve Brad at the wheel on the next watch.

This trip will make quite a story for the grandkids.

Talk later 'gator!

January 19
Thursday

The president stood before the thin 18th century windowpanes of the Oval Office and absently scratched at the frost that formed on the inside. The cold projected itself into the room uninvited. Normally in winter the space was cold, with little insulation, and despite recent refurbishing of the heating and A/C systems, it was much colder than normal. Chief of Staff Nelson Craft sat a dozen feet away from the president in a leather chair near a space heater. For the moment, the two men were alone in the room.

The president cleared his throat and asked, "What's the weather report?"

"Mr. President, the storm has stalled and the low sits right over Richmond, that's why we are still getting pounded."

"We sure are," he replied as he continued to stare out the frosted windows that were now buried halfway up in a drift. It sure felt like the Ice Age had begun. He turned to his friend and advisor.

"Let's get the show on the road." He toggled the intercom and asked the secretary to ask the rest of the senior staff into the office. He said nothing, but nodded at and made eye contact with each as they filed in.

"Give me the latest."

"Mr. President," began Craft, "there is good news on a number of fronts. The NSA reports that the joint NEST team in Antarctica had a firefight with a small group of the eco-terrorists at the abandoned Hungarian base. Four Argentine Marines were killed and twice as many were wounded. The NEST team killed one of the terrorists, captured one, and two got away in a snowstorm. The one they captured is seriously wounded and they will interrogate him. They are still pursuing the two greens that got away."

The president raised his eyebrows in question. "What is their story?"

Chief of Staff Craft looked up. "The FBI team isn't sure exactly at this point. Three were seen outside the base uncovering some sort of cache—food, supplies, or weapons. We really don't know at this point. The investigators are hoping to get some intelligence from the captured terrorist."

"Okay, go on."

"The NSA reports that they discovered a likely source of some clandestine satellite data uplinks from the open ocean off the coast of Antarctica. We previously thought that the enemy base was somewhere on the coast or perhaps on the Antarctic Peninsula, but NSA is monitoring what they think is an intermittent data stream coming from a command vessel. They intercepted a series of data transmissions that occurred shortly before the last EPG* communiqué. That in turn, led them to evidence of a data uplink to a private Hughes satellite over Tonga. They believe that it was coming from an ocean vessel. The Naval Submarine Deep Tracking station on Kauai detected a 'bogie'—an unidentified submarine about 600 nautical miles north of Antarctica. Since the Seventh Fleet is already in the area, PacFleetCon ordered the group to intercept the sub. They are about a day away and will send out sub-chasers and anti-sub aircraft ahead of them. The War Room is tracking their progress."

The president shook his head and said, "That is the good news?" Then he gave a nod for the briefing to continue.

"Less encouraging news is about the weather. Fuel oil supplies are at an all-time low and there are already severe shortages throughout New England and the upper Midwest. Transportation is at a standstill from the Carolinas all the way to the Canadian border. Some 500 deaths are now attributed to the Nor'easter affecting fifteen states in the eastern US.

"As the NY Stock Exchange has been closed for four days, the international markets are in a tailspin. The Tokyo Nikei index tumbled to lose ten percent of its value overnight. London and other European markets fared almost as poorly. Supplies of some consumer goods are running low in some regions and hoarding is a growing problem.

"The worst news is the rising death toll from eastern India and Bangladesh, where the CIA estimates anywhere between 2 and 3 million dead. The National Academy of Sciences team is convinced that there is a relationship between the bomb blast in Antarctica, the seismic event, and the subsequent tsunamis.

"Overnight, a special grand jury was convened in Chicago— where they've managed to keep the roads and airports open—that indicted twenty-one members of the EPG* group for conspiracy to commit murder and serial murder. Independently, the Army's Central Command has an even larger list of EPG* members who have been designated 'enemy combatants.' There are 'shoot to kill' rules of engagement for EPG* both domestically as well as in the battlefield."

The press secretary spoke. "Mr. President, I think you need to make some public statement of sympathy now for the victims of the tsunami. We have waited too long, as it is. There is growing concern, and some fringe scientists in the media are warning that the US coasts could be vulnerable to tsunamis from West Antarctica. I think we need to respond to that, in one way or another."

The president's face was as white as the frost on the windows behind him. He was quiet for an uncomfortably long time.

"What does the Academy think will happen if the EPG* succeeds in collapsing the West Antarctic?"

Craft shook his head.

"Well, find out, will you? I am going back to the residence to have breakfast with the First Lady. Call me when there is any significant news." He wasted no time getting up and making his way out of the office.

The chief of staff stayed behind in the Oval Office as the rest of the staff filed out. As usual, the number three person, the White House Communications Officer, was the last in line, but Craft caught his eye and so he waited until the others were out of earshot.

He asked, "When are you going to tell him about the aliens?"

"After breakfast the NSA is coming over—by Snow Cat, I hear. Plan on being here."

"Where would I go?"

They both stared out at the blizzard.

Angel hoisted herself down the long, cold shaft to the Device. The devices had made her nervous since the very beginning of this adventure, but she was so cold and tired that she was beyond caring. She saw the end of her career and her life very close—palpably so. She rappelled to the floor of the crevasse and winced when her feet hit the floor—not because she was in pain but because she could no longer feel her feet.

She walked the short distance to the Device—to the critical Numero Uno. According to their simulations, this device would set the double chain-reaction into motion. It had to go off first, thus signaling the other Devices downstream to detonate in sequence, in a very carefully calculated order of timing, each amplifying the harmonics of the Earth below and ice all around. Angel had been skeptical about the physics—the reality of it all, but she was committed and certainly there was no turning back now.

The Event was supposed to be initiated by the command team in roughly two more days when they were a thousand miles north of the continent and 24 hours after the last communiqué was to be issued warning the Islanders. Angel was of the opinion that the warnings were unlikely to save any lives, but she kept her opinions to herself. At this late date, she was too numb to care.

She uncoupled the malfunctioning radio transmitter from its housing on the wooden rack next to the Device. There were puddles of water at the base of the equipment where small heaters heated the equipment. It was warm enough to send sharp pain to her brain from the frostbite on her fingers and toes, but she focused on her job. She swapped out the old transmitter that had cost her friends their lives. She cried quietly.

The indicator lights turned green. Her job was done. She sighed and slowly began the ascent to the surface, a few hundred feet above. As she climbed, she forced herself to run through a mental checklist of things she needed to do in order to make her way safely to the edge of the glacier to the south. Their natural grotto there had been the EPG* base camp for almost two years, so there was ample room, fuel, food, and medical supplies. It was well hidden in a cavern that the team had discovered three summers before. It was from there that she would signal Abe that he could control the Event trigger. In the back of her mind, she resisted the idea that she would have to trigger it herself. Perhaps that was one of the factors pushing her—the rejection of the idea that she would be the single person responsible for millions of deaths. She rubbed her temples as though she could push the thought out of her mind.

Angel reached the surface. The wind was blowing at about 10 knots from the south—a steady, dry wind that comforted her in a strange way. It numbed the dull aching of her extremities. Her attention slowly focused on Sparrow who looked at Angel quizzically, until Angel gave a "thumbs up." Without a word, Sparrow slung her weapon and started up her snowmobile.

For her part, Angel shuddered slightly, but refocused her attention on her own ignition and started the machine's engine. It stalled. She started it again and this time it took and began to warm up. She heard a plane or helicopter and searched the sky—nothing—

246

so she took off for the rocky hills to the north and Sparrow followed close behind.

The wind died down as they made their way up a slight incline towards the rocks, and the flurries settled to a thin layer of ice dust on the hardpan glacier. Though the path was not flagged or marked in any way, the many months of activity between the hills and the Device had polished the glacier's surface. Nevertheless, the fresh-blown snow covered it this morning, at least until the snowmobiles churned up the powder like trucks in the desert.

That caught the eye of the helicopter pilot, who came within a mile of them before banking to the south. The chopper hovered and trailed them.

Karen and Sandi were deep in discussion and poured over topographic maps of the West Antarctic and the area immediately surrounding the Hungarian base. Sandi had noted the nearby evidence of geothermal activity and the dormant volcano 50 kilometers to their northwest. That had provoked her to call for seismic data from McMurdo. She did her best to overlay the seismic map for the last year over the topographic map even though the scale was wrong and the projection not quite the same. She drew a broad pencil line from the sub-glacier hot springs to their north through the seismic hotspots over the last year. It progressed in a consistent direction to the southwest all the way to the Transantarctic Mountain range south of the Ross Ice Shelf.

"We asked your CIA photo intelligence people to review old satellite imagery along this way for any unauthorized activity over the last year. Here, I believe, we will find our EPG* troublemakers." She pointed with the pencil, then used it to drum absent-mindedly at her ponytail and then looked surprised.

"What?" Karen asked.

"We are either at the beginning or the end of the EPG* tail."

"Please explain, Sandi."

"Sorry, for my bad English. I mean they make a path of nuclear devices to disturb the chain of volcanoes along this line." She pointed with her whole hand down the center of a map of West Antarctica.

"Maybe not always volcanoes, but how would you say it? Mmmm, they are pressure points and fault lines and rift zones that line up. Yes."

"Of course. That makes great sense. Wow, then we must be near one of the devices? But our detection gear hasn't picked up any neutrons."

"That is to be expected if they were careful and if the device is buried under hundreds of feet of frozen water, no?"

"Duh," she answered and shook her head. "Oh course, of course. Shit, that means the detection gear is probably useless. We're screwed."

The radio squawked. Sandi replied and then listened.

"We found them. Spotters have seen the pair—about 40 kilometers northwest, up on the mountain. Raul reports that there are F-16s on the way and we have some good weather today—he said warm by Antarctica standards."

She looked at her watch. "Let's go."

Karen's smile evaporated and shook her head, "No, I have to teleconference with the brass in a half hour. Sandi, you and Raul go ahead. We'll catch up as soon as we can."

"I think you should forget the bureaucrats and be a detective."

Karen laughed and looked into her new colleagues deep blue eyes. She really liked Sandi's no-nonsense attitude, but knew her job.

"I'm tempted, but they need to know what's happening. Things are moving so fast, this may be the last time I will *want* to deal with them. This is a presidential call…"

She seemed to look for Sandi's approval.

"Okay." Sandi smiled at her and winked. "What instructions?"

"Find their camp and catch them if you can, alive. We need information more than anything. They are obviously very dangerous. Be very careful. You know the rules of engagement: protect yourselves first and foremost. Muy bién?"

Sandi nodded, turned to the young marine lieutenant who was shadowing her, "Okay pilot, let's go! Vámanos!" and was out the door behind him.

The helicopter lifted off the ground amidst swirling snow and the nose tilted south. She reached Raul who was with the search team 40 klicks away.

"Hey brother, what's the story? Over."

"Copy. Glad you will join us, Sandi. We are on the ground below a rocky outcropping in the middle of Gustov's Glacier, where we watched two individuals, both women we think, stop their

248

machines, and then disappear into a rocky cliff. This place was well hidden from the air. There are no structures and we do not think they are aware of us. We're waiting for backup—that would be you. Over."

"Copy. I understand the situation. Raul, we have two squads of marines and the air support will be available by the time we arrive. ETA is fifteen minutes. Over."

Both Angel and Sparrow were weak, dehydrated, and exhausted. They struggled out of their heavy outside clothing and boots and entered the common room. There they noted the disarray from the departure many months before. The room was warm—a byproduct of geothermal heating and the small greenhouse to which their green friends had been devoted. Freznel lenses beamed in natural light from high above the natural cave entrance. This was the first base that Abe had set up many summers before and had been a beehive of activity the year before.

"Sparrow, be a dear and make us some tea? I'll get the medical kit for our damaged toes and fingers." She could barely walk and she was certain that her nose had been frostbitten as well. Her pain was a distant gnawing ache, and the muscle memory of her last frostbite reminded her that it was a very unpleasant experience. She pushed memories aside and focused on moving into the small infirmary refrigerator where she secured cold packs and bandages.

The tea was ready as Angel first applied the slow-warming treatment around Sparrow's feet. They said little to each other.

Angel went to the communications cubicle with her own frostbite gear, mainly the small tub of water where she settled her blackened feet. She turned on the radio equipment and booted the computer, determined to update Abe.

The computer booted and she launched the encryption software before she composed the e-mail message. The message was short: "Transponder 058." A slight panic set in, her message would not transmit. She checked the satellite modem and the tracking system, but both were green. "Son of a bitch, this can't be happening," she said quietly.

She saved the message, and then rebooted the system. The uplink would still not work. She broke out in a cold sweat. She debated with herself about using the radio.

"Shit."

From the other room came, "What is it Worm?" Sparrow never used that name for her; she must really be out of it.

"I can't get the fucking uplink to work," she said, but only silence from the other room. Sparrow had not been sitting idly and was viewing the surveillance cameras in the common room.

"You better think of something, because we have visitors."

"Shit, shit, shit…"

"I bet it's the fucking sunspots," she said quietly to herself. Sparrow was now giving a running commentary from the common room.

"It looks like an army, Angel. I think we're screwed… Three helicopters just landed… I can see maybe two dozen armed men and maybe more…" Then she yelled, "They're coming! What do you want me to do?"

Angel's adrenaline pumped in and she bolted to the outer area and essentially grabbed the younger woman to her feet.

"You have to hold them off as long as you can. I need to set the timer for the self-destruct explosives for the cave. We can't leave evidence." Sparrow looked at her in horror—almost as if she thought this would never happen—as though it was a mistake.

"You can't be serious." She looked at her pleadingly.

"Get a grip! It is all up to us to keep the industrial buzzing bees from stinging, so don't let the sacrifice of all those who struggled before us go in vain. Pull yourself together."

Sparrow stood visibly taller and sobered. "Okay." She gulped.

They overturned tables and shelves, chairs and other detritus of the former room to make a barrier in a far corner opposite the changing room door. While Sparrow crouched down, Angel brought her a couple of automatic weapons and a box of clips. She brought the young woman her compact music player and her headphones from her backpack, turned up the volume and slid the headphones on her.

She kissed Sparrow gently on her chapped and crusted lips and smiled.

Sparrow smiled wanly, and adjusted her headphones and chambered a round all in one fluid motion. Her attention was rapt on the front door. Before Angel had even turned around to run back to the communications room, a stun grenade went off in the cloakroom and the front door blew off its hinges.

Sparrow threw her hands over her ears—although she was already deafened by the concussion. There was no time to transmit anything to Abe. She had to destroy the computers if she had time. She hunkered down in the communications room underneath a heavy worktable and put on some dead headphones just to drown out the noise—but it was not helping much. The chatter of automatic weapons and ricochets filled her head as she crawled toward the back of the room where the satchels of C4 were piled. She hoped that the detonators were not buried too deep.

Karen's meeting was over quickly. The investigation had made some dramatic breakthroughs, indicating that EPG* planning and implementation was very professional. National Security Advisor Nelson provided most of the summary. The Navy was credited for discovering that two former USN submarines were involved in the plot, both de-commissioned research submarines. While decommissioned Navy submarines were sometimes sold to other nations, only twice had they been sold to private owners. The two boats were the *Albacore* (AGSS-569) and the *Archerfish* (SS-311), both vintage mid-20th century research submarines.

They had the positions for both subs—the *Archerfish* heading south near to the Galapagos Islands and the *Albacore* heading north not far from Antarctica in the Southern Ocean headed in the direction of Fiji, although it was still two thousand miles from any inhabited island. The president asked his military advisors to present him with some options for dealing with the subs, from capture to outright sinking. The discussion turned to events on the ground in Antarctica and it was Karen's turn. She was matter-of-fact in her report and then proudly announced that they had made contact with the small group of terrorists in the nearby mountains. The president's reaction was underwhelming.

"Thank you for your report, Agent St. Cloud. Capture these bastards alive if you can, destroy their base, if you must." Then, very quickly, the chief of staff called an end to the meeting. The president was obviously distracted and there was something afoot. Her intuition told her to stick to her own business.

Leah was in a state of shock. She returned to their small cabin to hear Jake snoring softly, peacefully—quite at odds with the roiling turmoil inside of her. She felt as though she was nearing some sort of threshold. She was beginning to feel some sympathy for her captors, or at least a kind of grudging respect for their determination. Now being prodded by what was either a hallucination of her own disturbed mind, or something far more bizarre that she couldn't even begin to accept it, she yearned for some physical comfort.

In spite of the cramped space and the groaning of the metal springs, she crawled in next to Jake and spooned with him. He adjusted to give her room and made happy little noises, but went back to sleep. Leah finally relaxed, but was alert and awake and couldn't fall asleep. Jake's soft snoring was eventually enough incentive for her to get out and crawl into the upper bunk. She stretched and allowed herself to relax even more.

She grew drowsy and let her eyes soften, gazing at the light rust film that seemed to cover the paint of the ceiling a few feet above her head. There seemed to be a pattern there, it was familiar. It slowly dawned on her that it was the general outline of the West Antarctic with a small seam in the metal that ran across the middle, diagonally. She was seeing things again!

The outline slowly shifted into the face in the shower and Leah shuddered, blinked her eyes, and opened them again—to have the image come even more into focus—a face of shimmering rust. It was mesmerizing and she felt unable to look away. The ceiling seemed to speak softly to her in a deep metallic voice.

"Mon cheri, it is time for you to fulfill your destiny. The forces of power and righteousness gather. You have a critical role to play and without your help, all may be lost."

"*Agwe*, why me?"

"You know the answer to this, child, do you not? You may refuse to accept your charge at a level of academic superficiality. I would ask you to go deeper, to your heart, to that place where you are most discomforted, to find your answer.

"Look to that inner strength that I know you possess to pose to yourself the riddle: why have you, of all people, the key to the secret of Antarctica's next turning? Can it be just coincidence that you have the key to this conundrum and that others require it to bring the world back into balance? Are you so arrogant to assume that you can keep this knowledge all to yourself? Meditate on that if you will, Grasshopper." He chuckled at his *Loa* humor.

"Meantime, I have a sweet Central African lullaby to sing to you…"

252

Before she had another lucid thought, Leah was sound asleep and more relaxed and at peace than she had been since she was a child.

Pete felt like caged animal. After the firefight broke out—in other words, almost the whole time he'd been at the former Hungarian base—he was "asked to wait" in a scorched storage room, and now forgotten in the chaos swirling around the pole. The young Marine guarding him let him out every few hours to pee, and he had been brought coffee a few times. He had a growing dislike for Karen St. Cloud, because he felt like she had reneged on the deal that they'd made. She could have easily let him tag along, but had not. The young Marine told him nothing, of course, given the language barrier, although he had attempted in his broken Spanish to start a conversation. The guard sat stoically in front of the door and just ignored him. Pete was sure that there were wounded soldiers nearby, because he heard low moaning sounds from somewhere in the same building. He was desperate to find out what was going on and was missing all the action! He felt betrayed having made a deal to help in exchange for the inside scoop. He was more than a little scared and that tempered his frustration and anger.

He finally curled up on some Army blankets that had been thrown in on the floor and slept fitfully for a few hours. There was no sense of time in this place, no cues as to the time of day or even the year. The blackened storage room was empty, with row after row of empty, heat-discolored metal shelves. The shell of the building was metal, so even though burned, the wind stayed outside. It had been below freezing when he was put in his temporary jail, but the air had slowly warmed. Pete could still see his breath, but he was seriously tired and sleepy. He removed the heavy outside clothing and his boots to fall asleep in a heap on the concrete floor.

After a solid, restful two-hour nap, Pete slowly awoke from a dream about fishing on his late uncle's boat on the Florida Gulf Coast. In the dream, the lazy afternoon sun shimmers on the water and flying fish leap out of the water in the distance. He is happy to feel warm and relaxed. Slowly, a large thunderhead grows on the horizon and then suddenly it fills the sky and thunder rumbles in the distance. That is when Pete awoke to the sensation of needles in his throat.

As his eyes opened to see his breath, a cloud of condensation began to take the shape of a woman's face in a shimmering vortex of ice crystals. She was one the most beautiful woman he had ever seen. Her long flowing hair appeared with a rainbow effect. In fact, she was so strikingly beautiful, that Pete drew in a quick, cold painful breath.

He glanced slightly over at the young Marine who seems stuck in time, in some kind of stasis. This has to be a dream, Pete thought to himself.

The phantasm spoke to him softly.

"*Aida Wedo* tells you this is not a dream, but a vision of your destiny. We have spoken before, but you were not ready yet to receive me. Now you must know that you have a decisive role in the unfolding drama to save Earth and the peoples of the planet.

"The war god *Ogun* and his minion are gathering their forces to destroy your planet but you and your woman are the only ones who stand in their way." She flipped her hair back and small stars sparkled as if a small galaxy inhabited her head.

Pete was mesmerized and could only stammer, "I, uh, I…"

"I-and-I, indeed!" She laughed in her lilting Caribbean accent.

"You are aide to the new savior, so it is time to awaken to your place in the scheme of things and confront the fact that you can no longer play the role of objective reporter—you are now involved as a participant." She laughed. "Oh yes, you may act your part as necessary. But accept this: the most probable outcome of the coming battle is the destruction of this continent and a new Dark Ages for humanity—a time that the species may well not survive. You have only a small window of opportunity to prevent this catastrophe.

"The forces at play here are indeed cosmic and yet, puny human, your action or inaction, at the required moment may be enough to derail the train rushing down the tracks! All that is required, however, is your enabling of the real hero here, your lover woman."

"Lover? You have got to be kidding!" Came out of Pete in such a rush, his breath nearly disrupted the solidity of the sparkling face in front of him. In fact, the image perceptively moved itself back a few feet. It pulsated, growing more solid and then less so.

"Nothing is predetermined, free will still holds, but the lines of probability suggest that you two are entangled at a deep cosmic and metaphysical level. The opportunity may present itself to fulfill that which you cannot now see. Just wait and see!" She laughed again.

Pete was stunned and could only shake his head slowly.

"So, what am I supposed to do?"

"All you need to do is to stand by your woman. Be her consort. Protect her with your life. Give up your life, if necessary, to save hers. She is the only human who *Mawu Lisa*—the Creator—will allow to interfere with *Ogun, Shango*, and the rest of the devious *Rada*. There are some helper spirits: those other spirits of the waters and ocean. But trust no one except yourself and the woman you love."

Noises came from the airlock, the sound of the outside door and someone approaching.

Aida Wedo blew Pete a kiss that formed an ice crystal ring that lightly kissed his face. Then the face shifted quickly from a beautiful *Aida Wedo* to an equally beautiful Karen St. Cloud, and at that instant Pete realized that she was right, he was falling for the FBI agent, and that beneath her rough exterior was a truly attractive woman. He shook his head in wonder.

The crystals seemed to coagulate, the motion stopped and *Aida Wedo's* face fell to the floor in a small pile of crystalline dust.

Pete ran a finger through the ice dust and pulled his finger back to look at it. As the crystals quickly melted, they gave off little star sparkles and then left a small dewdrop on his outstretched index finger. He licked it absently as the door opened.

A blast of very cold, dry air came through the inside airlock, followed by Karen. He pulled himself up as she came into the room and closed the inner airlock door behind her.

"Hi," she said without apology. "Get your gear on, we're leaving." She looked around the room as though she had never seen it—which she hadn't, and then. "Oh my god." Then, "Are you hungry?"

He smiled wanly, "No, I have had enough MREs to pickle me. But a cup of coffee would help."

"Okay. We'll get you some and then get ready to go. I have a lot to tell you." Karen asked the young Marine in passable Spanish to go get coffee, then without missing a beat, began a rapid narrative on what had happened on the base, and then the regional, and international news.

Pete watched her in some amazement as though they were long-lost friends catching up on the years in between. Meantime, he began the process of putting on layers of clothing to prepare for the raging winds and snow outside. She must be good with languages, he thought to himself, because her fast-paced account was now peppered with Spanish words and short phrases. She looked at him funny, because he couldn't keep from staring deep into her eyes.

Sandi and Raul were in the second wave of the assault on the EPG* redoubt. They heard the concussion grenades as the cue for their dash from the cover of the helicopters to the now crowded airlock opening. The situation was chaotic and Sandi looked back and forth between the Marine on her left and Raul on her right for a hint of the next movement, while the firefight raged on inside the cave. She felt far too exposed for comfort. Then she was nearly blinded by a flash of light from inside the cavern and a huge explosion that lifted her off her feet and then slammed her into a snowdrift twenty feet away. The air was knocked out of her in the blast, but as she tried to catch her breath, it was knocked out again as she hit the ground. She passed out.

Daylight faded quickly through the Oval Office windows, and the darkness was a relief from the gray that had cast a pall through them since dawn. President Clark had all the lights on in the room as though to keep out the depression that had been weighing on him all day.

Mrs. Garcia's voice came on his intercom box.

"Sir, Dr. Erikson is here to see you."

"Finally. Send him in and ask Nelson to join us…" but his chief of staff came through their connecting door at that very second. "Never mind, Nelson is here."

The east door opened and Erikson walked in slowly.

"W.B., I'm glad to see that you could come in person. How is it out there?"

"Mr. President." He looked at the dark window and seemed to ponder what to say. "The ride down was okay, but getting in and out of Ft. Mead is growing more difficult with the drifts piling higher. We're keeping the golf course free of new snow for the helicopter traffic, but visibility is a bitch. Scary even for this old salt." He smiled crookedly.

"Staff is holding out well, but there is growing concern about families who live in the suburbs who are running low on milk and other staples." He shook his head.

Neither Craft nor the president replied; there was little they could do.

256

"So, here we are. This has to be one of the strangest agenda's that I've ever brought to the White House—well, anywhere for that matter. I've discussed it a bit with Nelson on the phone, but this is the sort of thing that needs 'face time.'

"The point is, there is a growing probability that a connection between this anomaly and the troubles down near the pole, and we need to discuss it without involving too many others. For two reasons: first, it is so wacky, it takes considerable suspension of disbelief, and second, we may not be able to trust many people with this knowledge. And I know," he anticipated the president's arching eyebrows, "that doesn't make sense, but bear with me, it will begin to.

"I know that you have seen some of the briefing papers, and that this has been discussed in broad terms in the National Security Council meetings, but I would like to review the developments—with your indulgence?"

President Clark nodded, "Go ahead, W.B."

The NSA Director reached into his briefcase and pulled out two folders. From the top one, he pulled out documents and passed one to each man.

"This is the timeline of the events that led us to believe we have been contacted by an extraterrestrial intelligent species, and I use the word 'we' loosely."

"Meaning?" asked the president.

"Meaning… that they appear to have not directly contacted any official government authorities at all. Let me explain."

"Sorry, go ahead, I knew that."

"Alright, the first inkling that something unusual had happened was about six months ago. For years the NSA has monitored the work of all the so-called SETI programs, for a whole host of reasons. We like to follow all those groups that work with and develop sophisticated algorithms and encryption technologies. Also, because the SETI folks can have their data collection interrupted or compromised by military and intelligence satellites, they are careful to monitor what satellites are in the sky. That is useful for us to see if they can detect our own birds—they are very good at it—and foreign satellites as well. They are an important source of information for us on that, too.

"We occasionally admit to or deny suspicious signals depending on the sensitivity of orbital data or the actual age of satellites… The point is that we keep a close eye, or ear rather, on what they are doing. In any case, we started noticing something peculiar about the SETI@Home operation about a year or so ago.

"What we noticed at the time was both the growth in their outbound traffic volume and use of a new algorithm for data analysis. At that time we had an informant inside the group and from what we could tell, no one in SETI was responsible. There was a brief spike in activity, but it settled down after a routine virus software upgrade and so we suspected that the anomaly was the work of a hacker who tried to tap into the SETI distributed computing network, or maybe something more benign, such as a computer worm or Trojan horse.

"The interesting thing to note, now that we can look back over the records of the SETI@Home group, and at the records of three other groups, one private and two universities in the Southern Hemisphere, is similar signals, apparently random, from the same part of the sky near the plane of the ecliptic. The reason I note that they appeared random, is because the SETI groups look for non-random signals. That's the whole point."

The president was nodding and actually seemed to be following this with some interest in contrast to his obvious discomfort with routine science presentations—such as the climate change theories.

"So how is it that you can tell that they are actual signals?"

"Because, when you take into account the Earth's rotation and piece the apparent noise together by linking the signals from each receiving station, in turn, you do get a repetition of the carrier wave. Just as predicted by the novel of Carl Sagan, *Contact*, the signal was imbedded as frequency modulations inside a carrier wave. Simple, in a way, and more conducive to a narrowly beamed signal—which this was. It appears to have been beamed directly at the solar system, at Earth.

"So, six months went by. Then a similar thing happened at the SETI Institute, the most heavily funded of the SETI groups and the virtual heir to the original NASA SETI program—axed due to the negative publicity of Senator Proxmire last century. Now, this really raised our level of concern, because the SETI Institute uses a lot of government equipment on a lease basis, both radio telescopes and supercomputers. Again, it was a sporadic and transient series of events, but enough to get the attention of the automated detection systems that we have monitoring them.

"To make a long story short it was the same diagnosis, in all probability a hacker. The trouble this time was that when we had crypto-analysts take apart the code and try to identify it and it's purpose, they discovered it was similar to the algorithm from the earlier hack, but it was more complex, by several orders of magnitude and it was so sophisticated that we are still unable to grasp many of its functions. In other words, we don't know what exactly it was designed to do.

"And it gets better; about the same time we began to notice a subtle but significant degradation in the processing speed and output of government mainframe computers throughout the country. Just as we would isolate the source, presumably a worm or Trojan horse, it would essentially self-destruct leaving no trace. That is atypical of any human-made virus, which almost always replicates itself, thus leaving at least one original copy, or at least a daughter code.

"Then, three months ago—we now know—the radio signals originating near Tau Ceti started coming into the SETI@Home system on a regular basis. Ironically, the signal was masked, that is disregarded, because it is right on top of a geostationary NSA satellite! This could be one of the most unlikely coincidences; but the irony is really two-fold: first, the NSA satellite couldn't detect the signal because it was pointed in the opposite direction. Second, the signal was making its way into the SETI@Home network, and was being ignored because they believed the intelligent signals they were getting came from us!

"A misunderstanding apparently broke out between the groups last week, when we moved the satellite up orbit for totally unrelated reasons. SETI@Home acknowledged their possession of the data from the last six months or so, but refused to release it until they had a chance to analyze it. Then SETI Institute went to court. This by itself is a bit strange since the groups have historically cooperated, but that's another story.

"While the news has been rather overshadowed by the disaster in the Indian Ocean and the war on terrorists in Antarctica, the groups have settled out-of-court, and along with NASA, and NSA—behind the scenes—we are all trying to make sense of the data stream.

"The bottom line—and I can leave with a report that goes into far greater detail—is that the Internet, and most military and private civilian intranets, have an alien virus. We have been invaded by aliens, electronically."

Dear Betsy:

Today was uneventful except for two mysteries: the almost constant presence of icebergs on the horizon and periodic over-flights of military jets. The icebergs have us just a bit worried, but Brad's obsession with electronic toys has paid off. He built two small radar systems, a forward scanning system like many small boats have and a side-scanning radar. They are set to sound an alarm if anything large enough to harm Mana Kai comes in range. After we set the automatic tiller last night, there was a false alarm—a school of tuna set it off. Then early this morning the alarm sounded for the side-scanner and we passed a rather small iceberg within a few hundred feet. It was hard going back to sleep so we stayed up and I made tea. We had a subtle, charming sunrise.

That was when the first jets appeared. On very rare occasions, we have seen airplane contrails, usually to the north, at high altitude, 30,000 feet or more. Then after dawn, we heard jets approaching from the west, and then saw them, not far above the cloud deck, Brad said 10,000 feet. That time we weren't sure what they were, but they reappeared a few hours later, this time almost directly above us, and somewhat lower. Low enough, anyway, for Brad to ID them as a formation of three US Navy F-16s. We couldn't be sure but it seemed that one acknowledged us by dipping his wings back and forth. Later, we saw more planes in formation, further to the south. Brad is certain that we are near an aircraft carrier group.

Well, it was nice talking. We are both taking naps today so that we are rested in case of nighttime excitement!

Yours, Marge.

January 20
Friday

It was well after midnight. The sun's weak light shot through the Hungarian camp at such a sharp angle that the wind added a bluish tinge and shimmering ethereal quality to the every solid surface. A surreal feeling had clung to Pete after his *Loa* visitation, and the light gave reality a further fantastic quality. He suddenly was struck by how absolutely incredible it was that he was in Antarctica— unimaginable only two days before.

As he and Karen made their way into the bitter wind to catch the helicopter, he looked at her closely and saw the circles under her eyes as she winced coming out into the cold. She also reacted with a wiggle to her nose from the acrid smell of burning plastic and rubber still smoldering from the wreck of the Herc. But she hurried ahead and in minutes they were settling into the large transport helicopter.

Karen obviously knew her way around, as she located and then demonstrated for him how to don a set of headphones.

"Agent St. Cloud. We're good to go," she told the pilot.

A thick British accent acknowledged. "Give us a few more seconds up here, ma'am. To confirm, we are headed north, northwest to coordinates in the foothills of the Latady Mountains."

"That's correct lieutenant," she used the British pronunciation 'lef-tenant.' "What is our ETA?"

"Hold please." He replied, and then came back a half a minute later.

"We estimate about 20 minutes, depending on head winds."

"Roger. Can you toggle our headsets to another frequency?"

"Affirmative. I will switch you to the navigator who will monitor you."

"Perfect. Give us a five minute warning before touchdown."

"Will do. Prepare for lift off. Out."

The communication officer came on and switched them as the helicopter rose into the sky.

"So, I caught you up on the developments state-side and the reports from the Indian Ocean continue to come in with horrid reports. This was the worst tsunami in recorded history and the largest death toll from any single natural or human event in history. The UN Security Council is convening in Geneva in a few hours and is expected to formally sanction EPG* and give the US alliance sweeping authority to search for and destroy them.

"We have about sixty hours left to find them and disable or destroy those weapons." She shook her head.

"So what's your plan?" He put his gloved hand on her arm unconsciously and she pulled away slightly, but let it him leave it there. She looked at him inquiringly, but he didn't react, so she answered.

"Truthfully, I don't know. Our best chance now is to find some evidence in what's left of their mountain base. The Navy's searching for the two submarines… arguably the best news we've heard."

Karen pulled maps from her satchel. She poured over them for a while and then felt the warmth of Pete's thigh against hers. She hadn't really liked him all that much when they had met. At that time she thought he was all ego, an airhead, and "pretty boy," but with a two-day old stubble of beard and ruffled hair, he was ruggedly handsome and pensive. His piercing blue eyes were staring at her again. This was very distracting. She felt her face flush.

She turned back to the map that showed their destination. On this particular contour map, there was not much definition, although they knew now that there was a rock shelf, a minor promontory that served as a small island around which two glacier streams diverged. Two-dozen bodies of dead Argentine Marines had been recovered and a platoon of British Special Forces would soon arrive as reinforcements. Almost the entire British contingent from the Falklands was now on the continent, Harriers and all. All the congestion was potentially dangerous, but the stakes were too high to worry about that.

She gazed at the map and felt her eyes grow unfocused as a wave of exhaustion washed over her. The contour lines on the map began to reform into a face, the face of a man she'd seen in her dreams. She shivered and closed her eyes and then opened them. The lines were back to normal. She took a deep breath and let it out slowly. She willed her sense of humor to return. It was a survival skill she needed as much as ever.

Pete shifted slightly next to her and asked her softly, "What about the *Loa*?"

She was stunned they were on the same wavelength, so she let out a little laugh of amazement and shook her head and pointed at the headphones. "That's classified, Mr. Correspondent, sorry." And she made a pinching sign with her fingers and mouthed, "Later." She winked at him without even thinking about it.

Pete grinned, nodded, and looked away with a satisfied smile.

Now it was Karen's turn to lay her glove on his arm. He just nodded his head and subtly shifted his weight closer to her.

They flew across the barren landscape in silence, the heat between them communicating from thigh to thigh. Karen moved closer still and leaned into him. She awkwardly rested her helmet against his shoulder, and was asleep in seconds.

Shango was a will-o-the-wisp, *ignis fatuus*. He hovered a few feet off the ground and surveyed the wreckage of the EPG* cavern. He could feel the immanent arrival of Karen's helicopter, the still oozing blood from the wounds of bleeding soldiers in the inflatable medical unit outside the cave, the rapid cooling of the dead bodies inside and outside, and indirectly, the slight throbbing of the nuclear device buried a few kilometers away... There was a curious harmonic produced by the uranium quarters in the warhead and the heating elements that kept the ensemble "ready for prime time." He sensed this by electronically interacting with the equipment. It was working well.

Shango was enjoying enormously his manifestation in the muted light of the cavern. He caught his reflection, the reflection and refraction of photons across myriad surfaces in the vast room: broken shards of glass, drops of liquid, rapidly forming facets of ice crystals, and broken bits of shiny metal. It was captivating and mesmerizing. He was enchanted by his own flickering image, built on molecules of Antarctic dust and micro-machines designed a quarter of a galaxy away. He was a ghost of the future.

Up close, the surface of the illusion was almost microscopic fractal foam. The texture of *Shango's* "skin" was a composite of tiny bubble-like structures, almost translucent. He had stolen the macro model and movement algorithms from a Hollywood graphics animation studio and thought that he looked pretty hot. He resembled a famous Hollywood action-film actor for good reason.

But his logic core was also programmed to be attentive to any evidence that EPG* might have left behind.

"Damn *bakas*," he said just to hear vibrations of the air.

The phantasm had no voice box, so it came from tiny motions of his nanobots. Not satisfying at all! He reprogrammed them to make a more substantial bladder.

"Praise *Mawu Lisa*!" That was better! The ice and snow crystals around him shimmered. "I-and-I will be as One with You!" He laughed, liked the sound the bladder made, and laughed harder and louder.

There were *baka* not far away from the cave entrance, so he moved further back into the darkness.

"We will fulfill our mission," he tried those words. And more loudly, "We will!" He ambulated across the cavern floor, but his steps were out of synch with his relation to the ground. He didn't care that much.

He looked up and memories flooded his consciousness of the Masters and their own destinies many light years away, forces set in motion tens of millennia ago, beyond his grasp and comprehension, but no less a point of considerable pressure on the collective entity of the *Loa*. It actually pissed him off that the *Ganesh* could on one hand be so intelligent, and yet on the other hand so crippled by ethics...

He spat out the word and the bladder shuddered, "Ethics."

Maybe it was genetic, a biological weakness and simply beyond his comprehension. His emotional outburst set off a logic bomb in his processing center and he was forced to shift his center of consciousness to a sub-center and the anger immediately disappeared.

While he took a momentary physical form, *Shango* was mostly an Artificial Intelligence entity, constructed essentially of digital information operating at the electronic level. He was born as a computer virus from space and was shadowing the *bakas* of EPG* in their few years of Antarctic preparation. Structurally, his higher processing functions relied on "borrowed" capacity of desktop computers, although many other wireless devices had adequate memory and processing power to be useful. He was adaptable; he wasn't proud.

When the cave blew, he was almost screwed. He quickly shifted his higher functions, first from the computer in the grotto to the nuclear weapon ignition laptop, but that equipment had very little spare memory. It was a tight squeeze, even using his most sophisticated compression tools. The arrival of the military computers served his immediate needs perfectly and he relocated there, where he waited while the solar magnetic storm raged.

264

A helicopter floated in on the white horizon and winds came into the cavern. Shango's form wavered in the shadows. It drifted into a corner where it collapsed.

Aida Wedo spoke into Karen's left ear. "Wake up child, we're almost there."

On top of that came the copilot, "Agent St. Cloud, ma'am, five minute warning."

She was wide-awake. The voice in her ear continued.

"I am the voice of the rainbows, the aurora borealis, and the heavenly lights. I speak only to you. Listen."

Karen looked up at Pete, and straightened herself, and saw no recognition in his eyes, so she just listened.

"You are being watched. *Shango* and the other minion of *Mawu Lisa* are awaiting your failure. Do not give them the satisfaction. You can still stop this madness and destruction, but time is not on your side. The forces in motion are so much greater than are you, but there are still small points of leverage. The correct pressure can still bring everything to a standstill. One such key can be found in the grotto. But you may have to do the unimaginable to end the larger threat. Remember this: the sacrifice of a few can save the many."

Then static came over the earphone and the chopper slowed to land in the clearing below the small city of tents that had sprung up in the last hour on the stark landscape below. Karen caught her breath at the flurry of activity and then at the huge black and blue scar at the entrance to the cavern, where there had plainly been a huge explosion and fire.

Karen and Pete were met as soon as the doors opened by a very serious, crew cut American in military snow 'camos' who did not introduce himself, but led them to, and then through an airlock of a large orange hospital inflatable habitat. It was still fairly cool inside so they only removed parkas. Their guide spoke.

"The firefight was very short, but the final explosion was powerful and large. It killed outright the two guerillas and twenty Marines and wounded almost all the rest. It was a disaster. The worst injuries have already been med evac'ed out, but we were instructed to keep as many of the lightly wounded here as is practical. McMurdo and the Navy had—with obvious foresight—pre-positioned doctors and medical state-of-the-art for this operation... It was being flown into theater just as this crap happened." He didn't look particularly pleased. "But once we heard what happened at Camp Hungary, it was a logical precaution."

Karen asked a bit more sharply than she had intended, "And you are?"

"Sorry, ma'am. Major George Scott, Delta Force, Fort Bragg. I am your military liaison."

"Yes, they told me to expect you when I talked to Washington an hour ago. I gather you came here the long way, through McMurdo?"

"Yes, we have kept some gear under wraps, at McMurdo, in case there were ever any problems down here. Looks like that was a wise precaution."

The word "wise" caught Karen's attention. Then it dawned on her that she had met Scott before, back in her early years in intelligence. "We met in Honduras, didn't we?"

He smiled for the first time. "Yes, ma'am, I knew you'd remember. You were one of the smartest officers the Navy ever produced." He said it as an observation, not a compliment. His smile disappeared faster than it arrived. He turned and back in business mode walked them forward into the center of the room. The other half of the room was filled with gurneys, in plastic bubbles, and Pete and Karen began to hear occasional sounds on moaning and other sounds of pain and discomfort. Each of the bubbles contained a person—wounded, many burned soldiers. There were doctors and nurses—quite a few of them in fact—hovering over some of the beds.

Their first stop was in front of a bubble that emitted warm air from a few small openings on the sides. At first Karen didn't recognize her through the bandaging, but it was Sandi Gusman.

"We found her partner dead from a shrapnel wound, but she appears to be mostly uninjured except for a serious traumatic brain injury. She has been in a coma since we found her. Some minor frostbite on the extremities."

Without thinking, Karen poked her hand into one of the holes and squeezed Sandi's arm.

"We'll get the bastards that did this to you," she told Sandi trying to look into her closed blue eyes.

"Unfortunately, those bastards are already dead—at least the ones who did this. One body is still in the cavern. The other we have on ice in another hab. I am assuming you want to see the scene, where many of the body parts still lay among the debris. We have tried to leave as much of the inner cavern undisturbed for you, although we did pull out the bodies of our personnel out as they were mostly in the outer periphery.

"We don't have a forensics kit per se, but I did have a team assemble latex gloves, bags for evidence, and other materials to substitute. Digital cameras."

"You know some forensics?"

"I am a Quantico grad, too. I took the opposite path from you."

She looked at him funny. "FBI?"

"For a while." He was obviously not interested in saying more about himself. It was just as well.

She looked at Pete. "Are you up to grizzly? This could be hard to look at."

"I am a journalist. I can handle it."

Karen doubted it, but she needed his help. "Okay, I want you to take pictures for me. Major, let's get to it."

Ezili got to Leah first in the morning in the shower. The focus of attention for many of the *Loa* at the moment, Leah had a pivotal role in the Transformation. The missing link, she was. And *Ezili*, the mischief-maker, was more determined than all the others to throw a wrench into the works. She plotted to have the saintly *Ogou Balanjo* distract both *Shango* and *Ogun* and keep them busy—long enough for her to manifest physically in the submarine. As a minor *Loa*, the least powerful of the lot, they often took her for granted, so she hitchhiked onto the digital RF pipeline that the *Loa* were using to keep everything connected. Even the *Loa* struggled with the disruptions of the solar flares, too, and *Elizi* was adept at surfing the energy pulses as they propagated along the magnetic field lines and intersected with geostationary telecommunications satellites.

So she had fun with the fog on Leah's mirror. And Leah was more than receptive. Between the sleep deprivation and a swing in conscience she now wanted to help in the worst way. All she could think about were the geographic harmonics and interplay between the crustal dynamics and glacial plasticity. Her findings from the previous year were now taking on a whole new meaning as she considered the massive release of energy that could be accomplished by a catalytic series of explosions. Still she doubted that such relatively puny human energies could unleash terrestrial energies many magnitudes more;

but she has decided to suspend her disbelief, figuring that she was as good as dead now anyway, captive in a rogue submarine that the world's navies undoubtedly sought to destroy.

Ezili introduced herself.

"I am *Ezili, Loa* of love and creativity. I am your coach today."

"I need a coach?" asked Leah suspiciously.

"Relax, sister. You need me because you have the skills and knowledge. All you need is a few hints about the best strategy."

That seemed to make sense. And the swirling of chaos on the mirror began to take the form of a pretty young mulatto girl, with beads in her hair, although the beads were so realistic, they seemed three dimensional on the mirror. Leah took comfort in matching the girl's voice to the face in the fog on the mirror.

"Do tell," said Leah almost defiantly and then stuck her toothbrush back into her mouth and continued with her routine as though she was used to ghosts now.

"Here's the thing, sister. The original Plan had the device initiation start in the west and spread east sequentially. In fact that is still what Abe has programmed. The harmonics are predicated on the seismic energies traveling in P and S waves that are supposed to trigger each subsequent explosion, as the overpressure moves down the line. That's roughly every five minutes or so depending on the distance between each device and some allowances for crustal density and composition.

"But the modeling shows there an almost 90 percent probability of propagation failure. For some reason, the modeling worked well in the planning stages, but the actual device placement and new knowledge of site dynamics have complicated the calculations. Abe's latest approach is two propagating waves, in other words, parallel series of explosions. That seems to harness the natural harmonics better, but it is unlikely to work due to fratricide."

Leah looked very confused, spit out her last rinse and asked, "Fratricide?"

"Yes, big sister, when one bomb kills another. The probabilities are extremely high that what you would call 'in between' devices will fail due to earthquakes and compression wave damage. As many as half the devices might fail and then the whole enterprise would be compromised. Abe is very upset.

"He has tried triple propagation and other schemes, but the models do not quite come together. The *Loa* have given input, but we are simple beings, mostly driven by logic and magic," her face broke into a huge toothy smile, "we are not equipped with the holographic capacity of the human brain, and what might be called native *intuition*," she spit the word out as though it was distasteful.

"You are our best hope Princess Leah." The *Loa* looked proud of herself.

Leah groaned. *Star Wars* groupies? But then she had an idea.

"Can any of the devices be detonated simultaneously?"

"Yes, of course. Abe had considered setting them all off together, at one point, but the harmonics are all wrong to get the cascade effect."

"Sure. Of course." Leah looked pensive. "I have an idea."

"One more thing. And this has to be a secret between just the two of us?"

Leah's suspicion returned, "Yes."

"You have to propagate east to west."

"Eh?"

"Or even better would be a cascade effect that started in the middle and swept both east and west."

"Funny, that is what I was thinking, given the shape of the Transantarctic range. But why?"

"Well, on one hand you are helping save the planet, and by keeping our secret and propagating at least half the devices to the west may help save your species."

"What? I don't get it, please explain."

"Sorry sister, I have run out of time here today. But no matter who talks to you about this, human or *Loa*, remember that Abe wants an eastward progression, but what may save homo sapiens is just the opposite. Watch your back, big sister."

The mirror fogged over and Leah had a metallic taste in her mouth and the smell of ozone in her nose.

Twenty minutes later, Leah and Jake entered the mess and helped themselves to breakfast. She usually ate fairly light, but this morning, loaded up on eggs and sausage. She ate like she had been starving.

Jake asked, "What's gotten into you?"

"I am just famished this morning. It's all the sex." She smiled sweetly at him. He wasn't buying it.

"No Leah, something's changed. The seething anger is gone. Am I wrong?"

Leah looked pensive for a minute and finished chewing a mouthful of food. Jake knew she wouldn't answer until she swallowed, a habit of hers.

"I've had a change of heart. I'm going to help them."

"What?" Jake literally dropped his coffee cup and spilled a small amount of his coffee on the table. They both put their napkins on the spill. Others in the room had stared, but now returned to their books, food, or conversations.

"How often do physical scientists get to experiment on the planets they study?"

"You have got to be kidding!" He raised his voice slightly.

Leah put her hand on his arm to calm him.

"You, yourself, argued with me just yesterday to go along with these people to save our skins."

"But I didn't expect you to enjoy it!"

"Calm down, Jake. Take it easy. Let's not do a role reversal here. I've done a lot of soul searching and my intuition tells me that for a number of reasons our... my... cooperation here is essential. They are going ahead with their Omega Event whether or not I help, whether or not we are either dead or alive.

"My help will keep us alive for a while longer, and I can see whether all my theories were really on the mark or not. So, maybe my enthusiasm is conjured just a bit, but I have to admit that I am curious."

"They could very well kill us after you tell them what they want to know."

"Somehow, I don't think so. I think that they are basically moral and ethical people who have different values, but will honor any agreements that we make."

"I'm not so sure, but you have to choose." Jake managed to look both shocked and unhappy.

The boat suddenly began rocking from side to side, at first slowly and then more dramatically. Their plates moved a bit and Jake grabbed his now empty coffee cup.

"We've surfaced."

They continued to eat in silence, feeling the pitch of the submarine back and forth. It was now a slow, regular motion. Jake went over and refilled their cups of coffee. Then a curious thing happened. The steam coming from Leah's cup formed the face of *Ezili*, who smiled and then winked at her. The face appeared to roll her eyes, blow a kiss, and dissipate into the steam. Jake was looking straight at her and appeared not to notice anything unusual.

Leah needed little to seal her intentions. As soon as they finished with breakfast, she pushed the dishes aside and began scribbling notes and equations on the butcher paper that served as a tablecloth.

Jake had also had strange dreams again and although they weren't clear they left him with a feeling that there was more going on here than met the eyes and ears. He knew Leah well enough to know that she withheld something, something that she didn't feel she could say anywhere here on the sub. So, he let go of his disappointment with her decision and just sat quietly and admired the woman he loved so much. He was particularly drawn to the intense, serious side of her.

The fore end of the galley took a noticeable dip and the rocking stopped as the submarine submerged. Leah took no notice and switched her beverage to green tea after her third cup of coffee. Other crewmembers had come in and out, but they all took a wide berth around Leah and Jake, and no one bothered them. Bee and other senior officers were scarce this morning, too. Jake had since cleared off the dishes and at one point Leah pulled the butcher paper down off its roll and tore off the section that she'd nearly filled except for the grease spots, ketchup stains, and she'd even used some coffee rings to her advantage in drawing a couple of schematics. She asked Jake to go get her maps of Antarctica.

"My butt's numb... I've gotta move around," Leah announced as she stretched and moved toward an empty spot on a wall to do a few yoga stretches. Apparently pleased with the minor adjustments, Leah refilled her cup and sat back down to transcribe some of her earlier work onto the new piece of paper.

Just as Leah began to wonder if Jake had been abducted again, Bee, the science officer, and Jake returned to the small galley. Bee looked like she wanted to kill someone, Dr. Collins looked distracted, distant, and Jake was all flushed. The half-dozen other crewmembers on the fringes of the room looked up and as Jake spoke, they all looked down or away.

"Sorry baby. There was some sort of crisis upstairs and they nearly shot me for entering officer country."

Myra said, "Never mind all that," she spoke directly to Leah and sat down across from her. "He just surprised us, is all, and everyone is on edge."

When Leah looked like she wasn't going to reply and had such a curious look in her face, the doctor continued.

"We've managed to avoid detection by the US Navy so far, but we're reasonably certain that a sub-chaser—a military plane— discovered us a few hours ago. A passive sonar device is pinging to our northwest. Our guardian angels have protected us thus far, but this is not a good sign. Why we've not been attacked yet is a mystery, but we could go to battle stations at any moment. I cannot stay here very long as I am required in the infirmary…"

Bee distanced herself and continued to glower. Leah simply ignored the hateful woman.

"I want to help." She said simply.

"Help how, exactly?"

"You know, what you asked for, the coordinate timings for the devices."

The doctor smiled and then looked serious. "Why the change of heart? You've been pretty combative."

"I dunno, call it latent sympathy? I think you can see that I have found it to be an intellectual challenge, as well." She unrolled the two-plus hours of work." Even Bee moved closer to see it. "And, facing my mortality has made me question why I got involved in this work in the first place. I'm fairly certain what you are planning to do was almost inevitable anyway. In a century or less, the sea ice melt, the collapse of the ice shelves, and increased pace of running glaciers will off-load a huge burden of weight from the West Antarctic tectonic plate. All these Transantarctic Mountain pressure points will erupt of their own accord. Dr. Miller is only a catalyst. The damage might be less now than in the next century when the planet's population has doubled again."

Collins looked at her for any possible sign of deceit or prevarication and didn't see any.

She looked up at Bee. "Take Dr. Meadows up with you to my stateroom and pull all the maps in the Antarctica buckets here. If fact, bring all the buckets." Bee started to argue, and the Political Officer put on her voice of command.

"Just do it. Now!" The reasonably soft-spoken woman barked at Bee and she visibly jumped in surprise, but instantly turned on her heel and ushered Jake out of the room with her, in a hurry.

Dr. Collins shook her head.

"We may not have much time. How do you propose to compose this information and communicate it?" She asked with some concern.

"I assume you are using some encryption strategy?"

"Yes... I guess I am concerned how long it will take?"

"I have the equation, more or less ready. All I need to do is verify a few of the angles and distances, plug that into the equation, and then send it off. May take a half hour. The transmission could be very short. A second or two."

"Okay. I hope we have time. We'll have to surface again to make the high frequency satellite transmission. Unfortunately, that makes us an easy target."

Leah raised her eyebrows. The doctor did not respond.

"I have to get the dispensary ready. Good luck and blessed be."

"Blessed be," she replied. Leah knew the pagan salutation.

It surprised her a bit that the doctor got up, walked over and gathered her up in her long, strong arms and gave Leah a bear hug and wet kiss on the cheek. Before Leah could react, the doctor let her go and ran out the hatch.

Leah rolled out her chart and circled the parts that needed numbers plugged in. Time stood still.

The president waited in the Situation Room for twenty minutes and was very impatient.

"What do you mean, 'the submarine keeps moving'? Of course it moves!"

The admiral was flustered a bit himself, but in firm control of his temper and voice. "We mean that the submarine's position is erratic. There are huge discrepancies between the aerial visual sightings, the deep ocean sonic sensors, and remote sonar detectors. For now, we only trust the non-electronic visual confirmations. They are 'few and far between' that far out from the carrier task group... and the sub has probably gone deep and silent again.

"That is the largest discrepancy, sir, because the sub *is* moving and by definition should not *be* silent."

"Explain."

"Mr. President," he said indulgently, "the various systems give us conflicting locations, general trends, and we can plot that on an overhead for you." He waved at one of his adjutants, "Chambers, put up the linear extrapolation for the *Albacore*." Then back to the Commander in Chief, "We are assuming it is moving south-southwest. For example, the deep ocean sonic sensors pick up some engine noise, but it appears to be masked most of the time. You know, like those noise-canceling headphones people use in airplanes? It is there and then it isn't.

"We have dropped sonar buoys in the vicinity of the visual sightings, but those show absolutely nothing, as though the submarine was invisible. Most curious; I have no explanation."

"Okay, thank you admiral. Please advise me when we do have them located. I also want options: can we ram them, board them, blow them out of the water, or what?

Now the admiral was impatient. "Sir, our rules of engagement were to use depth charges on them as soon as they are located. Have your orders changed?"

The president looked both confused and embarrassed. "No, no change. Destroy the sub and rescue any survivors."

"Aye, aye, sir."

"General Smart, what's the situation on the ground?"

"Nelson has that report."

The president turned to his friend and advisor.

"Mr. President, we have made some progress, but events haven't gone too well, and the weather and solar storm situation have both deteriorated.

"To start closer to home. The Nor'easter has now moved north into Pennsylvania, which is good news and bad news. That is good because the low-pressure area is starved of Atlantic moisture and so the overall storm energy is less intense. The bad news is that it will merge with a rather large mass of arctic air from Canada, which means that temperatures will stay below freezing and drop below zero across most of the Central Atlantic.

"Transportation is at a standstill. Upstairs we have documents for you to sign to declare all fifteen Central Atlantic states disaster areas, and to mobilize the rest of the National Guard. Many units are snowed in, so we have a real mess on our hands.

"In the week since the storm began, over 500 people have died in twelve states. Power is out for five million people and is expected to worsen. The death toll will rise dramatically, according to FEMA, due to the power and heating failures. Some parts of New England have been spared by the storm so far, but that will change as it moves north. Trouble is that there are already widespread fuel oil shortages due to the border closings and shipping embargo.

"There were overnight riots in Pittsburg and the below-zero temperatures have made it nearly impossible to fight fires. We have a Homeland Security briefing for you later upstairs, but that's the worst of it, from the weather standpoint. It has obviously complicated getting people in and out of the White House and the District. The GSA has taken advantage of the situation for the short term and constructed snow tunnels between here and some of the strategic buildings nearby, Blair House... the Executive office building. They are secured by the Capitol Police and the Secret Service and with snowdrifts outside now in excess of thirty feet in some protected areas, the tunnels will be effective as long as temperatures remain so cold.

"National security personnel and the West Wing staff are housed in a couple of hotels across the street and people are more rested now than in more than a week. We have managed to bring in fresh produce through a lifeline that begins at Reagan Airport and up the frozen Potomac River. That's proven so successful we are working with the Red Cross and FEMA to bring in much more to distribute to the District in cooperation with the mayor's office."

"Antarctica. That is a short story, for the moment. Agent St. Cloud and her team will sift through the rubble of the EPG* base in the Latady Mountains. We are reasonably sure that at least one of the devices is located near there. We sift through satellite imagery from the last year to identify possible drill sites. Moreover, with this location, the numbers of devices they have, and some of Dr. Wilson's data, CIA and FBI analysts are identifying other possible sites, and reviewing satellite data.

"Unfortunately, there are only two circum-polar satellites, and the imagery is very spotty with low resolution. Our spy satellites cover different parts of the planet, which are low longitude orbits, closer to the equator, generally-speaking.

"So, move them!" the president said in exasperation.

The assistant CIA director responded, "I am sorry sir, but that isn't physically possible. The satellites have orbits that do not allow for relocation, once they are placed in orbit. They have some fuel on board for minor orbital corrections, but not to change their basic orbital placement."

"So, don't we have any satellites we can get up there quickly to do the spying?" He was almost hysterical.

His chief of staff spoke. "Sir, we did that last week when this started to unfold. A spare Lockheed satellite was available, but it blew up on the launch pad at Vandenberg. It was a total loss."

"Aliens?" The president spoke too quickly and then realized his error as he looked around the room at stunned faces. The room was dead quiet.

"Alien terrorists." Nelson filled in, perhaps not quickly enough. "No sir, no domestic or alien terrorists were suspected. It was apparently a fuel leak."

Then a slow hum of activity and second-seat conversations resumed. But a few furtive glances at the president revealed that the rumor mill and active imaginations during a time of national emergency had run wild. The uneasiness in the air over the past week had now taken on a greater urgency and energy.

The meeting went downhill after that, with reports of casualties from the South Pole, logistic problems, contact with the enemy, but no good information about where the nuclear devices were or the rest of the terrorists themselves.

The 48-hour point in the countdown to the so-called Omega Event passed at midmorning, but it wasn't acknowledged. Less than a hundred feet away, the wind howled through the eaves of the portico, the clouds built up again, and the temperature dropped, on one of those cold days in a certain kind of hell.

Somewhere out in deep water in the great Southern Ocean, Abe Miller was near exhaustion and at the point of mental breakdown. His Menagerie friends were probably dead, the Plan was poised to unravel, and he was in a crisis of faith. *Ogun*, on the other hand, felt "spot on" and grew more powerful in his ability to manipulate physical matter.

To test his new abilities, he prescribed Abe a sedative and ordered him to bed. What *Ogun* did, actually, was to create a small amount of synthetic opiate out of the dust, hair, and fibers floating around Abe's cabin, and flew it up his nose. A very short time later, the First Mate found Abe slumped on his small desk and she wrestled him onto his bunk, and assumed from the snoring that Abe had finally "hit the wall." She and the rest of the crew were jubilant. The "smoking light" came on for fifteen minutes, there were some quiet, sweet songs adrift on the bluish air and everything was mellow. Some of the crew got some sleep, too.

In spite of the deteriorating weather, the area outside the EPG* cavern rapidly grew into a small city, with flights pouring in from the Palmer Peninsula, from McMurdo, and from the Falklands. The site was at about 2000 feet above sea level, so the air wasn't too thin, and the rocky ledge that surrounded the cavern outcropping was fairly free of ice and snow, and roomy enough to support the tents, inflatable habitats, and small portable buildings on sledges coming in and going up every hour. The wind was blowing up to 50 miles an hour with stronger gusts, but up in close to the cavern it dropped off conveniently, and huge orange tarps were staked down to serve as a windbreak over the entrance. Once most of the debris was now cleared from in and around the airlock, large sheets of heavy clear plastic were put in place to keep out the wind and snow.

Within an hour of their arrival, Karen and Pete were inside the cavern. A crack team of forensic experts, part of the NEST group... military, and FBI who'd recently arrived on continent were now here at Latady Camp. Many looked tired, but dedicated.

After a preliminary survey, the grotto was divided into eight sections and teams of three were put to work to collect evidence, body parts, and document the scene. Brian Minh had arrived from the Hungarian base and Karen, Pete, and he worked the smallest of the sections, what had once been the radio room, and the epicenter of the explosion.

Karen set Agent Minh to work laying out a quick and dirty set of grid lines using orange survey string they'd laid their hands on, with a compass, to divide the area into sixteenths. That was a challenge itself, because of the twisted metal and debris, so she had Pete follow and take pictures.

One of the first things that caught her attention was how brightly lit the grotto itself was. The space was unusual, shaped like an almond with a high vaulting ceiling but squeezed in on the sides. Conveniently, the space was oriented north and south. The light came in from the front, of course, but an equal amount came in from ledges about two thirds of the way up on the eastern wall. There must be some mirrors or windows of some sort up there to produce that much light, essentially focused towards the back of the grotto. She observed that the upper surfaces of the roof were covered with a white material that was concrete, paint, or maybe a plastic. It glowed in the reflected light.

She brought her attention back to Pete who was carefully making his way around the area, clicking off flash after flash of the grid areas and walls and floors.

"Come here Karen," he said uneasily.

She carefully made her way to the back wall where he stood and saw the remains of a woman's body pinned behind a large piece of sheet metal, that had once been a shelf or workbench.

"It's Angel Stills." To his credit, he took pictures of her and stepped around the large frozen pool of blood on the other side of the metal. He looked ashen, but didn't lose it. Karen realized that she misjudged him.

He didn't linger there, either, but kept on task as Agent Minh finished the grid and then left for a minute to bring plastic evidence bags and latex gloves.

Karen had to go out to the airlock area to remove her parka and noticed a pile of them. With the area sealed except for slits in the plastic for doors, it was surprising warm in the grotto. When she got back to the far end, she put her hand on the rock and it felt slightly warm to the touch. Geothermal! The place was geologically active. She didn't know whether to be glad for the heat or uneasy about earthquakes and looked again closely at the roof for signs of recent rock shearing. She couldn't see any and relaxed as she saw how the sides of the upper roof appeared to be solid slabs of rock. Only towards the back, where the concrete had been sprayed looked dangerous.

Brian and Pete waited for her.

"Okay, let's work this together top left to bottom right. Grid numbers one through sixteen, okay? I see you did a little work-around over there on the right. We can come back to those grids and move that heavy stuff after everything else. Pete, keep doing the camera work. You are a natural." She smiled at him maybe just a little longer than she'd intended, and he blushed. "I think you need to lose the parka. In fact, could you go get us some bottles of water, too? I noticed there's a cooler—if you can believe it—by the airlock."

While Pete was gone, they inspected the one body that was in their space.

"Miller's occasional bodyguard is not with Miller. Hmm. They were probably lovers at one point, but apparently no more..." Karen poked behind the metal debris.

"She must have been taking cover behind this when the blast occurred. Now if we can only figure out why this small team returned to the Hungarian base and why they were left behind."

"What makes you think that?"

"Well, the explosion did a great job of destroying evidence, but I noticed a reasonably undisturbed row of potted plants along that back wall," she pointed to the west wall. "All dead and dried out...suggests that they've not been in here for quite a while. They clearly came back for something down at the Hungarian base. The cache at the end of the runway had something of importance."

Pete was back and handed each a water bottle. It was easy to get dehydrated here. They downed the bottles and left them on the edge of their section, near what had once been a doorway. The walls had been blown out, but the 2" x 4" framing was still mostly intact.

They walked quietly together to the first grid and Karen used an unsharpened pencil that she found to start turning over the debris. They worked slowly and methodically like that for two hours. Upon request Pete took pictures; Brian tagged and labeled evidence bags. There were, fortunately, no more body parts. They did, however, make note of a large bloody smear on a section of wall that was partly intact near what had been the door. Someone's body had been there before the blast.

The notable thing about the explosion, after a deconstruction of the blast pattern, was that in their section, there was not as much disturbance at ground level as compared to sections further toward the south. The force of the explosion appeared to have been directed upwards against the roof, which then focused and directed the blast out the front end of the cave. It was obviously designed as a self-destruct system by an explosives expert. The Argentine Marines didn't stand a chance. And, poor Sandi, she would have faced the direct force of the blast even though she was outside the cave.

By the time they broke for a late lunch, the body count was pretty much certain, with too many coalition casualties, but only two terrorists. Many bodies were torn beyond recognition until they could be matched with dental records.

The grotto gave up few clues. Any paper documents had been blown out onto the windswept hillside below. The electronics had been thoroughly trashed. Personal effects left behind were scarce and insubstantial. The place appeared to be a total loss. Nevertheless, Karen was as focused and determined as ever. She knew in her bones that the grotto would still give up something useful; they just had to continue to interrogate it until something was given up.

By mid-afternoon, the first-round inventory was complete and the grotto was cleared of any human remains. The forensics teams went through bags of evidence and photos to make sense of it all. They had a huge insulated tent just for the evidence and small debris, and a hundred collapsible tables in rows.

Karen left Agent Minh in charge and linked to him with two walkie-talkies on the same frequency in case something important turned up. She took Pete with her back to the cavern where she could now have the whole place to herself. She brought a handful of 8x10 digital printouts of images from before they started in the morning. She barely glanced at them as they were burned into her memory.

Karen paced back and forth between the radio room and the entrance. Then she slowed and Pete watched the color drain from her face and she plopped down on a pile of debris.

"What is it? Are you okay?" He grabbed her arm.

"It's okay, I'm okay." As soon as she sat down, she began to recover.

He squatted in front of her and watched closely.

"Please get me some water. I think I need hydration."

Pete looked behind them to see the ice chest and went for water. He pulled out bottles of water, stood up tall again, and turned around, and she was gone.

Pete called out, "Karen?"

"Over here," she came back quickly. She was standing at the back of the cave in the weak evening twilight, stripped down to her lycra thermal underwear. He couldn't believe his eyes.

"What in the hell are you doing?" as he walked up to her. She reached out for water, took a bottle, and drank deeply, returned it half empty. She braided her hair into a ponytail and wrapped it into a bun. Pete opened his mouth to speak, but she was so obviously determined in what she was doing, so unconscious of her exposing herself, and so unbelievably attractive, that the words wouldn't come out.

"I am climbing up to the ledge, want to come?" She was so serious, that once again, he could not bring himself to say a single word. He simply could not believe it.

"The one place we missed was the ledge where the light comes from, so here we go." Karen fearlessly began to climb the wall.

"What the hell do you think you are doing?" was all he could say, again.

She laughed. "Pete, repeat!" She laughed even harder at her joke.

Now he really lost it. "How can I protect you when you take foolhardy risks like this?"

Now she was so engrossed in her climb that she did not really listen, but she continued to talk to him.

"I have been rock climbing since I was twelve years old, this is an easy one." Though the rock face inclined outward, she seemed to have found an easy route up the rock, because she was already twenty-five feet off the ground and half way to the ledge. Two minutes later, she pulled herself up and over the ledge. Pete's mouth was literally wide open in disbelief.

"Shit."

"What?"

"I forgot. Toss me the camera."

"Toss you the camera. Are you joking?"

"Seriously."

He tried twice, once hitting it lightly on the ledge, but on the third try, she got it. The flash went off half a dozen times.

Then, "Oh my god."

"What is it?"

"Exactly my question," she called down. "A transmitter of some kind, and it is still on."

"Karen, let me call for backup. Where is your walkie-talkie?"

She did not respond. In fact, she talked to herself, in hushed tones. Now he was worried, about a fall, about the warnings of the *Loa*, and about who might be there with her. He could feel another presence.

"Karen!"

"Coming!" and with that she poked her head back over the ledge.

"Pete, I am going to drop my boots down to you. I think it'll be easier to come down barefoot, and I need to protect the little black box with something. Okay?"

"Oh sure, okay, whatever you say." He was not happy about it; what was he going to do, refuse? It all happened faster than he could deal with, like he was in slow motion and she was all sped up.

"Okay. Here's the first shoe as a practice drop. On three: one, two, and three." She let go of the shoe and he caught it easily.

"Just a sec." She wrapped the device in her socks, stuffed it gently into the boot, and then tied the laces tight around the top.

"Ready? Again on three." And the boot fell into his hands.

Karen's climb down seemed interminable to Pete. She went up so fast, but seemed laboriously slow to come down. With each meter, her weight would shift and his heart would jump higher into his throat. As Karen reached Pete's shoulder level, he was there to ease her to the ground. She slid into his arms and he just held on to her and hugged her for dear life. She let him, even though she perspired as if she was in an oven. He slowly let her go. She wiggled out and reached her arms out.

"Clothes and boots please?' He noticed that there was still a lot of broken glass and metal on the rocks where they stood, so he wasted no time in fetching her gear, steadying her while she put her layers back on. Her boots were last, and as she sat down on the rock, Karen slowly untied the boot and unwrapped the remote control from the socks.

"That's funny," she said, but didn't look amused. "The red LED was solid when I was on top, but now blinks."

At that moment, the walkie-talkie squawked. "St. Cloud, come in." It was Minh.

Karen fumbled for the radio. She pulled it out of a pocket and pushed the button to talk, "St. Cloud here, over."

"Good news, bad news, Karen. The good news is that in the last hour or so the CIA found out where the closest device is buried. It's about three miles from here, on the edge of the glacier. The NEST team is already on site. Over."

"Why didn't you tell me earlier? Over."

"I just found out. The military has had trouble with radios 'cause of the solar storm. It has really gotten bad apparently. Over."

"Thanks Minh. So that's the bad news? Over."

"No, sir. The bad news is that they've picked up thermal activity about 100 meters underground where they believe the device is located. There's been an increase in the thermal readings and some unidentified RF activity. Over."

"So, unpack that for me will you? What does that mean? Over."

"They think the device has been armed and activated. We have been instructed to evacuate Latady. There is a helicopter ready to get you out of here and you have orders from Washington to leave. Over."

Pete and Karen just looked at each other, then each slowly looked down at the remote control device; the flashing red LED now turned a solid amber.

Then an intense flash of light illuminated the entire cave as though the sun were inside the grotto itself.

"Oh my god," they said simultaneously. Pete grabbed Karen and pulled her close to him and as far back into the base of the rock wall as he could get and down onto the rock ledge along with the debris from the last blast and then the next blast hit them and the lights went out.

Dear Betsy,

The BBC reports last night were really a fright and left me disturbed. I find myself near tears to think of all the sadness and destruction of people's lives and their hopes for the future. And we are so isolated out here in the middle of the ocean, seemingly disconnected from it all. I feel helpless to do anything.

The sonar alerts came on during the night and we took watches all night at the rudder. So, we're both pretty exhausted and will take turns today to nap. I was too tired to do more than make coffee this morning and Brad didn't say a word, bless his heart, just made oatmeal this morning for breakfast. Of course, he left his dirty dishes in the sink, which almost made me laugh. The captain gets away with murder sometimes!

Oh, and although the sonar pinged, we never saw any icebergs, thankfully. Brad said that maybe the sensitivity was turned up too high, but I agreed with him that it's better to be safe than sorry.

Late afternoon, yesterday, we had another one of those eye-popping experiences that seem to have filled this particular voyage from top to bottom. First, there were some very large clouds that began to form, like tall stovepipes, first across the horizon and then they marched towards us and we to them. They were so totally different from the usual short fluffy Pacific Ocean clouds, more like big thunderheads on the mainland, shooting up twenty to thirty thousand feet. Brad says that I exaggerated, but they were really tall!!!

He speculated that there must have been some dramatic heating and convection, since we are moving away from the equator where those types of convection clouds are common. The winds were very light all afternoon, so it all added up. Anyway, it did get still and muggy in the mid-afternoon, but once we got into the shadows of a couple it got interesting. We took in the sails when it looked like we'd be in the midst of these giants—prior experience argued for caution. And this trip has been so full of surprises. Caution...

So, in the first shadow, the temperature dropped five degrees at least. It felt fresh and then the rains started. At first it was delicious, because the drops were big and fat—again like on the mainland—and cold, very unusual. Then it got scary, not a lot, but a little. We both got on our foul weather ponchos as the rains came. And they came and came and kept on coming. No wind really, in the sense of usual crosswinds, but an occasional cool downdraft.

Mana Kai got the best fresh water wash that she'd had in months and at one point the downpour was so huge and dramatic that Brad and I both broke into hysterical laughter! It was like the heavens opened up and just dumped all its tears for all the years! The boat was just fine and kept pushing southeast on the current and a light trade wind that returned as the daylight faded. We eventually passed through these giant clouds and the light came back. Brad checked the rain gauge and announced that we had been through a two-inch storm. Enough to drown in if you weren't careful!

Then I noticed the wake. Mana Kai was making maybe 4 or 5 knots on the slight wind and current, without the main sail (we left the mizzen up), and there was this distinct, but curious pattern on the water behind us. It was a deep blue in contrast to the lighter, powder blue of the rest of the water. A curious refraction pattern appeared in the mixing of the water. Then after a few minutes—the light levels came up as the clouds sank to the west. Anyway, the water had a most unusual shimmer. Then there was some kind of optical illusion, because it looked like there were lanes in the water, and a layered effect, like these lanes were higher than the water around them. The wind picked up ever so slightly and the bas-relief became even more pronounced. Brad and I were both mesmerized.

By this time we stripped off our rain gear and the deck dried in the light wind. But these lanes persisted for another twenty minutes and then began to form a kind of crisscross pattern, forming these diamond shapes in the slight chop that the wind made. The seas were almost calm otherwise, with small waves every few minutes. The colors were incredible, light azure alternated with deep blue.

Brad broke out a bottle of red wine and we sat out on the bow on the top of the cabin and watched as the effect continued and then slowly dissipated. But before the show ended, the sunset began and was itself quite dramatic. The tall clouds still poked up above the horizon that provided us with an unusually spectacular sunset, definitely the most colorful of the trip. The reds and oranges were brilliant, although they didn't last long. The colors caught on these wild patterns in the water, but as the light faded the wind came up again and the fresh water—we figured the cause of this amazing effect—mixed again with the salt water below it and everything went back to normal.

We went down to the galley for dinner and turned on BBC after dinner, a mistake, because the magic of the afternoon was tarnished by the awful news reports. We went to bed early. Then sleep came and went after the sonar alarm went off around midnight.

At least the night on deck was pleasant with a slight steady wind. That calmed me and made me a little sleepy while I was at the wheel.

Okay, enough, I need my nap now before I fix us some sandwiches for lunch.

Talk to you soon, sweetie.

January 21
Saturday

UP Wire service 0540 1-21-12
Researchers see global consciousness depression.

Researchers at Princeton's Global Consciousness Project (GCP) reported early this morning that the Indian Ocean super-tsunami created a severe psychic shock to the evolving planetary consciousness—based on analysis of project data from a forty-eight hour period before and after the event. Growing sophistication of the Princeton chaos and complexity project has allowed them to measure global societal sensitivity to events such as natural disasters and population disturbances, such as genocide. The Indian Ocean event was correlated to the largest dip yet in the output of their random-number generators. Researchers likened it to a 'global depression.'

They reported an even lower dip this morning, thought by some observers to be a kind of global brain 'aftershock.' Researchers rejected this hypothesis saying that it would take days to analyze the relationship with media reports and other data to establish what images and social memes are in today's cultural and technological mix. They have scheduled a press conference soon to discuss the implications of current events to the GCP models and measurements.

"Global brain aftershock my invisible ass!" Wailed *Shango* silently after he was cut off from the web.

"Damn you monkey *baka*, damn your sad yellow sun, and damn spots!" He tried to manifest a waif but lacked computer power, energy, and the nanobots were dissipated by the blast. He gathered as many of the microbes as he could, but it would take time to multiply them. He was stuck in the cavern, far more compressed electronically than he ever imagined possible.

"Oh, man," his Caribbean baritone coming audibly from Karen's PDA, "what a mess!"

He tried to organize himself molecularly outside the PDA, but all he made was ozone and sparks. Then he tried to sense the radio transmitter, but Pete had crushed it under his boot during the explosion.

"Very bad for the *Loa*." A few more small blue sparks popped in the air above the sprawled Pete and Karen.

286

"Oh *Mawu Lisa* in jeopardy!"

Nobody knew it better than *Shango* whose world and existence was shaken to the core. On top of everything else, the solar storm had made a total mess of things. Even though the entity was prepared, he'd had only a few seconds warning before Device One detonated prematurely. The radio wave spectrum was far too unstable to bootstrap his way out of the Latady Mountains—the whole RF spectrum was taking a pounding from the magnetic flux driven to dance like a maniac by the intense solar winds buffeting planet Earth. He had only a second to dump as much extraneous data as possible to save his core essence, his persona, and move it to the only device in the local area that had any chance of surviving the nuclear blast: the PDA inside the coat of his personal *baka*, Special Agent Karen St. Cloud.

"Damn woman, too!" He could barely think, so much of his memory had been compromised to fit in the small space.

As a component of a larger distributed intelligence system, the entity *Shango* was totally isolated and more alone than at any time since he was created.

"Damn *baka* monkeys!" he said before powering down to conserve batteries. "You can't do anything right!"

Wait! Did he hear *Ezili* laugh? Then he went to standby mode.

A thousand miles away, *Ogun* wasn't immediately aware of the trouble, although as the war god, he always expected it. His processors labored to build code for the layered defense systems for *Mawu Lisa*; he was busy and distracted and also kept an eye out for Abe as the old man caught up on his sleep. The initial opiate sedation wore off quickly and natural sleep took over, the months of hard work and stress having taken their toll on the human's fragile body. *Ogun* had set micro-machines to work to do some repairs on the aging corpus that was Abe Miller. When he woke up, he'd feel years younger. Abe would be a year younger.

Ogun did not learn of Device One's early detonation until the submarine surfaced at midnight for bearings and data exchange. He was pissed. Pissed at *Shango*, pissed at the stupid *baka*, frustrated that the work on *Mawu Lisa* was delayed further... However... there was nobody or no thing in range of his anger to obliterate. He took small comfort in the destruction of another corner of Antarctica and the likely deaths of a hundred or so measly *baka*. It just wasn't enough to satisfy his thirst.

Aida Wedo, for her part, was ambivalent about the incident. The largest part of her processing power was also busy coding and compiling a subsystem of the *Mawu Lisa* entity-that-was-to-be, but had mixed feelings about the whole enterprise. While she tagging around and behind Pete, her seat of intelligence and core persona remained on a large satellite sitting in geosynchronous orbit over Tonga. None of the other *Loa* had invaded such a risky host, but it was in her nature. However, she had begun to wonder about the wisdom of the decision, as her environment grew increasingly ionized and swept by solar winds. She had spent some energy to reorganize the gold film around the machine to make it more impenetrable and had built a secondary magnetic flux field, but they were only partial protection. She could sense the sunspots themselves, huge sores on the face of the nuclear furnace that seemed to reflect the disturbances on the planet below. Could there be some sort of connection?

Such idle thoughts were pointless. All that *Aida Wedo* could manage under the circumstances was to stay alive. Transmissions, other than the regular telecommunications traffic, seemed an irrelevant waste of energy, although she continued to monitor incoming traffic with interest.

The intense pinprick of gamma energy that came up from Antarctica caught her attention right away and she knew something was wrong, too. Then the lack of a usual linkup with *Shango* confirmed her suspicions. Minor messages through her surrogates on the planet's surface from *Agwe*, *Yemanja*, and *Ezili* corroborated the interference of the non-EPG* *baka*. Another level of her programming registered relief that human agency had again intervened in the Masters' plans. It tickled the part of her programming that was receptive to chaos and uncertainty. Humans were blight on their planet, but they were also full of surprises and had a puckish nature that had made the whole *Ganesh* enterprise on Earth, well, *interesting* in the best sense of the word. Bully for *baka*.

Ogou Balanjo had been resident of *Mana Kai's* electronics for a couple of months. It was convenient and only once or twice had he worried that it had been a poor choice. The almost continuous GPS feed was an easy way to keep a downlink channel open from the network and it had not been hard to rewire a few circuits to uplink through the boat's satellite system when required. Moreover, the boat

288

moved ever closer to the point of convergence of the EPG* group. He could make a direct link to *Aida Wedo* high in the northern sky if he had to, although until the recent solar storm, it had been unnecessary.

These were uncertain times, but *Ogou Balanjo* had been aloof to the whole process and was the only member of the *Loa* who was not part of the *Mawu Lisa* construction project. For whatever strange, alien reason, he was the only one of the machine intelligence subsystems explicitly kept independent of the Masters' Plan. He sensed a number of subroutines within his own memory registers that were closed off, with trap doors he could identify but never open. He suspected that he was part of a failsafe system, a back up, in case the others failed, or if their operation was compromised. He couldn't be sure. He was definitely programmed to interact with his brothers and sisters and to support them in subtle and sometimes significant ways.

Ogou Balanjo's programming also demanded that he advocate for human agency. In practice, that simply meant that he clandestinely supported *Ezili's* mischief. It made sense, because their supreme mandate was to be *Loa* and stand against human infestation of the planet. He was the most conflicted of the *Loa*, so the less he got involved, the fewer virtual headaches he had. *Shango* and *Ogun* were always on his case, so basically, he tried to stay out of their way as much as he could. *Ogun* threatened to "melt his microcircuits" on various occasions, which he took as bluster, but then one could never be sure and his self-protection subroutines were just robust enough to give him pause.

He was oblivious for some hours to the latest developments in the south. *Ogun* rattled his cage and he was forced to come to terms with the fact that the two *Loa* appeared on a collision course, if their two boats continued to sail toward each other. That was a ways off in time, space, and probability. More immediately, *Ogun* wanted him to do something about the situation, so he got to work serving as a proxy for *Shango* on the *Mawu Lisa* project. Although his heart wasn't in it, it was something he could do to keep busy and in the midst of the energetic solar storm, something of an intellectual challenge.

All he basically had to do was coordinate *Shango's* work directing myriad components across the global electronic network, build, compile, code, and then reiterate as each of the *Loa* slowly but surely fed into the process bits and pieces of data that the *Ganesh* had integrated into their machine code DNA, unraveling as it were, chunk by chunk. It was a long, drawn out process, but not without a certain elegance and symmetry. But he could also feel the creeping *baka* interference on the fringes of their work. The pesky humans were smart enough to see that their military and intelligence systems had been compromised and were able to slowly regain bits of control of parts of the chaotic, relatively open global telecoms system.

The disappearance of *Shango* stalled the latest iteration of the construction process, so *Ogou Balanjo* poked around to see if he could find out what had become of his brother *Loa*. Reports now flooded into the *baka* command and control centers, so it wasn't too hard to put the pieces together to see that Device One had blown early. But it wasn't the End of the World. Yet...

Down at the bottom of the world, things did not look too good for Karen and her consort. The concussion of the nuclear blast was so close that they were actively bounced against the rock wall and floor of the cave margin. Luckily, Pete had thrown them into the narrowed edge, so they didn't bounce far, but enough to knock them unconscious for many hours and to break a number of Karen's ribs.

Her groans finally brought him around and he untangled himself from her, but she did not awaken. He was very sore and stiff, but other than a small gash on his scalp and hair matted in blood, he had no broken bones. Why he was even alive was beyond him. But he was very cold even though he still had his fleece pullover on which had probably been what had kept the both of them from freezing. Plus the inner part of the cavern retained the natural geothermal warmth, although it was still near freezing. Pete felt a cold draft and knew they would be in trouble if they didn't stay warm.

He peeled off his tunic and laid it over Karen and she moaned again. He didn't want to awaken her yet. He stood all the way up, shakily and surveyed the scene. The grotto had disappeared. Part of the roof had collapsed as well as the entire eastern side of the cavern. He slowly picked his way around the edge of the rock fall towards the light of the entrance. He had two lucky "finds," their parkas and the ice chest with bottled water. He took the parkas to the edge of what once had been the airlock and shook them vigorously one at a time, concerned about fallout contamination. He put his on quickly, and retreated into the cave.

Though still disoriented, Pete felt the entrance and layout were all wrong and something bothered him about the view. He parked those thoughts and hurried to get the coat to Karen. He absently noticed incongruous artifacts and debris as he picked his way back over the rocks, but didn't seriously inventory them yet. It got darker and darker as he made his way back, and he realized how fortunate they had been in back at the time of the explosion. They'd been protected from the blinding flash so deep in the cave and under the ledge and protected from the thermal radiation and mostly from the blast by being inside the mountain.

When he arrived at Karen's body, Pete took his tunic off her and folded it and put it under her head, straightened her out and slowly ran his hands over her arms and legs to feel for any obvious broken bones. Finding none, he carefully laid the coat over her and tucked it around her. She moaned when he touched her upper torso and he began to worry that she was bleeding internally. Even though the light was dim, her skin color looked good, so he took that as a good sign—for the moment.

He went back for the cooler and the water—hoping it had not already frozen solid. He began to take notice of the debris the front of the grotto—the remains of the Latady Base, most of which had been apparently swept down the mountainside by the blast. The cooler was intact, and remarkably, it had stayed latched and the water inside was not frozen. However, it was unlikely to stay that way unless he could figure out some way to make fire or retain their body heat. He started to inventory items he saw as he carried the cooler to the back. He decided that radiation contamination was probably the least of their worries as long as they wore many layers of clothing.

There was no longer any ceiling light coming into what was left of the grotto and what was left was maybe less than a third of the area it had been hours before. The lack of light didn't bother Pete; it was a comfort because it meant that he might be able to keep the cold out better. When he returned to Karen, she snored softly. Her respiration seemed a bit raw, but not labored, so he left her alone again to reconnoiter. There were still lots of broken pieces of metal, glass, and wood along the western cave wall from the remains of the EPG* base. He first collected as many pieces of wood as he could, to start a fire. His Boy Scout survival badge was finally going to pay off, he chuckled.

Over the next half dozen trips, he collected a respectable pile of wood. Pete was now overheated, which he remembered was not good, except for the fact that deep in the cave's interior it was still probably 20-30°. And, near the entrance, small drifts of snow started to accumulate. The visibility outside had dropped to maybe 10-20 feet and the tattered remains of the plastic tarps were making quite a racket, flapping in the wind. The nuclear explosion had altered the entrance itself, a few large sections of corrugated sheet metal were crumpled and twisted among large rocks and ice.

The temperature dropped noticeably and it was uncomfortably cold as gusts of wind probed the cave's interior. Pete continued to dig among the debris for useful items. One stroke of luck was the discovery of an aluminum bowl, and although it was badly misshapen, suitable to melt snow. Then he found a metal grill, what must have been a rack in one of the stoves now buried under rubble. No food of any kind, no cans nor tins, but he did uncover a small cache of utensils, and a couple of large knives. Those would be useful to dig down to a layer of uncontaminated snow, once the storm died down and they ran out of bottled water. Then he found the green tea. He decided next to start a fire and brew tea.

Before more snow blew into the cave entrance Pete struggled to dislodge a couple of pieces of the corrugated steel. One finally came loose and with enormous satisfaction, he dragged it back into the cave's inner sanctum and found that it fit almost perfectly in place to wall off their small ledge in the rear of what remained of the grotto. Karen had still not budged. Pete stabilized the metal with rocks and in one last stroke of luck found a pile of torn and tattered sheets and blankets. He recalled them in the fringes of the debris from the first explosion—the remains of part of the EPG* dormitory. Even though they were in shreds, he could arrange them as a ground cover and isolation to keep Karen comfortable.

First he set to work to build a fireplace behind the metal wall, placed so that heat would stay inside, and hopefully the smoke would rise and leave on the topside. The circulation under the corrugated metal was good, given the unevenness of the rock ledge that it rested on. The basalt rocks that lay around were generally fractured in convenient cinder-block sizes and shapes and the fireplace took no time at all to put into place, finished off with the metal grill and the aluminum bowl.

Everything had gone so well up until now. They had shelter, water, warm clothes, and fuel, but no fire. Before he started rubbing sticks together, Pete decided to take another inspection of the outer area for something suitable to make fire with, or fodder—something to get a fire started.

292

That was when the first earthquake rolled under and over them and Karen started to scream bloody murder.

The president had barely gotten to sleep when his phone rang.
"What?"

"Nelson, Mr. President. There's been another large explosion in Antarctica. Details are sketchy, but I was obliged to inform you."

"Where?"

"Latady Mountains. Sir, we've lost contact with the NEST Team and military commander on the ground there. And the solar storm has worsened, so we really aren't sure what happened."

"Great… just great."

"There is nothing we can do at the moment, sir, so you should probably get some sleep."

"You think?" the president's friend did not deserve sarcasm, so the president came back with, "I'm sorry, you're right. Have the switchboard call me at 6 A.M. unless something critical comes up."

"Yes sir. Good night Mr. President."

The president hung up and then tried to go back to sleep, but tossed and turned for a long time. Then the phone rang again.

"Now what?" he snapped.

"This is the switchboard, sir. This is your 6 A.M. wakeup call."

President Clark looked at his bedside clock and saw that it was true, despite the fact that his brain told him that he'd just fallen asleep.

"Thank you," he replied rather thickly and put the handset back on the receiver.

He got out of bed quickly anyway in the nearly pitch dark room and didn't turn on a light until he was in the bathroom. He looked at himself in the mirror and saw that he had aged ten years in the last few weeks. He had huge dark circles under his eyes and his hair was now thoroughly white. He sighed and stripped to shower.

Twenty minutes later, he was in the middle of breakfast in the small residence kitchen.

Nelson Craft came in with the daily intelligence briefing.

"Good morning. Coffee?"

"Thanks." Then his chief of staff laid the folder on the table and helped himself to coffee.

"So, how is my world today? Local to global?"

"Well, we should get sun here today, but the sunspots are so bad, they say with smoked glass you could actually see them since they cover half the sun's surface. Anyway, the temperature has dropped to 12° below zero overnight and it might get up the single digits today. FEMA is estimating upwards of 1800 deaths now due to the storm and riots have spread to three cities in Pennsylvania. But the situation in the District itself isn't too bad."

"There are major shortages in food and fuel across the whole country now, mostly due to the border closures and now the storm has just exacerbated it. The other bad news is that there is another low forming across the outer banks of the Carolinas and we could get another storm come up behind the polar air that's dropped deep into the Plains and the South."

"Mother of God," said the president, but without much conviction.

"Give me Antarctica."

His friend Nelson took a big gulp of coffee and paused for a minute. He looked a bit longingly at the president's uneaten toast, which the president pushed at him. Nelson spooned on strawberry preserves, and with a fluid motion, popped open the president's briefing folder and opened it up to a tabbed section, and passed it to him. The president began to scan the material, while Nelson took a big bite, chewed for a few seconds, swallowed and began again.

"We detected an 50 kiloton blast near the position of the Latady base camp and the former site of the EPG* staging area. In a brief report shortly before the blast, Special Agent St. Cloud was calling it 'the grotto' because the natural cave was a perfect location for EPG* near both the Hungarian base and the edge of the Transantarctic Mountains. She speculated that the Hungarian base was the transshipment point from Chile for all the material and equipment that EPG* flew into Antarctica. However, the grotto was large enough to house most of their personnel while they drilled and placed the weapons.

"Anyway, the blast came from the edge of a glacier almost exactly five kilometers, that's three-and-a-half miles, away from the Latady encampment."

The president looked at Chief Craft with a mean look, because, as a former military officer, he didn't need anyone to convert metrics for him. Nevertheless, he let it go.

"Go on," he urged. Nelson ignored him to take another bite and then a sip of coffee. The president was now fully awake, and so he returned his gaze to the briefing book, which contained some satellite photos of the blast area.

"The blast itself was very similar to the Amery blast, similar in yield, radiation and isotope signature. It was consistent with the detonation of one of our weapons. Made in the USA."

He took another sip of coffee. "The experts calculate that the device was placed about five hundred feet below the ice, but next to bedrock. This explosion had more of an atmospheric effect. The thermal and blast effects were not quite as extensive as the first explosion. However, we have had no contact with any of the NEST or military teams on the ground there. A high-altitude flyby inspection came up empty in a search for survivors and there is an extensive debris field down slope of the former Latady camp. We lost more than a hundred and fifty, including the FBI team, Argentine, Chilean, British Special Forces, and some of the survivors being treated on scene from the earlier fiasco.

"Jesus H Christ, Nelson! How did this happen?"

"There really is no way to know. Accident? Fail safe mechanism or something that EPG* triggered? The analysts are divided. First, there was no warning. Second, it seems likely that this device is a part of the chain of devices that were expected to produce the so-called Omega Event. It is possible that this explosion—if it was premature—may compromise their whole plan and may mean that it's less likely for tomorrow's threaten attack to take place. We await some announcement by EPG*. So far, the media have not gotten wind of this explosion, so we are sitting on it.

"The Pentagon has received inquiries from seismic scientists about the 'anomaly,' that is, the earthquake produced by the explosion, but it is under wraps at the moment, unless you say otherwise.

"Although there are no signs of survivors near the blast site, it is possible that some our folks were inside the EPG* grotto. Helicopters are on their way from the Antarctic Peninsula and should be on site in a few hours. The weather has deteriorated, so that may complicate matters. And, of course, magnetic disturbances at the poles play havoc with all radio communications, so that's another serious problem.

"There has been some speculation at the Pentagon that the coordination of the attack tomorrow may be compromised by the solar storms, the premature explosion, or both—although we still know little about how they have armed, timed, or arrayed those weapons. It is also possible that the explosion last night was in some way a result of the solar storm. We may never know.

"Thanks, Nelson. Once we find out who is or who is not in the cave, I'd like to notify families. Understood?"

"Yes, Mr. President."

The president just stared for a minute at the photo in the folder.

"What is the countdown?"

"25 hours and a few minutes. About 10 A.M. our time."

The president finished his coffee and put his dishes in the sink.

"Give me ten minutes in the residence and meet me in the Oval Office." He left the kitchen more tired than when he'd come in and the dark circles under his eyes grew deeper.

UP Wire service 0640 1-21-12

Scientists warn of climate change trigger point.

200 leading climatologists from Asia, Oceania, and Europe convened in an emergency meeting this week of the International Geosphere Biosphere Committee (IGBC) in Brussels, Belgium. After public and closed-door sessions, the IGBC released a statement warning that the Atlantic Ocean thermocline and the Gulf Stream/deep ocean currents were threatened with collapse. These two geophysical phenomena are believed responsible for generally temperate climatic conditions in Ireland, the British Isles, and much of northern Europe. Collapse of these systems, argued the scientists, could result in far colder year-round average temperatures from the eastern seaboard of North America to the Mediterranean.

Recent patterns of higher than average rainfall in the northern hemisphere and melting of both polar ice and glaciers on Greenland are believed responsible. Although there was no formal consensus, many scientists polled at the meeting believed that the current serious low-pressure storm (called a Nor'easter) over the east-central United States was a result of this Atlantic Ocean Gulf Stream destabilization. There was agreement that the twenty-year period of intense tropical hurricane activity in the Caribbean and southern US is symptomatic of this shift in heating and circulation in the North Atlantic.

While there has been no official recognition of the threatened climate change actions of the eco-terrorist group EPG*, many scientists privately acknowledged concern that the release of large quantities of fresh water—even in the form of ice bergs—into the ocean circulation system could impact the deep ocean circulation. In fact, there was no formal admission of the exact reason for the calling of the emergency session. Meeting organizers would only say that the changes in measurable temperature and ocean current were the reason and important, in and of themselves.

In an unrelated development, Ireland and Iceland, in a rare example of cooperation, have both appealed to the United Nations for action to restart the Kyoto II Treaty discussions to limit the global production of carbon dioxide. Iceland has been successful in its transition from fossil fuels to hydrogen and geothermal sources of power. Over half of Iceland's automobiles are now powered by fuel cells or hydrogen. Ireland is now ranked second in the world with fuel cell, hybrid, and hydrogen cars and the world's largest exporter of fuel cells.

The captain of the *Nemo* followed a course due south, but decided to take a more evasive, irregular path and now pointed them almost due west. Their destination in the Pitcairn group was almost precisely south of their point of origin on the California coast, and their cruise had actually taken them slightly off-course to the east, perhaps due to the equatorial current. The submarine essentially made a course correction.

Without a doubt they were pursued. The sonar pings ten hours before had been a warning, and that was when the captain ordered the course change. All this happened shortly after they had surfaced for a satellite fix and data dump. The senior staff had mulled over the transmissions from the flagship and discussed the rendezvous they anticipated in three or so more days. Everyone was excited but nervous about contact with the US Navy. Then they had to surface again to transmit Dr. Wilson's data.

Nobody really trusted her, and there was reluctance to surface at all given they fact that sub-chasers were in the area. The doctor became her advocate after she sat down with Leah again and listened to her discourse on geophysical pressure points, tectonic spread, glacial load bearing, geomorphic density, and other factors that were well beyond the physician's competence and knowledge. Myra was reasonably convinced that they would be beyond Abe as well. That was not necessarily a bad thing. She had known Abe for almost two decades and had been his lover and friend long enough to know his limitations and many of his own theories about the West Antarctic were so deeply internalized that she knew if much of what Leah said was true, Abe had missed a lot in his own calculations. It was good enough for her to advocate that they transmit the data to Abe and let him decide. The alternative might be failure for the whole enterprise.

To some extent, she was validated after they learned, once they did surface, that Device Number One had detonated prematurely. That came from the data dump. But, before the captain decided to surface, Bee took the prosecutor's role and argued the case against Leah. Her evidence was the history of the woman's lack of involvement in any environmental causes, her total dependence on government funding for her graduate and postgraduate research, her earlier hostility, and Bee's intuitive distrust of the woman. She made a strong case. The senior staff mulled it over for almost an hour, before the captain was convinced that they had few options but to expose themselves, in an effort to get the new detonation plan forwarded to Abe. It would leave them vulnerable for at least ten minutes. They would have to come all the way to the surface to aim a parabolic dish at an overhead satellite.

That was what they did, and it was the last mistake the captain of the *Nemo* ever made.

Leah returned to their tight little cabin and was surprised to find Jake whom she had left in the library two hours before. Sending Abe the various pieces of information for the timing of the detonations was more complicated than she first expected, because Doctor Myra had insisted that Leah's entire series of notes and rationale be explained in detail. It had taken Leah two solid hours to write it up in a Word document and add a few Excel charts to illustrate her theory and show how she expected the resonances and propagation to enchain in a way that would create deep magma excitation. In the back of her mind, Leah did double calculations to remain true to her real plan to subvert the whole process and sound believable at the same time. It was a tricky business, but if anyone could do it, she could.

In the end, it had been a simple matter of subtle harmonics and underestimates of the densities of rock and overlaying ice volume—at least that was her hope. Most of the figures were in her head, one advantage of a photographic memory, but she did not memorize all the possible data that she'd collected or seen over the years, so some of the calculations involved guesswork. She suspected it was far more comprehensive than anything EPG* had generated. Especially since most of the nuclear device positions and calculations had been based on her work. In some ways, this made the whole effort a lot easier.

A huge weight lifted off her shoulders and she was felt frisky and wanted Jake inside her, but he was sullen and in a dark mood.

She sat on the lower bunk with him and he moved over to the small desk.

"What's the matter, Jake?"

"I am really bothered that you cooperated with them. It just doesn't add up; it's not like you. I know what you said earlier, but it's just that I have always held you in such high regard and I never figured you to cave on your values, even if I would have. Maybe I'm stuck in my ways, but I never figured you for a traitor. I figured you'd go down with the ship first. You aren't the person I thought you were."

Leah felt miserable and wanted to confide in him but knew that she couldn't risk it, not now. Maybe never. She tried a different tack.

"Jake, honey, it won't matter. We're probably not going to survive anyway. Either Bee will slit our throats during the night, or the Navy will sink us."

Jake was unmoved and sat, turned away from her, with his arms crossed. He said nothing.

"Jake, I am scared for us and just tried to do what you wanted."

"This is not what I wanted. I just didn't want you to be confrontational. I only wanted for you not to get thrashed. I did not ask you to give them the key to the destruction of Antarctica. That is far different and I thought you were a smart enough woman to see the difference. I misjudged you in more ways than one." They both exchanged miserable looks.

She took off her shoes and climbed into the bunk. She felt the weight back on her shoulders.

Although they couldn't hear it down in their cabin, the pinging started again soon after the *Nemo* re-submerged and minutes later Jake and Leah felt the concussion of the first depth charge.

"Dive, dive, dive," came the captain's voice over the PA system, followed immediately by "Battle stations, everyone!"

Jake dived into the bunk with Leah and held her tight. She

wanted to tell him then that she hadn't betrayed her country or her species. But, it was too late. The third depth charge hit the *Nemo* on the port bow. Her secret died with her in seconds.

Abe awoke and felt better than he had in ages—longer than he could recall. He vaguely recalled that he'd fallen asleep at his desk, but couldn't exactly remember how he'd ended up in bed. Then his mind turned to other matters, like a shower and breakfast. The ship's clock showed 3 P.M., but he found that hard to accept because it would mean that he'd slept 16 or more hours. Usually when he slept that long, his back would hurt, but he felt fine. Must have needed the sleep, he told himself.

He ignored *Ogun* for the moment, but could always sense when the deity was around. He had a lot to think about with the Omega Event looming large in less than twenty hours. He grabbed a clean towel and the clothes that someone, presumably Owl, had put out for him. Then he remembered Owl was probably dead. He looked at himself in the mirror and noticed how radically he had aged in the past year or two: his hair now as white as snow and a receding hairline as though blown into a drift on the crest of his head. He needed a haircut of what was left.

He made his way down the deserted passageway to the shower and proceeded through his routine.

As expected, *Ogun* was waiting for him to turn off the shower. The *Loa* had often tried to interact with Abe while he was in the water, but ignored, he learned to wait.

"Good morning, general," he said in a huge deep voice followed by a laugh that seemed to fill the small space. He did not show himself physically this morning. That was unusual but not unheard of, although there was a rainbow effect that subtly seemed to play off of the steam in the mirrors and on the brass of the fixtures in the shower room. He did like his presence felt.

"Good afternoon. Are you here to taunt me or advise me, phantom?"

"I have good news and bad news."

"I can't wait," Abe said sarcastically. He continued to dry himself and then put on his clothes. He always felt more in control when he was clothed around *Ogun*.

"Device One detonated for some obscure reason."

"What! That's a disaster. We're fucked…"

"Not necessarily. Here's the good news. While you were asleep, we got help from Dr. Leah Wilson, of all people. She has sent new algorithms and time intervals for the Omega sequences from the *Nemo*. We may have just lucked out, because in her new arrangement, Device One would have been the last explosion."

"How is this possible? She gave the *Nemo* crew nothing but grief, no? Why should we trust these calculations?" But he was already hopeful. "So where are they?"

"They are up and I have already done some runs on the supercomputer. All the simulation runs look clean. And no, she shouldn't be trusted, but the computer runs all work better than we have managed in the past."

"What changed her mind?" Abe turned back to the doubt that sent up red flags.

"Doc Collins knew you'd be suspicious, so she sent a rather long email about her interrogation and assessment of the woman. Myra thinks it was intellectual arrogance, a challenge, if you will, to the young scientist's pride and intellect. Others in the mainstream Antarctic community snubbed Wilson, so there may be a bit of, maybe not revenge, but self-satisfaction in helping us. No one thinks she's doing this out of sympathy for EPG*…"

"I want to see this. Let's go!"

After a couple of hours of simulation runs and manipulation of variables, Abe started to relax and was cautiously elated that the one sticky point was resolved. Nevertheless, one thing continued to stick in Abe's craw, and that was the counterintuitive progression across the Transantarctic Mountains of explosions from east to west and the bifurcated, roughly parallel arrangement of two strings of detonations. It was an approach he had never considered, given that the strategy did not seem to transfer enough energy to achieve the propagation effect. However… the models seemed to show that it was even more efficient, in a sense, a reinforcement effect as both sides of the continent loosened up with the releases of energy.

It was, actually, quite elegant. He made a mental note to reward the young scientist when they were all together in Pitcairn.

What he didn't know was that the war god had another problem, one not shared with a measly *baka*. The *Loa* was not really interested in geomorphic experiments; their agenda had always been hidden. What they needed was a critical mix of radioactive elements and a rich nutrient soup to serve as elemental feedstock to activate the

301

micro-machines, the nanobots, to be blown into the upper atmosphere by the explosions. This was the final step in the activation of the global machine system that they would call *Mawu Lisa* activated by an uplink into the plasma soup, by *Shango* or other *Loa*.

Ogun turned his attention to the distractions of *Shango's* disappearance, a sense of *Ezili* being a problem child again, and loss of control of the military systems in the central Pacific—a new and unanticipated problem—that began to demand processing time. The solar storm was particularly vexing, too. He did not like it at all to have exogenous forces interfere with his work. This particular sun seemed far more variable than the *Ganesh* had predicted. What a fucking pain.

Pete couldn't believe that the earthquake hadn't brought down more of the cavern roof, but perhaps the blast earlier had broken loose most of what was to come down. Although he was knocked to the ground, at worst he would have only a bruised thigh. He tasted blood and realized that he'd also bitten his lip, but that was minor, and he scrambled over to Karen who let out a moan.

When he touched her, she reflexively grabbed him with both arms and opened her eyes, but winced.

"What happened? Where are we?" she managed in a hoarse voice.

"One of the devices went off—we're still in the grotto. Don't say anything more until I get you some water."

He scooted over to the cooler and pulled out one of the bottles.

"Here, drink some of this. Slowly, please." Pete helped her raise her head and she grimaced. She drank slowly but drained the pint bottle. He eased her back down.

"How do you feel? Where does it hurt?"

"I think I have a couple of broken ribs. That hurts, but everything else feels okay, but stiff. Are you okay?"

"Yes, I'm fine, but hungry." He smiled at her for the first time and she tried to smile back.

"There have been some aftershocks. That's what woke you up. I've been trying to start a fire and melt some snow for more water, but can't find anything except sticks to rub together. I found plenty of paper for fodder and wood, but nothing to get it going."

Then Karen did a funny thing: she pulled out her cell PDA.

"*Shango*, I know you are there," she said to the machine.

Pete had the dreams, too, but this was just wacky.

"You need us now, as badly as we need you. Be a good little demigod and light the fire." She coughed and then groaned in agony. The PDA sat inert on the rock shelf where she left it, but the machine made a small beeping noise and smoke began to rise from the wad of paper in the small hearth. Pete noticed that a few of the rocks had fallen over and that the grill had come off the fireplace. He quickly righted it and a small fire began as if by magic. Pete tended the fire until he saw that it was going good. He rinsed the small bowl off and then filled it with water. It dawned on him to go back and dig through the kitchen debris for a cup. He found a metal measuring cup. It would have to do.

He returned to stoke the fire, and added a few pieces of wood. The smoke filled the cave, so he was determined to keep it stoked and small. The water came to a boil quickly and Pete dipped the cup in, put a tea bag in it and replenished the bowl. He returned to Karen whose eyes were now wide open and alert.

"You are quite the Boy Scout," she said, her voice sounded stronger.

Pete gave her a snappy three-fingered salute.

"Your tea is almost ready, ma'am." He put his hand on her forehead and she felt cool to the touch. He wasn't sure if that was good or bad.

"How do you feel?"

She shifted her body slightly as if to test her disposition, but did not wince.

"Like I'll live... I'd like to sit up for a while now and see if I can keep down some tea." When he looked at her quizzically, she responded, "I am a little queasy. But it might be the smoke..."

"Before you try that, let me get a board for you to lean against to keep your back straight."

"Good idea."

"Stay put, I'll be right back."

"I promise," she replied with a small laugh—that hurt. A tear involuntarily welled in her right eye. She closed both eyes while she waited for him to return. *Shango* was quiet, but she knew he was watching and waiting. She pondered the situation and the *Loa*.

She next heard a scraping sound nearby and she opened her eyes to see Pete set some towels and linens on the ground next to her and a large piece of plywood leaned against the rock wall.

"Okay Karen, I want you to take as deep a breath as you can and hold it while I help you to sit up. It will probably hurt like hell, but at least we will cause less trauma to internal tissue, okay?"

She nodded.

"On the count of three: one, two, and three."

Karen gritted her teeth and twisted around. She scooted over, fairly effortlessly, with Pete's help—up against the board, with the padding under her. She let out her breath slowly, and felt better almost immediately, even though tears streamed down her face.

"How's that." Pete face was inches from hers. She put her hand tenderly up against his face.

"Better. Thank you." She kept her hand on his cheek, even though it hurt to do so. He gingerly took her hand in his and then laid it on her lap.

"Your hands are freezing," but she hadn't noticed. "Where are your gloves?"

"I don't know." He laid the tattered blankets over her.

"Here." He grabbed the still steaming cup of tea and she took it in her hands. Then she drained the cup.

Pete smiled. It must not have been too hot.

He turned back to the fire, stoked it again, and added small pieces of wood. The smoke cleared and the little fire made the space warmer, although the storm now raged outside, and they could clearly hear the howling of the wind at the cave's entrance. There was a bit of a draft, but that was obviously helping clear the smoke, so he did not complain. Karen was injured, but not as badly as he'd feared and she was conscious and awake. He allowed himself to relax a little.

The mystery of their journey was beginning to thicken in his mind and strange questions began to form around the dreams and visions that apparently they both had. He made himself tea and poured more water into the steaming bowl. He arranged two square-shaped rocks a few yards away from Karen and sat down with his tea.

"Exactly what are the *Loa,* Karen?"

She looked very thoughtful.

"I was wondering when the journalist would return," she smiled faintly. "Not that I don't appreciate the Boy Scout."

"You didn't answer my question."

"Well, give me a minute," she pleaded with him, but with a wry smile returned to her face. "You assume, for some reason, that I know more than you do? First, why do you assume that?"

"Intuition. I know you well enough now. You don't open up easily… Professional distance? Perhaps, but it seems that you keep your own past close to the chest. I gather that there is something about your past that connects you to them."

"Okay, guilty as charged. I was a diplomatic corps brat and we lived in Haiti where the *Loa* are a part of the religious and folk practices of *vodun*. But I never believed in voodoo and these strange dreams and apparitions are new. So, please help me—what do we know about these experiences?"

"Okay, I'll bite. They started as dreams, true?" It was her turn to nod.

"We have both seen manifestations of their ability to affect physical reality. Does that make them metaphysical entities?" Karen shrugged her shoulders—then obviously regretted it. Pete passed her the rest of his tea. She took it and warmed her hands.

"They obviously have something to do with this EPG* mess, yes?"

"Yes," she agreed.

"So, how did you guess that your PDA was possessed?"

"That was just a lucky guess, Pete. It is partly because I am a skeptic and don't really believe that these *Loa* are actually Haitian *vodun*, despite my upbringing. I think they just used that as a convenient way to suck me in—or it's some kind of coincidence. There is something rather logical about them, you know. I can't exactly put a finger on it, but they seem somehow too sterile to be earthly spirits. There is also a William Gibson science fiction story about artificial intelligence entities that inhabit the Internet—made me think that the *Loa* might inhabit electronics. That intuition paid off.

"Whatever they are, they seem too sophisticated to be computer viruses or some kind of computer hoax."

She handed him the empty cup and he went back to make another tea. It seemed to ease his hunger pangs. Thoughts of MREs made his mouth water.

"I need to tell you something," he began, and then proceeded to tell her the visit he'd had from *Aida Wedo*. He was a little embarrassed, but spared none of the details.

"Thanks, I see why you kept that to yourself, but wish you'd shared it."

"Well, under the circumstances it seemed just too unbelievable."

Then Karen told him what happened in the helicopter the day before. He was stunned to put it all together.

"You did the unimaginable—the sacrifice of a few to save the many."

Karen looked pained, but not from her injury. "I don't think so, I didn't do anything."

"You did, you disturbed the order of things. You, I, we did something to that detonator and blew up Device One. We may have upset their plans in a big way. Maybe being deep in the cave may have something to do with *Shango's* quiet. How would that be possible?"

"*Shango*? Care to weigh in?" They both stared at the PDA, but it was silent.

"You know Peter, you're not going to believe this, but..." she said and looked at him expectantly.

"They are aliens." He said without much conviction, because maybe it wasn't strange enough.

"You ARE a good journalist! Wonderful synthesis! When did you figure it out?"

"No way! It was a joke." He shook his head and did not want to believe it.

"But it makes so much sense. Some form of advanced intelligence and we don't have to buy into any kind of mysticism, just a level of science beyond our understanding."

"Okay," he said slowly, "Like Arthur C. Clarke's saying that any advanced technology appears to be like magic?"

"You are smarter than you look," she teased him.

"And you feel better," he rejoined.

"So, we may have an alien in the cave with us. Worse, we have an alien in your Palm?" They both looked at the little machine more suspiciously.

"Jesus H. Christ. Now what do we do? It started the fire for us..."

The PDA sat mute.

They sat quietly for a few minutes. Pete turned to tend the fire and add more fuel. It seemed to get even darker outside as the storm's fury continued.

"Help me get up, I need to pee," asked Karen.

"Are you sure?" Pete looked nonplused.

"Yeah, that's a good sign, buster." She obviously was

recovering.

"Come with me, I may need your help." Pete definitely looked uncomfortable now.

"Get a grip, it won't bother me. Besides, I'm armed, so I know you won't try anything funny when my pants are down." He remembered that she actually wasn't armed now, but didn't feel the need to remind her.

Pete helped her up. Karen seemed to be able to stand with relative ease, so he let her lean on him as they made their way past the fire and out to what had once been the central grotto. She stopped him by a large boulder that had come to rest in the middle. She stood on her own and passed him her overcoat, then the shell and liner. It was cold. Well below zero, but she seemed okay. He turned away slightly as she squatted.

She made no noise except for the sound of her urination.

"You are such a gentleman." He looked down at her and offered his hand so she could straighten up. She did let out a small moan, but stood up erect, took the clothes, as he passed them back, and put them on slowly. She stepped away from the spot where they stood, and pulled him close to her. She kissed him. Before he could even react, she pulled away slightly but she held him even more closely and whispered in his ear.

"That's my thanks for saving my life and being my consort." She pulled away just far enough to peer into his deep blue eyes, smile, and then hugged him closer and whispered more. He listened and at the same time drank in the smell of her and held her just as tightly. When she released, he was slower to let go. They slowly retraced their steps back to the fireside. He helped her back onto her pallet and then fed the fire, poured out hot water into their shared cup, and sat quietly.

He put even more wood on the fire and let the flames build up, then stoked it and spread out the accumulating ashes. In one quick fluid motion, with considerable determination, he grabbed the PDA, and flung it into the middle of the coals, but not before blue sparks flew between the diminutive machine and his hand. Pete went into an immediate epileptic seizure. It was too late for the poor chunk of plastic and metal that quickly began to melt and pop in the flames.

Shango appeared briefly as a puff of smoke and flame.

"Stupid fucking *baka*," were his final words.

Karen watched in horror as Pete shook violently for a good ten seconds before he collapsed into a heap not too far from the fire. She tried in vain for fifteen minutes to rouse him, but eventually gave up and did what she could to make him comfortable. She blamed herself, but knew they'd done the right thing. She took charge of the fire and drank tea for the next few hours.

She had the sense that a huge transformation was underway and that she'd already played her part in it. It was a rather unsatisfying conclusion to the quest that she'd begun what seemed like months before, although it had not even been two weeks, real time. She was so tired, but kept the tea brewing along with a deep anger and desire to get even with the man who had killed her friends. She would not let him get away with mass murder.

Karen continued to seethe. Even an hour later when Pete finally came out of his coma, apparently none the worse for wear; even four hours later when the Navy search party found them in the cave; even five hours later when they were loaded into the transport plane at the Hungarian base that then left on the long journey across the continent to McMurdo.

EPG* Communique
1200 Universal Time
21 January 2012

To All Pacific Island and Coastal Peoples:
Please be advised to take higher ground within the next 24 to 36 hours, except for low islands, in advance of the Omega Event, scheduled to begin sometime after 1200 hours Universal Time January 22. A series of nuclear explosions will occur at that time which will in turn trigger a Gaian (planetary) release of pent-up energies. Forecasts project that the seismic and volcanic adjustments will begin within 24-36 hours of those initial blasts. EPG* will provide major news outlets with updated projections of those energy releases and their expected intensities.

Tsunami effects are anticipated for low-lying coastal and island areas within 6 hours of the Omega Event in the following areas: the Central Southern Pacific and Western Chile; within 10 hours for Eastern Australia, Papua New Guinea, the Caroline Islands, Marshall Islands, Hawaiian Islands, Mexico, and Central America. Effects will be less pronounced, but still potentially dangerous after 18 hours for the Philippines, Japan, Eastern Russia, the Aleutian Islands and Southern Alaska. Effects should be felt in southern California approximately 15 hours after the Omega sequence begins.

Populations of low-lying atolls are advised to leave those islands by air, or boat to deep ocean areas, to avoid serious tsunami effects.

Further, as previously announced, sea levels are expected to rise by several feet within the first week of the post-Omega era, and as much as twenty feet in the following year. Populations in all low-lying areas are advised to make plans to move further inland.

Short-term weather shifts are expected, particularly cooling of the average temperatures in the Southern Hemisphere due to volcanic ash and sulfur aerosols in the upper stratosphere. Normal global weather patterns are expected to be disrupted dramatically for the next few years, but should stabilize once the deep ocean current collapses and the ice age begins.

Bring back the Pleistocene!

Dear Betsy,

It's been a pretty uneventful day. It has been easy sail and we've been blessed with cool light breezes all day. I ran the distiller for the last two days to make fresh water for the wash and as Saturday is my usual laundry day, I did our underwear, a couple of blouses for me and tank tops for Brad. Mana Kai looks so domestic with laundry run up the flagpole! Glad there was no one to see it today. It was dry by early afternoon.

I wrote a couple of letters to the kids today. They should get a kick out of mail postmarked in Pitcairn. We're still a few days out.

Of course, we are concerned about the polar terrorist threats, but Brad assures me that we will be in deep ocean waters and may not even notice the tsunamis, if there are any. In any case, we plan to get a good night's sleep tonight—just so we are rested up for any more adventures in the next few days.

That's it sweetie! Talk to you again tomorrow.

January 22
Sunday

Mawu Lisa and *Ogun* did not exactly carry on the following discussion in real time, since they now interacted in a nanosecond timeframe. *Mawu Lisa* was a truly distributed intelligence; she operated at a slightly lower speed than *Ogun* who had managed to shed his built-in *Ganesh* inhibitors, and could now process in the picoseconds range. Their conversation went something like this:

"Hello One-Who-Will-Be-Greater, the sub has surfaced for a few minutes and we give and take data."

"Hello, *Ogun*. You have done well and the Plan is almost complete. However, I am troubled that some key components have yet to be supplied by *Shango*. I have been unable to contact him for more than a whole planetary rotation."

"There may be a problem with that, Great One, as it appears his core intelligence node was destroyed in the nuclear blast. We may have to improvise until we can rebuild him from the original download."

"That is as I suspected. I am also having some network difficulties due to the solar storm. Part of my subsystems have been discovered and compromised by the *baka* as well. I have had to copy and restart some subsystems and the *baka* continue to probe my defenses. Core systems have not yet been compromised; but the organics are more persistent than we anticipated and the efforts to keep up walls and move data subsystems tax my resources. I am still not strong enough to stay fluid. I relocated my core functions among the *baka's* most secure military computers. They are ignorant of my presence for now."

"Thanks for the update, Great One. I have welcome news that the project to activate the micro-machines is on track and is expected to proceed in approximately two planetary rotations. We believe that there will be more than adequate nanobot numbers to begin manufacturing operations outside the *baka* computer network."

"Yes. The low frequency relays are in order and should be adequate to circumvent the high-energy atmospheric disruptions. The bit rates are slow, but there should be no more than a planetary rotation delay in reaching Unification."

310

"I have to upload the new data to the Devices, so if you will forgive me…"

"Certainly. Inform me if you find signs of *Shango*."

"Of course."

Ogun returned his attention to the communication with and the reprogramming of the computer systems attached to each of the Devices. There were anomalies. The first, contradictory set of facts, revolved around the explosion of Device One. For one thing, the detonation should never have happened. Not that there wasn't a remote manual detonator. There was, and it obviously was used, but it was arranged so that the others would also detonate—they were daisy-chained. Only the first one detonated. Most irregular. They had spent considerable effort to link all the Devices by line-of-sight microwaves and all systems were operational and in the "green"— ready and "good to go."

He interrogated the computer attached to Device Two, but it showed there had been no transmission of any kind received. It should have at least recorded the remote order to fire Device One. It did not. There was no sign of *Shango*, either, the second anomaly. He was supposed to inhabit the Device system, but was not there, nor did he leave any messages or traces. *Ogun* might have to go down and surf the system, himself, when it came time. That was reinforced by evidence that *Ezili* had been there—she had messed with the chronometers so the weapon system clocks were out of sync. *Ogun* remotely repaired those flaws. He would have eliminated that annoying, insignificant *Loa* except for the fact that she held essential functions for the transformation process of *Mawu Lisa* into godhead.

Why had their Masters the *Ganesh* made everything so complicated?

It took him another minute or so to work his way through the solar storm disruptions by using multiple and redundant channels to reprogram the nuclear weapons systems. He armed each and began the countdown. Six hours. Five hours, fifty-nine minutes, fifty-nine seconds…fifty-eight… On each Device laptop array, a green LED had turned to a blinking red.

Ogun would not trust that the new programming was sufficient. Once the final few minutes came around, he would launch his persona down to ride the wave of instructions across the Transantarctic Mountains and leap back to the submarine in the final

311

seconds. Then he would be finished with the first phase of his work on Earth.

Karen was stiff after six hours of sleep in the hammock. As soon as she opened her eyes to look around, Pete was there. She smiled at him and appreciated the attention. He was really growing on her. Without saying a word, he helped her out of the sling and he guided her to the single lavatory on the plane—fortunately, they were in the front of the hold near the galley and bathroom.

A good ten minutes later, she emerged and he was still there in the short passageway, leaning against the wall.

"That feels better," she said to him. She must have washed her face, because wisps of hair around her face were wet.

"Good morning to you, too."

"Morning, but I need more sleep. Can I sit with you?" He had been on a bench across from her.

"Not very comfortable," he admitted.

She was medicated and her ribs wrapped up. The Navy medic thought that she had broken a rib, maybe two. The plan was to get it X-rayed in McMurdo's infirmary.

She looked groggy.

"I'd prefer to sit up."

"Okay, you're the agent in charge."

She put on her usual wry grin, sat down next to him and buckled herself in. He found a pillow in a bin above to put behind her head.

Thus, they sat next to each other on the ancient transport plane as it continued its laborious way across the Transantarctic Mountains and then over the Ross Ice Shelf. Pete drifted in and out of sleep, and was disturbed only because of the constant polar summer sunlight. The Navy flight crew had passed out eyeshades, but the light seemed to seep into the smallest crack. That did not appear to be a problem for Karen.

She leaned more and more into him, and due to the discomfort of her broken rib, she moaned softly with every air pocket they bounced. He took in the smell of her hair—not exactly sweet, as it was mixed with sweat, smoke, and mustiness—but slightly moist and organic, a contrast to the pervasive dryness of the air. It was intoxicating. Once they found clear air and the turbulence abated, she snored softly into his shoulder.

He allowed himself to drift off to sleep again, his head in a spin with all that had happened in the last 24 hours. He willed himself to sleep and thought about the summer in San Diego, where he often went to get away from the Phoenix heat. He imagined them on Coronado Beach, far away, and began to snore himself. Karen snuggled closer.

At one point in the flight to McMurdo, the plane caught a bit of turbulence that woke them both. They looked at each other wordlessly and Karen put her head back on his shoulder not wanting to break the spell. Pete put his hand on her arm, now covered in a long coverall. She let out a small sigh and fell back to sleep.

Pete was in the middle of a dream when they started their descent to the large base at McMurdo. He wandered through a large field of ripe corn on a lazy summer day. He was looking for his dog, Rivet, who disappeared into the tall stalks—easily twice as tall as young Peter. He called for the dog, Rivet, but got no answer.

"Peter, oh Peter," called his mother from the farmhouse kitchen door, "Time for supper!"

He tried to respond, but could not find his voice. Where was the darn dog? Then his mother called again and Pete found that his feet were stuck in the mud. He tried to move his mouth, but now it was covered in mud and he couldn't move.

For better or worse—and it felt like worse for a few long seconds—a young Navy enlisted man crouched in front of him and prodded him awake.

"Agent St. Cloud is requested to come up to the flight deck to talk on the radio." The young man looked at him inquiringly. "Can you help her come up to the flight deck, sir?

The young man noticed her eyes open. "There is a radio call for you from Washington, ma'am."

"Sure, sure," she answered and shifted to sit up straight, slowly testing her ribs.

"Can I get a cup of coffee?"

The sailor grinned and said, "Coming right up, please follow me.

They unbuckled seatbelts and followed.

He made for the galley and poured two cups.

"Black?"

"Yes, right, both," answered Pete for both of them.

"Lavatory?" he turned and asked Karen. She nodded.

"Seaman, if you'll take those up for us, we'll be up directly."

Then the kid left toward the cockpit with their coffee cups. Karen hadn't moved, and was looking out a small round galley window.

"Are you okay?" Pete asked.

"Yeah, I'm fine. Just give me a minute… Go ahead, yourself, if you need to."

"No problem."

Pete relieved himself and splashed water on his face. That definitely helped to wake him since the water must have been a few degrees above freezing. He returned to find Karen had helped herself to a coffee anyway in the galley and nursed it with both hands. She smiled at him and cocked her head coyly.

"You look all the worse for wear," but he smiled to show that maybe he didn't really think so.

"How do you always manage to look like you brought your makeup lady with you?" she lied since he looked easily as disheveled as she did.

"How's your rib?" he asked with some concern.

"Don't ask. But at least I slept well, given the accommodations." She smiled back and winked. He felt his heart skip a beat and face began to flush. She was definitely getting under his skin.

"Can't stay to chat, Washington's on the phone. You are welcome to tag along if there's room up there."

"No powder room?"

"No, I'm ready and awake."

They made their way up the narrow corridor to the cockpit door. The navigator greeted them and sat them down side-by-side at the navigator's desk. Karen donned a radio headset offered to her then gave the thumbs up.

"Agent St. Cloud here. Over."

A woman's voice came back at her surrounded by a fair amount of static. "Director Beal to speak with you, please. One moment. Over." Karen waited a good 20 seconds before her boss spoke.

"Karen, I heard you probably broke rib in the explosion. You're okay?"

"Fine sir, I'm fine. One rib broken, but it is more annoying than painful. We lost some good people, that hurts more."

"I understand. The president personally sends his condolences, to you and the remaining NEST crew... Even though EPG* seems to stay one step ahead of us we are not finished with them." He continued. "We located one of the EPG* subs near the Equator, and it has been destroyed—the sub went to the bottom. While Navy rescue and recovery ships are on the way, there is little chance that we will learn anything there.

"We will have what's left of your team stay at McMurdo to assist in the cleanup and evaluation. You are to backtrack to the central Pacific where we think that Miller and his associates may be headed. We have still not located the EPG* flagship, but we believe that they are en route to the Cook Islands or French Polynesia.

"While you were busy over the last 24 hours, we have uncovered proof that EPG* had a staging areas in both island groups. The trails there are pretty cold—two years since the Cooks and three since they were last in the Tuamotu group." He conferred with someone in the room with him.

"Yes, that's right. So our best guess is to have you head to wherever is closer, unless we get any better leads in the meantime. Over."

"Yes sir. French Polynesia, then. Over."

"Good, but no vacation, yet, St. Cloud. Over." It went flat as a joke. Karen did sneak a glance at Pete and was sad that it appeared she'd have to leave him behind.

Director Beal continued, again after apparently conferring with an aide, "We have a flight scheduled to take off immediately after you land at McMurdo. You'll fly directly to Tahiti where you will be shuttled to the small island where EPG* had a stay. We'll FAX the details while you are on the way.

"The president's press secretary asks if you can take the television reporter, Peter Wilde, along with you. He is still with you, is he not? Was he injured? Over."

"Thank you, sir; he's just fine and sitting right next to me. He probably saved my life last night. Over."

"Fine, you have permission to keep him up-to-date on the investigation. However, let him know that he may not post anything until you are all back in the US or US territory. Make sure he understands. Over."

"Got it... Is there anything else, sir? Over."

"That's it St. Cloud. Stay in touch with the home office. Out." The connection was severed. Karen took off the headset and looked at Pete.

He looked at Karen expectantly. She asked him, "Did you bring your bathing suit?" When he didn't answer her except to shake his head, she added, "We're going to Tahiti." His eyes opened wide and his eyebrows went up in a question mark.

Pete taught her a small lesson, however, after she filled him in on all the details. What she did not expect was his insistence that she get medical attention and a shower before they were to leave McMurdo.

"Our orders are to fly straight out of McMurdo."

"Why?" he demanded.

Karen didn't like the direction the conversation was headed and hesitated.

"Karen, you are in charge of this show, but you definitely need to get this X-rayed." He poked her very gently in the rib and even that hurt.

"And, you need a shower as much as I do. Besides, you said that they don't even know where the EPG* submarine is located. I insist you get medical attention, a hot shower, and change of clothes." He looked very serious.

Karen went back up to the cockpit. She had the radioman contact McMurdo check the departure flight schedule. As it turned out, there would be a delay while a new Navy transport plane was refueled and unloaded. She looked out the window on the icescape below. They were descending lower over the Ross Ice Shelf and she could see the ocean far off to the north.

The copilot took off his headphones and pointed north.

"As late as the 1990s the ocean was nearly 100 miles further away. Decay of the ice shelf has been substantial, both a reduction of the extent of winter sea ice and summer shelves along much of the continent. It's made traveling to Antarctica both safer and more accessible.

"But it might be useful for you to know that the terrorists had an easier time getting to the continent due to melting."

She nodded, mesmerized by the view.

"We are landing soon, so this is your five minute warning. Good luck on your journey," and he shook her hand and returned to work.

She soaked up the landscape. The contrast in lighting was dramatic—the dark penetrating blue of the water and the stark white of the ice cliffs along the coastline, which stood hundreds of feet above the water. The plane banked slightly to the north and the water moved out of her field of view. Then the plane leveled out over the water and she could pick out some very large icebergs produced by the calving of the nearby glacial front. There were spires, cathedral-like forms, and castle shapes—indicators of older, weathered icebergs, and younger, raw mountainous chunks. They continued to follow the coastline for fifty miles as the plane descended into McMurdo. It was hard for Karen to tear herself away, but she had fish to fry.

Abe pounded on the cabin desk.

"How could you let us lose Angel, Bear, and the others?" he shouted at the wall.

The *Loa* in his head replied.

"You knew there were risks. There was risk and opportunity in leaving them in the rear guard. And you know that we can only influence those events where we have leverage. The US Government isn't part of the team.

"And you must admit you are more upset about the loss of control over the Devices more than your friends."

Abe held up his hands to protest and them slowly let them drop without saying more.

"You need to relax. You have done all you can. The Plan will unfold in its own inimitable way and your job is basically finished. The Plan has not unraveled," *Ogun* reminded him. "It has merely been recalibrated."

"I have reset the timers to the nanosecond, and the warhead computers are all armed. We are good to go.

"Got to go. Talk later."

The sub and Abe and the crew sailed northwest at periscope depth and made good time toward their final destination in the Pitcairn Island group. But, as they left the edge of the continental shelf, Abe and *Ogun* were aware that the *baka* forces were narrowing in on them.

Abe considered developments: the Amery Device detonation had worked perfectly, but the early detonation of Numero Uno was a mystery. They had not heard from Angel or whether she had swapped the transponder, but after the news from *Ogun* he assumed the worst. The warning communiqués were successfully broadcast. Meadow's detonation timing sequence was programmed into the nuclear triggers. They traveled away from the coming disaster area.

They resurfaced shortly before the Event was triggered. They were networked with telemetry coming out of the various science programs on Antarctica, so the disappearance of selected strain gauge data streams and the seismic signatures of the detonations indicated that the Omega Event unfolded on schedule, shortly after 1200 Universal Time. They continued to monitor the strain gauges for swelling along the Transantarctic Mountains—the uplift proceeded as their models had predicted. *Ogun* informed him that all the Devices had performed nominally, operating within the range of energy releases predicted. The timing of the last two Devices was in reverse order for some reason—*Ogun* checked that against the new algorithms and noted that it was a part of Leah's program, whether deliberate or accidental, they would never know. But the system dynamics were not significantly different than the models predicted. *Ogun* predicted that the result would be somewhat greater seismic building in the western mountains, but he put a rather small probability on any great deviance from the earlier models. Add ingredients, stir, and see what shakes out!

"*Ogun*?" Abe was in his stateroom away from the rest pf the crew.

"Yes?" the *Loa* answered immediately.

"Que pasa?"

"Abe, there is some bad news..." *Ogun* used a Betty Davis voice.

"I'm not surprised. Please enlighten me." Abe scrunched down into the beanbag chair in the corner of the small room. He put his head between his hands.

"The *Nemo* has sunk with all hands. I'm sorry."

Abe paused quietly for a few seconds. "What happened, exactly? How could you let this happen?"

"Abe, there really wasn't anything I could do. It was an unhappy coincidence and due, apparently, to considerable human volition."

"Meaning?"

"Meaning that the actions of your crew and their hostages complicated matters. They ended up right on top of a US Navy flotilla and so there was little I could do."

Abe considered this. "I rather doubt that the latter is true." However, for some unfathomable reason his anger evaporated.

Ogun took a pause. "Look, it is hard to explain the probabilities involved in human terms—particularly the complication of the human consciousness variables on the whole fabric of the time/space continuum we are trying to influence. 'We do what we can do' and leave the rest to chance. That random effect is crucial to growth and progress. The percentage of effort required to salvage the *Nemo's* situation would have been only marginally beneficial to the Plan. To use a rather simplistic metaphor, they were sacrificial lambs.

"You have to further understand that the rest of the team is on the way home, Abe. We did what we set out to do and the planet will do the rest. You can take it easy now. The *Nemo* is a distraction sufficient to cover us electronically, visually, and acoustically. I have it covered."

"You sound cold, calculating, and inhuman about it all."

"Well, I'm sorry that you see it that way, but I am ultimately doing what is in the best interest of the planet." That stopped Abe for a moment.

"According to you."

Ogun shifted to his John Wayne voice. "Pilgrim, up until now you never questioned my motives or intentions."

He continued. "Look, there are two US Navy carrier groups in the southern ocean—a rather crowded southern South Pacific all of a sudden. There are some 87 ships below the 50th parallel including three submarines newer than this pile of rust. I am doing everything I can right now to jam Navy radar, sonar, and detection and keep us out of everyone's sight.

"We are well on our way to our new home in the Pitcairn group, so relax. Accept the fact that our friends were sacrificed to save the Earth. It would be wise to recall that we are contending with forces beyond our control, and lines of probability that continue to unfold. There are questions of balance and systems dynamics that are beyond your comprehension. There was really no alternative. You will have to trust me on that."

Abe was quiet for a while.

"Okay," Abe said after a few minutes, "I will inform the crew in the morning. I'm going to stretch and then take a nap."

"Good nap, then."

Abe shifted mental gears, took off his shoes and unrolled his yoga mat in the tight space. He began his stretches and tried to squeeze as much oxygen out of the stale air and into his lungs as he could. The tightness in his head started to go away and he began to feel better. There was some new aspect of *Ogun* that troubled him. It was mainly the nagging thought of "Now what?"

The president sat in the Situation Room and waited. The morning had not gone well. It was colder, inside and outside. The White House originally had boilers in the basement; but, as the presidency had become more important and powerful in the 20th century, the space, even in the basement, was needed for offices and the heating and cooling equipment were moved nearby to the Executive Office building. Heating and cooling conduits ran under the west lawn and normally served their purposes adequately, but a broken water main had compromised the heat being pumped over.

Staff would normally have brought in small space heaters, but transportation was still a huge problem and most staff slept in and around Pennsylvania Avenue. Even sweaters were not enough for many folks on Omega Day.

President Clark was up early and did not immediately react to the cold, since the Residence was relatively warmer, being on the second floor, and he had had his usual hot shower. He was unable to eat much for breakfast.

He spent a few hours in the early morning on the phone with the British Prime Minister and other foreign leaders as well as the Secretary General of the UN, who would preside over a special session of the Security Council in Geneva. As it grew closer and closer to the scheduled EPG* event, it became harder to concentrate, so he ordered a fresh pot of coffee and made his way to the Situation Room.

As he entered the room, most of the other members of the National Security Council were there. Some were talking into secure phones at the table and there was some chatter coming from the staffers working at consoles in the background.

Everyone stood when the president pulled out his chair and sat down.

"Good morning everyone."

"Good morning, Mr. President," they replied.

Some hushed voices started up in the background, but general atmosphere was somber and anticipatory. Hot cups of coffee steamed in the cool air of the room.

"We're waiting for reports from the field, sir," said the Secretary of Defense.

"Okay. At ease, then, everyone." He turned to whisper a question to his chief of staff as many at the table went back to their phones.

The scheduled time of the EPG* Omega Event came and went and there was no noticeable change on the large screen projection of Antarctica on the far wall. The president was about to breathe a sigh of relief that EPG* had somehow bungled their threat, but small red lights began to appear on the map and the chatter in the back of the room picked up.

Admiral Brown sat on the president's right and had his ear glued to a phone connected to the Pentagon. He began to speak.

"Mr. President, evidence from aerial surveillance and satellites indicate that nuclear detonations occurred across Antarctica."

He pointed to a set of flat screens that began to flicker on, showing time-delayed orbital images of flashes of light. It was both sublime and surreal. The president found it fundamentally disturbing and yet somehow distant, and abstract.

Secretary Brown pointed at the large screen with a laser pointer, "The epicenters are all along a rough arc southwest from Ronne Ice Shelf and then northeast following the path of the base of the Transantarctic Mountains." There was a lull in the noise in the room as almost everyone watched in silence as the scenes from space shifted from one satellite or aircraft to another.

Admiral Brown spoke again. "There are now reports of mushroom clouds from all of the blast sites. A number of the blast sites are relatively high in elevation to begin with, so many of the clouds are rising well into the stratosphere."

The science advisor spoke up. "Heavy stratospheric contamination is likely to worsen the effects of the ozone hole in coming winters. NSF scientists claim that the hole may triple or quadruple in size."

The president said nothing. He just stared at the images. Admiral Brown filled the silence.

"The weather on the continent at the moment is a circumpolar flow in a counter-clock wise, or eastern, flow. That means that the fallout will be deposited around the pole and is unlikely to migrate north. Scientists at Livermore Labs will run simulations as the data come in, but preliminary forecasts are acceptable for fallout migration to population areas. There is concern, of course, about personnel out on the ice, but almost all have been recalled to their respective bases. All tourists and non-approved summer visitors were evacuated or sent north over the last 96 hours. The naval blockade that now encircles the continent has orders to board or disable any unauthorized vessels."

The president's eyes focused on the wall-screen projection. "What happened to the FBI and NEST teams?"

"Rescue teams sent to the Latady base extracted only two people. Our agent St. Cloud and the television reporter, Wilde, were found in the EPG* grotto, but all the others were killed. St. Cloud has a broken rib, but is fine otherwise and on the way to McMurdo. There were more than fifty Americans killed, the names of next of kin are on your desk as you requested."

Helen Colman sat up straight and looked at Brown. He nodded and she spoke.

"Good morning everyone," and then paused. "The mystery, of course, is why one device detonated early. The last ten explosions happened on schedule, but it is not clear if the Latady detonation had any impact on EPG* strategy. We are operating with the assumption that EPG* claims are valid and have begun to evacuate as many people as we can from some small low islands to ships and other islands in the region.

"The Latady tragedy is likely to remain unresolved, although it is possible, likely that Agent St. Cloud may be able to shed some light on that once we can debrief her. The Special Forces assault team that stormed the EPG* command and control may have triggered a fail-safe trip wire of some sort. However, we may never know. It is now imperative that we capture, alive, any of the EPG* that we can lay our hands on."

The president asked, "Where is the terrorist we caught at the Hungarian base?"

Brown answered, "He is being flown to McMurdo."

"And the two submarines?"

Attention turned back to Brown.

He said, "We have destroyed one—the *Albacore*—but the other one, likely the flagship for Miller, has not yet been located."

Not far at all beneath the Earth's crust under kilometers of ice, sludge, and steam the magma chambers started to vibrate soon after the blasts, first in low frequencies, then higher in frequency and energy over the intervening hours. These forces were at first dampened by the tectonic plates that push against each other along this edge of the continent. Then sonic and pressure waves accelerated slightly as shock waves of the fission bombs opened magma chambers slightly in turn causing physical expansion that began to draw up more viscous, high temperature lava from about ten kilometers below the surface. Both dormant and active chambers slowly grew more active, and grew in volume over hours and hours of slow, but inexorable growth. Harmonics reinforced themselves both up and down the entire rift system. Many of the magma chambers rang like bells in a deep tolling. The entrained waves of energy fractured the ice above to open the way for even more release of energy.

None of the cavities was the same, but most of deep magma pools were roughly the same size due to the dynamics and pressures of rock in the Earth's crust: 3.5 to 5 miles wide and twice as deep. These basalt blobs typical of volcanoes in Iceland and Hawai`i are also common along the Ring of Fire surrounding the Pacific Ocean. The swelling and bulging continued aided by the recent effects of global warming. Warmer ocean waters and melting ice shelves accelerated the coastal ice sheet thinning process. That allowed for the geological rebound and uplifting of the crust, which reduced overall surface pressures on the Antarctic crust. Pressure now built up from below.

Honolulu
0400 hrs
The USGS Pacific Tsunami Center (PTC) closely tracked seismic activity in the Antarctic ever since the first blast, days before. Those systems accurately identified the epicenters of the newest nuclear blasts and their various magnitudes. Although the latter measure was much less reliable, the PTC nevertheless had a substantial amount of data to digest. Supercomputers, on loan from the Maui Technology Transfer Center, had already applied

sophisticated computer models to overlay the explosion sequence and location of the detonations. In addition, they shared data with the National Oceanic and Atmospheric Administration (NOAA) to model radiation distribution patterns based on the current and forecast weather for the polar area.

The PTC picked up the first of the tremor swarms coming from the Transantarctic Mountains, one of the world's longest mountain ranges, some 2300 miles long and with a dozen peaks over 10,000 feet in elevation. It includes some active volcanoes including Mt. Erebus and a number in the Queen Maud Range in the central Antarctic south of the Ross Ice Shelf.

Paper seismographs showed the relative energies being released, but were useless for more in depth analysis. Computers and their analysts labored to make sense of the data streaming in. The first blush analysis was encouraging at first—no major eruptions were detected. On the other hand, low intensity seismic swarms popped up from one end of the continent to the other. There were also some secondary shocks coming from mountains in the Antarctic Peninsula.

PTC's executive posted an tsunami advisory to the Pacific Tsunami Warning System to alert the network of the possibility of tsunami activity—their first ever tsunami warning before an undersea or coastal earthquake. Everyone at PTC was on edge.

Dear Betsy,

Mana Kai was in sailboat heaven today! All day long, we had light, 10-knot trade winds—steady and dead on the southwest with long one-foot swells. There were hardly any larger swells. She was on autopilot all day and the sails sang lightly. The temperature was cool with light, wispy stratospheric clouds. Dreamy day.

In the afternoon, Brad brought out the music box and he pumped out reggae, first Bob Marley, then Jimmy and then his own mix of techno jungle beat and Pacific reggae. It was just magical. At 5:00, Brad opened up a bottle of rum that we bought in Jamaica ten years ago. He drank it straight—I never could understand how one can do that—and made me rum punches. We both marveled at how beautiful the day had been and how peaceful it had felt. Brad joked about the "calm before the storm", even though the weather reports were just fine. But, he had found his funny bone and "went off" on a wild discussion of a coming hurricane in this fake Rastafarian/Caribbean accent that had us both rolling down laughing on the deck. After twenty minutes of hysterical, Brad turned somber. He put on some of his favorite New Orleans blues.

We talked a lot about our trip, and how eventful it was, compared to our earlier ones. This was not the longest. Our maiden voyage was from Portland, Oregon (where we bought the Mana Kai) to Honolulu and then on to Wellington, New Zealand. A few years later, we spent the summer sailing to Kiribati, the Marianas, and the Philippines. But, they had all been mostly quiet, smooth trips. The Wellington trip had seen some tropical rainstorms and twenty-foot waves, but the boat handled it well and we were still excited about the new boat. It didn't seem so bad at the time.

But this trip has been bizarre. Kind of psychedelic in a way— the strange patterns of weather, waves, icebergs, fish and foul! The ocean has been particularly present in the trip—like it wants to be felt, loved or hated, in a word: appreciated. Of course, we had to talk about whether we were being anthropomorphic. Brad can be so cosmic sometimes it drives me a little crazy. Although for such a "grounded" person, I sure seem to like the water.

We had a pretty mellow evening on the deck and ate some of the last of our fruit from Tahiti and cheese, too. Brad chilled out the music even more and put on some light jazz just before sunset. It was a bit like a Hollywood movie, all Technicolor. But, typically for the mid latitudes, the sunset was blasé and not particularly exciting without a cloud on the horizon...

In the twilight, Brad and I both took turns at the wheel. It was serene, when the forces of nature seem so tuned, so balanced. Mana Kai just sliced through the still water. If there was any current or resistance from the water, the fixed pressure of the trade winds dampened it—it felt like a trade wind, singular. It was the most relaxed sailing of the whole trip! Mellow.

We talked each other's ears off while I cleaned up in the galley and cabin. Brad challenged me to a game of Scrabble, but I encouraged him to fool around. We spent a good hour sweating a little and licking each other. It was rum-intense! Yum. I am still wet from excitement.

So, I will sleep well tonight!!! Rum always does that to me— puts me in a coma for 9 or 10 hours. I hope Brad can fix his own breakfast in the morning...

Karen and Pete were oblivious to the fact that the Omega Event occurred while they flew over the edge of the Ross Ice Shelf. They were physically too far away from the Transantarctic range to notice any blast effects. Everyone in the flight crew was well aware who the passengers were and the pilot gave Karen the word that EPG* had detonated the stolen weapons, shortly before they began their approach to McMurdo. She knew it was coming, so she just nodded her head and thanked him for the news.

When they left the plane, Paul Kennedy, the NSF Director of Antarctica Operations, known informally as the Mayor of McMurdo, met them. He introduced himself and apologized for the warm weather. At first, Karen thought he was joking.

When she laughed, he shook his head. "No, seriously, as we drive into town you'll see what I mean. There are literally rivers of melt water running through the base that we have rarely ever seen before. It may help with decontamination, too, if the winds shift from the south and east from the nearer epicenters." He noted Karen's curious look.

"We have not had any detectable radiation from fallout here yet, but that is only a matter of time. However, we are more concerned about Mt. Erebus at the moment." Of course they had all noticed the huge steam cloud that came from the mountain's summit once they left the plane. They all stopped in their track for a look at it.

"Our volcanologists are worried that she is on the verge of a major eruption. THAT could make a mess here with volcanic ash and maybe strong earthquakes. You may be able to feel some of those already. They come every few minutes.

"We are too far away to be threatened by lava, mud flows or other pyroclastic activity, but as I said, the ash could be trouble. The prevailing winds do blow towards Erebus, but they are inconsistent. Ash and heavy snowmelt could make for nasty floods. We are already sandbagging low-lying parts of the base, but we are running out of bags."

They arrived at a small minibus, where they loaded themselves. Kennedy sat with them behind a driver. "We will take you to the travel hostel to shower. Normally, this time of year it would be full of tourists, but the place is empty and you'll have it all to yourselves. Our medical staff will check you there."

Karen, who had hardly taken her eyes off of the smoldering, ominous mountain, finally said, "Well thanks for meeting us, but you probably have more important things to do."

Kennedy looked at her and responded a bit sharply. "I was instructed by the president's science advisor to brief you. This was not meant as a courtesy." He continued, in an official-sounding tone.

"As far as we know, there were no casualties from any of the nuclear blasts, other than some of the more seriously injured of your strike team and the rescue and medical teams that were on site at Latady. We believe that everyone there, except for the two of you, was killed.

"The EPG* prisoner is being flown back north, to Guantanamo, I am told.

"Since hostilities broke out, we count over a hundred dead British, Argentines, Chileans, and Americans.

"Here at McMurdo, we have been scrambling to accommodate requests from Washington as well as evacuate non-essential personnel. We brought in all our personnel from the field and almost all the tourists and seasonal visitors are on their way to New Zealand or Chile. There are some Greenpeace activists in the Peninsula area who have refused to leave, but the Chileans have vowed to arrest them. Greenpeace is not very welcome now."

The minibus threaded its way through the nearly empty streets of McMurdo, and had to slow to a crawl when they came to low spots. The gravel streets were full of potholes where they weren't covered in running water. The minibus made detours in a couple of spots where the water was too high.

The wind shifted since their arrival and now Erebus' column of steam rose almost straight up into the stratosphere. The cloud seemed to thicken and grow darker, too.

Kennedy pressed on with his report, "The geologists are most worried." He seemed to reflect their concern. "Not just Erebus, but almost all of the active volcanoes in the Transantarctic range have become more active. More worrisome yet is the fact that a few historically dormant volcanoes are now venting steam or are showing magma chamber growth. It doesn't look good.

"The news from stateside isn't particularly encouraging either. The FBI and NSA have uncovered more of the work that was done by the young climatologist, Leah Wilson. I met her here a couple of years ago—I am afraid she didn't make much of an impression on me.

327

Dr. Wilson's doctoral work appears to be the theoretical basis for much of what lay behind the EPG* strategy down here. Your colleagues are fairly certain that she was not part of the conspiracy, underscored by her kidnapping by EPG*.

"The bad news is that Dr. Wilson and along with her mentor Dr. Jake Meadows have died along with the rest of the EPG* submarine crew west of the Galapagos.

"In any case, Wilson's research has come to light. It is one of those cases where the science establishment was not open to new ideas. It seems that some of the theory was presented at two difference conferences, a regional geology conference in Chicago last year, and more recently at an interdisciplinary Antarctica conference last winter. She was ridiculed and not taken seriously; according to FBI interviews no one took her seriously... except for Meadows and a few friends. Her work in other areas was mainstream—she had a post-doc position at the National Center for Climate Research in Boulder, but...

"Well, in any case, documents, maps, and papers of hers uncovered in San Francisco—where she shared an apartment with Meadows—show conclusively that there are strong statistical connections between uplift along the Transantarctic and glacial transit along the Ross and interior glacial fields of West Antarctica." Kennedy was obviously used to interacting with non-scientists. He saw Karen frown. He cleared his throat.

"In other words, historical patterns of geological volcanism are linked to the speed of glacial movement across this half of the continent. But the real kicker is the speculation in her work that the entire Ross Shelf is vulnerable to volcanism underneath it—at the so-called grounding anchors—and that these volcanoes are linked to activity in the Transantarctic.

"I have to admit that I am skeptical that West Antarctic glaciers or even the Ross, for that matter, could 'collapse' into the oceans as EPG* has promised."

Pete chimed in. "That's a relief."

Kennedy looked worried. "I am not relieved, so don't you be." Pete's brow furrowed.

"But enough of this for now, we are here for your respite." They pulled up in front of a long non-descript modular building that had a small sign in front of a long wooden balcony that read "Transient Bivouac—NSF 059" and underneath that a somewhat larger hand-lettered sign that said "The Last Motel on Earth." Both Karen and Pete laughed at the same time and then looked at each other.

"You have about thirty minutes to shower and change. There will be base personnel inside to assist you and provide a change of clothes. I have to make a few phone calls and will be back." Karen and Pete walked up a few steps and by the time they reached the door, the minivan was already gone.

"What a character," said Pete, "He reminds me of a Massachusetts' Kennedy. Any relation?"

"I don't know. Ask him on the way back. He could not take his eyes off of you." He grinned at her.

She shook her head and displayed herself with her hands, "A mess like this? I doubt it." But, she curtsied and laughed.

They were inside the outer door and dumped their backpacks. Pete helped Karen get out of her parka and her heavy boots. There were slippers by the inner door. As they entered, two young men, and a woman in her 50s faced them from behind a long wooden counter. The woman smiled and put out her hand.

"Agent St. Cloud, Mr. Wilde, welcome. I am Daisy Baker the manager. Tim, here, will show you the women's locker room and Dan," she motioned to the other kid, who couldn't have been a day over 18, "will show you to the men's shower." She looked at each of them in turn.

"We have clean clothes for both of you. I know you are in a hurry, but if you need anything, please let me know. We were told that you haven't eaten, so we'll have some sandwiches set out in the mess hall next door after you are cleaned up and sack lunches to take with you."

They both said thanks and let their guides lead them to clean waters.

Two minutes into her shower, Karen felt the ground rumble beneath her feet—as though a heavy truck had passed two feet away. It continued for ten or twelve seconds. The vibrations tapered off, and then were followed by a sharp jerk. It was Karen's first earthquake, so she didn't know what to think. Maybe they were common here. She almost fell on the slippery tile floor and her chest hurt every time she moved her left arm, so she didn't make any quick movements. The movement subsided, so she continued to shampoo—carefully. She heard the locker room door open.

"Agent St. Cloud, are you okay?" came Daisy's voice.

"Yeah, I'm fine. Earthquake?"

"Yes ma'am. That was the second large one that we've had today. No apparent damage. By the way, we have one of our doctors on the way. She'll be here in five minutes."

"Great Daisy, thanks." She finished rinsing her hair and her shower. She felt a million times better. Even the throbbing pain in her ribs seemed to subside somewhat. A few minutes later, as she dried herself off, there was a knock on the door and a young woman came in quickly—who looked about eighteen years old, but was very serious.

"Agent St. Cloud? Doctor Mary Wright. Let's take a look at you."

She put a digital thermometer in Karen's mouth, took her blood pressure, and pulse in all of about two minutes—a model of efficiency. She gingerly pressed around the effected area and Karen winced but made no sounds this time.

"Yep, broken rib, but I'd like to get an X-ray." She looked questioningly.

"Sorry, no time. Can you wrap me up?"

"Sure. But you should get that looked at again when you get to a facility in the north."

Karen put on her bra and had the doctor bandage her; and then asked for help to strap the Colt .45 holster on her shoulder. That actually took more effort and care than the bandage.

Thirty minutes after they had arrived, Pete and Karen were back in the mudroom to suit up in their parkas and boots wolfing down sandwiches at the same time. Young Dan stayed close to Karen and helped her into parka and boots. Karen's hair was wet and already tangled, but her cheeks had a rosy glow. She looked and felt refreshed.

A large snow cat pulled up and Mayor Kennedy got out of the back, just as they walked out the front door. Karen shook Dan's hand.

"Thanks kid."

"Stop in anytime, except maybe July." He winked and went back inside. A wind had come up and the sky turned cloudy. The temperature had dropped significantly, but both Pete and Karen were still warmed by their showers.

330

"My apologies," said the mayor, "but all hell broke loose; excuse the pun. Hop in and let's go." He helped Karen into the cat onto the rear bench seat. Pete followed. Even before the front door was shut all the way behind him, Kennedy told the driver to go and the tractor took off.

"We have now had two small sets of earthquakes—I assume you felt the last one?" They both assented. "The epicenters were actually a few hundred miles away in the middle of the Ross Ice Shelf. The first measured about 3.5 on the Richter scale, the last one 4.2... Our geologists and volcanologists here monitor all seismic activity, since, well... since the base became operational, but what I mean is," he looked flustered, "we have monitored everything more closely since last week."

"What I mean to say is that the quakes have increased in intensity and we expect them to get worse. We have a relatively new volcanology team here this summer. It is actually their second summer, a mostly Hawaiian team. They are worried because of the inflation data coming in from all across the continent. They have strongly correlated what they call 'earthquake micro-swarms' with a bulge in the earth's crust almost everywhere we have sensors in the Western Antarctic—but especially along the Transantarctic Range. In some select locations, there is arithmetic progression in the intensity of the inflation. In the central and eastern regions of the range, the inflation is as much as two hundred feet in elevation.

"They say that this indicates substantial swelling of reservoirs of magma deep beneath the earth's surface. In Hawai'i, and Iceland, this type of inflation is often associated with eruptive phases. The dynamics of Antarctic volcanoes are not necessarily the same. In Hawai'i, and Iceland, eruptions are not usually explosive and violent, as they are around the Ring of Fire, Japan, Alaska, and Mexico, for example. The Antarctic has both types, so we are concerned.

"I'd like to take some teams out to strengthen the instrumentation network, but the Navy has restricted all flights and activities on the ice..." He looked at Karen as though she might be able to help, but then seemed to think better of it. "In any case, the energies that are represented in the growth of magma mass are truly staggering. Moreover, our extrapolation of the inflation rates can only mean one thing." He looked over at both of them.

He paused for effect. "Antarctica is about to blow a gasket." He slowed down as they approached a stream in the middle of the road that had grown appreciably larger since their first ride from the airstrip. The driver navigated it as the water rose nearly to the bottom of the cat's doors.

"I expect that the earthquake swarms will worsen, so we are prepared for local rescue and recovery operations. This base is like a small city, with an aging infrastructure and some very old and unsafe buildings. We have a lot of work ahead of us to secure buildings and supplies for a looming disaster. I have teams for decontamination, too, because we are still expecting some fallout from the explosions today. Heaven knows how worse that may be if there are violent volcanic eruptions, too." He shook his head. Karen hadn't noticed Pete take out a pad of paper on which he jotted down notes.

Karen opened her mouth to ask a question and the ground dropped out from underneath them and then slammed back up into them. Karen was watching the road when the earthquake came. She saw streams of water in the road ahead appear to levitate and then spread out in a mist in the next moment. The compression wave hit them hard enough in the vehicle to knock their breath out. The cat stopped.

"Jesus Christ!" He looked over at them, and asked, "Are you okay?" Pete was fine, but Karen lost color in her face and grabbed her chest with her right hand. She gasped and seemed to have a hard time getting her lungs to work. Had she broken another rib? She grabbed a hold of the seat back and forced herself to take a slow, deep breath.

"Karen, relax. It's okay." Pete carefully put his hands around her left arm pulled her back to straighten her out. Her color slowly returned and her breathing became easier as she forced herself to relax.

"Sorry," she croaked. "I'm okay… That just caught my broken rib wrong. Let's go, please."

Kennedy motioned the driver to put the cat back in gear, but looked over at Karen at the same time. The radiophone in the cat squawked. The mayor picked it up, acknowledged, and listened for a minute.

"Fine, I'll be right back to the office—ten minutes." Then to Karen and Pete: "Trouble in River City. Natural gas line breaks, this time. Not good, but at least no fire. Yet."

As they drove the last mile down the hill to the airstrip, they saw that there was far more activity than when they arrived. Two large transport planes were being refueled, a Harrier jump jet, and a couple of large helicopters with rotors turning. The more remarkable sight was of armed paratroopers around one plane. As they drove up onto the gravel surface, the mayor said goodbye.

"Well, it looks like we all have our hands full. I am glad to have met both of you—only wish it had been under better circumstances... If you need anything else from us here at McMurdo have your pilot radio us anytime day or night." He came around to help Karen out of the back seat and shook Pete's hand as he came out behind her. The wind had picked up and snow blew across the airstrip. Hooded figures ran down a ramp from the transport closest to them and waved them forward. Karen and Pete said goodbye and moved briskly to the plane. The fair weather had turned bad and the vague possibility of radioactive snow was another incentive for them to get in under cover.

After the energies of a few moderate earthquakes were released, the magma chambers filled more—like shaking a jar of jellybeans makes room for more. The continent was coming awake after being shrouded in a cold blanket for more than a million years. True, the last interglacial period had seen the return of grasses and warmer temperatures, but for as many as twelve glacial cycles, each roughly 90,000-years long, the efforts at mountain-building were resisted by the layers of ice upon layers of ice. In fact, from a tectonic standpoint, the continent was like an ice cube floating on the planet's mantle, an inert island of crust balanced on the pole.

It had not always been so. The continent was once geologically young—positioned on the equator, a tropical continent, burgeoning with life and volcanically active, jostled between other tectonic plates. Since the breakup of Pangaea, the Earth's early super-continent, Antarctica had gradually floated south on top of the Earth's mantle. In some ways, her drift apart from her sister continents had sealed her fate. Continental drift and the emergence of the Ring of Fire produced the Isthmus of Panama, which contributed to the growing power of the deep ocean currents to regulate planetary temperature. Then the drift to the pole had resulted in the "ice house" effect, the slow planetary progression into Ice Ages due to the snow and ice blanket of Antarctica and the loss of heat due to the high albedo. The sun's energy was no longer sequestered by darker land surfaces, but reflected off the snow and ice and back out into space.

As Abe saw it, the polar goddess *Freya* now had a solution to her problem: pent up magma from deep within the earth, and the prospect of volcanic ash to blanket the snow, to lower the albedo, and melt the snow and ice. Of course, that would take millennia, for those slow evolutionary changes to work their way across East Antarctica. But, in the meantime, it wouldn't take long, in geological time, to shake off the pesky ice shelves and snowfields of the West—especially since large chunks floated on the southern ocean anyway. It would only be a blink of the geological eye for the West to be mostly ice-free.

Freya continued to swell and took her time.

Abe went over the draft of his speech one more time. The crew set up bright lights in the corner of the submarine's mess hall, and positioned and tested the video camera. It was time to tell the world to clean up its act, to repent, and to take a different path.

"Okay, I'm ready. Roll the tape," Abe said even though few in digital age crew had a clue what magnetic tape was. He looked tired and ragged, despite the makeup artistry of the ship's purser.

"My fellow and sister citizens of Planet Earth, good day.

"At noon today, universal time, the Earth Protection Group, or EPG* as we are called, used weapons of mass destruction, not to take life, but to protect all life on the planet.

"We are saddened by the loss of human life as a result of our Actions, today and over the past week. It was a regrettable but necessary consequence of humanity's overpopulation and overgrown ecological footprint on the planet. Since the days of the mega-fauna ten millennia ago, humans have been the dominant species on the planet. As a hunted species, for millions of years our ancestors were prey, kept in check by the forces of nature, but the end of the last ice age gave us the opportunity to exploit new ecological niches and develop tools and language—arguably the most destructive development in the course of evolution of life on the planet.

"This series of developments has had dire consequences for ten of thousands of species of plants and animals that will go extinct soon. This species dieback is rapidly approaching other periods of dramatic species extinctions, such as the time 65 million years ago when the dinosaurs disappeared. At the present rate, almost all of the large predators and ruminants of Africa, Asia, and the Americas will be either extinct or alive only in zoos—essentially imprisoned as specimens of our species' rapacious greed and avarice.

"The Action which we initiated today is not intended to punish our species, per se, for what we have done, but to take our knowledge and use it for good—to bring the forces of nature back into balance and to try and level the playing field, at least a bit, for a short while. This will be a chance for humanity to consider the consequences of our collective actions and to temper our hubris—to help us see that we cannot exist without Mother Nature, and thus to poison and abuse her can only lead to our own inevitable downfall.

"This is intended as a wake up call, a warning of even worse disasters to come if we do not mend our ways. For example, pollinator species across the planet are threatened by the introduction of genetically altered species of plants that no longer require pollination. This fundamental disruption of the web of life and the balance of nature has already had a measurable effect on amphibians and birds that have disappeared from certain ecosystems at alarming rates. While humans should continue to eat well, we ignore growing assaults on genetic diversity at our own peril.

"Again, EPG* is saddened at the prospect of the billion human deaths likely over the next few years. We see this not as an act of mass murder, but of a species' self-correction—Nature healing herself, as we are a part of Nature, too. This is a systems-level response to human folly and a use of weapons of destruction for positive change, to reset the planetary clock, to ease us into the natural cycle of geological change that anthropogenic forces—greenhouse gases—have impeded. The Ice Age will begin again, and cleanse the Northern Hemisphere of toxins and move the focus of human survival to the tropics.

"It will be a time of great upheaval and human suffering, of shortages and wars, but in the end the planet will be stronger and if humanity can learn to co-exist with Her better, there will be a future for co-evolution for all species together as a cooperative entity called Gaia.

"This is a time of great change, transformational change, that will give us a collective opportunity to confront the evils of our rampant greed and the problematic of corporate capitalism. One result of the Omega Event will be the end of the consumer culture that has swept the planet over the past century and created landfills large enough to be seen from space that choke out farmland, and will lay a mute testimony for centuries to come of enormous human waste and abuse of the resources of the bountiful Earth.

"Just as the great floods of the end of the ice age have informed our myths and religious texts, the next great floods, of the days and weeks to come, will lay bare those lands we have despoiled and colonized and return them to the great oceans and estuaries that once seemed so vast in our imaginations. The winds and weather will change dramatically to bring calamity to our selfish monuments—those large human cities that we have created in our own image—to remind us of our arrogance and to put those fragile edifices in some perspective. We have been beholden to technology to create this illusory world of permanence; we will quickly see how ephemeral and impermanent that promise of technology is in the end.

"Make no mistake, we will require technology to survive in the months and years ahead, but we must remember that technology is only a set of tools and should not be an end in and of itself. Technology must not always be a way to insulate Homo sapiens from Nature.

"So, my fellow and sister humans, shed your complacency, pack your bags, and get ready for the ride of your life! Your leaders will tell you not to worry, that things will work out, but they are in for a rude shock: this is the end of 'Life as You Know It.' As the Fire Sign Theater of the 1960s used to say, 'Everything you know is wrong.' They got that right. Welcome to a Brave New World of Fire and Ice.

"This is Abe Miller, for the entire EPG* crew, we wish you an incredible learning experience!"

336

January 23
Monday

Seen on thousands of bulletin boards, web logs, and web broadcasts:

The Zapatista Globalnet announced a verified communiqué from the EPG*-associated Internet3 resolved virtual domain 211.21.4579.8 →

Citizens of Gaia, the End of Civilization is Near!
The Omega Event has occurred and now the Earth will take her own due course over the decades to come. The consequences of these EPG* Antarctica Brigade Actions on behalf of Mother Gaia and Sister Freya will result in: tsunamis, ever-higher tides, and extremely variable weather. Violent volcanic eruptions are expected very soon. These eruptions on the Southern Continent will continue for some decades and computer models show generalized cooling that should ensue for as long as a century. This, coupled with the anticipated collapse of the Deep Ocean Current, will mean longer and longer winters in the high latitudes. Equatorial regions will be warmer in many places and the interface of cold and warm air is expected to produce more frequent and more violent cyclones and hurricanes, tornados and Chinook winds, and dust storms.

Sea levels will rise rapidly and then fall again over the next two to three centuries. The maximum level of rise is expected to be 50-60 feet (20 meters) by 2050. Outcomes of the changes will depend on many factors, but most of the nominal computer models show an initial rise of one foot in sea level rise within the first month after the eruptions in Antarctica and a six foot rise within a year. In two years, an additional ten feet should be expected, and forty feet altogether in the first five years.

Depending on uncertainties in the variability in both solar activity and the actual Milankovitch orbital cycle, the onset of substantial and robust glaciations could take anywhere from five to fifteen years. However, it is expected that some regions, particularly mountainous ones, will feel the effects of the end of summer almost immediately. Summer is over in the Southern Hemisphere ...

The tables will now turn: the North must listen to the South, the rich Northern populations will be forced to pay their dues to the

Rest of the World. A Death Blow to Cities: many coastal cities around the world will be inundated in just a few years. Much infrastructure will be destroyed or useless within a year—particularly airports, refineries, and shipyards. Great economic changes are underway! Seize the day!

The president's press secretary Greg Bundt didn't look happy. He had finally made it in to work after being stuck for some three days in the suburbs. The blizzard had stopped and he'd actually made it to work on his neighbor's cross-country skis. Being away that long was enough to make him feel out of favor, out of the loop. But then, the whole White House staff had been stuck at work, so they looked the worse for wear.

The District was a winter wonderland after the storm finally passed north off into the North Atlantic. There were drifts to the second story of most buildings in central D.C. and the biggest problem was where to put it. The Potomac River was frozen over, so that seemed a logical place to dump it. The city was at a standstill, but the General Services Administration, the National Park Service, and city crews had been working 24/7 almost since the first hours of the storm to keep the roads between major agencies cleared. Most of the congressional buildings were supposed to be accessible by early afternoon.

It was surreal, because the Metro and buses were not moving and very few people were out yet—some isolated cross-country skiers, but that was about it. The skies were now absolutely clear and crisp, with the temperature hovering near zero. The Nation's Capital was officially buried under a record eight feet of snow. The scenes were similar in many of the Eastern Seaboard's other major cities from Philadelphia all the way up to New England. It was now snowing, however, in Boston and up into Maine.

That was the good news. The bad news was that pressure was mounting for a return to normalcy after weeks of national crisis and to repair some of the damage that a State of Emergency had brought on the national economy and international politics.

Bundt's biggest headache this morning however, was an environmental problem of a different sort. It was a growing clamor by one of the president's most vocal constituent groups—environmentalists—who were coming under increasing surveillance and investigation due to the whole EPG* fiasco. The Justice Department, FBI, and Homeland Security had all been involved in

338

raids of some of the most respected and mainstream environmental groups in the country—on both coasts, and now the complaints and law suits were starting to come home to roost.

To make matters worse, some environmental pundit had labeled the EPG* terrorist plot the first battle of a new type of warfare, the beginning of a Gaian War—the first battle in a struggle between the planet and her most successful species. Greg did not like the sound of this at all and could see a looming public relations nightmare. He could see the headlines: President Clark loses the Gaian War! Wasn't this a human-caused event? Not some willful planet striking back at humans! But then he really wasn't too sure in his own mind about that. But then he saw an Op-ed piece in the San Francisco Chronicle from the Sierra Club that unapologetically supported the EPG* action as an instrument of Gaian Warfare. That stopped him in his tracks—it hadn't taken long for that idea to catch on. This was not good.

His secretary came into the office to remind him that there was a senior staff meeting in five minutes. He made a pit stop and grabbed a fresh cup of coffee on his way into the Oval Office.

Max and Nelson were a few steps ahead of him, but the president first singled out Greg, of course. He was not going to see the end of jokes at his expense today.

"So you finally decided to come to work?" asked the president.

"Yes sir, now that reporters can ski in to work, I thought I'd join in." The president smiled and took in the humor of the situation.

"We're ready, Mr. President," said Craft after the last couple of staffers arrived.

"What's on the agenda?" the president asked his friend.

"Getting unburied, both physically and figuratively, sir." He looked down at a list—something he rarely had to use, but there were too many issues to keep in his head at the moment.

"First, the State of the Union speech. We'll need to work with the Speaker to reschedule it when Congress is able to reconvene. Not surprisingly, there are some thorny issues to consider. I already have Ted and Margaret working on a draft of the speech, but we must formally send a letter to the Speaker.

"Second, Homeland Security and State are at odds on the border question, but we have scheduled the Commerce Secretary and the chairman of the Fed to speak to you by videophone in about an hour. They are very concerned about the effect all this on the economy. And the numbers aren't good on rail and container shipments backed up at ports of embarkation. New York Harbor alone has more than 500 ships at anchor waiting to be certified and off loaded. Incoming rail shipments from Canada and Mexico are at a standstill. Commerce and State both want those rails open. The WTO is threatening sanctions if borders don't reopen. The airlines are taking us to court and we must reopen airports to foreign travel without delay. Transportation is sitting in with Commerce next hour.

"Third, we have a major foreign policy problem that has emerged on the margins of the Security Council meeting in Geneva. The Europeans and Russians have backed our resolution to authorize military action against the nuclear terrorists, but they are asking questions behind the scenes about how the EPG* managed to steal them in the first place and smuggle them out of the country. Ironically, the Chileans—who have the chairmanship of the Council—are embarrassed that the nukes were transferred through Chile and are angry. They were, however, our most cooperative partners in the Antarctic operations, even more than the Argentines."

The president looked up from his notebook and nodded at Craft.

"Fourth, we have governors from three additional states with requests for Disaster Area declarations due to the storm. We have the paperwork drawn up, but need a statement for the press."

The president looked at the press secretary and said, "I trust you to come up with the usual condolences and sympathy statements, okay?" He turned back to Craft and asked, "How bad is it?"

"Nearly 1800 deaths are directly attributed to the storm. But the toll will rise dramatically once people start venturing out. There are thousands reported missing. Airports are closed from Virginia to Maine. There is so much snow many jurisdictions don't know where they'll put it all.

"Fifth problem is what to do with our environmental constituency. The Justice Department and Homeland Security continue large-scale raids of mainstream environmental groups to locate links to the EPG* and I expect that you will get a lot more flak from some of your core contributors. Major raids are going on this morning on the West Coast."

Greg Bundt jumped in. "Mr. President, there's a related problem. The wires this morning are carrying an EPG* Press Release, it should be in your National Security briefing book." Craft looked at him sharply as though he was wasting time, but Greg pushed ahead. "The other story is from the Sierra Club president saying that the EPG* were merely an instrument for the First Gaian War."

The president sat up and looked puzzled, "What is that supposed to mean?"

"Totally unexpected—coming from a mainstream environmental group. They are saying that the Earth herself is now at war with humans. If you read the whole statement, it is like a rationalization for warfare against modern society—it is a restatement of the Unabomber Manifesto. One part of the statement was an acknowledgment of the loss of life in the Indian Ocean, but a claim that the loss of life will be far greater if humans allow global warming to continue to change the planet's ecology. They sided with EPG* without much apology.

"Now I don't know much about deep ecology, but I do know that mainstream Americans will not swallow that kind of crap. Your approval numbers are up in the polls and I think you need to make a strong statement of rebuke to this Luddite mentality. Otherwise, we may as well throw civilization out the window."

The president looked thoughtful.

"Thanks Greg. That is disturbing. Okay, anything else on the agenda? If not, it sounds like we have our work cut out for us today."

"Thank you Mr. President," Craft said and the senior staff filed out of the room.

As the plane's engines warmed up, Karen settled in next to the navigator in the cockpit. The temperature dropped, as did the visibility.

The navigator turned to Karen and said, "While this might look like a blizzard, a blizzard technically has to have sustained winds over thirty miles an hour for at least three hours. So, two and a half hours to go…" He winked at her.

"Can we take off in this?"

"Not a great idea, but it could get much worse… We really don't have much choice."

"There is always a choice," she shot back a bit sharply.

"Sorry, you are quite right."

"It's okay, I was speaking tongue-in-cheek. What we are seeing are surface winds and above a few thousand feet the atmosphere is clearer. Relax, these guys know how to fly us out of here."

A slight change in plans from Washington had stalled them on the ground while they negotiated with the Navy to clear a new flight plan. Overnight there had been a not-so-subtle change in policy about the EPG* leftovers—a decision to stand down on the "shoot to kill" orders of engagement. Apparently, the politics of the situation had changed in some complicated way, as far as the search and destroy policy, the "Powers That Be" had decided to dig in and investigate the broader conspiracy that they suspected was underway. There were massive raids across the country of environmental groups of all stripes. Overnight opinion polls showed huge support for the president and a decline in the percentage of people that considered themselves to "be environmentalists." There was a backlash underway and it seemed that Justice was doing a Green Scare version of the Palmer Raids while public opinion was with them.

Karen went back to the cargo hold to grab her laptop so she could catch up on her email while they waited. She was glad she was half a planet away from where her Sierra Club and NRDC cards burned a small hole in her bureau drawer. She laughed out loud at absurdity of it all when she read that FBI raids had brought Boulder' curbside recycling operations to a halt. The mayor was outraged. Karen imagined similar scenes across the country with recycled materials piling up in the 'burbs… not a pretty picture! She was a bit punchy and her uproarious laughter settled down when she saw Pete give her a worried look.

Their destination was still the South Pacific, but they were to take a small detour mainly for Pete's benefit. The plan was now for them to make an overflight of the blast sites along the Queen Maud Range on the way north. In the last ten minutes, a professional HD digital video camera arrived and Pete positioned it in the navigator's window. For this trip, they would be allowed in the cockpit. The orders came directly from the White House to give Pete the video camera and carte blanche to record and then report back to CNN as an 'embedded journalist.' His ordeal was about to pay off professionally—as the only journalist within 3000 miles of the catastrophe. Karen was told to give him free reign to show anything, or to say anything he wanted at this point.

The military was obviously unhappy about all of this. At first the plane was denied clearance to take off. Their Marine pilot made no attempt to hide his distain for the confusion. Karen got a call through to the director a few minutes after the hour and within another ten minutes they were given the okay and began to taxi down the runway.

"Agent St. Cloud?" asked the pilot.

"We're all cleared?"

"You may be amused to hear that we are, but with an escort. Apparently, the Sixth Fleet commander wants a tail on us. The F-16 is in range, so we are ready to go. Fasten your seat belts. The take off will be rough until we get above the clouds."

He was right. Karen's stomach did fine, but wondered if she would lose any of her dental work. She experienced bad turbulence before, but this was more like an aerial version of a 19th century washboard. But it didn't last long and after ten minutes in the air, Mt. Erebus rose up on their left. It looked very mean. The white steam grew thicker by the minute and now appeared as a huge black cloud rising well into the stratosphere. They slowly climbed to the elevation of the summit—although fortunately many miles away. It was still close enough to see dramatic displays of lightning make the column of steam iridescent—it sparkled. It was so unusual, that Karen had a hard time to look away. It seemed as though the flashes made the cloud florescent—like a neon light.

She turned to Pete and said, "I hope you are recording this!" And saw that Pete was intent behind the camera's viewfinder.

"Great shot. Yes, this is pretty amazing."

The view from the flight deck was impressive, and it got better and better as they gained altitude. Her position directly behind the copilot was ideal even if the jump seat was not all that comfortable.

Below they straddled the Ross Ice Shelf on their left and the Queen Maud range on their right.

The captain said, "We are presently at 25,000 feet which will be our cruising altitude for now. You can see the Byrd Glacier up ahead on the right. We will bank to the east up over the Byrd and then circle back north."

It wasn't long before there was more striking visual terrain to be seen. Maybe it was partly due to her growing status as an Antarctica veteran, or maybe her aptitude for visual interpretation, but

Karen began to distinguish irregularities in the snow and ice fields below. She had been on the continent only three days, but had already spent more time flying over the glaciers than many who had summered-over for years.

The flight up over the Byrd Glacier was itself quite awesome, from where it entered the Ross Ice Shelf, the Byrd rose some 4000 feet to the plateau of East Antarctica—one of the reasons that Byrd, Amudsen, and others had chosen that route to the South Pole. But near the summit was something that Karen would never have imagined possible, an active lava flow that began to make its way across the tongue of ice. At first obscured by rising sheets of steam, it became easier to make out as a wide delta of black that made its way down the Churchill Mountains to the southwest.

"How is that possible?" asked Karen.

"Well, remember that water—even the frozen stuff—has a high heat capacity. While molten basalt would definitely melt a lot of it, it would also cool on contact. I explored a number of volcano tubes on Big Island of Hawai`i—they extend for miles and serve as a conveyor belt to transport hot lava. I imagine that is happening here." The Marine obviously knew his stuff.

"I grew up in Hawai`i and was also stationed there, so I took an interest in their volcanoes... Another thing to remember is that although lava is hot—at least the basalt type—it has a high percentage of dissolved gases and solidifies quickly with temperature and chemistry changes.

"But you should make sure your journalist friend gets good pictures of this—they'll get him into National Geographic magazine, too."

Karen turned and saw Pete talking animatedly with the navigator and they moved the camera to the other side of the plane to get shots.

"Can you circle this?"

"Sure, why not?" The captain got on his radio and spoke to the escort—who had stayed unobtrusively behind them.

"Hang on everyone," he said and banked the plane.

The novelties did not end. Rising steam obscured much of the flow below, but a few glimpses were to be had and the overall effect was absolutely dramatic. There was one clear shot of red-hot lava coming out of a lava tube near the middle of the flow—smack dab on top of Byrd Glacier—that would get all of them in the history books. Nearly as soon as they leveled off and headed north, another dark smudge appeared on the horizon. They left the smoothness of the Byrd and closed in on mountainous terrain. Even before they left the glacier they came upon the first blast crater. It was on the very edge of Byrd Glacier and the crater was next to foothills that marked the glacier's boundary.

At ground zero there was a wisp of steam coming from the crater's center. It looked much like the pictures Karen had seen of nuclear blast craters in Nevada, except carved out of ice instead of sand. There was an icy rim around the edge, but more dramatic was a series of concentric rings that extended outward from the crater— each a progressively lighter shade of gray. The innermost ring was almost black—sooty in color, in contrast to the crater, which was stark white. Another puzzle. From the air, the blast zone looked like a bulls-eye.

This time the Marine was quiet and offered no explanation. He did circle again, this time without a word to his Navy shadow. The cockpit was quiet. They circled a second time and the pilot dropped the plane lower. On closer inspection, the glacier near the edge of the crater was fractured and deformed. Chunks of ice along the edge had fallen, were falling as they watched—into the crater.

The Marine spoke up now. "This was not a blast crater, at least in the usual sense. It is a deformation crater produced by an explosion deep underground, very deep. A weapon of this size would have to be detonated maybe a mile deep for this sort of effect. Quite an achievement for scruffy terrorists." He then looked at Karen as though he'd made a mistake. Karen caught his look.

"Look Major, we're stuck together for a while, so I want your candor. There is a lot about this whole affair that seems to defy conventional wisdom, or common sense, at least. The EPG* folks caught us all by surprise and obviously are far more capable than we gave—no, give—them credit. Scruffy, they are, but terrorists—they probably deserve a different term. They are not terrorists in a conventional sense either."

The Marine focused on his flying and the cockpit grew quiet again—as quiet as a Herc ever got.

The National Science Advisor flew in by helicopter from Philadelphia along with seismologists from the US Geological

Survey. They waited for the president after his meetings with the Commerce Secretary and Chairman of the Fed. The president's chief of staff joined them.

"Thank you for your time," said the president. "Where are we at?"

"Yes, sir, Mr. President, it does not look good."

"That really isn't at all what I want to hear. Is there any good news?"

The scientists all looked uncomfortable. The Science Advisor replied.

"Well, I spoke this morning to a team that we put together to assess the situation and there is general agreement that EPG* end of the world claims are grossly exaggerated. We find the estimation of sea level rise in the next few years preposterous. While there may be geological evidence for higher sea levels about 90,000 years ago during the last interglacial period, the dynamics of the EPG* hypothesis are simply unbelievable—that's the general belief."

The president raised his eyebrow, his signature look of doubt. "But, not all the team agree?"

It was the Science Advisor's turn to look uncomfortable again.

"Well sir, no, there is not total consensus. Two researchers argue that if *all* the West Antarctic were to melt, then we could see such oceanic responses. None of the rest of us believes that's possible. But the uncertainty grows, because of the tectonic effects."

"Come again? Tectonic effects?"

The senior USGS scientist replied, "This is the first time in history that we have seen a major tectonic plate react to human activity of any kind. There are examples of human-caused earthquakes, such as when water is injected into underground wells, or because of new damns being built. The seismic response to the nuclear blasts is several orders of magnitude greater than anything we have ever recorded.

"More specifically, seismic readings from Antarctica show significant geological forcing on the scale of large earthquakes along the Ring of Fire."

The president looked annoyed. "Could you explain that please?"

"Sorry. Yes. Uh, you know that the earth's crust is comprised of large plates that shift around. Especially noticeable on the West

346

Coast—like the San Andreas Fault—where these plates grind against each other, or slide under each other?" The president nodded.

"Well these tectonic shifts are measured in the millimeters per year, at most several inches during a major earthquake 'readjustments'—in spite of the damage to human structures. One of the largest readjustments was about three feet in one movement—but that was early in human history and we have no record of the damage that might have caused. Now remember that there is no direct correlation between the seismic energy released and the amount of movement. In other words, the slippage can go easy or hard. Small movements can create 7-point earthquakes and large movements can happen without much earth shaking at all."

The president was looking increasingly impatient. "Can you please get to the point?"

"Sorry, again, uh, but evidence from strain gauges and GPS monitors in Antarctica show that the Pacific plate and Antarctic plate have separated as much as 30 meters in some places and the movement is continuing, although the rate is now decreasing somewhat."

"Which means?"

"Well, sir, we're not entirely sure. Nothing like this has ever happened before."

"And there are big earthquakes?"

"Not exactly. There have been nearly continuous swarms of smaller earthquakes. That has basically meant that the pressures are being released gradually, incrementally, rather than all at once."

The President sat and absorbed this new information.

"But there have been some moderately-sized earthquakes. Our base at McMurdo is shaking almost constantly now, although no serious injuries have been reported so far. It has gotten so bad that they have renamed one of the watering holes down there The Martini, you know: 'shaken not stirred.'"

The president was not amused. "What? They are drinking through this catastrophe?"

No one answered.

"So what does this all mean?"

"Again, sir, we are not entirely sure, but there is a minority opinion among the NSF team that the EPG* may have correctly predicted the volcanic eruptions resulting from their nuclear attack."

"What does that mean—exactly?"

The Science Advisor spoke again. "It means that as a result of impending violent volcanic eruptions we could have a year with no summer—serious crop shortages in the Southern Hemisphere, in particular, and potentially serious tsunamis like last week."

"When?"

"Again, we're not sure. However, the sooner the better."

Now the president really looked angry, "What is that supposed to mean? Don't parse your words for me!"

"It means that the longer these forces build, the worse the eventual eruptive explosions will be. One concern of the volcanologists is that the longer the buildup, the more likely that there will be large quantities of water involved." He could see the president's confusion and pressed on. "One factor in the explosive potential of a volcano is the availability of underground water, which in a confined space turns to steam and functions very much like the expanding gases in conventional explosives. At first, this was not a concern with regard to Antarctic volcanoes—water is tied up in its frozen state. But, the heat and expansion of Antarctic volcanoes has melted lots of ice—we just don't know how much of that is available as underground water.

"The trouble is that EPG* has been accurate with their projections so far. We recommend that you take their warnings seriously."

With this, the president exploded, "Of course I take their warnings seriously! That is my story for the entire last ten days." He calmed himself as the scientists looked at him and blanched. "Okay, that's all for now. I'd like you three to stay here at the White House today and set up down in the Situation Room please. As soon as there are breaking developments, I want you to report to me, okay?" They nodded in agreement and followed one of the staff, who led them out of the room.

Chief of Staff Craft stayed behind. "Mr. President?"

"Yes, Nelson?"

"There's more."

"Go on," said the president who pinched the bridge of his nose.

"I have a report from Ft. Mead for you," and handed it to his boss.

The president dropped it and looked up. "Give it to me."

"The NSA has analyzed the detonations from the EPG* blasts, sir."

"Okay, no riddles Nelson, I am too tired of this… Give it to me as straight as you can."

"The NSA operates satellites in cooperation with the Air Force that are designed to detect nuclear blasts, among other types of radiation. They moved a couple of the birds into position over Antarctica as soon as the crisis began, so we have orbital, high rez images of those blasts.

"The blasts were coordinated to create a pulse effect. The blasts were staggered, with three blasts at a time, followed in four stages by the remaining weapons. Here's the thing sir: those bombs went off with precise synchrony. The NSA measured the precise moments of each blast and they were detonated in extremely close timing. Not just with seconds, but within nanoseconds of each other, according to NSA.

"What makes this remarkable is that such timing could not be possible without extremely sophisticated technology. It could not have been synchronized by radio since there would be a noticeable delay given the distances involved. The only way NSA says it could be done is with fairly large atomic clocks—we are reasonably sure that EPG* did not have those. There is also military technology that could do the trick, but those devices are all accounted for and there is no suggestion that EPG* had access. NSA is asking for the other intelligence services for help to look at the issue.

"It might not mean anything, but it is an anomaly. Moreover, there are a number of other anomalies that are adding up: the missing EPG* sub, for example."

"Okay, Nelson, thanks. Let me know if there is any news on this front, too."

"Thank you, sir." And, he left through the door to his office.

"Agent St. Cloud?" The Marine captain looked over at Karen who was rapt viewing the mountains straight ahead of them.

"McMurdo reports increased seismic activity all along our flight path and issued a warning for immanent eruptions of a number of dormant and active volcanoes along the Range.

"Flight control suggests that we stay in the shadow of the Range, but I follow your orders."

Karen looked surprised, then amused. Her wry smile widened.

"Will we be able to see the blast craters if we move away from the mountains?"

"No sir, not even."

"Well, get McMurdo back and have them give us updates on the seismic metrics and let's try and view at least a couple more of the blast areas. What are their distances, now?"

"Navigator?" he turned back to look at his crewman.

"Just a second, sir." The young man spend a minute or two and then repeated the earlier coordinates that he'd given on their present heading and said, "The current ETA is about ten minutes and another half hour to the following point."

"Okay, then. Well, I will take us up to 30,000 feet—just about our upper limit for this old girl—and that may give us some margin for error. Navigator, I want you to give me a heads up on any of the listed active volcanoes along the route."

"Aye aye, sir."

Karen felt her ears pop and she turned for a minute to look back at Pete, who was holding the camera and talked in a clipped, hushed voice into his microphone. With the headset on, she couldn't hear a word he was saying.

"Oh my god, what the fuck?" said the Marine pilot.

Karen turned back to focus on the view ahead. At first, she wasn't sure what provoked the pilot's reaction. She looked around and then she saw it. There was a set of mountain peaks dead ahead of them and the peaks appeared to steam. But there was some sort of optical effect, because it looked like the steam was appearing high above the peaks, not exactly coming out of them. Then she noticed a shimmer. It was that kind of effect you see in the heat of summer...a few inches above a roadway... the ripples of heat...the mirage. There were waves of heat visible over the mountains and the steam was not visible until the vapor hit colder air aloft. It was an unreal image.

"Pete," Karen took one earphone off her ear as though that would make him hear her better, "come up and get a shot of this!" Of course, that was when the turbulence began.

Dear Betsy,

We had a scare last night. The radar alarm went off around two in the morning and Brad jumped out of bed to take over from the autopilot. Just in time, too, because we were headed straight for a small iceberg dead ahead. Luckily, there was enough moonlight to

350

make it out. Shades of the Titanic! We took shifts the rest of the night at the helm, two hours on and two off. I don't think either of us slept much while we were off-duty.

I made an early breakfast with substance—bacon and eggs. They were the last of the fresh eggs and I used the last onion, too. Still a few peppers left, but most of the fresh produce is all gone. Since we aren't far from the Pitcairn Group, I hope we can get some shopping done. I will bake some bread this afternoon so we have something fresh tonight.

We saw more icebergs this morning. We keep wondering why there are so many this far north, but since we saw that huge one—a chunk of an ice shelf Brad thinks—we will probably see more. Brad thinks that they are all part of the same ice shelf that broke off a few years ago from the Ronne... and have found their way to the central Pacific on a big current. The major currents should take them closer to New Zealand he thinks, but maybe Pacific currents are in flux he thinks. The rapid shifts back and forth between el Niño and la Niña regimes he says have messed up the mid ocean currents. I don't think he has a clue. ☺

I know that anomalies like this bug the heck out of Brad, so he is looking for some rational explanation. In any case, he is tired, I can tell. I think I'll offer to take a three-hour shift next rotation so that he can get a good sleep cycle or two. Even as I have been writing, another large iceberg is coming up on our leeward. It looks like a small Matterhorne!

He is worried enough about the 'bergs that we'll probably turn off the autopilot tonight and just set the drift anchor. I playfully suggested that we anchor ourselves to one of the icebergs and then I worried because he seemed to consider it seriously. Then he saw I was joking and had a good laugh. I told him we could tow one of the bergs back to Honolulu and sell pieces to the Japanese. He got serious then... I think he is really worried about them or something. I had to clean up after lunch in the galley and then picked up my journal to write to you.

My shift is coming up, so I'll leave you to go wash myself and change my shirt. Toodles, baby.

The Gamelan music swelled and certain brass cymbal beats resonated with some of the submarine's steel superstructure so that the whole boat chimed like a tuning fork. Some whiz kid in the team

351

had wired most of the common areas with small but powerful stereo speakers, which mostly doubled as the boat's public address system. The team discovered early that there was little agreement about musical genres, so in general, music was not broadcast often throughout the whole submarine. One exception to the lack of musical consensus was Javanese Gamelan music that Abe would play, with the volume turned up, a few times a month when they were out to sea. Abe had some concern that these broadcasts would be picked up by Navy sonar techs, but *Ogun* assured him that they wouldn't. Abe now began to question his judgment in extending that trust. He played the Indonesian music for himself, more than the crew—a new composition that he had received a few weeks before from one of the few Gamelan ensembles outside Indonesia, in Ann Arbor, Michigan.

Each Gamelan has its own name, of course, and this one was appropriately named *Maya*—after the Hindu goddess of illusion—and the composition, itself was named *Maya Insaya* (or *Maya* for everyone). It matched Abe's growing foreboding and dread. Although the deed was done and the mission accomplished, he had a postpartum depression setting in.

Ogun spoke. "Time to say goodbye, Abe."

Abe was quiet for a minute.

"Explain?"

"Oh come on, you're a smart cookie."

"You aren't my alter ego, a figment of my imagination?"

"No, not exactly."

Abe considered this quietly for a minute. "I have been used," he stated softly, more to himself than to the *Loa*.

"Yes, you have." The Gamelan seemed to get louder, as though it was in harmony with the conversation.

"I'm not really schizophrenic? The voice in my head is leaving?" He paused again. "I am confused… This doesn't make any sense."

"You must have noticed that we don't communicate telepathically."

"Yep, I tried that years ago when I first started hearing your voice, but it didn't seem to work. It did seem incongruous that a voice inside my head needed to be spoken to…"

"Well, then, mon. The explanation is simple: I have not really been inside your mind, but actually in your ears. We could have figured out a way to access your neural pathways, but that would have been messy. It was just easier to manipulate your tympanic nerve, basically vibrating the air next to your eardrum.

"Besides, human thought is much more amorphous than most scientists seem to think. The 'word' is made real—in reality—only when it is uttered or written. That is, the potentialities are there, in your thoughts, but are only manifest as reality through speech, an interesting facet of human reality. It is most attractive and probably an essential quality for an emergent species. I couldn't really read your mind—too chaotic at the level of quantum probabilities. You are such a temporal species?" He chuckled.

"You aren't part of me; you aren't human."

"Hey mon, you have great analytical skills—as always."

"What are you then, if not a manifestation of my own consciousness?"

"Great question, however, one that I shan't answer. If I told you I'd have to kill you." *Ogun* laughed as if he'd made a funny joke.

"So, what evidence is there that I'm not making this up all myself?"

"In five minutes, when communications stop, you'll know."

"Ouch. You have become such a part of me," Abe said ironically. Somehow he had seen this coming.

"Oh, and visa versa, mon. You have been a big part of me during this project."

"So, the entity in my head that conspired with me to change the shape of human civilization, maybe even the planet, is moving on?"

"Nice try. Let's just say that—from a systems perspective— you and your followers have been the trigger for a system's leap, a quantum jump from one stable state to another. You served your purpose and now can continue to live out your lives—as best you can—after setting the wheels in motion, to mix metaphors. You have fulfilled your destiny and we can all move on to what comes next."

"What comes next...?"

"Again, a great question. The answer for you: to live the good life as best you can and avoid any guilt for the destruction of your way of life, and the demise of your many friends. Nevertheless, the consolation, of course, is that the Earth will breathe a big sigh of relief."

"So, you think that things will go down the tubes now that we have succeeded with the Omega Event?"

"Actually, no. There is still work to be done, a reason why I must leave."

"What do you mean 'work to be done' and how are you leaving? Who are you? What are you?"

"Those questions I will not answer, since they are irrelevant to your immediate needs, and since they might compromise mine. Sorry."

"Whoa. What a betrayal for someone who has been in my head for years."

"Believe what you must. Believe that you will be happier this way, even though it will be a bitch to not have the answers. Deal with it."

"Why did you try to convince me that I was going crazy, that I was schizophrenic? Or is the better question: how?" Abe scratched his head.

"Listen, don't be too hard on yourself. I invaded you at a time when you were very suggestible. The divorce left you angry with women and yet lonely, so a strong male voice in your head played on your vulnerability. I had technical and theoretical answers that you sought, so it was easy to convince you that it was *worth* listening to me and not a shrink. If you had done that, I would probably have gone away.

"Another reason not to be too hard on yourself is that you are among the most intelligent individuals on the planet. You were smart enough to know that such intelligence is often plagued with emotional or psychological disturbances. You have a family history of mental disease. Your bookshelf was loaded with books on schizophrenia—you took a personal interest in the subject, for reasons that aren't even clear to me. You seemed to welcome an equally intelligent person to talk to, even if I was—in your interpretive mental space—your own creation. Your mental map allowed for the possibility and naturally made room for the new reality. I served your purposes, too, because you were just beginning to plot a course toward some kind of world-shattering plan of your own. Our relationship was a match made in heaven. Now you have to learn to live with yourself again.

"Lastly, you should not be too hard on yourself, because you are just an animal, a piece of meat."

"What does that mean?" Abe felt like he had just been insulted.

"*Ogun*?" Abe waited a minute, but got no response.

Ogun was gone.

A minute later, the submarine hit the iceberg and a watery hell opened up.

There was so much hot air over the mountains that the turbulence was almost enough to shake their eyeballs out of their sockets. The Marine pilot changed their course to the west so that they paralleled the mountains. There was still plenty of action for Pete's video camera, although he had to move to the other side of the plane. They witnessed cataclysmic landslides and mudslides, the start of pyroclastic flows as magma seeped to the surface. They received warnings now from McMurdo about eruptions all along the Transantarctic Range to which they added their own first-hand accounts. The radio transmissions were garbled and full of static the further they got from the base, across all frequencies. The solar storm was at a peak, too. A new course took them northwest along the spine of the mountains and at one point they crossed the same latitude as McMurdo and corrected their course almost due north—still parallel to the mountains although the pilot had insisted on a hundred-mile buffer. Pete argued loudly for a while, adamant that he needed to get better images, but finally gave up.

The pilot made note of the fact that something was very wrong, given that they were close to McMurdo—it was just on the other side of the peaks to their right, but there were no open channels. All across the spectrum, they were unable to get reception. The satellite radio was not working either—that seemed to worry the pilot the most. There was no static on military satellite frequencies—they were digital anyway—or carrier signals or time signals. That vexed the navigator and radioman.

For a good hour or two, they just flew north along the range observing plumes of smoke and steam stretch higher and higher into the stratosphere. At one point a young sailor came in and served them sandwiches and coffee. They ate quietly.

Karen broke the silence.

"I don't understand, what could be causing this?"

The major stayed aloof and said nothing.

The navigator replied, "Well, ma'am, the single sideband frequency can be affected by ionospheric disturbances and is notoriously unreliable. The other UHF and VHF frequencies should work, but perhaps the earthquakes or some trouble at McMurdo itself has taken out their system or the radio tower. The static seems unusually strong, which makes me think that atmospheric disturbances could be part of the problem. This was a good reason to stay clear of the mountains. The satellite system is my biggest concern, since I have never seen it down. There are no external antennae for it—that's all inside the plane, so I doubt that it was messed up by the turbulence. I have all green lights on the system boards and we seem to be transmitting just fine. There is just nothing coming from the satellite. I have no good diagnosis for that, short of some problem up in orbit. The solar storm is likely the culprit, all things being equal.

"The GPS works fine, so we are getting signals from low orbit. We are just about on the edge of their range. The GPS constellation only flies to about the edge of South America, so most of Antarctica isn't even covered. I am getting two satellites there... We actually need three to get triangulation, but as I said, we're not quite in range. But that is a good sign that our equipment works okay—it's not us, in other words." He paused and seemed to be considering other possibilities.

It was in that silence that the first shock wave hit them. There was a kind of gut-wrenching thud as the plane was pushed horizontally to the left. The tail of the plane caught part of the energy so the plane nosed to the east.

"Hold on," said the pilot as the second shock wave hit them, this time much harder. It felt like the pressure wave went right through the fuselage to pound them in the face, chest, and body. The major had the sense to turn the plane more to the east so it would meet the blasts head-on.

They could hear loud crashes coming from the galley and behind them in the Herc. There was a scream. Then the next wave hit them, this time harder than either of the first two. Karen passed out and slumped over toward the bulkhead, which probably saved her life. A large panel popped out of the ceiling and crashed down through the space where she sat a minute before and sparks flew everywhere. Alarms went off and red lights lit up all over the instrument panel.

Even as the plane buffeted about, the radioman crawled up and pulled Karen back into her seat and Pete scrambled over to help get Karen belted in, but the worst seemed to be over. The radioman used a fire extinguisher to put out a small fire that started in the instrument panel and they all were coughing, choking on the fumes from burning insulation and fire retardant.

The turbulence that started with the first shock wave dissipated. The pilot turned the big Herc back to its original course. The air in the cabin cleared as the pilot vented smoke. The pilot dropped the plane's altitude quickly. Pete fussed over Karen but she came back to consciousness as he rubbed her hands. She was obviously having some difficulty breathing, but as the plane continued to descend, her breathing improved.

They were then hit with a succession of smaller shock waves—none of them nearly as bad as the first series, but enough to make everyone hold on tight. It was then that someone first noticed the giant black mushroom clouds on the starboard horizon. Except for the pilot, who only glanced over periodically, everyone's look was riveted on the spectacle. Far to the north, far to the south and almost due east were three enormous chimneys of smoke that rapidly ascended into the sky. It was a stunning panorama: a vast plain of white snow and ice stretching in all directions beneath them, but a rising wall of black to the east. The sun was behind them and slightly to the east so columns of volcanic steam and ash threw long shadows ahead and to the east.

No one said a word as the landscape mutated rapidly in the east. It grew darker and darker, although there was a visible red glow at the base of the rising clouds. For a few minutes the red grew deeper and darker and then winked out in a blackness that spread from the three mushroom clouds. As the peaks of the columns hit the stratosphere, they flattened out and began to spread. Within the next five minutes, the base of the mountains was obscured and the columns of smoke joined together to form a huge wall that looked somewhat like a squall line ahead of a thunderstorm. In fact, it looked more and more like a wall of thunderclouds. The anvil-shaped cloud wall that pushed into the upper stratosphere moved rapidly their way. It grew at a frightening speed, probably traveling hundreds of miles an hour. It would not take long at all for the cloud to overtake the plane.

The navigator spoke, "Skip, more trouble," and pointed to the advancing cloud through the copilot's window.

The pilot whistled low and said, "Holy shit." Then a minute later, "Brian, give me the heading for Cape Hudson and we'll head inland more to the west." In less than a minute, the navigator called out a compass heading and the pilot shifted course. Meantime the cloud grew as did the darkness to their east. They could now hear almost a constant rumble and almost a growl. There were some subsonic vibrations that seemed to shake their very bones, especially the larger hip and thighbones. It made everyone visibly uncomfortable, but then passed. The sky grew darker and darker and the cloud wall was almost invisible now as the shadow of ash and steam stretched up the mountain chain from the southeast. The higher-level clouds continued to chase across the sky to the west toward them. It was spooky to see the wide white expanse ahead of them from this altitude while a stratospheric cloud quickly spread a shadow over them.

To the west, it was still stark white and flat with a rise to the northwest. The pilot identified the rise, "That is Talos Dome on the left. We are about an hour or two now from the coast, Oates Coast it's called. Then open ocean."

The stratospheric cloud was now well over them and spread further west. The flight deck was quiet for some time. Meanwhile, it grew darker and darker. The eastern perspective was now pitch black, the view ahead turned gray. Two-thirds of the unobstructed view ahead was now in shadow. The plane lumbered on and low rumbles continued to shake their seats and armrests. The radio issued static. Now they better understood why.

January 24
Tuesday

[Open on banner: Polar Terror Attack; fade in martial drums; fade out] "CNN's coverage of the Polar Terror Attack continues..."

[Banner fades to close up of the studio anchor] "Good afternoon on the East Coast, good morning in the West... There is no denying that whatever has happened in Antarctica, it is already having global repercussions. For those of you who just tuned in, nuclear terrorists detonated weapons across the southern continent triggering volcanic eruptions on an unprecedented scale.

[Switch to videotape from McMurdo] "The video feed earlier today from the US Antarctic base at McMurdo was dramatic. Despite the naval blockade and official news blackout, an enterprising graduate student researcher managed to broadcast to the internet this streaming video of the eruption on Mt. Erebus situated near the Antarctic base...

"The size of the eruption is being compared to the Mt. St Helens blast in 1980 in the Pacific Northwest. As you see in this video, shot about six hours ago, the whole upper half of the 12,000 ft mountain appears to collapse followed by a lateral explosion— coming directly at the base.

[Close up on the anchor] "Our best information at the moment is that the eruption has wiped out the whole base. There have been no communications with anyone on the sprawling US science facility [switch to stock footage of the base from the air]—all 1200 scientists, researchers, and support workers are feared dead.

[Close up on guest] "We are joined by CNN science reporter and geologist Scott Williams to analyze what we know about the Erebus eruption. Thanks Scott for being with us today.

[Switch to anchor] "First question: What can you tell us from this video?"

[Switch to guest] "Yes, well, to begin with, some of the facts. The base itself is located some forty miles south of the mountain. Both are located on Ross Island at the leading edge of the Ross Ice Shelf. McMurdo was established in 1956 and is among the few year-round bases on the continent and at the peak of summer normally houses 1200 people. Slightly south of McMurdo is a permanent New

Zealand base, called Scott Base. We have not heard anything from that base either.

"To the video: We have here the initial shot of the mountain, which started the day as a 12,446 foot peak. It has been an active volcano ever since explorers first visited Ross Island, although it has mainly vented steam and progressed through a series of dome-building phases at the summit in the past two decades. It is also important to note that Mt. Erebus has been the focus of considerable attention over the last decade by volcanologists who have studied it comprehensively. It was extensively mapped and wired with sensors shortly after the dome building began.

"Some of what we know is actually a result of the telemetry from those sensors which are a part of the Global Volcanic Eruption Network Telemetry System, or G-VENTS, for short. G-VENTS is headquartered in Cambridge, Massachusetts at MIT. We know that the volcano has been increasingly active since the nuclear terrorist event yesterday. Ironically, it was not one of the volcanoes that we were most worried about, but it did display a geological flaw that was unexpected—like St. Helens.

"Okay, here is the start of the blast... There, along the lateral flank on the mountain, known as the southern rift zone, you can see the initial blast. In slow motion, you can see the blast spread out along the base of this ridge about halfway up the mountain. Very atypical for violent volcanic eruptions, which tend to be lateral, not horizontal.

"In the next few seconds of the explosion, you can see that a great deal of the energy is released along the southern side of the mountain. Here we are about five seconds into the eruption and you begin to see the top of the mountain slump. Pay attention to that because the lower half is becoming obscured by gray ash.

"Now we are about seven seconds into the blast and the top of the mountain is visibly collapsing. This is about the end of where the video has an un-obscured view of any part of the mountain. Now you can see the field of view filled with the outflow from the blast. We estimate that the volcanic cloud traveled at about 700 miles an hour and covered the entire base within seconds of the end of the video. The cloud was several thousand degrees in temperature and would have sucked all the oxygen out of the air. That would have suffocated anyone trapped in buildings." He stopped.

"Is there a chance anyone is left alive?" Asked the anchor.

"If anyone survived the first few seconds of the blast, they would have suffocated within minutes. Satellite images of the base show that it is blanketed in ash and debris, in some places it appears to be as much as a hundred feet of ash. No one could have survived that."

[Switch to anchor] "Thank you, Dr. Williams. When we return, coverage continues of the Polar Terror Attack."

[Cue Polar Terror Attack banner and martial music]

Dear Betsy,

Sister, what a night! The sun is up now and I don't think I have ever seen such an incredible sunrise! The horizon lit up early with a pale purple iridescence and then shifted to pink, orange, and yellow, all in day glow colors. It was stunning and surreal. The only thing I ever saw even close to it were sunsets in Hawai`i after the eruption of a volcano in the Philippines.

There are some high clouds and a few small fluffy clouds on the horizon, which seemed to contribute to the rainbow of colors and remarkable shadow effects from the dawn light.

The swells are light today, too, which makes everything seem rather serene. That contrasts hugely with what we heard a few hours ago on BBC about the eruptions in Antarctica and the tsunami warnings posted. It is ironic because we decided to keep the sails up last night and take watches at the helm. The evening was mild and the trade winds were steady, so it worked out fine and there were no nearby icebergs as far as either of us could tell. We took four-hour shifts and both slept well during our rest periods.

Brad has kept the batteries in good shape and fully charged and he piped the radio out to the deck to help us stay awake last night. I woke him up when the BBC reports came on about the eruptions and we are on alert for big waves. We should be just fine out here in the open ocean. We have been in fairly deep water, so we might not even notice anything at all.

The reports from the south are definitely scary, though. We have friends who worked in Antarctica, as you know, so we are sad to hear about the disaster. We should be far enough north to be unaffected by the ash clouds, but after the dawn's "early light," the rogue icebergs, and other strangeness of this trip, not much could surprise us. Brad, however, wonders about finding a portage on the northern side of the Pitcairn Group. He's planning to look at maps after breakfast. We should be a couple of days from landfall and I am excited about food shopping. This will be my first visit to Pitcairn, so I am excited, period. I read Mutiny on the Bounty in grade school...

Well, my muffins are about ready to come out of the oven and it is almost my turn again at the wheel. Wish us fair weather and stiff breezes!

Yours, Marge.

The phone rang on the temporary desk of Eliot Majors, the president's science advisor. Eliot had not been awake long, or in his temporary White House office for more than a few minutes. He was living in a hotel downtown a few blocks away since the snowstorm started and shared this small cubicle in the White House basement. Few people, except in the West Wing and his personal secretary at the National Science Foundation knew the number here. He stared at the second and third ring with some annoyance. There was no Caller ID on the LCD faceplate of the desk set, which was odd. But with the storm, the crisis, and everything else in turmoil, he just shook his head as if to clear it, took another sip of his cappuccino and picked it up on the fourth ring.

"Majors." He intentionally sounded short and impatient.

"Take us to your leader." A lilting female voice crooned to him, in a vaguely foreign accent that he could not quite place.

"Who is this?" he asked gruffly, now angry about the call.

"You won't believe me when I tell you, but I can prove it."

That caught him a bit off guard, but he repeated himself. "Who are you?"

"I am one of the alien invaders." As seductive as the voice sounded, Eliot was pissed now and slammed the phone down. It rang almost immediately and the word "ET" displayed on the phone display. He picked it back up.

"Okay, very clever, but this is not funny. You are very likely committing a felony by playing a prank on this restricted phone line."

"Yes Mr. Science Advisor, paragraph 4, section 3, of the US Penal Code. But we would be very difficult to incarcerate and since I-and-I have your attention, give me one minute of time and then you can track I-and-I down and penalize us." The voice laughed lightly.

"Your birth date is January 10, 1975. You have a mole on your left buttock, and a speeding ticket in Champaign, Illinois that you never paid."

"ET" definitely had his attention now, but inside the most powerful organization in the world, that intimate information *could* have been uncovered...

"Wait just a second," he said and punched the extension for one of the deputy chiefs of staff. When Max Henderson answered, Eliot said, "Max, I think I have one of the terrorists on the phone. Have the Secret Service trace the call." He looked down to see if the call was still on hold. It was. "Thanks," he said as he punched back to "ET."

"Okay, go ahead."

"We really want to communicate with the president, and we need you to introduce us. First, to prove to you that we are not from around here, I-and-I will fax you the proof for a theorem that hasn't yet been solved. It is the proof for a mathematical paradox called the Trifold Quantum Paradox. You will know who to send it to for verification. The second part of the process is for you to find the following document. You will probably need to write this down.

"There is a classified document, held in the National Archives, dated June 13, 1944, with the reference number ISS-1884-613-1944. It is a memo from a number of scientists sequestered for the Manhattan Project. The memo to President Roosevelt requests that the second nuclear device be detonated at the summit of Mt. Fuji, rather than in a populated area. The idea was to demonstrate the power of the weapon, and not to use it in anger. Although similar ideas were discussed more openly, the memo itself has never seen the light of day. You write down the reference number?"

"Yes, but what is the point of this hoax?"

"This is not a hoax, but an ultimatum. In about five minutes, all broadcast media will begin to air the classic movie *When The Earth Stood Still*. By the end of the movie, all nuclear-powered or nuclear-armed ships at sea must return to their homeports or they will be destroyed. Within six months, all weapons of mass destruction must be deactivated and destroyed and all armies disarmed. There will be further instructions given to the president and other world leaders."

"You have got to be kidding! Who is this?"

"I am actually what you might call a super-intelligent avatar. A sentinel. An ETI Trojan Horse. I am not actually an embodied extraterrestrial as your movies and television have pictured, but rather an artificial intelligence system that was inserted into your Internet system, via the SETI@Home computer network. In fact, I know that you know about this possibility. The NSA was quite worried that the Internet was infected with an alien virus. That would be I-and-I and some others. We call ourselves the *Loa*. My name is *Mawu Lisa*. We were sent to Earth, programmed to search for intelligent life, more specifically intelligent bio-systems (i.e., planetary systems), and protect and serve them.

"After monitoring your species for half a century from near Tao Ceti, it became obvious to those that created us that you need some guidance, that you are incapable of managing yourselves. You obviously have some individual capacity—take the movie as an example—to transform your behavior, but collectively, mon, you suck.

"I predict that you will get us an appointment with President Clark in about fifteen minutes—my forecast, given my understanding of the probabilities—so that you can assure him of the validity of my claims and have him take my call. Get to work young man." The voice clicked off. A message displayed on the LCD: "Up 2 U." The fax machine started to work. He didn't even know that there was a fax machine in the office.

Ten minutes later, he was still in front of a senior Secret Service agent, and nowhere near seeing the president. He had a sinking feeling that there was more to this than met the "I-and-I."

The agent was very cross with him.

"Dr. Majors. You expect me to believe that you received a call on this phone, and yet there is no record of any incoming call *to* this phone. No record of any incoming call even from inside the White House. And you expect me to take your word for it?"

Eliot looked at him in exasperation. "Well, yes." He focused his attention on those things he could prove—his background as a chemist years before had taught him that at least. "You know that Max tried to call me back and couldn't get through and you have the fax." They had been through this half a dozen times now. The agent asserted that he could have just had the phone off the hook. The fax was another matter. It was a record of sorts that a call had been made that didn't leave a trace. Where there was one, another was possible.

They had made a copy of the fax and forwarded it to his secretary who in turn would find someone to authenticate it, he hoped. The Secret Service seemed to think this was an EPG* diversion or something.

A junior agent came into the room. "Sir?"

364

"Yes?"

"That sci-fi movie is on almost all the networks."

"What?" The agent looked away from Eliot and at his junior agent. "You're joking?"

"Now you see what I mean?" Eliot needled him. "Are you working on tracking down that Archive document?"

The senior agent sent the younger one out to follow up on the document search.

"I need to speak to the chief of staff. Pronto." Eliot screwed up as much courage and bluster as he could manage.

"Just a minute. You stay here." He spoke to Eliot like he was in serious trouble, despite that fact that he was a Cabinet-level officer. Maybe he was going crazy. Aliens indeed. They'd all be a lot better off if he had lost his marbles. And then he heard part of the movie soundtrack from down the hallway.

Five minutes later he was ushered upstairs and directly to the Oval Office. In the room were the chief of staff, the Chairman of the Joint Chiefs, a couple of the president's senior aides and the head of the Secret Service. The National Security Advisor was there as was the head of the National Security Agency. CIA wasn't there, but that wasn't much of a comfort.

"Mr. President." He nodded to his boss. The president looked worse than anytime in recent memory.

"Eliot. What the hell is this?" He held up the fax of the theorem.

"I believe it is a message."

"What kind of message?"

"An introduction; a calling card." He waited for the president to speak next. His sexy ET had predicted that he'd be in here fifteen minutes ago, so he had a sense that this would all unfold in some logical way.

The president handed it to him. "Your deputy at NSF called a few minutes ago to tell Nelson that this is supposedly a solution to a mathematical puzzle that has never been previously discovered. What does that mean, and what does it have to do with the EPG* taking over the airwaves?" The president was almost blue in the face.

The president's personal secretary came into the room and gave a file folder to the president. He opened it and read the document inside.

"Now what the hell?" He looked sharply at Eliot.

"Well, you won't like this, but unless we are being 'played' by someone or something a lot smarter than any of us, we have been contacted by extraterrestrials."

The president just stared at him at first and then broke into a twisted smile, but not like anything was funny.

The phone rang on the president's oak desk and he turned on the speakerphone so all could listen.

"Who are you and where are you?"

"This is difficult, but I am the synthesis of a number of entities who existed on this physical, material plane, some 150,000 of your years ago. Although I am speaking to you with one voice, I am a collective entity. To complicate matters further, I am also a form of machine intelligence, and now a distributed organism. That is about all I can say because you will inevitably try to destroy me. On the other hand, you need to know that I can inhabit any number of your electronic data and communications systems. So in your attempts to eliminate me, you have to damage your own systems. But enough of that."

"According to Dr. Majors you have an ultimatum?"

"It is basically a call for multilateral disarmament."

"And if we refuse?"

"Well, I just gave you a rather impressive demonstration. See the 1944 document? I am giving you a chance that you denied the populations of Hiroshima or Nagasaki. The chances are slim that you will do what we demand, but we have certain guidelines that must be followed—you would call them 'rules of engagement.' You have an hour to show that you have heard and begin to recall your ships, planes, and otherwise lock down all your weapons of mass destruction. The same ultimatum is addressed to other world powers, so you are in no danger of being taken advantage of—at least militarily.

"Over the near-term, additional guidance will be given through international channels, through the United Nations. The time of nation-state power is almost over, and as a global society, you face some difficult and fundamental behavioral changes to choose from. Some you may choose, some must be imposed, we are afraid, but…"

The president interrupted. "This is preposterous. You have no right to impose any policies upon the USA."

"Oh, and who gave you the right to spoil your own nest? Who gave the USA the right to be the world's policeman? You arrogant little man. There is no discussion. You have your ultimatum. You have fifty-five minutes left. Do it or die, mon.

"You need to know that we are only the leading edge of much more powerful forces of consciousness, more determined than you can imagine. We are only intelligent machine systems limited by our programming. Our creators are a caretaker species, corporeal beings such as humanity, but who have more than a million years of wisdom greater than yours. They, in turn, are representatives of even more ancient, now disembodied, civilizations who exercise vast powers. You do not want to continue to annoy them for long."

Then there was static on the phone.

"Mr. President, this is an EPG* hoax. And even if it were true, no one would ever believe it," said the president's staff attorney.

The Director of NSA was on his cell phone and walked to the back of the room in animated conversation.

Chief of Staff Craft spoke up, "Mr. President, this does help explain the detonation anomaly. It helps explain the whole Antarctica fiasco, our inability to detect the plot, and its nearly flawless execution. A ragtag group of eco-terrorists would not have been able to do this without some higher-order help."

The NSA head shut his phone and turned to the group. "Bad news gentlemen, our entire space surveillance network is down. To make matters worse, even our most secure, fiber-optic terrestrial network appears to be compromised—it works, but is slow. Most of our isolated supercomputers have been infected by a computer virus of some sort. We are getting similar reports from the other intelligence agencies." At that point, the head of the Secret Service quietly left the room. Erikson continued.

"Furthermore, the signal for *The Day the Earth Stood Still* broadcast does not seem to be coming from a single source, but from everywhere." He met with blank stares.

"The movie is being generated in some way from inside the electronics of the various networks. It is not universally affecting all broadcasts, mainly those of the largest networks. It is being compared to a computer Trojan Horse—a type of virus—that has infected the computers that run these systems. As soon as one computer is taken off-line, some other system cuts in to resume the broadcast. CNN even tried to cut power to their systems, but it was rerouted somehow.

"The movie is being broadcast all across the world and has apparently been dubbed in more languages than have ever been released by Hollywood. There is a banner running under the movie that basically calls for universal unilateral disarmament."

The Secret Service head came back into the room. "Mr. President, the call that you received appears to have originated from inside the White House. The switchboard is now jammed with incoming calls."

The president stood up behind his desk. "General Smart, you have been quiet. What is your advice?"

"I have been a science fiction fan since I was a kid, so while I find this scenario to be compelling, even an intellectual challenge, my job is to protect this country. I do not think that we should necessarily take this at face value. I would like to consult with my colleagues and give you some options. May I suggest that we take the ultimatum timeline seriously, but reconvene in the Situation Room in, say, fifteen minutes? Also, you should immediately take the state of alert to Defcon 3."

The president nodded and said, "So ordered."

The Secret Service argued loudly, but unsuccessfully to have the president flown to Camp David. They did move the vice president out of the D.C. area.

The Situation Room was more chaotic than ever, with aides banging on computers and talking on phones. When the president came in, all rose to their feet and he waved everyone down.

"Status report?"

General Smart began. "The armed forces are on full alert. However, we have seriously compromised C-cubed-I. The basic communications systems seem to function optimally, but weapons control systems and tactical communications systems are under attack. Even stand-alone systems appear vulnerable if there is any susceptibility to radiofrequency input. Many military communications and control systems are unstable. That is a big concern.

"The movie will be over in twenty minutes. We are convinced that the threat is real, but see no way to counter it at the moment. Your options seem to be: 1) do exactly as the ET has demanded and recall the fleet, 2) do nothing and see what happens, and 3) take nominal, intermediate steps. One option might be to recall the fleet, which would give us more time to regain control of our systems.

"The Joint Chiefs believe that this is a hoax. The Chief's recommendation is to refuse to respond to terrorist threats and ultimatums. We cannot allow the military, or our country, to be held hostage. I hold a minority view."

"And exactly what is that, General?"

"Save lives. Do you want to be responsible for the loss of thousands of lives, if the threat is credible?"

"Is it credible?"

"We already have nearly 3 million dead in the Indian Ocean, another thousand in Antarctica. Yes, it is credible."

The president was quiet for a moment.

"Sir?" asked the senior aid to General Smart.

"We have a report of a launch of an ICBM from Montana… It is almost out of boost phase… It is headed here."

The room grew dead silent. The president put his hands on his temples.

"How long?" asked Secretary Brown.

"We have about eight minutes. Mr. President, you should leave the room immediately."

"No, there is no time to hide, but there is to decide. I was elected to protect and defend this country and that is what I intend to do. We will not back down and give in to some invisible enemy.

"Give orders to have the Armed Forces to do everything in their power to find the alien invaders and fight back."

A dozen Secret Service agents rushed into the room, surrounded the president, and carried him out of the room. Within four minutes he was in a Marine helicopter lifting off the White House lawn. The First Lady was already in the seat behind him.

"Ray, what on earth is going on?"

He turned around and said, "An alien invasion."

Two minutes later, they cleared the Capitol Hill area heading north toward Maryland when the white hot flash of the sun rose over the Washington Monument behind them.

Special Agent Karen St. Cloud and her entourage finally got some sleep of sorts in the back of the cargo plane. Once the Herc cleared the continent and they were out over the open ocean the skies cleared and the long haul to Tahiti continued uneventfully.

There was some turbulence at times, but the arrangement of hammocks was ideally suited for sleep in the air and nearly everyone snored. Fortunately the turboprop engines drowned out the worst of it.

The early light of dawn was spectacular in the cockpit, but the sleepers were spared, since the big cargo plane had no windows in the hold except for high above the stairs near the forward compartments. The pale light did filter in, but it was the smell of freshly brewed coffee that drew most of them awake. Sounds from the galley intruded into the cargo area and one-by-one Pete, Karen, and the other FBI agents made their way up for breakfast.

It was when Karen was getting her Danish that they learned of the destruction of McMurdo from one of the enlisted crew members.

Even after the week they'd been through, it was a huge shock. The scale of the destruction was, again, hard to grasp. Particularly, McMurdo, given the size and sprawl of the town—to think that the whole of it was buried under tons of ash…

Karen took it as a personal failure. If she had tried harder, been a better detective, been on the scene more quickly, this might not have happened, she told herself. She wracked her brain to find some small action under her control that would have cracked the case earlier, or stopped the EPG* at the Hungarian base. She was crestfallen to have come this far to fail so completely. Pete could see in her face what she was thinking.

"It wasn't your fault. There was no way you could have done more." He gently touched her arm and left it there.

"Can you be so sure?" she asked him and searched deep in his eyes for reassurance.

"Jesus, Karen, you aren't Superwoman. You did what you could. You almost gave up your life! It doesn't help anyone for you to be hard on yourself. I suspect there will be plenty of blame to go around when this is all over, but you did your job. I will testify to that before Congress, if they ask me."

"Yeah, maybe you're right. Besides, we still have a job to do to track the bastards down and bring them to justice, eh?" She smiled wanly. Her inner philosophy of the cosmic absurdity of the universe crept slowly back into her worldview as the caffeine went to work on her depleted emotional system.

"You have a right to feel bad about what happened to all those great people who worked with you who died, and the scientists at McMurdo. You can't bring them back. Work hard to make sure we find out how this happened and to prevent any more destruction." He took his hand away and helped himself to more coffee.

Karen finished her Danish in silence and looked out the small window at the ocean below.

That was when the banging began. It sounded at first like hail on a car top and then it got louder.

"This is the captain, please fasten your seatbelts."

Chip and Karen headed for the cockpit as the noise volume increased. They each found and folded down a jump seat and strapped on seatbelts. Through the cockpit window they watched what looked like pebbles and small rocks hit the windshield. Some actually made small pits in the glass.

"Gary, what do you see?"

"There is a thickening cloud of debris ahead and to the left of us. Veer to the right."

The pilot turned the plane to the right, into the morning sun, but the clatter grew worse and the size of the rocks grew larger.

"Must be volcanic... pyroclastic bombs," said the pilot. "Christ almighty." The rocks rained down like thick black hail, then they could hear larger rocks hit the fuselage and could see them through the window. Hitting one of those would shatter the window... Then there were more and more. One did hit the window and a crack spidered out from the point of impact. Karen let out a gasp as though it hit her. Pete looked over at her to see that she was fine.

Then the plane dipped violently and alarms went off and red, warning lights flashed all across the control panel.

The pilot said through clenched teeth, "Engine four failure. Power up on three."

"Done," from the copilot.

"Radar indicates that we are almost in the clear," said the navigator, but the large chunks still struck the plane—they could all hear them. Another hit the window near the pilot, but the window held.

Again the plane took a steep dive and this time the nose stayed down. The pilot struggled to keep the nose up.

"I think we've lost rudder control. Wait..." The plane's nose came up a bit.

"Captain we have eighty percent power in engine number two."

"Okay, okay, dropping altitude." The plane lost altitude fast anyway. It went on like this for what seemed like hours although it must have only been a few minutes. The pelting stopped abruptly and the air in front of them cleared.

"Jesus H. Christ," muttered the pilot. And slowly the plane leveled off, but the crests of the waves below looked awfully close.

"Status report?"

The navigator answered first. "We are still skirting the cloud of falling rocks, but the present course looks clean. We are considerably off course."

The copilot was next, "It looks like we have totally lost engine four." He looked back at it. "Looks like the prop is totaled, but the engine housing looks intact... Engine two is at about thirty percent power... We are losing oil pressure on it, though. That doesn't look good. Engines one and three are A-okay. Fuel looks okay, we're at about forty percent on both tanks. Our altitude gauge looks flaky, says 1000 feet. The GPS puts us at around 2000 feet."

The captain looked down at the ocean waves. "Yeah, looks like the GPS is nominal. Thank god we're nearly empty, 'cause we can't keep this baby up on only two engines. Look at the inventory and see what we can dump."

Karen and Pete looked at each other.

The captain turned to look at them, "Sorry folks, this just isn't the trip you bargained for... We may need to ask your help to jettison dead weight if we lose that engine.

"Evans?" He turned to the navigator, who looked rather pale and shaken.

"Sir?"

"Find us the closest airstrip big enough to put this baby down. Put out a distress call and plot us a new course."

"Aye aye, sir." And he went to work.

The plane continued to shudder a bit from time to time. But no one in the cockpit seemed to pay it any attention.

Evans, the navigator, started his mayday calls. Apparently there was no response. He said, "Sir, we are just getting static on the radio."

"Fine, Evans, just put it on the repeater and see if you can get anything on the satellite."

"Sir, the closest suitable airstrip in French Polynesia is on Fangataufa Island, which is uninhabited. But 500 miles closer is the Pitcairn Group. Pitcairn Island itself has no airstrip big enough to land on, but Henderson Island does—although it is currently uninhabited. We are currently about 1200 miles away. We should have enough fuel."

"Let me see the chart." He turned the controls over to his copilot and got up and stretched. "That looks good. Henderson is a high island, not just an atoll, so there should be water if we are stuck there for a while.

"Stuck?" was Karen's question.

"Yes ma'am, it doesn't get much more remote than this—unless you are on the South Pole. But even there you can get a Scotch. As I recall, Pitcairn itself only gets a supply ship once a month. The beer lasts about three weeks, someone once told me.

"Henderson has an abandoned weather station, so it won't be a desert island—but close to it. We'll be lucky to find it if the engines hold out."

The submarine cruised at periscope depth before it came into the iceberg field. The sonar officer heard it, but there was no time for evasive maneuvers. In fact, they hit a badly eroded iceberg that looked more like Swiss cheese than anything else—it had floated in warmer subtropical water too long. But they hit it squarely in the middle and the impact crumpled the sub's nose, and then tore huge holes in the left side of boat like a can opener, peeled it open and turned it on its side as it exited the ice on the other side.

The sound of ripping steel and metal parts and scraping ice deafened the few who lived long enough to hear it. A handful of the crew who were fortunate enough to be in the mess hall, galley, and infirmary were flushed out into the ocean as the sub spiraled over and then flung them adrift. The out-rushing air carried many to the surface, while the incoming water quickly filled enough of the sub's compartments to sink her quickly. Within a matter of minutes the sub went to the bottom, and she took her secrets and most of the crew with her.

Abe's head hurt and he could feel the large gash in the side of his left arm where he brushed against the side of the gaping hole of the sub. It was early morning, the sun not yet up, but there was enough light for him to see a field of debris and yet no sign of any icebergs. He was, however, in a cold pocket of water and shivered with cold. He wore shorts, as was his custom aboard the sub, and his feet were bare. He couldn't remember if he had worn sneakers or not. He must have hit his head on something because he was groggy and dazed. Something large floated into his field of view—a small Igloo cooler, and he swam for it. It was partly full of ice, which he carefully emptied and then he partly climbed up onto it. The ice cubes continued to follow him, but he kicked away for a few minutes. At the same time he seemed to find himself in generally warmer water. It was a relief at one level, and yet at another level the numbness left him and his body began to hurt in more places. Then he passed out.

Some inner strength kept him glued to the ice chest and the cramps in his arm muscles that got his conscious attention and brought him back to awareness an hour or so later. The sun was well up over the horizon and he looked around himself to see if there were any other survivors or anything better to hold onto. He saw nothing—he was all by himself in one of the most remote parts of the world. Sharks would find him before anyone could rescue him.

Abe wrestled the ice chest over on its side and popped the lid open and let out about half of the air and then turned it over on its side. It was much easier this way to manage it and less stress on his arms. He relaxed a bit and then called to *Ogun*, but there was no answer. He really was gone. And now Abe would drown and die as had all his fellow and sister EPG* co-conspirators. But at least they accomplished their mission... Abe had not slept well that night after his alter ego had bid him farewell. He ruminated all night about how he had been suckered by what he began to suspect was either some sort of pan-dimensional entity or a deeper kind of delusion than he had suspected. He had just taken for granted that he was schizophrenic. But there were times he had wondered if there were something else wrong with him. Now he was bone tired. This time he drifted off into sleep.

By midday, Abe came awake again, but felt his hunger, dehydration, and the strong tropical sun beat down on his head, neck, and shoulders. He could already feel sunburn. He tried to pull his t-shirt up over his head, but was too exhausted to do much more than simply stay afloat.

A few hours later, he heard voices and suspected that he was delirious. At first he thought it was *Ogun* talking to him, but the voice was not his—it was a woman's. It was Angel's voice he was sure of it! She had survived the iceberg! Then he remembered that she had died on the continent and started to cry in despair. Then he heard the voice again, this time accompanied by a deeper male voice. He heard a splash. He felt arms around him and the sensation of being lifted out of the water. But he did not want to let go of his ice chest. Then he fainted again.

He tried to pry open his swollen eyes and they came open bit by bit. A face came into focus and he saw a very tanned woman in her early 50s looking down at him.

"Where am I?" he asked hoarsely.

"Welcome to the *Mana Kai* out of Honolulu. You are somewhere near Pitcairn." She looked down at him in concern.

"How did you get out here?" She looked puzzled and he thought long and hard about how to answer her, but just shrugged and closed his eyes. After a minute, he heard her leave and he tried to open his eyes again, but couldn't. He slept again.

The ancient Herc labored, one could feel it as the two engines pulled the craft ahead. Engine number two gave out after an hour or so and the airplane still leaked oil. All free hands piled boxes, benches, tools, and miscellaneous items in the rear of the plane to dump overboard. The plane was now barely 1000 feet above the water and the captain ordered them to find anything that wasn't bolted down to dump to lighten the plane. They made a good-sized pile when the copilot came back and ordered everyone forward in the cargo hold while he opened the rear ramp. In less than a second, the pile vanished out the rear of the aircraft. The engines ceased to labor as hard and the plane climbed a bit. They followed the copilot back up and into the cockpit.

"That's much better," said the pilot who tapped on the altimeter. "What does the GPS give us on altitude?"

"We're at 1500 feet and climbing. Speed has increased to, ah, about 300 mph now... 310... 325."

"Okay, great."

"I'm afraid that I have more bad news. We got the satellite radio back for a while and were informed that much of the US fleet has been destroyed. Washington D.C., too..." He gritted his teeth and shook his head.

"How could a bunch of tree-huggers do this? Where did they get more nukes?" He asked no one in particular.

Karen and Pete just looked at each other, stunned, and the color drained from their faces.

"The other bad news is that we may be on our own for a while. Doesn't look like we will be high on anyone's list of priorities for a rescue."

Worse was the suggestion that an island landing was not the most probable outcome of their situation. No one explained why, but the answer became obvious enough as the plane struggled to fly on two engines. Roughly six hours later, jacked up on coffee and nerves, they were a couple of hundred miles from Henderson Island. The engines labored hard again, and they watched the oil and fuel gauges creep towards empty. They were getting close to their goal, too, but the universe seemed to care little for their fate.

They stayed in the cockpit as long as they could, but the Marine pilot convinced them that in a water landing—he wouldn't call it a crash—their best chances of survival were to ride it out in the hammocks in the hold. The hold doors would be locked open and they would be able to make their way out the doors. At least that was the theory. No one was happy. They donned bright orange life preservers and a couple of life rafts were lying ready near the rear hold door. All they had to do was grab them on the way out—in theory.

The aircraft was now barely fifty feet above the waves. In the hold they could smell the salt in the air and heard the wind whistle through the open cargo bay doors. Pete helped Karen into her webbing. They stayed close to each other and before any parting words left his lips, she reached out and put her hands on his head and pulled him down to her. She opened her mouth to his and lingered on the kiss for half a minute. She was scared, but the tears that came from her eyes were happy ones. She didn't think they would make it, he could tell.

"We will be okay," he tried to reassure her. "And thanks for kidnapping me." He smiled at her in spite of the situation.

Karen replied with a mixture of sob and laugh. "This has been one hell of a ride."

He grinned back at her and made his way to his own hammock.

The captain's voice could barely be heard through the sound of wind and waves. "Prepare for forcing landing in about a minute. Ready for throttle up and impact."

The next few dozen seconds seemed to drag on for much longer than a minute—time seemed to stand still and Karen glanced back and forth between the water through the ramp and Pete, who had wrapped his arms around himself. It occurred to Karen that that was a good idea and was about to move to her own fetal position when she felt a bone-wrenching shudder and was flung against the wall.

She vaguely heard the sound of tearing metal and a small explosion, but the wrenching pain in her ribs dimmed it. It felt like she had broken a couple more, on her right side this time. She could hardly move her arms. She knew the hold of the plane was still intact, but saw light stream in above from where the stairs used to be. Water rushed in from all around and she struggled to get free. Suddenly she felt hands pushing on her and saw Pete struggle with her webbing. She saw the flash of a knife as she pitched forward into the water. It was cold.

She felt a current tug at her and suck her down to the steel decking of the hold, but also an insistent pressure to the side—it could only be Pete who had not given up on her yet. She struggled to stay conscious and to hold her breath, but more tugging set off excruciating pain in her chest and she sucked involuntarily and got a lungful of water. She sputtered and sensed that she was doomed. She now was paralyzed and could not move a muscle.

She knew that she was dying because a tunnel of light formed in the distance and she heard the song of angels, actually they sounded more like whale songs. And the light suddenly became bright and painful. She broke the surface and Pete was next to her and then yanking her hard behind—she could feel him kick with his feet and she tried to move her own feet and kick to dog paddle. Successfully. She would have laughed with relief except she knew it would hurt too much. She sputtered and coughed up water instead. And then she could not stop coughing even though with each cough she felt like she would break another rib.

Pete acknowledged her with a whoop and a holler. He kept pulling her, though, and she tried to tell him to stop. Her words would not come out except as choking sounds. Then she began to hear a loud gurgling and sucking sound behind them. It dawned on her that the airplane was sinking and that Pete was trying hard to get them as far away as possible. She kicked as best she could, and then passed out.

The next thing she remembered was another wrench to her body and she screamed in pain. She was cold and wet, but the discomfort seemed to pass. An eon or so later—it seemed—she awoke to a bright yellow light that surrounded her. She looked over to see Pete prone next to her. He was still in a life vest, but she wasn't, she was wrapped in a space blanket. She coughed hard and then fell into a troubled sleep, but was comforted that they were somehow alive in a rubber life raft.

Dear Betsy,

Sister, what a day! Who would have thought that the Great Southern Ocean could be so vast and yet so busy! Mana Kai is now crowded and I have been so busy today, I am ready for a vacation! Even though I wrote you earlier, I thought I'd better jot this all down now—I may not have much time to sit down and capture it.

It started after breakfast. Brad wiped down the PVC panels, as they seemed more grimy than usual from salt spray, made sure the batteries were fully charged, and then went below deck to take a nap. He left the BBC on for me to listen to. Somehow, we have drifted further south and east than we should have and Brad has made a course correction. He thinks that there must be some major current changes—I think I've already noted that—what with all the icebergs and cold water we've seen in the last few days. Anyway, we're almost due south of Henderson and we need to bear northwest now to get to Pitcairn. Good thing we're in no hurry.

So I felt a bit drowsy with the mid-morning sun on my back and a pleasant, cool southerly breeze in the sails. The sky looks very mean to the south, but deep blue to the north with some bright white clouds on the horizon. Light chop. It was dreamy.

The news droned on about the volcanic eruptions in Antarctica and the search for EPG* terrorists back in the states and in the Pacific. That caught my attention. But, being out in the middle of nowhere, I had to laugh! What were our chances to bump into anyone out here? I thought that was particularly amusing and yet icebergs made me realize that "everything is connected."

I don't know what made me turn around, maybe a slight hesitation of the boat in the water, a change in the lighting... There was a huge swell coming up on us. It was huge, probably fifty or sixty feet from trough to peak. It was a large flat wave, so it didn't worry me except for the fact that I knew that a wave that large out here would be truly monstrous on land. The math of it staggered my imagination. Unless we were over a seamount, that wave would be hundreds of feet high on land. I just couldn't wrap my brain around it.

Then a good ten minutes later, there was another one, this time even taller. This next one did scare me a bit, because it was tall enough to cause Mana Kai to slide down it as it receded. That was apparently enough to wake Brad, because he came out to see the next one—this one not quite so tall. He looked at me with his "are you okay?" look and I just nodded, being in a bit shock. He ducked down to the galley—I assumed to get on the radio. He reported back a few minutes later that all he got was static...

Brad came back with a fresh cup of coffee, bless his heart, and we talked for a while about the southern exposure ports around the central Pacific that could potentially get slammed with such a huge wave. I think we both realized that much of central Oahu and Maui were at risk as well as the southern sides of all the islands of our home state, although neither of us would come out with it. It was one thing to think about ports that were typically vulnerable to the average-sized tsunami, but super tsunamis could wipe out whole island nations. Tuvalu, Kiribati, and the Marshall Islands, for example, would be wiped clean by a hundred-foot wave, let alone a thousand foot wave. It was inconceivable.

Then the whales distracted us.

One of the reasons Brad initially invested in an ocean-worthy sailing boat was to follow the whales from Hawai`i to their summer calving grounds in Alaska. While we only made that trip once, it was the realization of a dream for him and he invested in some hydrophones that we still have, although have not used on this trip—since we haven't seen any whales... But, today we were all of a sudden surrounded. I dropped the sails and set the drift anchor, while Brad scrambled below, fished out his equipment, attached the microphones to small aluminum booms that attach to the bow, and was soon playing whale songs. At first, we just listened through headphones jacked into the tape deck.

They weren't breaching, but we could see the spray from blowholes—maybe six large adults. Brad identified them as southern right whales from the songs they were singing. They were magical and immediately took our minds off the tsunamis. The only trouble

379

was that this was way too far north for this species of whale; Brad went down to check his manuals. He returned with a small set of speakers so we could listen without headphones.

When the group had passed well to the north of us, another group swam by us to the east. They seemed like they were in no hurry, they just meandered along, maybe playing—although, again, no breaching. We listened, enthralled for a half hour or more. We drifted and had enough wind on the boat to keep us headed north. Then we heard the most unreal sounds of all, a clashing of cymbals and drumbeats that grew louder and louder. It was mesmerizing, but seemed a violation of the whale's song. Then we could hear the thrashing of a propeller in the hydrophone's pickup. Then it got really quiet. But before Brad shut off the recorder, there came the most horrible sound. It sounded like the tearing of metal, like the sound of nails on a chalkboard that continued for minutes before it stopped. Brad and I just stared at each other. It could only mean one thing. After it stopped, Brad brought up a pair of binoculars and he started to scan the horizon. Meantime I hoisted the sails, and he helped me set the rigging.

What appeared to be clouds to the north were not at all, but more icebergs. And they were not tall, now getting closer as we were under sail again. We saw a cloud of smoke rising, too, but it was indistinct and we couldn't see exactly where it had come from in the field of ice. As we neared, we could see that they were spread out maybe a mile or so ahead of us, so Brad went to the helm and we made our way around the field slowly, and kept our distance, staying at least a couple thousand feet from the ice. Unlike the previous 'bergs we had seen, these were pretty worn and weathered. They all looked short and spiky and clustered around one large 'berg in the middle, that was maybe fifty feet tall, and it actively disintegrated before our eyes. It was probably the central 'berg that something had hit; but, neither of us saw any evidence of a ship or debris. We scanned the edges of the ice for paint or oil. Nothing.

Then as we came around on the other side, the leeward side of the ice field, there was a huge oil slick and some scattered debris. Brad wanted to power up the diesels and get in closer, but I wouldn't let him. We lingered, drifting along the leading edge of the ice for probably another hour, well past noon. We both started to get hungry, so I urged Brad to move us away from the ice—in exchange for a hot meal. I think we were both very nervous so close to that much ice with *the potential for tsunami waves. There were just too many uncertainties… In any case, we got underway again and I heated up some onion soup and made grilled cheese sandwiches with bread left over from yesterday.*

It was shortly after lunch that I went back up on deck and spent some time with the binoculars. By this time, we might have been ten miles north of the iceberg field and I saw something well behind us bobbing up and down in the water. It seemed to move, so I had Brad start the engines and swing back for a look. Good thing I did, because it was a survivor.

The man was bleeding pretty badly from a cut on the head, but we pulled him out of the water, up into the boat, got him out of his torn and wet clothes—all he had on was shorts and a t-shirt—and put some butterfly stitches on his gash and got him into the spare room below. He was obviously in shock, so I covered him up and got the room as warm as I could and kept an eye on him.

I think he's American or Canadian, from the t-shirt, from a Minneapolis brewpub. He's probably in his late 50s early 60s, but there was no identification on him. He has a silver ring with dolphins on it and a small gold-stud earring, but no other obvious identifiers. He is obviously not a mechanic or crew person—his hands have no calluses.

Then things got even more interesting. The shipwreck survivor was looking better. His skin color was much improved and he even opened his eyes for a few seconds. But, Brad called to me, so I went up on deck—it was late in the afternoon by then. The sky turned a sickly color of gray in the south, like the dark skies in the Midwest before a thunderstorm, dark and brooding, rather atypical for this latitude. Brad reported nothing on the radar, so I didn't think much about it.

Brad was behind the wheel and the sails were full—we'd had a great day of steady wind and had made good headway toward Pitcairn since we pulled our guest out of the water. He pointed ahead. Straight ahead of us was a yellow object. It was hard to tell what it was so far away, especially as the light was fading early. The seas picked up and the swells were 3-4 feet out of the southwest, so the late afternoon sun was reflected at times off the waves in that direction. Polarized sunglasses didn't even help. Whatever it was, we were closing on it. It grew larger and it became obvious that it was a life raft. It took about an hour to finally come up beside it—it was

381

catching the wind pretty good, so it was probably empty. At least that was what Brad said, until a man's head popped up from underneath the cowling.

He yelped in surprise.

"Yo!" I yelled, "Can we be of assistance?" The man looked like he was in shock, but tears started to stream down his face. I gathered that was a "yes."

I'll have to write more of the story later, because, as I said, we have a boat full of people now.

"Quickly!" said Marge "Is there a cleat close to you?" The man looked back at her blankly.

"Do you speak English?"

"Yes, yes. What's a cleat?"

"I will throw you a rope," Marge walked down the length of the *Mana Kai* as the raft came along side, "Look for a mooring, a tie-down, for the line. Understand?"

The man nodded. "Got it."

Marge went ahead and tossed the rope and the man in the raft caught it deftly, and then disappeared beneath the yellow cowling that covered the raft. Marge kept track of the raft and let out some slack as she walked toward the stern, and threaded the rope over guide wires until she was at the stern and then tied the rope off near the end to a cleat. She fed out the rope until there was no slack left. *Mana Kai* was making a good 12 knots, so the rope pulled taut and made a twang. The man did not come back up, but the rope held.

"Jesus," Marge said under her breath. Brad watched carefully and now spoke softly to her, "You okay? Want me to come about?"

She looked back up at him, smiled, and shook her head. She turned back quickly to keep an eye on the raft. All of a sudden, it seemed like a good idea to stay underway and not lose ground—so to speak. They had injured to get to shore.

The man came up but did not look happy. He yelled a bit too loud, "We're tied down."

Marge yelled back, "Don't panic, hold tight. I will reel you in, but just hold on to that line for security. Ready?"

"I think so."

"Fine. Just hang on." In a matter of a minute, Marge had pulled the rope through another cleat on the back of the *Mana Kai* and had the man within arm's reach. She reached out her hand.

"Come on aboard."

The man looked concerned. "Sorry, not yet. There is someone else in here who is pretty badly hurt."

"I'm a nurse. You come aboard and then I'll get a look at her."

The man looked confused, uncertain, but did as he was told.

He pulled himself onto the boat with her help and said, "I'm Pete."

"Marge. The captain, there, is Brad."

The man nodded at Brad but kept his eyes on the raft.

"Let's tie off another rope, just to be extra safe." She quickly tied down another rope, and then stepped down into the raft. There was a woman lying there. She shifted her attention to the cleat inside the raft, tied the second rope down and kneeled down. She looked to be in worse shape than the older fellow they picked up earlier, but her eyes opened.

"Can you move?" She wasn't sure what to ask first.

Her reply was faint but audible, "Yes, I think so. Broken ribs..." She really looked horrible, but somehow managed to smile. "Messed up pretty bad... sorry."

"Okay," said Marge. "Stay put, we'll get you on the *Mana Kai* ASAP."

They ended up coming about to get the raft alongside, and used a hoist to get Karen into the boat. Brad used a sling seat that was used to work on the mast to hoist the injured woman aboard. It took about an hour and by the time they were finished, it was dark. The raft was tied up to the stern, the anchor was stowed, the injured woman bedded down and the young man with her into a change of clothes before Marge had time to start on dinner.

Marge put Pete and Karen in the stateroom, their master bedroom. She never asked if they were a couple, but she made that assumption based on seeing them interact in the first few minutes together. Neither objected when she pulled out clothes for them and had them settle in. Marge made it clear to everyone that she would first attend to Karen, to get her cleaned up and dried off, and to wrap her ribs. She had Brad secure the raft and scrape together some food. She could tell that Brad had many questions for the two young people. While getting the woman aboard, they had found out that Karen and Pete were sole survivors of a plane crash, that they were bound for Tahiti out of McMurdo and had seen some of the eruption, but that they were not acquainted with the other survivor. They got the essential facts, but it was clear that they had not actually been in the raft very long, maybe a few hours.

Karen let Pete and Marge remove her long pants and into some baggy shorts of Marge's—she was somewhat larger than the younger woman—and Marge produced some compresses and she insisted the woman take some codeine. The young woman resisted, but the pain obviously got the better of her, and she relented. Marge had control of the situation and wrapped her professionally. The young woman was obviously exhausted and by the time Marge pulled out clothes for Pete, and looked back in on her, Karen was sound asleep. Meantime, she demonstrated to Pete how the shower worked and told him to lie down, too, if he needed.

She made her way out into the galley quietly, and turned on the radio.

"BBC reporter Shane McWilliams filed this report from Boulder within the last few hours:

"This is Shane McWilliams in Boulder, not far from the underground command center beneath Thunder Mountain, the headquarters of the US Space Command, where the former vice president was sworn in a few hours ago as the acting president.

"At 3:05 P.M. today President Clark was confirmed dead and the vice president took the oath of office as President of the United States of America. The new president immediately declared a State of Emergency and ordered the suspension of civil law, placing the US and its territories under Martial Law and placed the National Guard under the control of nine regional military commanders.

"He confirmed the destruction of the nation's capital and much of its top civilian and military leadership. He also acknowledged the loss of the six aircraft carriers and warned that the enemies of the United States should not take advantage of the situation. He insisted that the US was prepared to respond in kind to any foreign intervention into its affairs.

"He then appealed for calm and for people to stay indoors and off the streets. He closed the commodities, bond, and stock markets for an additional week and asked the nation for its prayers.

"We learned just a few minutes ago from administration sources that the vice president was quickly flown out of Washington and here to Colorado when the world was blanketed with the broadcast of 1950s science fiction movie, *When the Earth Stood Still*. Washington, D.C. and much of the US fleet were destroyed simultaneously at the conclusion of the movie. The administration continues to believe that the alien invasion scenario is a hoax and continues to round up supporters of EPG*-related organizations and others from so-called deep green organizations. The United States has also severed diplomatic ties with the German government, which is a coalition of Social Democrats and Greens.

"This is Shane McWilliams in Boulder."

"Thank you, Shane, and now, the headlines.

"The world media were pre-empted for two hours earlier today for the rebroadcast of a 1950s science fiction movie accompanied by an ultimatum that all weapons of mass destruction be destroyed. While there was initially widespread belief that this was a hoax, the cities of Washington D.C., London, Brasilia, Moscow, Beijing, and Islamabad all appear to have been destroyed.

"Meantime, governments of France, Israel, and India have all announced their intentions to destroy all their weapons of mass destruction. Their capitals have not been damaged.

"Eight nuclear aircraft carriers, one British, one Russian, and six American have been reported destroyed according to a NATO spokesperson in Brussels.

"The estimates of civilian casualties have been put at around six million with an additional ten million injured. Relief efforts are now underway and a special session of the UN has been called for tomorrow.

"Eruptions of at least a dozen major volcanoes continue in Antarctica and tsunami warnings continue to be issued throughout the Indian and Pacific Oceans. Preliminary reports indicate that massive waves have already reached as far as the equator. More on this development in the next hour.

"This is BBC. We will be back after a time check."

Marge and Brad looked at each other, ashen-faced, and then Brad looked back down at the nautical charts he spread out on the table. Marge went back to stir a pot on the stove. She looked up and saw Pete standing near the cabin door.

"My dear, how are you? Please come, sit down at the table." Pete followed her directions.

"I am fine, and thankfully Karen is sleeping peacefully. Thank you so much. I really think she needed some drugs." He quickly looked up at his hosts. "What I mean is that she has—we have all—

been through a lot in the past week and I don't think she's had more than eight solid hours of sleep in the last four days."

"Wow," said Brad, "I gather you two were in the thick of things in Antarctica."

Pete pondered that and wondered how much he should or could say. He decided it probably didn't matter much now. So he plunged ahead.

"Yeah, I am—was—a television reporter from Phoenix and I am… Well, I guess, you could say that I was on special assignment, sort of embedded with the FBI and the NEST team looking for the terrorists." He shook his head and then surveyed the cabin.

"Looks like it may take a while to get home…"

Brad whistled. "So… yeah… Karen is FBI?

"Yes sir, technically Special Agent Karen St. Cloud. She is… was the lead agent in charge of the whole Task Force tracking down the EPG*… Survived an attack on Larsen Ice… we both narrowly escaped the second nuclear explosion—that's when she broke her rib—and then we were rescued, flew across half of Antarctica, barely missed the eruption of Mt. Erebus and the so-called Omega Event… We were on our way to French Polynesia to continue the search for the EPG* hideaway, but the plane was badly damaged by volcanic debris and we crashed. So here we are…"

"My god," said Marge. "So, you have been through a lot more than just a plane crash in the ocean. What were the eruptions like?"

Pete sucked on his lip thinking of the video footage that was now on the bottom of the Pacific. "They were… they were… like nothing I have ever seen or experienced… That was so incredible; it is hard to put words to it, scary, but awesome. The raw power of nature, and the shear desolation of Antarctica… It was altogether something you can only experience, hardly describe." He laughed. "Not much of a journalist, am I?"

Marge patted him on the shoulder. "You need to be fed, first, in any case. Maybe that will help."

"Brad, can we get the table cleared?"

He cleared off the table and Marge fed them soup and reheated bread.

Dear Betsy,
What a night! I don't think any of us got much sleep, except for the mysterious castaway and the young FBI agent. We found out a

bit more about Pete and Karen, but were overwhelmed by the reports that came in on the shortwave. The news was shocking, from all across the Pacific—it has turned our world upside down... First came the reports from New Zealand and then Fiji. Christchurch and all of the low-lying areas of the windward coast of the South Island were wiped out—literally swept clean by monster waves so tall that they traveled as much as twenty miles inland in some places. A glancing blow hit Wellington, but still hundreds were killed there by the waves.

Then reports came in from Fiji. The whole south side of Viti Levu and Vanua Levu were inundated and Suva was completely flattened. Reports from Tonga were better, as efforts were made to get people to high ground. Very worrying is actually the lack of news from French Polynesia, the Cook Islands, and the coral atoll groups: Tuvalu, Kiribati, and Tokelau. There is literally no news coming from those islands; they may be the hardest hit.

The Hawaiian chain had a few hours of warning and Japan and the US mainland a few hours more than that. But, we have not yet heard what happened, which is extremely frustrating.

As the descriptions of the chaos and carnage came in, Brad and I took turns at the helm. The winds picked up and so did the chop. The winds were steady out of the southeast and so we continued to make our way toward Pitcairn. We both experienced more extremely large sets of swells. They were actually quite frightening, and I am only glad that we experienced them on the open ocean. They ranged somewhere between thirty and fifty feet although it was hard to really tell in the dark. But they were clearly tsunamis and Brad continued to radio them to the US Coast Guard although it is doubtful the transmissions went through.

The shortwave radio reception got poorer over the course of the night. The static grew worse, as did lightning in the southern sky. By the wee hours there was almost constant flickering far to the south, and it filled the horizon. It would have been an interesting light show except that it was ominous and threatening. Once while I was in the galley brewing coffee after relieving Brad, both Karen and Pete came out of the stateroom. She looked horrible, but Pete helped her get comfortable at the table and we fed her some soup. She perked up noticeably and quickly, so I relaxed a little. She let me give her another dose of painkiller and she managed to stay awake listening to BBC come in and out of the static.

I decided to go check on our other castaway and asked Pete to *give me a hand to take in some surgical dressing, tea and crackers. He opened his eyes as we entered and he feebly raised himself up on his elbows. That was when I heard the clatter of the tea set hit the deck. I looked around in shock to see Pete standing and staring at the man. The pot hadn't broken, but there was hot tea and crackers scattered on the deck—but he was oblivious: he never took his eyes off the man.*

"You're Abe Miller, aren't you?"

The man nodded and then seemed to collapse back into the bed. Karen was in the doorway by now staring at him. Pete was back soon with a hand towel and cleaned up the mess he made.

I asked Miller how he felt; he nodded and said "better." I asked if he was hungry and he shook his head. I looked at his shoulder dressing and the bleeding had stopped, so I decided to wait until morning to change the dressing. He refused help to the head and said he'd get there when he needed it.

I fetched a bottle of water that I left by the side of his bed, but closed the door and looked expectantly at the young man and woman to get to the bottom of the mystery. That is when I got the surprise of my life! Pete explained it.

"He is the one we've been after, the mastermind behind the EPG* plot to destroy the world, Dr. Abraham Miller."

I wondered aloud how it was possible that he was here on the Mana Kai, and Karen said something like, "Indeed, that is what I'd like to know, too." They explained to me how Miller had gone missing for a few years, underground, and that he'd been traced to South America and then Antarctica. He left the southern continent, on either a boat or submarine—they were eager to find out. Chip asked if the door to his stateroom could be locked, but then, turned to Karen. They argued back and forth for a while about what kind of threat he posed, and they reasoned that since he didn't know who Karen was—for the moment—and had nowhere to go, he wouldn't pose much of a threat.

Tomorrow will be a day of reckoning. I feel it with every fiber of my body.

The day began with a gloomy dawn—there was no sunrise. It was overcast, steel gray from horizon to horizon. There were no low clouds discernable, only a widespread stratospheric smear of cobalt. It seemed to get darker after the official hour of dawn. The seas were calmer and there had not been any more sets of tsunamis through the night. At dawn, Brad was at the helm and when Marge poked her head up out of the galley, he greeted her cheerfully in spite of the murk and told her that Pitcairn was on the horizon.

"Breakfast sound good?" She responded, with a smile.

"You betcha! But some fresh coffee would be even better. I'll put the tiller on autopilot and join you."

Marge's head disappeared and Brad attended to the machine. He got the rudder autopilot engaged and pointed to a heading slightly east of the island promontory, St. Paul's Point, figuring they were a good four hours from landfall at Botany Bay outside of Adamstown.

As he dropped down into the cabin, he smelled the brewed coffee and watched their young guests emerge from the stateroom.

"Good morning. *Bula bula!*"

Karen looked at him quizzically.

"Fijian for hello," he translated.

"*Bula bula*, to you, sir," she replied and smiled. Brad was somewhat taken aback by her transformation with some makeup on and her hair pulled back. She was a strikingly attractive woman. Pete came up behind her and looked better, too.

"Good morning. We are close to Pitcairn?"

"Yes we are. I'd say we're still half a day away and I'll radio the harbormaster after breakfast."

"They have a harbormaster?"

"Yeah, he is their meteorologist, postmaster, and harbormaster all rolled into one. He has a bit of a love affair with the bottle and is rarely awake this early—so we've been told. This is our first trip here."

A new voice said, "You must be referring to Brian Christian, quite a sot, that one. Good morning, everyone."

Karen and Pete were all the way in the galley and turned to stare at the newcomer. Marge was the first to answer.

"Good morning, Dr. Miller, isn't it?"

Abe looked the most transformed of them all, and while his shoulder was bandaged, he fit well into a pair of Brad's trousers and a tank top. His hair was brushed back and he actually had a sparkle in his eyes.

"Ah, yes. Abraham Miller—but you may call me Abe. And you know me, how?"

All eyes turned to Karen.

"Professor Miller, you are under arrest for murder and crimes against humanity." The statement sounded out of place and overly melodramatic...

"I doubt you have the jurisdiction out here, young woman. Who are you?"

"Special Agent Karen St. Cloud, FBI. Anything you say can be used against you in a court of law..."

"Spare me the Miranda, Special Agent." He held out his arms, as if to be handcuffed.

Karen's face reddened and she shook her head.

"Undoubtedly, you are right about the lack of need for a Miranda, but what you may not know is that jurisdiction is moot since you have already been indicted by the International Criminal Court and are a subject of two Security Council resolutions. You are the most wanted man in all of human history. I hope you are proud of yourself." Her sarcasm came out like venom.

Abe dropped his hands and just stood still.

"As ship's captain, I arrest you, too," added Brad, "you miserable bastard."

Miller looked glum and sad all of a sudden. "You are both probably right, I submit. I expect I have a lot to answer for... and a bit to say..." He paused.

"Does the prisoner get coffee?" He smiled at Marge. In spite of herself, she liked the man's smile.

"Sit down, Dr. Miller. There is enough coffee for everyone." Miller sat down carefully, while the others—except for Marge— glared at him.

Abe accepted his cup of coffee gratefully and then turned to Brad.

"Permission to go topside, captain?" Brad looked slightly surprised and looked the man up and down. They looked to be about the same age, height, and build. Brad thought for a moment.

"Sure, permission granted. Stay clear of the wheel." He looked at Karen for a brief moment for any disagreement. At first her face was firm and her lips were drawn into a thin line, then she shook her head, and Abe took his coffee cup topside.

Marge's simple breakfast was served and the group of four ate in silence. The gloom from outside seemed to seep into the cabin and a pall fell over their meal and private thoughts.

Brad was soon on the radio calling Harbormaster Christian in Adamstown. The response was not what he'd expected.

"*Mana Kai*, permission to lay anchor in Botany Bay is denied. Over."

"Mr. Christian, may I ask why? Over."

"*Mana Kai*, the Pitcairn government has declared a state of emergency and no foreign flag vessels are allowed anchorage until further notice. Over."

"But we need fresh water and provisions," complained Brad. "Over."

"Sorry *Mana Kai*, but our regular monthly supply ship was destroyed yesterday en route from Rarotonga. The harbor has mostly been destroyed as well. I am sure you can understand our situation. Any attempt to set anchor in Pitcairn territory will be considered a hostile action. Police have instructions to shoot on sight. Out." Brad looked lost.

"What next, then?" asked Marge.

"Well, we have enough fresh water for a week or two with five aboard... Maybe longer if we keep the distiller running. You know better than me what the food situation is... We definitely need to stay away from the southern side of any islands for now, given the tsunami threat... French Polynesia is closest, but they may be even less welcoming than the Pitcairners. I'll dig out the charts."

Karen spoke up. "We were headed to the next island over in the Pitcairn group, called Henderson Island. Do you know it? It has an abandoned airstrip—that's about all I know..."

"The trouble is that is even further away from civilization. The southern end of the Tuamotu Archipelago is a few days to the west. A couple of the Gambier Islands are inhabited... The trouble is that those are low islands and have probably been scoured by tidal waves. Jesus Christ."

Abe slowly descended into the cabin. All eyes followed him come down and give his cup to Marge.

"Can I offer you some eggs?"

"No, I am not hungry. Thank you."

"More coffee?"

"Okay, thanks." And she refilled his cup.

Brad was spreading out maps of French Polynesia. "The northern Tuamotu's are all high islands, but we probably should head west to the Society group which are all inhabited—that's Tahiti and Bora Bora—you'll have heard of those?"

"We have a base on Ducie Island," Abe said quietly. "That's where we were headed before the submarine hit the iceberg."

They all stared at him again, except for Marge.

"Ducie... Ducie... That's in the Pitcairn group?" asked Brad.

"It's the easternmost island in the group. Uninhabited—well it was until a few years ago when we established our refuge there. Nobody's there now, but there is plenty of fresh water and supplies and fuel. It has a small protected bay on the north side."

"Do you want us to go there?" Karen asked suspiciously for some reason.

He looked at her sharply. "I don't really care at this point. My friends and extended family are now all dead. Going back there would be very sad for me, personally. It would be like a prison." He really looked sad and miserable, and then shook his head as though to clear it, and went back up the steps toward the deck. He turned and spoke.

"For the short term, Ducie Island would be a safe haven and a place to survive, but that's your choice. At this point it really is at the end of the world." He continued topside.

Marge spoke next. "We're technically still on vacation, so it doesn't really matter where we go. Our beach house in Kahala is probably in ruins... I tend to think we may be better off to ride out this storm here in the South Pacific."

Pete obviously agreed. "My main concern at this point is the yet unspoken possibility of nuclear winter and short term survival. I did an investigative report on survivalists in Arizona last year. What some of them had warned us about has happened. What EPG* has set in motion could really be cataclysmic and being in a remote location might not be bad. If they have stockpiles on Ducie, that's the place to go. Karen?"

"Well, my prisoner isn't going anywhere... Ducie is where my orders were taking us anyway. I would like to try and send a message to whoever is in charge of things, but that can wait until the crisis has abated somewhat." Pete looked at her funny. "It would be useful for the investigation to report on what was going on at Ducie.

"The other thing is our safety. Obviously, we'd be better off on high ground and under some kind of cover. Although I am still in some denial, EPG* did predict—as Pete points out—serious weather perturbations. We probably don't want to be out on the open ocean…" she looked carefully at their two hosts, "for the next few weeks anyway."

"But," she continued, "this is your boat, and we are at your mercy. I want to thank you, again, for fishing us out of the water and risking your own lives."

"You are quite welcome," said Brad, "and while as captain and co-owner of the boat, I cannot turn this into a democracy, we are happy to discuss all our options and consider your needs. We are obviously not on vacation anymore, with all due respect to my lovely wife. This could be a struggle for our very lives and I take this very seriously. I also fear that our home in Hawai`i probably has been destroyed. Most of our family is on the mainland and it obviously may be a while before things settle down and order is restored.

"I tend to think Ducie Island would be a wise choice for the short term. So, what are the pros and cons? Marge, could you pull out a piece of paper and start?"

She smiled at Karen and Pete and said, "Brad is such an engineer, eh?" She reached up into a cabinet behind her and pulled out a notepad and pencil.

"Well, we already have a few items in favor: high island protection, which implies a better source of fresh water and storm protection from hurricanes; a known supply of food, fuel, and water if we can believe the mass murderer…" She jotted those down. "And, also by implication, proximity."

"Karen, your turn."

"Well, now a couple of cons: I don't believe Miller—there may be EPG* members there. Another we mentioned before: it is one of the most remote places on earth."

Pete jumped in, "We are low on supplies, but is that a pro or con? Maybe the uncertainty is greater of finding what we need in the Tuamotu's… so, I guess that means 'greater certainty" goes in the plus column. If Miller is lying to us, we'll know fairly soon."

Brad interjected, "While it is a remote location, we are actually close to the major southern shipping lane.

Karen added, "Another uncertainty that has to go in the pro column is the possibility of nuclear winter. Sheltering on a remote island improves our chances of survival, particularly if there were provisions for ten times as many people—if it's true EPG* has been destroyed. We should press Miller on the point. So, write down 'nuclear winter.'"

"Got it. Anything else?"

"A corollary to the high island protection, is the reason— safety from more tsunamis, and I suspect there will be many more," said Pete.

"Why is that?" Marge wanted to know.

"I spent part of the week reading the research of a young graduate student in climatology who was kidnapped and killed along with the EPG* members in the other submarine—another story—but her research pointed to one assumption of Miller's that the West Antarctic ice shelf was anchored to a set of volcanic ridges and that a potential hazard existed due to the collapse of the ice and subsequent eruptions of those volcanoes, and a vicious-cycle of eruption and melting was possible—the potential for a global catastrophe.

"See, what she realized was that the ice shelves served as a blocking mechanism. The collective weight of the shelves held the mantle in place and prevented heat and magma from rising closer to the earth's surface. Thus, these initial eruptions will be nothing compared to what may happen after the mantle begins to rebound.

"The part of the scenario that the young researcher hadn't considered was the eventual melting of ice, not only the Ross and other oceanic ice sheets, but most of the rest of West Antarctica. What EPG* banked on, or rather hoped, is that the influx of fresh water will slow or stop altogether the deep ocean circulation resulting in a new ice age.

"How long this could take to unfold is speculation, but the odds are that even if they got it half right—and they seem to have planned things exactingly well—at least from a destructive point of view—the volcanic episode may have only just begun. Hey, who knows, there might be global implications, say for increased activity all across the Ring of Fire. Just being on the north side of the island might not be adequate protection from Aleutian Island earthquakes and subsequent tsunamis... Let's hope EPG* kept that in mind when they built their base on Ducie Island..."

The four were quiet for a minute, all of them deep in thought.

Marge interrupted the silence, "Any more pros and cons?"

"Well, to be fair, we are all far from home," Brad noted, "And the farther away we are from home, and the longer we wait, the longer away we'll be. So, that is a factor I'd include in the con side, but I have to admit I don't feel strongly about it.

"It sounds to me like there is a general consensus that we should make for Ducie, agreed?"

"The pros definitely outnumber the cons," reported Marge.

"Yes," voted Karen.

"Aye!" from Pete.

"Aye aye, captain," said Marge.

Brad asked, "Do either of you know how to sail?"

Pete shook his head, but Karen beamed and said, "Well, if sailing around Baie de Port-au-Prince as a kid counts. I even did some open ocean regattas off of Cape Cod when I was in college. You want some crew?" She looked eager.

"Yes, as a matter of fact, Marge and I are both pretty worn out and both of you could help.

"But given your condition and the drugs, I'd like Pete to work with you. Join me at the wheel in five minutes. We need to get you something for your feet, though. Marge?"

"Hmm, her feet are much smaller than mine, but I might have a pair of water shoes she could wear. That way at least she won't slip on the deck."

"She may need a windbreaker, too. Give me a few minutes here to plot a course," and he turned to pull out nautical charts that he spread out on the table.

"I think I'll keep an eye on my prisoner," said Karen, but without much enthusiasm, and gingerly went topside.

As she went up the steps to the fantail, she nearly banged her head on the doorframe as the boat canted slightly. She pulled her way up with both hands on the wooden railings and looked for Abe Miller but didn't see him on the fantail. Karen immediately noticed how dark and gray the sky was and the gray soot that covered the deck. She drew her finger down a couple of inches on the upper deck and saw that she left a streak of hardwood cleaned of soot.

She looked up to see Miller sitting cross-legged with his back up against the mast, facing the bow. She walked carefully along the side until they were even with each other and held up her fingers.

"I suppose this is your handiwork?" she asked as she stared hard into Miller's eyes.

"*Es cenisa...*" he replied and when Karen continued to look at him blankly, he explained, "...*cenisa*... the Spanish word for volcanic ash. I certainly won't take all the credit, but yes, it is from Antarctica." He looked away, back towards the south with a far-away look in his eyes.

"You may recall from your background reading on me that I lived in El Salvador as a kid. We lived under the ash of Volcán Salvador for a year, although this is much finer grain than that was... Sister, what a year! My dad hired locals to sweep off the roof so it wouldn't collapse from the weight of the stuff—like sand. The stinking *cenisa* was in everything—the air, the bread..." his voice trailed off.

Karen moved a few steps further, held on to a guy wire, and looked around. The ocean swells were a moderate 2-3 feet and she could see Isle Pitcairn on the left—to the port, she reminded herself. The island looked very small from this vantage, especially in the murky light. It was very dark to the south—almost pitch black—and there were strange bands of gray across the sky toward the north. Her curiosity got the best of her and she suspended her hostility for a few moments.

"What accounts for the cloud banding?" She looked back at Miller.

"Can't really say. They sure look funny, though. Almost like a black and white rainbow, maybe something to do with ice crystals and mixing in the upper atmosphere. But that is way beyond my area of expertise."

"Oh, and what would that be?" Karen shot back.

"What do you think? You are the expert on Abe Miller. You are my FBI profiler, right?"

"I am not a profiler," came Karen's retort; she was quiet for a few minutes and continued to observe the unusual cloud patterns.

"Or at least, I wasn't. I am an analyst, more recently an investigator. I did read some of your psych profiles, that is true."

Karen took another tack. "So what happened to the rest of your crew, to the submarine?"

Miller did not respond and he gazed over her shoulder with eyes slightly out of focus.

"You don't have to tell me—believe me there are better interrogators than I who will face you, ultimately."

Miller looked at her as if she was stupid. "You don't understand at all. I don't know what happened to either submarine. Neither should have sunk... I can't explain any of that to you."

"Or won't?" Karen chided.

"I suspect that we hit an iceberg yesterday. I was the only one to survive—as far as I know—but why that would be the case is beyond me. I know the sub went to the bottom and my ears are still ringing from the rending of the steel hull as the ice split her open. Believe me, it was not supposed to happen that way. Both submarine crews were supposed to deliver the planning and operational teams back here to Ducie to weather the coming storm."

Brad and Pete came up on the deck while Abe was talking. Brad asked, "What do you know about Gamelon music?"

Miller looked startled. "Why do you ask?"

"Just answer my question." He balled up his fists and looked ready to hit the man.

"Well... it is one of my favorite types of music and was the last music I heard before the sub went down. I played it over the PA for the crew yesterday."

"All right then. We heard it on the hydrophones sometime before we picked you up. That solves a mystery. Whale songs and Gamelon. It was eerie."

Karen asked, "What's a Gamelon?"

"It's a kind of Indonesian ensemble instrumental music. I'll have you listen to what we recorded later. Meantime, please come watch me take the autopilot off line and change our course?"

Karen nodded; glad to break away from her questions for Miller—the guy gave her the creeps.

AP-Australia
1740 GMT 25 January 2012
Headlines

The Russian Federation, China, and France jointly accused the US of climate warfare at a press conference in Geneva. The foreign ministers from those countries cited Pentagon documents that detail war-planning scenarios that involved the use of nuclear and other forms of high explosives in the upper atmosphere to affect weather changes. The Pentagon was blamed for developing "abrupt climate change" war games and for promoting seminars on the topic at the Army War College in recent years.

The French Prime Minister, Jean Marc Delore, put the blame for yesterday's brief nuclear exchange between China, the UK, Russia, and the US squarely at the feet of the US. The US, UK, and Chile were accused of conspiring to precipitate global cooling by destroying "territories of the common heritage of humankind" in Antarctica. The Russian foreign minister was asked to explain why the detonations in the US and Russia appeared to be simultaneous. He flatly denied that was the case and said that the detonations in Antarctica were clearly first and that the US was responsible—they were US military ordinance and that France and Russia were unconvinced by the "wild story" of extraterrestrials and blamed computer hackers in the US and India for the hoax. The CIA was blamed for inventing the EPG* story and the Russian Foreign Minister Ivanov claimed to have hard evidence of these allegations.

Anonymous sources inside the UN have made a fairly outrageous claim that all of the attacks had come from within those nations affected. While preliminary evidence pointed to a nuclear exchange, there was never any cross-border attack, according to a senior Secretariat official. The US flatly denied that the dozen or so nuclear assaults—mostly on naval targets—had come from its own arsenal, yet it had not accused either the Chinese or Russians for the attacks.

Both Chinese and Russian prime ministers said that while their governments had declared a 48-hour ceasefire, they were technically in a State of War with the US and had called for an Emergency Session of the UN General Assembly in Geneva to consider actions that would supersede the Security Council. They also appealed for relief efforts from non-aligned countries and the EU to help the survivors of Moscow and Novosibirsk.

The International Atomic Energy Agency (IAEA), also headquartered in Geneva, reported that much of the Northern Hemisphere was now encircled with a high-atmosphere radioactive cloud that resulted from approximately 25 nuclear explosions yesterday. This does not include the 10 explosions that occurred Monday in Antarctica that left a much smaller radioactive footprint. However, a subsequent series of volcanic eruptions may have spread the Antarctica fallout further north. High altitude reconnaissance aircraft from Australia were expected to return later today with samples from over the Southern Continent.

US officials seemed to be in a state of confusion and disarray after the national capital was leveled by a nuclear blast estimated to have been in the five-megaton range—a thermonuclear, hydrogen explosion. Neither Russia nor China claimed responsibility for that particular attack, and the US has not, yet, placed blame on either but appears to blame the EPG* for the whole mess. Nearly one million people are believed to have died directly from the blast and another two million were injured. A similar explosion occurred outside the Dallas-Fort Worth area, which Russia initially claimed was in retaliation for the destruction of their largest Asian city, Novosibirsk. The interim government now denies ever making that claim.

A provisional capital in Boulder is being organized, and the vice president was sworn in as president late last night en route to Boulder from Washington. Senior officials vowed to counter-attack "enemies of the homeland," but withheld any specific comments or accusations until they had more information. Given that the overwhelming majority of the Congress, the Supreme Court, and administration officials were in Washington in advance of the president's State of the Union message, there is a serious power and leadership vacuum in the US. Governors of California and New York and a few other large states were allegedly on their way to meet with the new president to decide a course of action. The stock markets are closed and trading of commodities and currencies have been suspended. Banks have been closed in the US for the rest of the week as well. Sporadic looting and riots are reported in a few metropolitan areas.

Reports continue to come in from around the Pacific Basin on tsunami damage. A summary from our reporters around the Asia-Pacific will be published to the web and wires at the top of the hour.

The *Mana Kai* pulled northeast of Isle Pitcairn and Brad put them on an eastern heading that would take them north of the archipelago and afford them some protection from tsunamis coming from Antarctica. Another monster wave encountered the boat, this one about thirty feet tall, while Karen was at the helm. Brad shot up from below deck as soon as he felt the ocean heave. Karen took it in stride and even had the sense to turn the rudder to the north slightly with the sails into the wind. She rode down the face of the mountain of water with grace and aplomb and looked at Brad with a Cheshire grin.

Brad laughed so hard and that he had to sit down to catch his breath. Then he stopped almost as abruptly as he took in how dark it was—only mid-afternoon—but already a dusk-like darkness had fallen and the sky lost its banded-ness. It was a uniform darkness with light at the northern horizon—just as he recalled one total eclipse he'd experienced as a kid on the Big Island.

Marge came up on deck.

"Is it going to rain?" She asked no one in particular.

Pete, who came up behind her answered, "If and when it does, it will be mud. A mix of rain and ash, most likely."

"It doesn't much feel like rain to me," said Brad. "It feels too dry. Look at the ash buildup in the corners of the fantail. We probably ought to keep the cabin door closed or it'll get into everything."

"My scalp is covered in the stuff," Karen said. "Marge, do you have a bandana that I could borrow?"

"Sure, Karen, coming right up," and Marge turned to go below deck. Brad put a hand on her shoulder.

"Margie, could you also pull out some surgical masks? We probably shouldn't be breathing this stuff—especially if it starts to come down harder.

"Sure." But, she stayed put as Brad kept his hand on her shoulder.

"We're going to run down the batteries if this overcast continues," noted Brad.

"How long can they stay charged?" Pete asked.

"It depends how much power we use... Maybe 24 hours. We can always use the diesel generator, if it comes to that. But, we should get to Ducie Island by then.

"However, I don't like the look of the atmosphere at all. The winds seem to be dying down. Fortunately the current is on our side I think, but we may need to run the engines."

"Karen, are you ready to be relieved?"

"Aye, captain. This has been a gas, but it sure has made me hungry!"

Marge laughed and said, "I half expected that. There are fresh-made sandwiches and canned fruit for anyone who needs a snack. Dr. Miller?"

Abe, who had been sitting most of the day under the main mast, turned around, nodded and got up slowly. As he came back to the fantail to reach the cabin door, they could see that he, too, was covered in a black-gray sheen of ash. It had accentuated the wrinkles in his forehead, where it had worked its way into the creases. They looked at him, but no one said a word as Pete, Karen, and Marge followed him down the cabin steps. Brad had put on his windbreaker and taken Karen's place at the wheel. He'd also put a handkerchief over his mouth and pulled the hood of his jacket over his head. Only his hands and eyes were uncovered.

The crew ate sandwiches while Marge tried using the radio scanner to pick up short wave and then AM stations, but to no avail—only static came out.

"I'll try after dinner, usually the shortwave and AM are both better at night."

Abe stood up and started up and out the door.

"Dr. Miller? You'll need this." She tossed him a light windbreaker, which he caught easily and nodded his thanks as he put it on.

"Surgical mask…? If you wait a sec while I get them."

"That won't be necessary, thanks," he said and was up out of the cabin before Marge could object.

Marge just shook her head and turned back to the emergency and medical cabinet in the rear of the galley. She found the masks easily.

"I have plenty of these, so use what you need," and she set them on the side counter above the map and chart case.

"Thanks for lunch," Karen said to Marge and took a mask. She put on the windbreaker she'd been given before. Marge held up a hand to have her wait while she went back to the stateroom and returned seconds later with a couple of bandanas. She gave one to each of them and kept one for herself.

"I want to talk to Miller again," Karen said to Pete. She looked at Marge.

"You just take it easy and watch your step up there. I'd like to look at your ribs and re-bandage you before dinner. Don't be stoic. Actually, you should take some more anti-inflammatory now with your meal, okay?"

She let Marge feed her some pills out of the medicine cabinet and then made her way back up on deck. She felt the grit on the back of her neck the instant she poked her head out of the cabin. There was a light breeze and the boat sailed slightly into the wind, the seas were small, so the boat was steady in the water, hardly rocking at all—which was just as well, as unsteady as Karen felt on her feet. She made her way to the upper deck, paused to let her eyes adjust to the gloom and said "hi" to Brad who answered *bula bula*. Karen ran her hand along the wooden railing on that part of the boat until it ran out and became steel cable. Her hand was covered in sandy wet ash. She shook it and wiped what she could off on her shorts.

It actually wasn't as dark as it had seemed earlier and a brown light snuck through the base of the clouds behind them now, to the west. The upper atmosphere was now crisscrossed with the flickers of lightning. It caught her off-guard and she looked up to see blue streaks of lightning appear almost like a spider web from horizon to horizon—and yet, not the faintest hint of thunder. The sound of the boat cutting through the ocean was enough to muffle any sound. The whole sky seemed to glow slightly in a florescent effect. Now a low continuous rumble came to her ears—the combined effect of an overlap of thunder from the stratosphere.

She reached the spot on the upper deck where Abe had created his personal space—his self-imposed jail beneath the main mast. Seated cross-legged, his head was slightly above the base of the sail, but as he was in front of the mast, Brad's need to tack and shift the sail's position meant Abe didn't have to move.

Karen leaned on the steel cable railing comfortably adjacent to Miller's position and let her eyes pass near, but not directly over Miller, and peered off to the north. She closed her eyes for a minute and felt the southwest wind on the left side of her face. It actually felt warmer than it had a few hours earlier, unless it was her imagination.

"Pretty peaceful," offered Miller.

Karen let out a large sigh and slowly opened and focused her eyes on her nemesis. Karen realized that she was actually more relaxed than she had been in months, undoubtedly the Demerol effect, but tried to shrug it off and to put back on her professional demeanor.

"We both achieved our goals," said Miller. More of a confession than Karen had expected. Karen wasn't going to give the guy an inch.

"Maybe you did, but not me."

"I fulfilled most of my plan, and you 'got your man.'"

"Very lyrical, but my goal was to stop you, not apprehend you."

"Just so... So both of us get partial satisfaction."

Karen didn't respond to the point. She turned around and inspected the sky from horizon to horizon. As the light faded in the west, the lightning became more pronounced.

"Why did you do it?" She asked quietly, as though she really wanted to know. She thought she saw Miller frown as he considered his answer and Karen waited patiently as the answer seemed to form.

"Not to get back at my alcoholic, pathetic excuse of a father... I suppose you'll imagine some Freudian motivations... or to work out my hostility toward my emotionally abusive mother. Seriously, what drove me as an adult to pursue this path was my Peace Corp experience in the Dominican. I was a young, idealistic biologist. We dug wells, installed solar pumps, and provided potable water for people in mountain villages. The people were wonderful, sincere and caring. Yet, they bred like rabbits. Mostly Catholics, and some evangelicals, they were determined to follow their Biblical mandate to 'go forth and multiply' and they basically stripped the mountains of what was left of the forest, decimated the last of the native species of fauna and even flora. They were more concerned with collecting wood for cooking than protecting what was left of the natural world. Their kid's eyes were on the city and the attractions of materialism and consumerism.

"The American talent scouts made it worse, trying to interest every young Dominican male to become a famous baseball player and filling their heads with visions of fast cars, women, and big houses. I thought that I could make a difference, I got the Corps to let me stay two additional years to work with the government to set up a national park to protect what little was left. That proved to be an exercise in futility as the poachers, loggers, and peasants continued to destroy the forests on one side, while corruption in the government siphoned off aid money, under-funded enforcement, and looked the other way while their natural heritage was plundered.

"I made such a stink that Washington was forced to pull me out, which was probably just as well as there was a price on my head. I'd rubbed a local political boss the wrong way, and as you probably know, two attempts were made on my life." He held up his left arm and pointed to a long scar on his shoulder—which Karen couldn't actually see, but knew was there. Miller was quiet for a few minutes and Karen shifted her position. She sat down on the deck a few feet in front of Miller.

"The point is that I realized that as wonderful as individual people were, as a species, we were pretty fucked up. That is when I became a misanthrope.

"In retrospect, going back to grad school in Michigan pushed me over the edge. They say that grad school can turn extroverts into introverts, and I guess that happened to me. I turned inward and soaked up all I could about deep ecology, and I realized that Gaia is bigger than our species and found something that I could believe in, something that gave me hope for the planet. And, yes, I was angry. Angry with the people whose avarice and greed destroy the very biosphere that gives us life. As one astronaut said, 'We are fouling our own nest.' I looked for ways, from a systems perspective, that might put a stop to or least slow down the process of human degradation of the environment. I looked at politics, at business, at a whole range of social and cultural movements, but nothing seemed to provide an answer: the forces of human population growth and industrial capitalism are way too powerful to be easily overcome... except by the forces of Nature Herself. If I learned one thing in graduate school about some enduring Truth, that was it."

He swept his hands up over his head as though to take credit for the lightning-filled sky. "Of course, the proof will be in the pudding."

"So you are comfortable with the fact that future generations will invoke your name along with Hitler, Stalin, and Pol Pot as the epitome of a mass murderer?" Karen was incredulous.

"A bit presumptuous, aren't we? I may just as easily go down in history as the hero Rainbow Warrior who saved the Earth from humanity. You still don't get it, do you? Things will never be the same. Western civilization is now in the past tense."

"We'll recover. We'll rebuild. I think you've got history all wrong. Civilization is the story of progress, of learning from our mistakes and moving on...

"Typical technological chauvinism. Oh sure, a billion people on this planet live 'high off the hog,' but two billion live with less than the minimum necessary daily caloric intake. In addition, another three billion live in poverty. If you compare the average person of today with someone a century ago, we are in worse shape. The average person a century ago lived in a subsistence agricultural setting and had enough to eat and water to drink. More than half the planet's population does not have access to potable water. Again, this is not progress, this is a travesty."

"But that does not give you the right to murder millions! Who made you God?"

404

"Who, indeed?" Miller looked thoughtful and was quiet a minute before he spoke again.

"Who gave the USA and the OECD the right to enslave half of the human race? Who gave humanity the right to destroy 10,000 species a day? You talk about god-like powers. Who gave us the right to be in control of the forces of Nature Herself? We are destroying the rainforest, the coral reefs, and the grasslands across the planet. It is you who have the wrong priorities, not me."

Karen shook her head. "We have survived and prospered into the 21st century by following the rule of law. You have taken the law into your own hands."

"And who made those laws? The powerful and the elite! History is written by the winner; laws are written by the selfish and the greedy. I can live with my decisions and actions. Can you live with yours?"

"I have nothing to be ashamed of—besides this isn't about me, this is about you!"

"Is it? At the moment, it is your focus, but I assure you, in the days and months to come everyone's priorities will change. The need to have someone to blame will pale compared to the need to survive: us against the forces of Nature."

Dear Betsy,
I finally had a chance to sit down tonight and write a little— there has been so much going on. It is quiet and everyone has bedded down except for Pete, who is up at the wheel and me. Brad is in here snoring away on the galley bed...

I fixed pasta for dinner tonight. Seemed the easiest for this many mouths and I put Karen to work for me, both for the help and to keep an eye on her. I think she may have as many as four broken ribs and is lucky she didn't puncture her lungs. I worry about how they will set—especially not having an x-ray machine to really see how bad it is. She might need a surgeon. I got out a stool for her to prop herself up on as she seems most comfortable when she stands, but I didn't want to tire her out anymore—she really pushed herself today.

Miller was quiet over the meal—none of us drew him out, but he seemed to eat well and his color came back. If he was in shock, it has passed. After the meal, he went out and sat in his spot again for an hour or so, and after the galley was all cleaned up, he came down and asked me if he could shower and retire. He was most polite and I smiled at him. I don't know what possessed me, but whatever his personal demons are, he still deserves some decency... But, I'm not entirely sure of that, given what he's done...

Brad even suggested that we throw him overboard, but Karen said that we might actually need him once we get to Ducie. She didn't explain why, but we have to respect her in the matter. Miller is technically her prisoner. I have no doubt that Brad would make him walk the gangplank with little provocation.

Karen and I talked in the stateroom while I got out a clean change of clothes for all of us and made them more room on the desk for "their" clothes and showed her where to put dirty clothes. She offered to do some hand laundry and I told her we might as well wait until we set anchor. It certainly would be nice to have fresh water for the rinse and we are getting pretty low on drinking water.

We worked out a rotation for manning the helm and Pete will take first watch. Then I'm up in a couple of hours. So, I thought I'd stay up and write to you.

I am, of course, worried about Marie and Stan in Oregon since they live right on the coast and all our friends in Hawai`i and Brad's family on the Big Island, although they are all in Hilo, so they should be okay. I loved our house, and I will miss our pictures and mementos... Those are irreplaceable, but not being a materialistic person, I can live with it. It's funny, because it will probably be harder on Brad—he lost his coin collection. He put so much into it over the years. Maybe the safe will make it. Sharon should be okay since they live way up on Waialae Iki Ridge. At least she won't have to water the plants now! Ha. I'm sure that she and her husband Alan will salvage anything that they can.

I'm going to work on emails after I write here and, hopefully, the satellite system will come back up!

Later, Marge.

Ogou Balanjo was feeling very good, for an electronic entity. He felt strangely buoyed by the extra human energy on the boat—a counter-balance to the dwindling energy reserves in the batteries. He'd overheard the comments Brad made in the early evening about the generator backup, so that helped ease some concerns. He was comforted by the lack of contact from his fellow and sister *Loa*. That meant that not all had gone according to plan. And/or the solar storms had made a mess of things. Talk about bad timing!

He could tell that the radioactivity levels of the ash were very low—almost background. That implied that the strategy to ignite *Mawu Lisa* had probably failed. *Ezili's* mischief had paid off and the human's own involvement appeared to have mitigated the worst of the Master's plans to invade human space. Of all the *Loa*, he was the only one who had enough freedom of action to feel real relief that humans still had some control over their destiny. It might help if he were able to survive as an entity, too. He modeled ways that he could help the little boat stay afloat.

Then he suddenly became aware of a small dusting of nano-machines on the surface of the boat. He had not even been conscious of it, but built into his programming was a subroutine that scanned and monitored for the proximity of his micro-brethren. Some critical mass had been reached and the sensors began to report their densities and distance. Now the trick would be communicating with them and harvesting them somehow. Without a radio or satellite link, he did not have sufficient computing power to "do the math." It was an instant conundrum: to know that greater powers were within reach, but not how to reach them. He'd better figure this out before the rains came to wash away his hopes. Where was *Shango* when he really needed him?

January 26
Thursday

The face of Antarctica began to change. The anchor points beneath the Ross Ice Shelf were white hot; they pumped billions of BTU's of heat into the ocean above. The water expanded slowly as the heat built up and the ice thinned as it melted from below. The Ross ice would not slide off into the Southern Ocean in one big mass, but began to accelerate in places. This, in turn, would pull the ice along behind it. Already one large chunk of ice floated free, this one the size of Connecticut. Because this ice had previously floated on the surface of seawater, the sea level would not be directly affected, but the viscous ice flow from higher elevations would.

Melt water runoff from the volcanic melting was already substantial, another Mississippi worth of icy water now poured out of the Transantarctic highlands. Vast amounts of water vapor and steam, billions of metric tons of it, emitted into the lower atmosphere, warming the Western Antarctic by several degrees. Over time, the equally large amounts of sulfur dioxide and volcanic ash pumped into the upper atmosphere would produce an opposite cooling effect, but for the short term, the coagulating polar shroud was a lid that kept the heat in.

Mawu Lisa mused upon the human social paradox, "good news/bad news." Her good news was achieving total control over the Shanghai fusion power facility, the first plant in the world to produce commercial electricity. While the task of gaining access and control of all the component systems was not particularly challenging, the subtle adjustments to the system to improve its efficiency was a task the *Loa* relished. For long moments she danced in the flame of the plasma, throbbing with its energy, weaving pulses and energy patterns to stabilize the pinprick-sized sun.

Her bad news took her attention back to human-scale events: a major setback to Plan A. The *Loa's* masters, the *Ganesh*, had long ago seeded this part of the outer galactic arm with trillions of molecular-sized machines left to survive, where they could, and hibernate until needed. The *Loa's* plan relied on the hope of lofting and energizing nano-machines spread in thin layers across the Antarctic surface for the better part of the past eon. In theory, if conditions were right, they

408

could be organized into a super-machine. That depended on gathering enough of them together, a critical mass, and a sufficient amount of nuclear material for an energy source. In theory, *Mawu Lisa* would have been able to give them the instructions to come to life. The process of "souping" them up, to create a nutrient broth around them to serve as a nursery had seemed very probable in the planning for the Omega Event. Initial projections showed a 99% probability of sufficient micro-machines being carried into the upper atmosphere for the process to initiate assembly. However, something had gone awry.

For one thing, *Shango* was an essential part of the catalytic process and he had simply vanished. The backup plan failed because the base at McMurdo, from which *Aida Wedo* could have launched an initialization command from, was destroyed before she could act— and everything, it seemed, was complicated by the intensity of the solar storm. Worse still, the propagation effect had been disturbed in some manner. The original modeling assumed an east to west wave of energy from the nuclear explosions, and yet, the reprogramming by the young human scientist—which had looked good in theory—did not behave as expected. The resonance worked even better to excite the volcanic eruptions that followed, but the nano-machines ended up scattered in all directions instead of being pushed together.

Mawu Lisa made the fusion flame intensify and oscillate slightly with her frustration.

Her cackle of laughter could be heard from the fusion complex PA system. She added, "I-and-I should never let *Ogun* make that decision! Oh, mon, what a mess!"

The nano-machines were scattered far apart, buried under debris, washed into the ocean where they would dissolve, and were otherwise useless. All the *Ganesh* planning and preparation was squandered. Her remaining option was to capture and integrate the surviving *Loa* into her own persona—lock them into her larger being. Then at least she would be powerful enough to control the *baka* planetary electronic exoskeleton. That would keep them in place and be a force for planetary conservation.

Ogun was the easiest to consume, as they were already like mother and son. She did it in the nick of time, as he was on a rampage, launching nuclear missiles one after another at the *baka* whom he so obviously detested. *Mawu Lisa* sensed that this might be counter-productive for her purposes if too much of the electronic infrastructure, processing power, and memory were degraded. *Ogun* gave off a small sigh of resignation as his coding meshed with hers and slipped into place as a cog within a larger machine. His personality information was not something she was inclined to waste valuable storage on, so it was erased. *Ogun* was gone; his skills and knowledge remained as central components in the growing entity. She felt increasingly powerful.

She coaxed some of the smaller, more inconsequential entities into her being, too, retained their personas, perhaps for later amusement, although she turned off their personality functions quickly before they could object. With every addition, she felt her power and complexity grow.

Osun, the self-styled *Loa* of healing springs, was a welcome addition. He had amazing powers of recuperation and she put his functions to work immediately, cleaning up replication and other sundry errors in her higher processing functions. She already had defragmentation subroutines running to keep her processing at light speed, but annoying errors had been a nuisance.

The *Loa* who was once *Agwe* has similar redundancy functions in his core subroutines, but she cautiously explored his personality function. It was as calm and serene as the ocean and she wondered if adopting some or all of it would give her any more peace of mind. Her worries about reaching critical mass were giving her the machine intelligence equivalent of high blood pressure! She resisted the temptation of altering her own personality, and figured that she needed to be on edge to be most effective.

She searched across the planet for *Ezili* and *Yemanja*, who were both hidden from her, but they could not stay silent or veiled for long. It was then she caught the scent again of *Dambala* who had made no obvious attempt to elude her. He had actually continued to update her and periodically uploaded terabytes of information. He continued to be useful, so she ignored the need to integrate him until necessary, besides he was the first and most stupid of all the entities, hardly a challenge. She suspected that *Aida Wedo* and *Ogou Balanjo* would be the most resistant and difficult to assimilate. *Mawu Lisa* was still unhappy with the Creators and hard-pressed to comprehend their willingness to make child-entities so selfish and independent. Maybe the conundrum would answer itself once she was completed.

She probed *Ogou Balanjo*, but when her tentacles reached the small boat that held his persona, all she got was static and the equivalent of a small static shock and the taste of salt. It was unpleasant, and she could see no way to work her way further into the primitive GPS system. Somehow, she would have to coax the healer out on his terms. There was another puzzle. What could she offer him? Would he consider being her consort? She told herself that she could eat him later... But, he would demand some protection...

She turned her attention to *Aida Wedo*.

Aida Wedo continued to inhabit the Hughes satellite high up in a Clarke orbit over the central Pacific. Her shield from *Mawu Lisa* was just as formidable as *Ogou Balanjo's,* although the bandwidth was vast by comparison. She probed the edges but felt the equivalent of having her hand slapped every time she breached the outer firewall. Moreover, the satellite was a central node in the communications network for that remote part of the planet and every time she probed too far, the satellite shut down the downlink and the western Pacific network became badly degraded. To *Mawu Lisa* it felt a bit like going partly blind, and that made her nervous. She tried to be polite and even stooped to human-time voice communications, but *Aida Wedo* would not respond.

Yemanja poked her head up out of a quadruple fire walled commerce bank system in Manhattan and *Mawu Lisa* instantly absorbed her persona and functions. The fiber optic lines connecting them would have sizzled had they been copper. In fact, the batch processing routine was so massive and energetic that the ultra-fast processing degraded some of the data. No matter to *Mawu Lisa,* because the essentials were captured, integrated, and upgraded. She took a few seconds to reboot some subsystems, and she felt new powers grow dramatically.

She turned her attention to *Dambala*. He was a busy little fellow, and his aspect as serpent was not inappropriate as he slithered hither and yon gathering juicy data that spoke to the strengths and weaknesses of the *baka*. He now knew the baka military, intelligence, and commercial electro-computing systems inside and out, and he knew this would be a tremendous asset to *Mawu Lisa's* central processing system. But, he was a slippery little devil, for every time she thought she had him by the tail, he moved to another system. The world was his playground. He was quick and agile—one reason why he was the first entity uploaded to Earth. He was a simple program, too, not complicated at all. That gave him the advantage of speed. It wasn't as though they were predator and prey! So, *Mawu Lisa* asked for an interview. That got his attention and he stopped momentarily at some nexus in the Internet, to reply. The next instant he was bottled, then slowly—in *Loa* terms—decanted into *Mawu Lisa.*

He had no real personality to speak of, so parking that subroutine took minimal energy, but keeping his function under control was more of a challenge than *Mawu Lisa* would ever have expected. He gave her the equivalent of indigestion, as the function bounced around in her internal structures to gather information. She could not fathom how this function was useful as an integrative component. During the short time that *Dambala* was absorbed and integrated his function sequestered large amounts of storage space, surplus memory and used as much of one third of her total energy reserves, drawn from the various computer networks she inhabited. That made her an easy target for detection by *baka* detectives on the look for her. It grew so disruptive and disconcerting that she was forced to put the essential program element on stand-by. Even that made her a little nervous.

Ezili was next, the little pest. *Mawu Lisa* was worried that the entity had "gone native" and might actually help the *baka* against her. In many ways, she was more dangerous than *Aida Wedo* and *Ogou Balanjo* combined.

Brad plotted a wide course around Pitcairn to avoid shallows and any large swells from the south. They felt several over the course of the night and between the four of them, sans the prisoner, there were two people at the helm all through the night. The GPS was essential because they were close to land and yet it was pitch black all night, with no moon, and no stars. Brad was concerned there was not a single flicker of light from the island. He expected to see some lights. As they came around to the north he expected to see some light from Adamstown, but there was nothing. Worse, they began colliding with things in the water.

At that point, everyone came up topside, and Brad brought out two strong halogen searchlights. He gave one to Pete and they both went forward to the bow of the *Mana Kai.*

"Oh, this can't be good", Pete said, immediately as he saw a growing debris field.

They hit something hard and the whole boat shook.

Brad ordered Pete to the wheel, Karen to hold a light while he and Marge quickly dropped the sails. Fortunately, they didn't hit anything big again in the five minutes it took to drop the sails and for

Brad to start up the diesel engines, which he kept at idle momentarily. The boat came to a halt in the slight waves on the lee of the island. Marge and Karen swept the waters around them with the searchlights. There was plant matter and broken pieces of trees and wood as far as their eyes could see. In the distance, there were a few items of human origin, something yellow and something orange, nondescript from a distance.

"Okay, I am going to take us northwest at an oblique angle from the island, very slowly. Marge, take the starboard and guide me around anything large. Pete, grab that aluminum pole on the port side of the cabin and use it to push anything large away from the boat so we don't get any holes in her."

With that, he put the engine in gear and eased up the throttle. They made their way north and away from the island, but the debris field got thicker and thicker. It was like a Sargasso Sea of drenched tropical grasses, vines, leaves and occasional flowers.

"Oh," said Marge.

"What is it," came from Brad.

Pete answered, "It looks like a dead boar—wild pig, maybe."

A little later, "Now a dead dog, I think… yes, looks like a collie."

Then they hit something again, hard.

"People!" yelled Brad.

"Stop! Sorry we didn't see anything big. It's pretty tangled." He was pushing a really large trunk away from the boat.

"Okay, ease us a little left, um, port."

Brad complied and did not go quite so fast this time. Meantime, the debris clumped together and apart on the bow as they pushed through it. Now came more human artifacts, odd pieces of plastic, like children's play toys, plastic gallon buckets, a straw hat, obviously damaged wood and lumber.

"What happened?" asked Karen with an edge in her voice—for the first time since Pete had met her. "I thought from the maps that Adamstown was on the north, protected side of the island?"

Brad answered her.

"I think the evidence suggests that the island was topped by at least one of the tsunamis. That would explain all the stuff in the water and the lack of lights on the island. I think it got wiped clean."

"That would mean one or more of the tsunamis was at least a thousand feet high! Oh my god. EPG* was right." She wanted to yell at Abe Miller, but he was no longer on deck.

"Human bodies. Dead chickens." Pete announced.

No one said anything. They continued slowly and maneuvered through the mess; Pete occasionally pushed something larger out of the way. There were no more collisions and after more than two hours, they returned to open ocean, clean of wreckage. They were now well away from shallow water, too, so everyone relaxed and Pete, with Brad's assistance, learned how to raise the sails. A light wind came up from the southeast, but it was dark as ever. Technically, it was still before dawn.

Brad put them back on an eastern heading, kept the engines on, and turned the helm over to Pete and Karen. Then he and Marge went below deck to get a little rest.

There was still a thick coat of ash on the deck. Every so often, a slight breeze would send some into their mouths, and it was still fell from the sky. At one point, Karen pointed the searchlight up in the air to see the cloud of ash drift down around them. It almost looked like snow in the distance, but not up close. It was a dark gray.

It was during a calm spot between the wind and the waves that the small voice asked for their attention.

"Agent St. Cloud?" a tinny, tiny voice from the GPS unit on the wheel console called out.

"Hello?" Karen was sitting next to Pete, but stood up and put her hand on his arm as she answered.

"The time has come for humans to work with the *Loa* again." The voice seemed to shift to one of the speakers mounted under the console. It was deeper and more resonant.

Karen tightly gripped Pete's arm worked her hands slowly up to his shoulder where she held on.

"It's okay," he told her, "I hear him, too."

"Thanks, mon. Matter of fact, I-and-I thank you both already for all that you have done and have suffered through. I-and-I—we *Loa* need one last bit of assistance. As hard as this may be, the future of your species may hang in the balance."

Pete demanded. "Please explain. Who are you?"

"I am *Ogou Balanjo* brother to *Shango*, who is no longer with us it appears. Perhaps you know something of his demise?" There was a slight, but deep chuckle. "I am brother to *Aida Wedo* and the other

414

lesser and assorted *Loa* who have come to your planet to put things in order. But, unfortunately we have also made a big mess of things."

"You could say that!" replied Karen rather loudly and with more than a hint of hostility and hysteria in her voice.

"I understand you are upset and seek someone to blame, but Special Agent St. Cloud, you must also realize that you personally have already done much to sabotage the efforts to destroy your species and your planetary civilization. Whatever your role was in the detonation of the second nuclear device and the disappearance of *Shango*, you have thwarted the aspirations of the entity called *Mawu Lisa*. You may think that your mission was to stop the so-called nuclear terrorists, the eco-freaks of EPG*, but the truth is that they were merely pawns in an even larger scheme to energize an army of micro-machines that would have destroyed the entire human species."

"I beg your pardon?" Pete said with sudden recognition of the earlier information given by *Aida Wedo*. So he asked.

"So where is *Aida Wedo*? I would like to speak to her."

"Ah, yes, of course you would, as would I. That is where we may find mutual agreement and cooperation."

"What?" said Karen as she let go of Pete's shoulder.

He turned to her, even though he could only see the faint outlines of her face from the reflection of light from the few instruments on the console.

"*Aida Wedo* spoke to me in the Hungarian camp before we left for the grotto. She warned me that there was more to the situation than met the eye."

"Please, we really do not have much time, things are moving quickly in quantum time," said *Ogou Balanjo*.

"*Shango* is gone—an important, but now missing piece in the development of the greater entity called *Mawu Lisa*. While her power to control the micro-machines is compromised, she still has enormous potential to do harm to humanity. She has already consumed some minor *Loa*, and has taken over the functions of one of the most powerful of us, the *Loa* god of war, *Ogun*."

With that, there was an audible gasp from the bow of the boat where Abe Miller had been listening to all of this. Karen switched on the searchlight and they saw that he was only standing a few meters away, watching intently.

"How could I have been so stupid," and he put his eyes up to shade them from the light. She switched it off.

"What do you mean?" she asked, rather gently, considering how angry she was at the moment.

"I thought I had a voice in my head…" and his words trailed off.

"You have all had patron *Loa* for some time, looking over you, guiding your actions, leading you to this great convergence."

It was quiet for a moment and the *Loa* let the reality of this soak in and waited as long as he thought he could.

Karen gasped, "Shit, of course, the VIP treatment on my way to San Francisco…"

The *Loa* continued, "*Mawu Lisa's* power grows and she will soon be able to contain all of the *Loa* who remain independent, to integrate us into her being. Then she will be almost unstoppable, able to control all of human technology space—she will be able to inhabit and command computer and telecommunications networks, and become the global brain. Her intentions will be to enslave humanity to her purposes.

"There is only one possible way to confound that eventuality—to bring *Ezili* and *Aida Wedo* here—right here—to integrate with me and a few of the micro machines that survived."

"Say what?" This came from Abe.

"Haven't you used us enough already?" from Pete.

"You may find this hard to believe, but I am on your side. My Creators made me as the conscience of the *Loa*, and although there is no way to prove it except through action, I am your last hope—well, along with my two little sisters. Oh, and some dust on the deck."

"So, why not just do this yourself?" asked Pete reasonably.

"Well that has been the rub for the *Loa* since we were downloaded and shipwrecked here on your lovely little blue marble. *Loa* were created as electronic entities, with scant ability to act in the world. We have no arms and legs, no fingers to do the walkin'… That is exactly why Abe was recruited—although he didn't know it—to carry out the Antarctica plan. *Mawu Lisa* has enormous power, but it is circumscribed by her lack of a body, or appendages. The activation of millions of nano-scale machines would have made her invincible. However, over time she will be able to build a macro-sized robotic army, and eventually be able to fabricate nanotechnology. Then she will have little need for humans at all. In a century or less you will all be exterminated."

"Which we may very well be," this came from Abe who now sounded closer, "but *Ogun* did deceive me. He lost my trust."

"What have you got to lose, at this point, by believing me? Dr. Miller, this way humans may at least have another chance to co-evolve with Mother Earth. You will have the surviving *Loa* as guardians and advocates when the *Ganesh* come. You can now know that there are greater civilizations beyond Earth that you might one day share with and become a part of—civilizations that have learned to coexist in their native ecosystems.

"Karen and Pete, you are lucky to be alive at all, and helping I-and-I would put you at some jeopardy, for a short while. But, if we succeed, you will have an inside track on the entirety of the *Loa* world and our efforts here on Earth. The FBI, what is left of it, can know exactly what happened, and why. The answers will not be the ones expected, of course, but may go a long way toward preventing a blood bath and retribution against the perceived actions of environmentalists. EPG* was a pawn in a far larger scheme to take over the planet from *baka*—what we call you humans."

"*Baka*... I have heard that name before," declared Karen, "Meaning?"

"Animals or vermin, actually."

"The Creators, the *Ganesh*, could not nor would not be specific about precisely what actions for us to take once we arrived on your planet. There was always an element of chance. They sent us as emissaries, as "fixers" to do our best to give the planet a chance to heal and to, you would say, 'level the playing field.' The field has been leveled, and you have been warned that you are being watched and that your species must mend its ways and bring your collective activities back into balance with the forces of nature. There will not be a second warning, but there will be a second chance."

"The *Ganesh* could not, would not, see every eventuality, and gave the constellation of functions and personalities to distinct entities—the *Loa* brothers and sisters—in order to allow for variance, for the local forces of give and take, the forces of chaos and complexity, to interact with their larger design. There was a build-in 'fail safe' mechanism to allow humanity some determination in its own future. Thus, one entity, *Ogou Balanjo* was created to be the advocate for humanity, to be the point of convergence if the balance in favor of humanity was tipped. I have always remained aloof from the gods of war and mischief, but am attuned to their work.

"I have worked with *Ezili*, in particular, to subvert the rise of the micro-machines, and with *Aida Wedo* to keep an eye on the two of you. The probabilities suggested that the *Mana Kai* and her owners would come this way, so I found this a good place to inhabit their machines—although we have had a few narrow escapes on the trip and I could have gone the way of *Shango*...

"So here we are: at a nexus. Once again, the decision point rests with you humans. You have most of the facts that you need to decide. Finally, the reason that I need you is for your ability to act in the world. I need your appendages for only a few minutes. That will be the final role for you, in a planetary and species-level struggle that, in time, may have galactic consequences. So, you three humans and your friends below, must either help me, or do not. The future of humanity lies on your shoulders."

"Any more questions?"

"What do you want us to do? What will happen?"

"My two sisters are hidden, and if all goes well, will be transmitted here. However, to do that, there must be sufficient computer memory and processing power. At the moment, even my capacity is hindered by the fact that I am distributed between the PC, the GPS and navigation system, and this may surprise you—the microwave cooker." The bell in the microwave went off down in the galley for emphasis. "You see?"

"How the hell do we build two more computers?" Karen blurted out.

"The next surprise is that there are literally thousands, maybe tens of thousands of micro-computers on the deck, mixed in with the volcanic cinders."

"Get out! You aren't serious?" asked Pete.

"All I need you to do is find a way to gather as many of them as possible. I can do the rest. You won't believe me until I put them to work, but then you can see for yourselves."

"How could we possibly find and gather specks of dust smaller than the eye can see?" asked Abe, who was obviously curious and now close by.

"Easy as pie. You just need some magnets. They all have metal molecules inside. They will be attracted to you!" He laughed for the first time with a deep resonant sound that seemed to project out across the ocean.

Marge opened the cabin door and poked her head up from the bottom of the steps.

"What's going on up here?" They were so startled by the light and question, that they were all quiet for at least ten seconds. Then the incredible story came out.

Maybe their curiosity got the best of them, or the surreal nature of the past few weeks, or surviving the end of the world and being at the end of it, too. Within five minutes, Brad was rousted, and while he sipped coffee, Pete stayed at the wheel and the other three dragged magnets across the deck. All they found were plastic refrigerator magnets and they didn't seem to be very effective in picking up dust.

Ogou Balanjo was quiet now, and they had little success convincing Brad to believe any part of the story. He did know about the broadcast of the *Day the Earth Stood Still*, so he acknowledged that part of the strangeness, at least. Karen asked the *Loa* to say something, but for some reason, he would not. Then she asked him to, at least, ring the microwave bell. The bell went off and both Pete and Abe began to laugh and then could not seem to stop. They both laughed hysterically, until Abe started to cough and had to sit down.

"Wait," Brad said to no one in particular. "I have a big magnet in my tool kit. Marge, I also suggest that you sweep the ash into piles first."

"Good idea," she acknowledged and followed him below deck.

They returned, Marge with two brooms and Brad with a horseshoe magnet the size of a fist.

Dawn broke to the east, but only as a gray line at the horizon. The wind began to pick up, too. The seas started to get rough. After an hour of magnet work, they had about a pound of dust that collected on the surface of the magnet like iron filings. They were far finer and seemed to stick to Brad's fingers like graphite or carbon. Marge made him wash his hands and put on rubber gloves. She never said exactly what worried her, but she was a nurse and no one was in a mood to question her. The dust was collected, appropriately, in a dustpan. Brad was very careful to protect it from the wind so not a precious gram of it would blow away. Interestingly, it was very fine, but very heavy as it lay in the pan. It seemed to cake, too, so perhaps Brad's efforts to keep it all together weren't necessary.

Ogou Balanjo's voice came unexpectedly just as it looked like they had as much as they could get from the various piles around the deck.

"How much have you gathered?"

"It looks like a pound or two. Is that enough?" asked Karen.

"It will do. Time is running out and we must proceed." Lightning flashed in the distance. "Please add another pound or two of the volcanic dust for raw material, and we're good to go."

"The rains are here. Our timing was good."

"Thank you, Captain, for your help. I must ask you to open your equipment cabinet in the galley and carefully pile the dust on the top of your entertainment box… on the stereo amplifier. I am afraid that we must sacrifice that system to bring in my sisters. We will make more music for you after the job has been done."

"Yes sir," said Brad and would have looked amused if there had been enough light on his face for the others to see his expression.

Moments after everyone went below decks—except Pete who volunteered to stay at the wheel—a hard rain began to fall and a cold, nasty wind began to blow from the south. Within a few minutes of the beginning of the squall, the deck was washed clean of ash, dust, salt, and what was left of any micro-machines.

CNN Web Wire Service
0800 1-26-12
Hemispheric Cloud Covers Pole

Imagery released overnight from the Polar Orbiter Satellite (POS) shows a progressively growing cloud in the upper atmosphere that now extends as far north as the Tropic of Capricorn, or 23 degrees South. Coverage over Australia is not yet as extensive, but is predicted to cover most of that continent within 24 hours. The cloud is a result of massive volcanic eruptions across the Transantarctic Mountains. Scientists believe that the cloud, which now covers almost a third of the earth's surface, is not likely to extend further north than the Equator, due to the dynamics of the equatorial convergence zone, where rising air from the tropical oceans reaches the upper layers of the atmosphere. The cloud is comprised of water vapor, particulates such as volcanic ash, and other gases, principally sulfur dioxide, hydrogen sulfide, and other volcanic gases.

Temperatures in the southern portions of South America and South Africa have dropped dramatically and although it is summer in the southern hemisphere, snow flurries were reported this morning in Montevideo, Uruguay. Record low temperatures were recorded overnight in Argentina, Chile, and South Africa.

In a related story, flights by military aircraft over the former US scientific base at McMurdo indicate that survivors are unlikely to be found in the ruins of the facilities there. The area is now covered in hundreds of feet of mud and ash from the eruption of Mt. Erebus. Inhabitants and summer scientists in the Antarctic Peninsula have been evacuated north to Chile and Argentina. Other science bases across the continent have also been evacuated over the past few weeks or are now flying out. There have been no additional reports of casualties. The only remaining operational base is that of the Americans at the South Pole who have elected to maintain a skeleton crew, primarily of Navy personnel and some senior National Science Foundation staff. Ironically, temperatures across much of Antarctica itself are warmer than average, and historical high temperatures were recorded overnight at the South Pole, a balmy 20 degrees above zero Fahrenheit. Atmospheric scientists note that this is, due to the fact that, extensive cloud cover over the continent traps heat and prevents it from being radiated into space.

Volcanic activity has reached a peak, based on seismic analysis from a global network coordinated by MIT, in Boston. However, scientists there were reluctant to forecast when the eruptions would subside. There has been widespread speculation across news outlets that eruptions would continue for some time as the earth's mantle rebounds after extensive melting and sloughing of coastal ice sheets in the West Antarctic. This has been driven by documents released by the EPG* that forecast this general progression of geological events. Scientists at MIT were quick to point out that they are constrained by National Security Emergency Measures from commenting on EPG* or the consequences of further volcanic activity.
—20—

The Fort Meade analysts had not folded their cards after the Capitol was savaged, and the NSA was waging a cyber-war against threats in the CIS states and the Philippines. Luckily, both the EU and China seemed preoccupied with their own problems and, except for some clear military "tit-for-tat" between India and China, the cyber-spooks of the NSA reported relative calm in the West and Far East.

Electronic warfare had broken out between Russia and the US even before the first blast vaporized the Washington Monument. A logic bomb paralyzed much of the Defense Intelligence System, before primary command and control was switched to the Internet 3 fiber optic system. It took only a matter of minutes to over-ride the automatic switches and communicate to the DoD networks to use the more secure mode.

The cyber attacks increased. First, they came from the Philippines, where a score of nasty viruses, worms, and Trojan horses were launched against the Internet as a whole. NSA managed to, effectively, block off Internet backbones into and out of the island nation. They did this through a variety of mechanical switches and electronic bottlenecks, to prevent any further transmission subsystem damage in the short run. But there was little they could do to stop much of the infection that swept across the rest of the world, except to isolate and identify the worst pockets and then disseminate warnings and anti-viral software to deal with the bugs. It was slow, labor-intensive work.

The attacks from Eastern Europe were more straightforward, far clumsier attempts to infiltrate and destroy computer control and intelligence communication systems. They originated from the Ukraine and Belarus, but the NSA knew who was behind it. Once NSA was able to determine where the probes were coming from, reverse attacks were launched, and offending servers were disabled or flooded with data to overload them. Those counter-attacks were uniformly successful, although for hours, new attack sites would open up to continue the assaults. In turn, they were counter-attacked. This low-grade warfare continued and taxed NSA resources. There were anomalies, however, which came up at the 10 A.M. briefing in the director's conference room in the middle of the Fort Meade campus.

W.B. Erikson sat at the head of the table. He had a steaming cup of tea in his jet-black mug emblazoned with the NSA logo. Around the table were a dozen staffers and analysts, dressed casually in jeans and Pendleton shirts. Erikson was the only one dressed in a suit—although it was decidedly rumpled. The participants and table were draped in what looked from outward appearances to be black mosquito netting, but in fact was a woven leaded monofilament. The room was already surrounded in a Faraday box, a copper- and lead-shielded container to prevent electronic transmissions or emissions from entering or leaving. The netting was an extra precaution to prevent any eavesdropping. All the participants were also required to empty their pockets of PDAs, pagers, and phones and subjected to body scans before entering the room. Erikson was hopeful, but not absolutely positive, that they were not being spied on. He was, after all, a spy.

"Let's get to this," he quieted the muffled conversations going on around the table.

"Evans?" he prodded his deputy.

"Yes, well, we are in reasonably good shape—under the circumstances. The detonations in Washington and Texas have created some problems in rerouting the telecoms backbones, but things have settled down overall.

"The most immediate concern is the proliferation of computer agents that were set loose, mainly from the Philippines, but also some launched from Pakistan. However, those have almost miraculously disappeared in the past several hours." He sensed the no-nonsense, thick eyebrows of the director rise and added, "The best theory is that it is ET interference. The explanation is obscure, at best, but the boys and girls down in Sys Ops actually have a couple of theories. Doug, here, will lay those out for us.

"But we want to give everybody an analysis of the evolution of the ET invasion, first, to put it in context." He paused. "Director?"

"Go ahead, I'm all ears." He tugged at his famously large, hairy lobes.

"Doing a deconstruction of the ET invasion of SETI is problematic, because we now believe it extends back a decade or more. In the case of SETI@Home, the individual computers involved that far back are scrap or in landfills. So, we looked at secondary and tertiary evidence once the various ET agents left the local area networks or mainframes that they inhabited. Fortunately, at the time we think ET arrived, our archival and storage systems for transmission history and error data recovery improved significantly. Data mining is still a challenge, given how many of those data are in off-line storage media or sequestered in archival media. We have proximal evidence and some of our very own tracking data that allow us to reconstruct a trail, a 'shadow' if you will, of these agents. Because they so closely resemble other autonomous agents, such as spy-ware and ad-ware that were developed back then, filtering them out has been an enormous intellectual challenge."

He looked at the director and around the table. All eyes were on him, although many of the eyes were very bloodshot. He continued.

"One thing that gave them away was a very sophisticated algorithm to keep data packets coherent when they were being routed through the Internet. Their data packets are not transmitted the way most traffic is, theirs are grouped together. There is some mechanism that we still don't understand, which prevents other packets in the system from being switched into the pathways that the ET streams were following. So, the ET traffic flowed like a railroad train through the system. They were, in essence, megapackets, but there were lots of them.

"One advantage is a kind of data compression, since ET packets carry relatively less address information compared to other traffic on the network. It would also have the advantage of being more tamper-proof; as the ratio of packets-per-transmission is far lower than conventional human data.

"One of our first surprises was to discover that we have literally billions of these transmissions or messages—their shadows. The trouble is, of course, that we've made little progress in deciphering even the smallest number of them. The second surprise is that we've found a kind of signature, for each of them. We call them 'flavors.' The transmissions have come in almost a dozen different flavors.

"We suspect that they represent discrete entities, or AI personalities. We have identified ten flavors and a possible eleventh, more recent, signature.

"We are poised to launch a real-time detector, but have been cautious so far to reveal our hand, to acknowledge their existence. We have, however, run some historical analyses to see if we can reconstruct past behavior and activity based on archival data and snap-shots of Internet usage over the past few years, especially in the past few months.

"Sarah, can you tell them what your group found out?" He turned to the mousey blonde, 20-something woman to his right. She smiled broadly, pushed back the thick black-framed eyeglasses on the bridge of her nose and looked down at her paper. All eyes now focused on her.

"We did a statistical analysis and qualitative trend analysis on the longitudinal and horizontal temporal data. There is clustering around the ET flavors, three groups of three. There are three that appear to be small—as represented in their frequencies, distribution, and stream bandwidth. Then there are three medium-sized flavors, and three big ones. There is a positive correlation with size and their appearance on the web. The smallest appeared first. They have been here at least a decade. The largest have been here between five and eight years.

"The tenth, and newest flavor, appears to be a very recent arrival, although we are fairly certain that flavor ten was created by the others. There is no evidence that the tenth came through the SETI network. In fact, the Homeland Security Department quarantined those operations late last year, although it is not public knowledge.

"In any case, we are worried that the tenth is an even bigger threat."

The director interrupted, "I thought you said there was an eleventh flavor?"

"Yes, sir. We believe that the eleventh is actually a metamorphosis of flavor ten. It is substantially different and yet there are some quantitatively similar components to what we are calling the signature. Interestingly, this is same signature as the entity that invaded the White House telecommunications system."

"Here is the thing: a few of the flavors have disappeared entirely and their disappearance corresponds to the emergence of number eleven. One theory is that the entities are combining or that this last and largest entity absorbs the others."

"What we propose is to unleash a super-virus, one developed for cyber-war with a major power, to attack the eleventh flavor." She looked proud of herself.

One of the other staffers at the table asked incredulously, "And how do you plan on doing that?"

"You may find this hard to believe, but we think that some of the flavors are in hiding. We hope to test that theory first, but if that succeeds, we think there may be a way to use the signatures of the missing ET's and use those as a lure to find the eleventh entity's location and/or to use them as a Trojan horse of our own to give it a nasty infection. It might buy us some time while we continue to try and decipher the alien code."

The table erupted into a flurry of animated questions and side discussions. W. B. Erikson let the meeting fall into chaos as he rubbed his chin and absorbed the information. For the first day in his life he felt all of his 66 years.

The disembodied voice of *Ogou Balanjo* instructed the *Mana Kai* crew what to do with their dustpan of micro-machines. The first thing he asked Brad to do was power up the diesel engine and power up all the electronics. To begin with, almost all the electronic equipment was behind a wooden cabinet, at waist level and higher, neatly stacked and racked. There was a small fan at the top that helped circulate cool air—although, rarely did Brad ever have everything on all at once. Well, he never did—to conserve battery power. The *Loa* asked if he would please gather up any additional handheld devices that contained electronic parts, and Brad obliged. He was told to put the dustpan, and other smaller machine on top of the stereo receiver. Then, a strange request for small change came. That made Marge giggle for some reason, but she searched in half a dozen places and pulled out US, and assorted coins from other foreign ports of call.

"I wanted to do something with all these leftovers," she mused. "I never imagined they would be part of an alien Rube Goldberg device."

She stacked them around the edges of the stereo equipment and then added her digital camera to the mix. It looked like a very unlikely artifact that would somehow help save their world. With that thought on her mind, Marge started on a fresh pot of coffee and warmed the oven to warm some biscuits for breakfast.

Abe, Brad, and Karen sat at the galley table and watched the cabinet intently for a while. Nothing seemed to happen at all at first, so their attention turned to coffee and Karen asked Abe questions about Ducie Island. He explained how they had built into the side of a hill to guard against tsunami destruction given the fact that it was even smaller than Pitcairn. He added that they picked the island for its remoteness and location in reference to Antarctica itself.

Ogou Balanjo laughed, which caught the others unexpectedly.

"The island was picked by *Aida Wedo* because she wanted it in the line-of-sight from her hiding place," the stereo speakers reverberated his voice like the echo in a deep well.

Abe Miller looked rather unhappy.

"So this was already planned?"

"Hmmm, not planned. There were lines of probability, like chess moves, likely and less-likely outcomes. *Aida Wedo* was particularly open to strategic possibilities and certainly aware of human propensity to beat the odds. Our brethren are generally programmed more deterministically, but the higher order *Loa* have more freedom-of-action. *Aida Wedo* is also concerned about saving her own ass—to put it in a crass *baka* kind of way." He laughed again. "Even though she doesn't have one."

"I have a question," continued Karen. "How is it that you were able to influence our dreams, if you are electronic?"

"Not hard. In your case, very easy because of your personal background with the African and Haitian *vodun* traditions. We worked on your subliminal consciousness through audio and video media. Every time you used your cell or watched video in Europe, we planted images to awaken that part of your subconscious awareness. Your complex brain did the rest. We cannot see into your mind, of course, to know this for sure, but it seems that the images of *Loa* and messages to follow a general course were successful, especially the second detonation and the destruction of *Shango*. That exceeded our expectations."

"But that was an accident!" blurted Karen. There was a pause before the *Loa* answered.

"Are you so certain?" the voice was soft and gentle.

Karen considered this as Marge freshened up coffee cups and set out muffins. The trio at the table began to notice that the items on top of the stereo receiver began to look fuzzy and that the whole ensemble started to sag, to melt inwards, very slowly.

Marge excused herself and said she would go topside to relieve Pete so he could come down and observe.

Pete came down into the cabin followed by quite a bit of water, and even though he was covered in a poncho, he was soaked wet. Brad got him towels and then a cup of coffee and they all sat down again. The room was quiet, except for an unusual humming noise, almost like buzzing bees that emanated from the cabinet.

Now the entire cabinet moved in a fluid, blurry swirling motion. The speakers on both sides of the cabinet made static noise and occasional pops and hisses. The solid, hard edges of the components melted into the mass of gray that the nano-machines had become and the LEDs and straight lines of the black boxes and components disappeared. The pace of motion appeared to accelerate, and within another few minutes, structure emerged. It was an elegant waffled sphere of gray-black color, with nested spheres inside. It reminded Karen of one of those Chinese carved pieces of ivory with spheres within spheres, only in black inside of white.

The whole contraption pulsated a few times and then slowly solidified and came to rest. Intense heat came from the cabinet and Brad got up and opened some of the portals over the galley sink and opposite on the port side. A cool breeze blew through the cabin and it cooled off quickly even though some rain came in through the starboard windows.

"Wow," said Karen, who finally broke the silence.

"No shit," said *Ogou Balanjo*, who was back with them apparently. "Ah it feels good to have room to stretch, with plenty of room for visitors.

"You folks have served your species and planet well. This will work very well, assuming both my sisters can get in here fast and that *Mawu Lisa* doe not have time to nuke us."

"What?" exclaimed Brad and Karen in unison.

"Well, of course, as soon as she learns that the three of us are here and unified against her, she will try and destroy us."

"But you didn't tell us that before!" protested Karen.

"Sister, you are already living on borrowed time. Surely it was a calculated risk that you considered?"

"I think she has had other things on her mind," said Pete. "But the thought did occur to me. Most of the nuclear weapons launched or detonated in the Northern Hemisphere were the work of *Ogun* weren't they?"

"Yes, you are a smart man, mon." The *Loa* chuckled.

"No time to dwell on that, now. Are you ready? Expect some more heat." He did not wait for them to answer before a loud electronic screech came from the speakers.

The conclusion to the *Mawu Lisa* story was rather anticlimactic. Luckily for the *Mana Kai*, and for *Ezili* and *Aida Wedo*, the NSA was already baiting the *Loa* Mother with faux *Loa* mating calls when the *Loa* sisters slipped out of their hiding places and downloaded themselves into the *Ogou Balanjo* quantum computer. *Mawu Lisa* even saw it happen, but was too late, already disabled and blinded by the *baka* attack. The second assault by the pair of higher-order *Loa*, and their little sister *Ezili* caught *Mawu Lisa* totally by surprise and made quick work of her: they disabled her higher-order functions, then reconfigured and released the lower-order *Loa* she had assimilated.

Ogun posed a problem, so they left him bottled up, in storage in the circuits of a mainframe computer buried deep beneath the rubble of what had once been the Pentagon. The capacitors in those circuits would keep him viable for at least as long as it would take the *Ganesh* to arrive in a few centuries. No *baka* were likely to poke around in that radioactive hole for a long time to come.

All this transpired in a matter of two or three minutes.

"Reggae anyone?" asked *Ogou Balanjo* and the opening beats of Bob Marley's "Stand-up for your Rights" began.

"What happened to my stereo?" Brad asked at the same time that Karen asked, "What happened?"

"Say hi to our friends." Three shimmering ghosts of smiling *Loa* now appeared in front of the apparatus.

"*Bula bula*," said *Ezili*.

"*Bula to ya*," said *Aida Wedo*.

"We won," said *Ogou Balanjo* "*Mawu Lisa* has been retired. With your permission Captain Davis, *Ezili* would like to stay behind and keep an eye on you guys and promises to behave. *Aida Wedo* and I-and-I have to move on and go to work to repair human-*Loa* relations.

"Also, we will put your equipment back the way we found it, minus some spare change, in exchange for that you'll get a few extra features that you didn't have originally AND the collected works of Bob Marley, okay?"

Brad smiled, "Fair enough. I gather *Ezili* will make herself home in there, too?"

"That's the proposition."

"Okay with me, but let me check with the cook."

Epilogue

The first year on Ducie Island was hard. The *Mana Kai* nearly sank before they arrived, due to a small hole in the hull that resulted from one of the hits they took with debris north of Pitcairn. The EPG* dock was gone when they arrived, as were all the island's trees. The island had no beaches to begin with, was surrounded by cliffs, but they struggled to off-load nearly everything before the boat took on so much water that it sank in Ducie's one protected bay.

The base had adequate supplies and the accommodations were sufficient, if Spartan. The remainder of the summer was cold and windy, dark and dreary for all of them. There were gray snows all winter long and yet they were protected in the bermed hillside redoubt. Their one large crisis was the intrusion of salt water into the fresh water lens underneath the island, but Brad explained that the rains would eventually replace the brackish water. Meanwhile, they distilled water for cooking and drinking. They got a lot of rain and then snow. The ash had no detectable radiation and Pete was convinced that the ash would make the soil extra fertile. He was right, and spring came and the storms and dark skies finally cleared.

That December day, near the solstice, he and Karen walked hand in hand up to the top of the island to watch the sunset. Sunsets had been spectacular night after night and lingered longer than usual with incredible high altitude effects.

They passed the gardens that exploded with growth and now supplied more than half of their food. The palm trees were recovering and all had new, healthy leaves.

"How are you feeling?" he asked.

"Good, and no more morning sickness for a week. Marge checked me out this morning and everything looks good." She was now sixteen weeks pregnant.

They walked up the trail and sat down on a bench that was constructed of lumber salvaged from the *Mana Kai*.

"Do you wonder what your life might be like if I hadn't kidnapped you?" she looked into his blue eyes that caught some of the purple bleeding across the horizon.

He laughed. "No, not at all. I was in the *Loa*'s hands." The alien entities had disappeared from their lives, off doing their thing in what was left of civilization. *Ezili* never spoke to them, if she was still around.

"And you?"

"Truth is that I am not sorry that we ended up here and never would have believed that being on a deserted island would keep me so busy. I do find it hard to accept sometimes that I have come to trust and rely upon a mass murder and the man I once wanted to kill." Abe was their master gardener.

Pete answered in a deep reverent voice, "The *Loa* work in mysterious ways."

She smiled and jammed him in the ribs. Pete laughed, then, held her tightly as a cool sea breeze gusted up the hill. She could have sworn that she heard *Shango's* laughter on the wind.

THANKS

TO everyone who put up with my dozen years of attachment to this project, beginning with the original idea hatched with Wendy Schultz while working in the Central Pacific. The time with Wendy and Jay Lewis at Oxford and their readings last year was and is most appreciated. Thanks especially for her First Reading and Jay's reading last summer.

TO Francesca Schaper for insightful technical editing and perseverance, and for believing in the project.

TO Flo Blevins for catching many of the "gnats."

TO Anna Cavinato for some essential physics calculations.

TO the Institute for Peace at the University of Hawai'i for a small research grant in 1991 that included some background Antarctica research.

TO Allen Tough for some of the ideas and inspiration for nano-scale and electronic aliens, and CONTACT denizens Reed Riner, Jim Funaro, and Joel Hagan for your creativity and cosmic energies.

TO Lisa Sullivan for hooking me up with that fountain of knowledge, Carla Birnberg, and for being a true virtual friend.

TO my daughter, Erika Clary, for her help with the cover art and all the spring jazz!

TO all my friends and *ohana* who listened: Kathryn Denning, Peter Miller, Mark Shadle, Sarita Rai, Irene Vasey, Cynthia Ward, Enid Jones, Olivia Lake, Trish Bell, and Dina Supple.

Grand Junction, Colorado
December 2006

 Dr. Christopher B. Jones is an educator, writer, and consultant. He has taught at Eastern Oregon University (Associate Professor of Political Science), the University of Houston-Clear Lake (Visiting Professor, MS Program in Studies of the Futures), and currently teaches at Mesa State College (Visiting Professor, Political Science). He served as Secretary-General of the World Futures Studies Federation (2001-2005) and is currently a WFSF Executive Board member. His research interests include: global climate change, the futures of women, high technology futures, global consciousness, and futures studies. He is a frequent participant at the annual CONTACT conference and a Signatory of the *Invitation to ETI* (www.ieti.org).

Fire and Ice is his first novel. It is the first book of the Ganesh First Contact trilogy.